Gale Borger

Totally Fishy

Disclaimer:
Any references in this "fish tale" to real persons or places
are used in a totally "fish-titious" manner, or a whale of a tail.

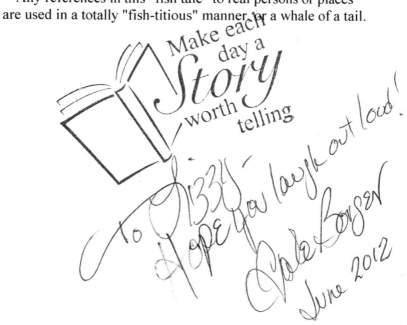

Make each day a
Story
worth telling

To Dizzy –
Hope you laugh out loud!
Gale Borger
June 2012

TOTALLY FISHY
An Echelon Press Book

First Echelon Press paperback printing / 2011

Cover Art © Nathalie Moore

Echelon Press
9055 G Thamesmeade Road
Laurel, MD 20723
www.echelonpress.com

ISBN: 978-1-59080-746-0

Printed in the United States of America

10 9 8 7 6 5 4 3 2 1

To my rock, my favorite fish guy, and my husband, (Captain) Bob, and to Shannon, wonderful daughter and always in my corner, I love you both.

I'd like to thank the multitudes of fish keepers and hobbyists who have touched my life. Your expertise and willingness to share knows no bounds. Special thanks to Steve Schindler of Tropical Oasis Exotic Pets for getting us started in the fish hobby and to Frank Falcone, who inspired my love of Cory catfish.

Thanks also to Karen, Sean, Nathalie, and all of Echelon Press for their wealth of knowledge and never ending support. If not for you, I'd still be treading water.

1

Slogging his way over soggy ground, tripping over tree roots the size of his thigh, and hacking his way through an endless wall of vegetation was not what Dr. Evo Castillo would call a fun-filled afternoon. Sizzling heat, accompanied by outrageous humidity, made him the main course for everything that bit, stung, or sucked blood. Hot, dirty, and pissed-off, he trudged on, thinking about air-conditioned offices and a cold American beer.

Evo hacked his way forward, muttering to himself as his temper gained momentum. "It's not like anyone is dead or anything. I really don't see what the big rush is."

He stumbled over something that was wise enough to move out of his way quickly. "Seventeen years working for Maldonado Oil and where am I?" Grumbling, Evo hacked another ten feet and stopped to wipe his brow with a soggy, gloved hand. Breathing hard, he consulted his compass and looked around, as if he could see through the thick stand of foliage in front of him. "Almost there."

His sweaty assistant, Luis gave him a hopeful grin. "Really?"

Evo looked again. "Well, sort of."

Luis sagged and shifted his backpack "Do you know where you are, Dr. Evo?"

"I'll tell you where I am." Hefting the large machete, Evo once again began the slow process of hacking his way closer to Maldonado Oil Site 151. "I'm slogging my way through five miles of Venezuelan rainforest to check out another damn anti-oil complaint."

Temper flaring, Evo grunted as he dodged another flying branch, and slashed his way forward. "Dr. E. M. Castillo–" Hack, pull, toss, *grunt*. "Renowned scientist–" Hack, *grunt*, pull, toss. "Environmental Liaison and mosquito fodder extraordinaire–Hah–*oof*."

He stumbled and fell to the ground. Kicking out, Evo tried to dislodge his foot from the stump he'd tripped over and met soft tissue instead of wood. "Damn stump!" He looked at his caught foot. "What the–"

"Dr. Evo, are you okay?"

Sitting up, Evo stared at his feet as the bile rose in his throat. "Oh, crap, I spoke too soon. Luis. Come quick!"

Crashing through the brush, Luis almost fell over Evo. He skidded to a stop and stared at the scene in front of him. "Hoo boy, Dr. Evo, that's quite a stump, all right."

Scooting backward, Evo dislodged his foot and Luis grabbed the camera. Lying in a heap on the jungle floor was a human thigh and part of a lower leg, encased in olive drab and relatively fresh.

"My God, where the heck did that come from?"

"I would think, Dr. Evo, it came from some poor dead guy, but I think the bigger question is who is he?"

"Not to mention why is his leg lying here in the jungle? Maybe the back pocket is still attached to the, uh, rest of him here. How about if you take a picture to show how we found him, call Alfredo so he can alert the authorities and I'll look for an I.D. and mark where we found his leg."

"Okay, boss." Luis pulled out the camera and snapped several pictures of the leg and the surrounding jungle. He called his brother Alfredo, who waited at the Land Rover where Evo and Luis had entered the jungle.

Alfredo sounded chipper when he answered. "Luis, good to hear your voice. Are we still on schedule?"

"Alfredo, my brother, a small glitch in our plans."

"Is there not always a glitch?" Alfredo chuckled. "What is it this time, Luis?"

"A stump."

"You call me about a stump?"

"No, no. Not a tree stump, a leg. Well, part of a human leg."

Alfredo sat up at full alert. "A leg?"

"Yup. Just his leg."

"His? You know it is a man?"

Luis lifted his hat with his free hand and scratched his head. "I think so. It looks like a manly leg to me."

"I will tell the police."

"Yes. Dr. Castillo wants you to call the authorities. We will clear the area. Tell them we have pictures and will mark the site with our emergency flags. They will be able to spot the site from the air."

"Where's the rest of the body?"

"Don't know, but Dr. Evo and I have to move on before the dark sets in, so get going."

"Okay, okay. Tell the good doctor I am on it. Give me the coordinates."

Luis recited the location of the body part and clicked off the cell phone. He wandered to where Evo stood over the leg, his hands on his hips, jaw tight. "All taken care of, Dr. Evo. Alfredo will handle it from here."

Shaking his head, Evo squinted into the sun as it began its descent to the western horizon. "Damn. We need more time. That leg could disappear any time out here. "

"We can recon the area, but a wild animal must have eaten the rest of him. I do not see a trail anywhere, so what was he doing way out here anyway?"

"I don't know, Luis, but there was no identification on the body, so we may never know. I set the flags and I have a smoke pot lit, so if the wind holds steady, they'll find the area

7

easily. Come on, we need to get moving before dusk or we'll be jungle fodder ourselves."

Cramming his old ball cap on his head, Evo hefted his backpack and machete.

Taking his foul mood out on the plant material blocking his way, Evo wondered for the hundredth time what the heck he was doing out here. Fieldwork like this was for younger guys, fresh out of the university. Evo remembered his days newly out of school, broke, driven, and willing to do just about anything to jump-start his career and make a name for himself. He thought nothing of spending weeks under the worst conditions known to man just to spend hundreds of hours compiling research no one cared about to write a report few read, on the environmental impact of drilling in a particular area.

These days, Evo had a corner office in a beautiful high-rise in Lima that he never saw, a membership to the most posh health club in the city he never used, and a plush condominium few could afford, in which he never slept.

His little brother Tony was working on his final research project before graduating with a doctorate specializing in fisheries and soil and water management. He'd currently partnered with Dr. Samón Fernandini, a brilliant-but-bitchy tree-hugging ichthyologist with the Peruvian Environmental Agency. Tony thought she was a goddess. Evo saw her as a tight-assed, wicked-mouthed, pain in the ass—but with great tits.

Evo stopped again to catch his breath and slap a monster mosquito as he fantasized about Sam's excellent pectoral muscles. Slamming the machete into a log, he uncapped his canteen and took a long pull. Though he kept in great shape, he realized his breathing came harder than usual and he sweated like there was no tomorrow. *Must be a coincidence that I'm breathing hard and thinking about Sam's bra size. Geez, Castillo, you need to get a life.*

Letting his assistant take the lead, Evo ran a wet cloth over the back of his neck. "Damn this humidity."

Watching his assistant move rhythmically through the rainforest, chopping and pulling without complaint, Evo once again thanked his lucky stars he had hired Luis and his brother Alfredo all those years ago. *I need to be more like Luis. He never complains about anything. He's got to be as sore as I am, but look at him.* Chop, pull, toss, chop, pull toss. Evo raised his sore right arm and halted in mid-swing. A sudden muscle cramp shot pain through his shoulder and he dropped the huge blade.

Evo grabbed his shoulder and howled. "Ow, ow—damn! Shit. Shit!"

Mother Nature must have heard Evo cussing, because at that moment she set out to drown one environmental scientist in the Venezuelan jungle. The skies opened up and all thoughts of Samón Fernameanie, the bitch-thyologist from Peru, washed out of his mind. It poured as if Heaven itself turned on the holy water spigot full force.

Instantly drenched, Luis looked back to see the boss jumping around in the downpour, holding his shoulder and dancing in what looked like some wild ancient ritual. Luis opened his mouth to enquire, but thought better of it and waited for Evo to vent his temper to the sky.

Shaking his arm, Evo ranted to the jungle, "Nothing has gone right since we left Peru the day before yesterday!" Cramp easing, Evo slowed to a stop. He lifted his face to the sky, and slowly turned in a circle.

Water cascading off his body, he yelled to the tops of the trees. "Well happy horse hockey, can this day get worse?" He closed his mouth a millisecond before the bird poop fell from the tree and landed on his forehead with a resounding splat. Luis stood and watched in horror, waiting for the explosion he knew was coming.

Evo stood rooted to the ground and closed his eyes in resignation. "Thank you, I'll remember not to ask *that* again."

The torrents of rain beat down on his head. The bird poop slid over one ear and plopped onto his shoulder, leaving a gooey white trail quickly washed away by the monsoon. That corked it. Evo tore off his favorite baseball cap and spiked it into the muck at his feet. Swearing and stomping, Evo railed at the world and sent Luis diving for cover.

Several wet minutes later, anger spent, Evo stared at the muddy mess at his feet. He realized too late that he would need his favorite hat later. Sighing, he dug it out of the muck and held it in front of him, rinsing it off the best he could in the rain. He slapped the filthy hat on his head.

Evo peered through the underbrush and sighed. "You can come out, Luis. I'm done now."

Luis peeked from under a banana frond and grinned. "That was a good one, Dr. Evo. You sure told off Mother Nature, no?"

"Yeah, but the bitch wins again. That's what I get for tempting the 'Yes, things *can* get worse' theory."

Grabbing the machete, Evo resumed his trek through the muddy jungle. Taking out his frustration on the jungle flora, and trying to avoid the fauna, Evo muttered to himself, "Yep, that's what I get—nothing but water down my shirt, mud up my ass, and crapped on by Birdzilla the shit monster." He winced and grabbed his burning stomach, "Not to mention a mother of a bleeding ulcer."

Not realizing he'd stopped, Evo had become so wrapped up in self-pity he jumped and yelped when Luis tapped his shoulder. Huge, round chocolate eyes gazed up from under a dripping pith helmet. "*Senór* Evo, uh, I have been thinking. It is raining like the cats and the dogs. Can we go home now? Maybe we could try again tomorrow. Alfredo will wonder if we drowned."

Sighing, Evo checked his watch and looked at their coordinates on his GPS. His foul mood vanished. Evo pulled a slicker out of his pack and draped it over Luis. "Not on your life, my friend. We are not doing this trip again. We are going to finish here today if it kills us. It's been raining like this for almost a month, and Maldonado wanted that report on his desk last week. I'll call Alfredo on the cell and get an update on Peg Leg back there."

Luis sagged and Evo patted his shoulder. He flashed Luis a bright smile and tapped the GPS. "Look on the bright side, we're almost there."

"Wonderful." Luis tried to smile.

Evo hiked his collar and stared wide-eyed as a chunk of mud fell off his nose and slid down a front tooth. He spit out the offending mud (at least he hoped it was mud and not leftovers from Birdzilla) and tied the slicker under Luis' chin. Evo turned and tromped onward, content with the thought that his assistant must think him totally bonkers.

Fifteen minutes later, the rain stopped as suddenly as it had begun and the bugs swarmed in like it was bargain day in the human flesh department. Slapping another mosquito, Evo's good humor took another nosedive. He swore a blue streak. *This is not funny anymore. Damn wanna-be environmentalists. Why can't they just stay home?*

"Fun and adventure, eh, Luis? Dragging our equipment through miles of rain forest, muck, and bugs–again."

"*Si, Senõr* Evo. Alfredo and I are happy to slog anywhere you go."

Evo sigh. "I know my friend, what would I do without you two?"

"Don't know, Dr. Evo, probably not have so much fun like we are now? Speaking of fun." He swatted yet another mosquito. "Why the long hike through the jungle? Are we sneaking in the back door?"

"Yes, and I'd rather not alert anyone to our coming."

Luis knew the tedious routine by heart. They'd interview a couple of locals, take a few pictures, and write *another* report to *another* special interest group who claimed their goats were dying because the sound of the drilling gave them brain cancer or something equally stupid.

Evo passed the bug repellent to Luis, who gratefully covered every exposed area of skin before handing the bottle back.

Tucking it back into a side pocket, Evo zipped the backpack and hoisted it over his shoulder, checked the GPS, and started forward. "We should be within a quarter mile."

"Oh, boy." Poor waterlogged Luis gave a world-weary sigh and moved ahead.

Evo made to follow, but found his rubber boot stuck in the mud. He grabbed the top and pulled as he lifted his foot. The boot made a sucking sound as he finally pulled it free. *Good thing I have a decent boots and hip waders. I'd be dead in the water without them. I even got 'em on clearance.*

Evo thanked God for online shopping or he'd be traipsing through the jungle naked. *Talk about interesting public relations.* Evo shopped a plethora of wilderness outfitter stores, but considered himself a loyal Gander Mountain junkie. He sure would like to see that store in person some time. Maybe he would just take off and go to the States–Wisconsin it was. The weather would surely be better than here this time of year.

The thought of trading his present fate for millions of stars, roaring campfires, and a new *Carhart* jacket lightened his nasty mood considerably. Evo could almost smell the steak sizzling.

Hearing a shout, his thoughts crash-landed him back in the hundred-degree heat of the jungle. Luis stood up ahead waving frantically. It looked like more black mangrove slop ahead, so they must be nearing the site. He couldn't hear the drilling from here, but one could never tell by the noise in the jungle. It could echo through the rainforest for miles, or the canopies could buffer noise and make it come from a different direction all together. His mission was supposed to be a secret–allegedly it came directly from Maldonado-Nunez himself.

His immediate boss, Hector Chavez, was the only guy between Evo and Nunez. Many higher-ups thought Evo should have received that promotion six months ago, but it had gone to Chavez, and Evo had to live with it. Funny, he'd been relatively content with his job before then.

Maldonado-Nunez had been accused by various individuals and special interest groups of being a polluter and burner of rainforests. Some declared Nunez guilty of irresponsible mining practices, dumping mining refuse, oil and chemicals, a polluter of small lakes, rivers, and streams, and probably kicking puppies and pinching small children as well.

Evo's job was to investigate those charges and make any adjustments at the site or in personnel needed to rectify the situation. He was a troubleshooter and a master at conflict resolution. He worked with environmental agencies to assure compliance, as well as being a liaison between Maldonado Oil and the media, and handling problems with subcontractors and other companies on site.

Evo, however, considered himself, first and foremost, a scientist. Narrow-minded people like Fernameanie thought him a traitor to work for an oil company, but Evo had endless compassion for the preservation of all life forms and for the environments in which they exist. Working for "the enemy" allowed him the freedom to do what he did best for the natural world while keeping a finger on the pulse of a huge conglomerate, which had the power of destruction and devastation of the natural world at its fingertips.

Evo would then report back to Chavez on the situation, what steps he'd taken, and what still needed to be done to make things right. *All this for six digits, no time off, perpetually soggy clothes, and a bleeding ulcer. Oh boy, I'm livin' the dream.* He grunted as he hoisted his equipment over the last fallen tree into the clearing. He stopped dead as he took in the scene before him.

"Whoa, what the heck?" He scanned the shoreline of the lagoon. Thousands of dead fish lined the narrow vegetation-strewn beach, their silver bellies shimmering in the waning sun.

Evo neared the beach and the smell of rotting fish almost knocked him over. "*Whew-wee.* Did I say thousands? This looks more like *hundreds* of thousands."

He stepped close enough to get a good look at the dead fish. At first he couldn't believe his eyes. He picked up one tiny body and examined it. "Luis, look at this! I gotta call Tony and Sam."

Evo dumped the fish in Luis' outstretched hand. "If I'm right about this, no one in the fish world is going to believe it." He turned and trotted up the beach, dropping his pack and reaching for his cell phone.

Luis looked down at the dead fish. "What are they not going to believe, little one? That you are dead or that so many of you perished here?" He watched Evo's animated gestures as he talked on the phone and opened the backpack at the same time. Turning the little fish over in his hand, Luis became more puzzled over Evo's excitement. He shrugged. "What makes you so special, little fish? You look like a strange guppy to me." Luis turned from the beach and made his way to Evo.

Luis watched Evo unpack his portable table and testing equipment.

"Luis, I just called your brother and told him what we found. He's still waiting with the Jeep at the drop-off point. He's going to meet us at the rendezvous point in an hour. I told him we'd keep in touch. I'll try my brother again–there was no answer."

14

"Okay, Doc. I'll set up the testing equipment and get the camera."

The two men set up near the tree line and returned to the water. They each reached a gloved hand into the pile of dead fish and pulled random samples from along the beach. They stored each sample and labeled the containers. Luis took pictures of the shoreline, and focused the camera across the lagoon. What had originally looked like a serpentine of bubbles and small debris was revealed in the zoom lens of Luis' camera to be a long line of dead fish floating toward the shoreline where Evo and Luis watched in silence.

Luis sighed. "There are so many. What could have killed them?"

Evo shook his head. He left Luis to take more pictures, a feeling of dread coming his initial adrenaline rush caused by the thrill of discovery. His ulcer sang as his irritation rose. "What the heck could have done this?" *Could it really be the drilling this time?* Evo tried his brother's cell phone again to no avail.

Slapping his phone shut and fighting the anger rising to the surface, Evo rubbed his stinging stomach and trudged back to his portable lab. He pulled out a magnifying glass and examined his first sample.

He confirmed his initial identification of the little fish as he took in the small, streamlined body, forked tail, and bright colors. Sparkling calico patches of green, orange, black, and silver winked in the sunlight as Evo scribbled in his notebook. "Look at these."

Luis bent over the table. "They are wild guppies, no?"

"No, they're Endlers, Luis. Endler Live Bearers. They look rather like guppies, but they're supposedly extinct in the wild. This must be a cache no one knew about. What a find!"

"I am sorry, sir, but they look like guppies to me."

"It had better not be the drilling that killed them." Evo

stared at the dead fish, as if waiting for them to reveal the truth. He deliberately controlled his breathing, trying to rein in his growing ire.

Luis stared at the tiny fish with its clown-like colors. "I have heard of such fish, sir. I thought the Venezuelans killed them all with lake pollution. A garbage dump runoff, yes?"

"Yes, looks like someone killed this lake too. The complaints are legitimate this time. The locals weren't crying wolf after all." Evo ripped off his glasses and pinched his nose between his fingers. He looked around for signs of runoff, tire tracks, any indication of human interference.

"Cry wolf, sir? Wolves did not do this. Maybe the oil wells…"

"Luis, I didn't mean actual wolves; it's a figure of speech." At Luis' blank stare, Evo sighed. "Never mind, my friend." He turned back to the lagoon. *Who the hell would do this?* He looked down the shoreline, hands on hips.

"So what now, Dr. Evo?"

Evo started and Luis jumped back. He dug into his backpack, pulled a water test kit from its depths, and began analyzing the water. Luis' eyes widened as the colors changed, indicating the presence of heavy metals.

Evo blew out a puff of air and ran a hand through his hair. He shook with rage as he scribbled in his notebook. When he belched and grabbed his burning stomach, Luis backed away, giving Evo room for the impending eruption which, Luis knew from experience, was again only moments away. Evo leaned both hands on the table and muttered to himself. *Here it comes, three, two, one, and…*

"Damn poisoning sons-a-bitches!" Evo slammed his notebook shut. He spun away from the table. Luis flinched as Evo continued to yell and kick the sand, sending a spray into the air. He grabbed the mud-caked khaki ball cap from his head and slapped it against his leg. He stared at the hundreds of thousands of dead fish and flung his arms wide. "Shit," he yelled. "Shit, shit, *shit*!"

Evo fumbled in his pocket for the antacids and popped four. "This could have been the hallmark of Sam and Tony's careers. Endlers found in the wild. What a discovery. Fat lot of good this does anyone now. I can see the headlines now. Oil Interests Create Dead Endlers"

He stomped back to the makeshift lab. "This is great–just effing great." Evo began stuffing things back into their packs. "Whoever did this is going to pay."

Leaving Evo to his one-man rant, Luis backed away and quietly began to put the specimens on ice, packing them carefully to prevent further damage. He also waded into the water with a net to retrieve live fish. He used their bottled water supply to float them in breather bags, hoping some would survive the trip to the lab.

Evo looked up from his backpack to find Luis back at the shore. "Luis. What are you doing now? Those fish are a dead issue. We need to get out of here and get to the drilling site."

"I am taking samples, Dr. Evo."

"We have enough samples. Come on. We're behind schedule as it is."

"Dr. Evo, I know if you were not so angry you would have found live fish and taken samples. I am only doing what you trained me to do."

Evo stopped. "Live–"

"See?" Luis held up his net, and Evo saw four wriggling bodies in the net. Luis dropped the fish into the container and dipped the net back into the water. "You can see there are very few, and they might not make it, but it is worth a try, you always say. It is the way of science."

Evo gazed into the sample container. Some of the little fish perked up in their new environment, while others struggled to hold on to life. He placed the container in the rack and joined Luis in a quest for any survivors. "I'm sorry, Luis. I let my temper overshadow my priorities. I'll mark the samples. You keep searching."

Luis sighed and continued the careful back-and-forth motion of the net, lost in thought. It was very discouraging for him to watch this beautiful habitat destroyed under the guise of progress, or global competition, or whatever excuses the OPEC idiots used these days. No matter what they called it, it all came down to big money. Billions worth of oil and mining, and everyone wanted in on the big bucks.

The Americans screamed about prices, but sold their oil to other countries. South America was rich in oil, but slow in production and no competition for the big guns in the Middle East. With the government and private corporations fighting for control, everyone loses. At this rate, South America would never produce enough to meet world demands. In the race for billions an "anything goes" attitude prevailed. Shortcuts were taken and as a result, the environment suffered. With that kind of money talking, no one listened as the environmentalists cried out. At least Maldonado didn't clear-cut and burn thousands of acres each day like some large corporations. Luis and his brother took these jobs because they believed they could make a difference. Like Evo, they'd had about all they could stomach of progress.

Luis looked at the container in his hands and watched another Endler give up its fight for life. "No one cares about you, but us," he said softly. "Unlike cute baby seals or the great leatherbacks who have world-wide funding and media attention, you have only us." He gently packed the doomed fish away. "That means you are in big trouble, my little friend."

Evo looked up and saw Luis talking softly to the fish in a bag. He hefted his mountain pack over one shoulder. "Sorry, Luis, but we have to wind this up. Any time you're ready."

Luis looked up. "Oh, no, Dr. Evo, go ahead and yell some

more, I have found more live bodies, so will catch up with–"

Something plopped in the sand at his feet. Luis looked down. "What was that?"

Evo looked over as the sand sprang up at his feet. "What the heck?"

He bent to look and a blast of heat surged past his ear. In a split second he registered, "Bullet!" At that moment, the tree behind him exploded, sending shards of blasted bark in all directions.

Evo hit the ground rolling "Luis–*down*!" Luis hit the sand and gunfire sent sand flying up in small tufts all around him. A test kit exploded and Luis' canteen jumped when it was hit, draining their precious fresh water into the sand.

"Get out! Get Out!" Evo hoped Luis could hear him above the rapid tattoo of the automatic fire. Grabbing his pack by the strap, Evo belly-crawled into the jungle. Sand kicked up around him as he scrambled for cover. He lurched into the weeds and ducked behind a wide tree. Ripping open a cargo pocket, Evo pulled out the .45 he carried in the field. He checked the clip and slammed it home. Flopping onto his stomach, he took a bead on where the gunfire came from and emptied the clip. Luis scrambled into the weeds next to him as Evo loaded a second clip.

Evo gasped. "Luis, how many are there?"

Cool headed, Luis leveled a look at Evo. "I think only two, but cannot be sure. Do not worry, I will find out and take care of them." Grabbing the shotgun from the side strap on his pack, Luis disappeared into the jungle. *That's what I love most about you guys.*

Evo looked around the trunk and about jumped out of his skin when the blast from Luis' shotgun went off very close to his position. "Luis?"

"One down, Dr. Evo," Luis quietly replied. "That means there are at least three–the other shots came from the other side of the lagoon. Take care and do not move from here."

Evo heaved a sigh as the bark above his head splintered. He backed off and rolled to the other side of the trunk and yelled, "Hey. Who are you?"

No answer.

"We mean no harm. I'm Dr. Evo Castillo from Lima. Why are you shooting at us?"

No answer.

Evo wondered where Luis was. He thought he'd give it one more try. He picked up his ball cap and waved it in the air. "Anyone there? Hey, can we talk? You've got the wrong guy."

Bullets flew past his hand, grazing a knuckle. Evo sucked in air between his gritted teeth and grabbed a rag out of his pack. He tore it up with his teeth and wrapped his bleeding hand. He picked up his ball cap and his eyes grew wide. He stuck a finger through the still smoking hole in the bill. "Shit, my favorite hat. Now I'm pissed."

Shotgun fire had him scrambling again, hoping to find Luis in one piece. Evo waited, sweat dripping into his eyes. Keeping the gun trained on the spot where he thought the ambusher was, Evo held still while he anxiously waited to see or hear movement in the jungle. Seconds ticked by and his patience grew thin.

A rustling to his left had him swinging around, bringing up his weapon, Heart in his throat, finger on the trigger he paused one split second.

"Dr. Evo, I got the other one too."

Evo flopped on his belly, squeezed his eyes shut, and breathed hard. "Are you sure, Luis? There could be more."

"I am sure, Dr. Evo. I walked along the beach to make sure the shooter was dead. There is no one else. No I.D. on the shooter, but he's wearing the same military uniform worn by the old rebels and shooting at us with an American M-16." He scratched his bald head. "So they must not be very well funded guerillas, yes?"

"Probably got the M-16 from his grandmother's garage sale. Seriously, good job, Luis. That could be significant later. For right now, let's get the hell out of here."

"We are not turning back?"

"Not on your life. We're going ahead as planned. I want to know who those guys are. No one knew we were here, so why were they at the lagoon? Coincidence? Or worse? Who wants us dead?" Evo hefted his backpack and trudged on.

Luis picked up his pack and the specimens. Watching Evo forge ahead, he sighed. "Dead fish, dead doctor, dead Luis. I wonder if we will ever get home." Threading his arms through the straps, he hoisted his pack and followed.

Somewhere in Southeastern Wisconsin

The late fall afternoon warmed our skin as we sat around in camp chairs in my mother's back yard. The lazy afternoon, in addition to the copious amounts of beer we had consumed, added to the comfortable feeling of being among close friends and family. Our particular circle of chairs includes me, Buzz Miller, retired detective, and number one of four daughters. On my left is FBI Bob, who we worked with last month capturing a murderer.

Bob joined our little community recently, and is doing a great job of pretending to ignore my pain-in-the-ass youngest sister, Al. The funny thing about Bob (aside from his lack of taste in women) is he could pass as a younger clone of our local Sheriff, J.J. Green. It drives some of the older gossipers of our town crazy–as if they aren't crazy enough already.

J.J. sits to my right. Now J.J. is a story unto himself. I feel a little soft and mushy looking at him now, must be all that beer I drank. Anyway, when the women in town describe J.J., they say he looks like Tom Selleck and has that easy-going

Andy Griffith type of personality. That combination makes him perfect for the job of Sheriff and irresistible to any female between the ages of nine and ninety. My sisters and I have known J.J. since we were kids, and believe me when I say that underneath his easy-going and handsome exterior lurks an evil mind. He might have everyone else fooled with those adorable dimples and "aww shucks" persona, but we know the real James J. Green. He always ran off before getting caught. He wasn't smarter. He could just run faster.

If the older generation knew half the stuff he pulled when we were younger, they'd have never elected him sheriff. Heck, he'd have spent more time in jail than he does now.

Oh, but how the women love that man. Young or old, they turn to mush when he walks into a room.

One look from those crinkly, humor-filled eyes, or a glimpse of those deep dimples on his Marlboro Man face would make one of those high-powered corporate chicks from the city start knitting baby booties.

It was a sad day when J.J. went off the market and up and married June Tabbot thirty years ago. Some major loser knocked her up and J.J. came to her rescue. He gave her his name, a good home, and he gave her son legitimacy and a great father. All June ever gave him was a hard time. She ran off with a water softener salesman three years later, leaving Adam with J.J. with no one ever hearing from her again. Bitch—good riddance.

The fact is, the day J.J. became single, every breathing female within a 40-mile radius came into heat, and the local gossips (and we've got some *professional* gossip mongers in our town) claimed they wouldn't leave J.J. alone until they found him the perfect woman. A feat that turned out to be harder than it sounded, because J.J. has remained single since the day June ran off.

Joanie, at the Post Office, claimed she would sort mail

wearing latex gloves because of the nasty perfume on some of J.J.'s mail. She claimed that one day she walked into Sal's Diner for lunch, and Joy Broussard told her she smelled like a French whore, while my mother wanted the name of her new perfume. Mom cinched it for Joanie, because everyone knows my mother has almost no sense of smell. When she *does* claim to smell something, there's either some summer visitor wearing nasty perfume that would gag a maggot, or eau-de-dog-crap on her shoes.

Lately, the geriatric crowd has again taken up the "find J.J. a nice girl" cause. Granddaughters, nieces, family, friends-of-cousins-twice-removed-daughters-in-law's-step-children—you name it; they're lined up and ready to say, "I do."

The scuttlebutt down at Sal's Diner is that up until a month or so ago, the "Mrs. J.J. Green Wannabes" took to staking out J.J.'s house. I heard the poor guy has to recon the neighborhood before he feels safe enough to go home at night. Hah! Made me almost feel sorry for him—please note I said *almost*.

I mentioned Green's devious mind. I should have guessed something was up when on more than one occasion he had me pick him up on the next block while his squad car sat in his driveway. I saw him sneaking out from behind Mrs. Kelly's Hydrangea bush, but when I asked him about it, he said he'd lost his wallet. I might have commented that I thought it more likely he'd lost his marbles. He claimed he had none left from hanging out with us—smart ass.

I've also noticed lately, I've come under fire by some—actually most of the eligible women in town. Leigh Swanson, the buxom beauty who owns the local beauty parlor, *Ready, Set, Blow*, pretended not to see me at the drug store last week, then she *accidentally* cut a large chunk of hair off the back of my head three days ago. Peggy Weller pretended not to see me when I tried to say hi to her at the grocery store, and Ellen Madsen (whom everyone in town considered the frontrunner in the "Go for the Green" stakes) *accidentally* dropped a large rock on my foot at the hardware store's garden center last week. Coincidence? Even in my worst state of paranoia, I think not.

A curious person might ask what happened to account for the recent assaults on my poor person. Considering I'm at least ten years older than most of them and about one (alright, two) sizes wider across the butt, I should never have figured into the equation. Being the crack detective I am, however, I finally figured out that the blame falls squarely upon James Joseph Green's shoulders. That is, my mom told me the women in town blame me for sneaking through the back door and stealing J.J. off the shelf.

As untrue as the story might be, the little rat-bastard Green must have planned the whole thing from the start, and being the unsuspecting dupe, I waltzed right into the trap.

It began when J.J. asked me to help with the investigation into the murder of my mother's neighbor last month. I did, and noticed somewhere along the way J.J. became a little more playful, as well as a little more attentive to me than usual, especially in public. I admit I ate it up, never stopping to wonder what the most gorgeous man this side of Lake Michigan was doing with an average-looking, newly inducted member of the AARP, with flyaway reddish-brown hair and a family full of crazy people. I mean, we've hung out all our lives, and the most romantic we'd ever been happened playing Tarzan in the old barn with a rope on the old hay pulley between the lofts. One day, he ruffled my hair one time too many times and made fun of my Tarzan yodel. I shoved him out of the hayloft and the pansy broke his arm when he landed– as if it was my fault he couldn't have landed on his butt instead of his arm.

Back to my story, it all culminated one afternoon right here at Mom's, out in back of the barn. Okay, I know what everyone is thinking, but honestly, we had a dead horse, a dead man, and half the town as chaperones, so let's all keep our minds out of the gutter, shall we? Anyway, in front of half the town plus the news media, J.J. grabbed me, pulled me close, and whispered in my ear. The fact he was talking about murder didn't matter, the damage was done.

He made it look like we were all cuddly and couple-like, and suddenly we became front-page news. My humiliation was complete when the gossip at Sal's said he'd uttered sweet nothings in my ear, leading the women of the town to try to do me in. Then their mothers started giving me the evil eye, and I was sunk. Explanations were useless, and my own mother refused to confirm or deny any rumors. That was certainly good enough for the gossip mill, so Green and I became the new town soap opera, *As the Stomach Churns.*

Taking another swig of beer, I stared at the culprit in this saga. Thinking about that entire episode made me pissy and I gave J.J. the stink eye as I touched my toe to his camp chair and tilted back in mine. I've got to give him credit though. J.J. can sure keep up the facade like a pro. He grinned at me and I sucked on my beer. I gave him an insincere toothy grin and he laughed, patting my ankle affectionately, as if he meant it.

He smiled like a contented old lap dog and leaned over to fluff my hair. Again. This caused a ripple of comments to flow through the crowd and I sighed. *Might as well give up, or break his arm again, Miller.* I was too content to argue, and to be perfectly honest, I kind-of enjoyed the temporary notoriety it afforded me, bad haircut and all. Feeling comfortably muzzy, I grinned, leaned back again and scratched the ears of my Newfoundland, Wesley. Wes was showing me the love, and leaned his 160-pound frame against my knees.

At once, I had a slight feeling of vertigo, and that feeling didn't come from a bottle. As Wes wallowed in doggie bliss, he leaned more of his weight against my chair. My feet slowly left the ground as it shifted to the left and back. I leaned forward and kicked my feet, trying to regain my balance without spilling my beer (we do have priorities in Wisconsin). As my chair passed the point of no return, my arms flapped in a drunken imitation of a dog paddle and my toes fluttered helplessly in the air.

"*Whoop*." My feet flew up. Wes woofed, excited at the prospect of playing tackle.

J.J. finally noticed I had a problem when I punted his beer across the yard. I toppled to the left and it flashed through my mind the picture I would make rolling ass-over-teakettle down the hill with a beer in my hand.

Without so much as missing a beat in the conversation, my sister Mag's boyfriend, Ian, reached out and shoved me back toward the upright position. J.J. grabbed my foot as it swung by, and pushed Wesley over as he righted my chair.

As my chair hit the ground, he grabbed the beer out of my hand, pointed at my face, and said, "You owe me one, Miller." He fluffed my hair, swigged my beer, turned, and resumed his conversation with FBI Bob. The crowd, "*Ooo'd*."

"*Whew*. How many coupons for that ride?" I blinked and tried to clear my head. I looked across the yard and saw my Bulldog, Hilary, lapping up the remainder of J.J.'s beer. She loved beer, even though it gave her gas, so it was always a good idea to curtail her drinking habits. There's nothing on earth worse than Bulldog beer farts in a small room. I strolled over and picked up the can. Hill looked up at me with those sad eyes of hers. She heaved a great sigh and passed some wicked gas. She looked around as if she couldn't believe something like that could have come out of her butt. She gave me an accusing stare—like I had anything to do with it.

"Yes, Hill, you did that, but you could have at least been polite enough to share it with J.J." I made my way back over to our group.

Hearing J.J.'s name, Hilary perked up, waddled after me,

and parked herself on J.J.'s foot. He leaned over and rubbed her ears. "How's my best girl, Hill? You're the prettiest girl in town, ya know?"

I smiled at the two of them. He sure loved my dogs. I guess that's something.

My mom sat a few feet away with her friends and I heard Joy say in a stage whisper, "Gerry, did you hear that? J.J. just told Buzz she's the prettiest girl in town."

I suppressed an undignified snort and poked J.J. He nodded and smiled in acknowledgement as we eavesdropped on the geriatric wild women.

Mom sounded doubtful as she replied, "You sure he was talking to Buzz?"

Jane nodded and said, "He always was a smart feller."

"Who's a fart smeller? Is it that damn Bulldog again?" Mary Cromwell sniffed the air and took another swig of beer.

A small stream of beer shot out of J.J.'s mouth as he tried to hold back a laugh. I pinched him while Mom scowled at her friend and shushed her. "Mary, not so loud. We were talking about J.J. and Buzz."

"J.J.'s a fart smeller? Boy-oh-boy, what those youngsters won't do for entertainment these days. I can tell you one thing though." She leaned forward and poked a thumb to her chest. "In our day we had better things to do than sniff someone's farts." She sat back and grinned.

Jane's hands fluttered in Mary's direction. "Mary, Stop!"

"Stop? Stop what? We're talking about farts. Now I like a nice long fizzer every now and then, but just lately I've been getting a little juicy…"

"*Mary!*" Joy, Jane, and Mom looked horrified.

J.J. snorted and beer shot out his nostrils. He began to cough and I slammed him on the back. Bob barked out a laugh and Al looked horrified. J.J. gasped for breath and dropped his forehead on my shoulder. He shook with silent mirth.

27

Mom's friend, Jane, bit her lip and sent a worried look our way, but she must have figured we were preoccupied and tried desperately to shush Mary. "Mary, be quiet, I mean it. One more crack like that and–"

"Yep, I know just what you mean, Janie. I like to crack one off every now and then, just like you. Sometimes I save 'em up if I know I'm going to be in an elevator. You know, so everyone is looking around wonderin' who did it." She slapped a scrawny knee and guffawed at her own joke. "No one suspects the little old lady."

"Mary!" This time all three women yelled.

"Oh, Jane, Joy, get off your high horses. You did it right along with me back in the day, and you know it. She pointed at mom. "And you, Gerry Miller, remember the frozen food section of the grocery store? Wow! If those turkeys weren't already dead, they would have been after you cracked off that doozy."

She turned to us, but contrary to Mom's protests, Mary waved her off. She took another swig and belched loud and long. "It was later in the evening after we'd eaten polish sausage and sauerkraut over at Bodgie Burns' house. We went from there to the Herr-ee Chest for some Weiss Bier.

Good old Gerry forgot to get the lemons. Boy did we have some major boomer-action going on after that."

Mary blinked myopically at the small, humiliated group of women and continued. She pointed at my mom with her bottle. "Hah! Gerry here got the munchies so we decided to stop at the Pig a few towns over. Anyway, we had to cheese it really bad, so we ran around to the frozen food section where we thought no one would be. Just as your momma cracked off the cheezer of the century, Old One-Eyed Larry came around the corner." She looked at my red-faced mom.

"Larry didn't know what hit him, 'cause you laid that rattlin' whopper on his blind side. That old boy whipped around

28

and tripped over your feet. His skinny ass flew through the air and he landed right in the chicken livers."

Mary guffawed as we piled on top of each other trying to stay quiet.

"Yup, old liquored up One-Eyed Larry swore his dead daddy had come back to haunt him, so there he was, a-layin in the frozen chicken livers a-prayin' to God for salvation. You wouldn't believe the things he confessed."

She was holding her middle and laughing so hard she could barely speak. "*Hah-ha*–he thought Ger's gas was fire and *ha-ha*–brimstone. He was a hollerin' and a-prayin'. He–*hah-ha*–couldn't–*hee-hee*–get out of the freezer. He looked like a beached whale floundering in the frozen foods, so we pulled him out and ran like heck."

By now tears rolled down my face and the entire yard full of people uproariously hooted and guffawed. Mary played to the crowd and my mom looked around for a hole to crawl into.

"*He-hee*–Old Larry, he smooshed some of the meat cartons he laid on and had chicken livers flash frozen to his butt. *Ha-ha*. He stumbled home and every hound dog in town followed him, nipping at the chicken livers. Last seen Larry was praying the hounds of hell wouldn't chew off his leg."

Mom looked ready to faint, and Joy got up and put her hands on her hips. She lifted a finger to Mary, about to let fly when Mary's son, Ted Puetz hurried up to the group. "Mother, for God's sake shut up! Have a little decency for once."

Mary gave him an evil glare. She stood nose to nose with Ted and wobbled a little before she poked him in his ample belly. "You may be town constable, young man, but if you speak to me in that tone of voice again, I'll (*burp*) kick your butt into the next zip code. Do you understand me?"

Ted actually scuffed the grass with his toe. "Yes, Ma."

"Okay then. Us girls were just talking about how smart J.J. is to be chasing after Gerry's daughter, and we got a little carried away, so go run over there and grab me a beer like a good boy."

We all stared silently at Mary: our mouths hanging open like a bunch of Bluegills on a hook.

"And another thing." She snatched the beer out of Ted's hand. "You're in U-nee-form! What are you doing with a beer in your hand? What happened to professional ethics around here?" She spun around and took a swig of the confiscated beer, giving us a wink and a grin.

Ted turned a blotchy shade of purple and stomped back toward the grill.

"Putz." Mary snorted as she flopped back into her chair.

At that J.J. lost it. He roared with laughter and I joined him. Apparently everyone in the near vicinity heard the exchange and uproarious laughter echoed off dad's barn.

My sister Fred and her old college roommate Sam walked up and Fred said, "What's so funny?" The laughter began all over again.

2

Evo grabbed his cell phone from the cargo pocket of his pants and took it out of the waterproof bag. He tried Sam Fernandini's office and was told she was on vacation. He swore and ranted some more before he called his brother's home phone, rewarded with his voicemail–again.

He waited while his brother's lengthy message blabbed in his ear. Probably got some bimbo over there. Tony always has a girl stashed somewhere. *Sam's on vacation. Tony's not answering his phone.* Evo's jumbled mind flashed red as he wondered if Tony and Sam were together. *Stupid! It's none of your business. Why would you even care? Tony is free, rich, and single, and Sam is beautiful; a bitch, but beautiful. What is she doing with my little brother anyway? I'll wring her unprofessional cheating neck!*

Evo barked from Tony's answering machine. "Dammit, Tony. Where the hell are you? This is Evo. Dump the bitch and pick up the phone–this is important. The good news is, I discovered a small, secluded lagoon in northeastern Venezuela overflowing with beautiful Endler Live Bearers."

Tony made a flying grab for the phone, still dripping from the shower. The answering machine squealed and Tony swore. He fumbled with the phone as it slipped out of his wet hands, hitting the table with a crash. He picked it up and dried it with a bath towel.

"Evo, is that you? What are you yelling about? Did you say you found wild Endlers? I ran in from the shower and only heard part of your message–hold on a second. I'm standing here wet and in my skin."

Tony heard Evo mutter, "Like I wanted to hear that," as he

31

picked his towel up off the floor and wrapped it around his hips. He turned on the speakerphone just in time to hear Evo yell, "Too much information, kid. Get some pants on. Tony grabbed his digital recorder. "Evo? Hold on. I'm going to record this so I don't miss anything."

"Are you alone, Casanova? Because this is huge, and probably should stay between us until we can track down Fernameanie. Uh, you don't have any idea where she is, do you?"

"Yeah, yeah, I know where Sam is. She's out of the country on vacation. It was just me and my fish tank last night, thank you very much. *Hah*! I slept with the fishes. *Ha*! Sometimes I kill me. Anyway, whaddaya got going there, Big Cat?"

"Geez, you sound more American every day, you idiot. Mother would kill you. Anyway, I'm investigating an environmental complaint lodged by some locals so I snuck up the backside of one of our drilling sites in Cumaná, Venezuela. I came across a black mangrove lagoon just overflowing with Endler Live Bearers. It might be a part of Laguna de los Patos, but I doubt it. I don't think I am that far north. I'll give you my bearings and if you would chart it for me, I'd appreciate it."

"No problem, Evo." He wrote down the coordinates. "So, what happened? What else did you find?"

Evo popped another antacid and walked to the shoreline, staring at the devastation. "I found hundreds of thousands of *dead* Endler Live Bearers, that's what I found."

"Oh, shit, are you kidding me, Evo–*dead* Endlers? The entire lagoon is dead, or just part of it? See if you can salvage even a few. Boy, after Sam and I discovered that the good citizens of Venezuela built a garbage dump adjacent to the only lake where Endlers existed and wiped them all off the face of the earth, I thought we would only see them in captivity. If there are any salvageable fish, it's nothing short of fantastic,

Evo!"

Evo shifted his phone to the other ear and began to pace. "Tony, Tony, listen to me. These fish may all be dead, too. Luis skimmed the lagoon for live fish, so I hope some make it home. Literally thousands of floaters are washed up on the beach as we speak. I got pictures. I'll send some to you.

"We have got to get a hold of Fernandini and we have to keep this quiet. Only you, Luis, his brother Alfredo, and I know so far, and I'm not talking to anyone until I find the source."

"What about the samples?"

"I have samples of both water and dead fish. I'll bring Alfredo in to help with the diagrams and soil samples while I look for the connection and interview the locals. Is there anything else you would need?"

"Yeah, to be there in person, and to get Sam back from the States."

"She said she wanted to visit there again someday. Didn't she go to undergraduate school or something up there? Funny, I was thinking about her and Wisconsin earlier."

"You were thinking about Sam in the jungle, Evo? I thought you barely tolerated her." Tony scrunched up his eyes, waiting for the explosion.

"I do, er...I did. Uh, never mind—leave her out of this. What the heck is she doing way up there, anyway?"

"She's visiting her old college roommate, Fred Miller and her family. I guess they had a lot of classes together until Sam split off and specialized in fish. Her friend Fred—"

Evo interrupted, "What the hell kind of name is Fred for a girl, anyway? Is she some kind of woman who wants to wear the pants all the time? Probably dresses like a man too. I hear a lot of that goes on in the States. Now it comes down here with Fernandini being called Sam. Next thing you know, Mother will want to be called Melvin."

"Sweet Virgin Mother, Evo. Are you 40, or 140? Fred is a

nickname, like Tony. When people are close to one another and they love them, they give them nicknames. Fred's whole family has nicknames. There's Buzz, Al, Fred, and Mag.

"They call their parents, *The Bill and Gerry Show*. Hell, Mag is short for *The Maggot*. I've spoken with most of them and cannot wait to meet them. You're such a tight-assed Neanderthal!"

"I am not! I tell you, Tony; you know it's my life's dream to meet a woman named after a disgusting little worm that feeds on necrotic tissue."

"Good Lord, Evo, lighten up. Mag would surprise you, but I am happy to hear you want to meet the Miller family."

"Isn't the Bitch-thyologist supposed to be here working on your project? Come on, Tony, I'm counting on you getting your degree so we can make our plans a reality. How can we start our own business if the key to our success lies with a woman more interested in shopping for shoes in the States than finishing crucial research?"

"Evo, don't call her that, and she's not a shoe-shopper. It's not like that at all. Sam hasn't been on a vacation in years, the opportunity came up, and we're stalled in the research until the final water samples of the test lakes come in at the end of the month. I was invited to go, too, but I declined so you and I could hang out, so get your ass home."

"Oh." Deflated and irritable, Evo lifted the bill of his muddy ball cap and scratched his forehead. I'm sorry, Tony, don't mind me, I'm probably just jealous. I *do* know I'm wet, tired, shot at, and I want red meat and a beer. Shit, I think I need a vacation too. Tell you what, don't worry about me. You should go to the States. I won't even be back until the end of the week, or so, and I am not good company for anyone–just ask poor Luis and Alfredo."

"Shot at?"

"We're okay."

"A long shower, a Band Aid for the bullet hole and a large chunk of cow and you will once again be a lean, mean party machine, my man. You get back here on Thursday or Friday, and I will add your ticket onto mine. What day will you want to leave for Wisconsin?"

"Leave for where? What the heck are you talking about, leave for Wisconsin? I'm not going to the States with you, Tony. I'm in the middle of a job here. I have an inspection to conduct, reports to write, media to contact, and probably some damage control to deal with. I probably won't get back to Lima before Friday."

"Great, our flight out will be Friday night. Just think of it, Evo, fresh air, bon fires, beautiful women and American Football–and you have to admit, you love American beer, my little suds sucking sibling."

"Alright, alright–I'm convinced. I'll admit I'd love to go, but I can't just drop everything and take off for the States. The only things I have with me are field clothes and dead fish."

"You got vacation time coming?"

"Yeah."

"You got money in the bank?"

"Too much."

"Figures. I know your passport is in order."

"Of course it is, but Tony…"

"*But Tony,* my butt! I'll even pack for you."

"Hold on a minute; don't you dare touch my underwear! Brother or no brother, I'll beat the crap out of you if you mess with my stuff. That itching powder episode still gives me nightmares."

"Aww, c'mon, big brother, can't take a joke? That was years ago."

"Seems like last week. Besides, how the hell do you know what to pack, anyway?"

Tony laughed. "Do you own anything but field clothes,

blue jeans, and polo shirts?"

Evo thought a minute. "Uh, no."

"There you have it. I also hear there is a *Gander Mountain* real close to Fred Miller's house. The original store was built about four miles from White Bass Lake. I can pack light and you can shop there. How cool would that be?"

"Tony, you're an ass, but a convincing ass. I think I'm going to the States on Friday. What the hell; go ahead and throw some stuff in the suitcase under my bed. I have a pre-packed hygiene case in the bathroom cabinet, but I mean it; stay out of my drawers–literally! I'll buy what I need in Wisconsin. I don't want to take a chance you'll somehow sabotage my underwear and I'll end up in some American hospital with raw balls. I'm sure they sell underwear and socks somewhere up there."

"Got it, but you hurt my feelings." Tony heard Evo snort and ignored him. "I'll call your secretary and take care of all the preparations. You just show up at my place on Friday."

"Will do. My credit cards are in my safe; I'll need those too."

"You trust me with your credit cards, but not your underwear?"

"My credit cards won't give my genitals a wasting disease."

"Aww, come on. It wasn't that bad."

"Yes it was, and I still haven't forgiven you."

"You're a hard man, Evo."

"I thought I'd never be hard again after that last fiasco."

There was a short silence on Tony's end. "No kidding? Geez, I'm sorry, Evo maybe I went a little overboard in the itching powder department. You really rotted off your winkie? I mean, the flag flies at half-staff?" He chuckled and Evo rolled his eyes. There was no stopping Tony once he was on a roll.

"The little soldier stayed at parade rest?"

"Tony…"

"The old peter putzed?" He chuckled harder.

"I'm not kidding, Tony."

"The willy nillied?" Tony guffawed.

"*Tony*!"

"Uh, oops. Sorry, Evo. What were we talking about?"

"Retrieving my credit cards from the safe."

"Oh, right. What's the combination?"

"The combination is Great Aunt Sophie's birthday."

There was silence on the other end. "Sophie's birthday? Why ever did you pick that?"

Evo was glad no one but the dead fish were around to witness his embarrassment. "It's the only six numbers in a row I ever remember. I had to remember that date under the threat of death. To miss that old woman's birthday is to poke a sleeping crocodile with a sharp stick–you get your head bitten off by three generations of female members of the family."

Tony hooted. "Evo, you kill me. It *has* been too long, my brother, I cannot wait until Friday. If you get in early, call me."

"Okay. Hey, Tony, one more thing. Luis knows about the site. Maybe we should keep him and his brother close. While I'm gone they have no work anyway–I'd bet they'd love a trip to the States. Put their tickets on one of my credit cards. We'll put them up in a hotel or something and we'll show them a good time up north."

Evo turned and shouted to Luis, "Hey, you and Alfredo got any special plans for the next week or two?"

"No, *Señor* Evo," Luis called back. "We go where you go."

"Good, because I'm going to the United States, and you and your brother are coming with me."

Luis stared at Evo, and with childlike wonder said, "Disney World?"

Evo cringed. "Maybe, we'll have to see, but we'll be near

Chicago."

Luis did a little wiggle. "*Woo-hoo*. Chicago Cubs. Chicago style hot dogs. Blackhawks. Bulls. White Sox. Chicago style pizza. Chicago style football... Da Bears!" Luis sucked in a breath and looked at the cloudy sky. He closed his eyes, smiled, folded his hands as if in prayer, and said reverently, "Snow."

Evo shook his head and chuckled. He turned back to his phone. "Looks like we have traveling companions, bro. Luis wants to see Mickey Mouse and snow."

Tony said, "Yeah, I heard him. Snow, *hmmm*. I never thought of that. Alfredo once told me they signed on with you because they wanted adventure. Well, I guess they are about to have an adventure, alright. Do they have snow in Wisconsin this time of year?"

"I don't know. I'm more concerned with protecting the brothers from media attention and whoever might have shot at us."

"Right you are. This could become sticky if word gets out, and depending on what you find, it could become dangerous. I'll take care of the travel details, and have everything ready. You take care, big brother. No Superman stuff, hear?"

"You got it, little brother; bye for now."

"Bye, Evo, be careful, and be safe."

"Hey, Tony, just one more thing; I mean it–keep your fingers off my underwear."

Evo could still hear Tony laughing as he hung up his phone.

3

Tony hung up the phone and leaned on the back of his couch. He had his work cut out for him. Where he didn't quite lie, he did exaggerate a little. Tony picked up the phone again and called his work. He told them he would be out of country with his brother for a couple of weeks. He called Evo's secretary, Elena, and told her the same thing and asked if she could swing some time off for Evo. She put him on hold while she checked her computer and assured him she could clear Evo's schedule for almost three weeks. Tony practically jumped up and down until she made him promise that Evo would get his ulcer looked at while on vacation.

That made Tony stop. *Ulcer? Big brother-solid-as-a-rock-Evo has an ulcer?* Good thing Tony was sitting down. Getting Evo away from work sounded more and more like a good idea. Evo shouldn't be working for the *enemy* anyway. Why he did escaped Tony and made Dr. Sam crazy. It couldn't be the money. Hell, Evo already had four more dollars than God did. He never took time off so he didn't spend what he made; let alone what he'd inherited. *He busts his ass for some millionaire who could give a shit, and now he's making himself sick. Idiot.*

"Looks like it's time for *Almost*-Doctor Antonio Enrique Moronez-Castillo to step in and save the day. Maybe I can marry him off to some beautiful, outdoorsy American woman– Wait! Maybe I can marry him off to Dr. Sam. Would that not be poetic justice? Then Evo could settle down and earn his ulcers the old fashion way; with a wife, ten kids, a hundred fish tanks, and a dog."

Tony was beyond excited as he pushed off the back of the couch and practically skipped down the hall to his office. His towel dropped somewhere along the way, but by the time he realized it, he had procured a private plane to Milwaukee, rented an SUV (who knew what kind of bad highway led to the wilds of Wisconsin?), and had MapQuested directions from Mitchell Field Airport to White Bass Lake, Wisconsin.

While his directions printed, he ran to his bedroom and pulled on a pair of ratty looking shorts. Good thing money was no object, he thought, as he rummaged through his closet for a suitcase. They would buy what they needed for Luis and Alfredo in Wisconsin. The brothers would probably get a kick out of an American wardrobe for their first American vacation, anyway.

The following day Tony took care of the money and passports. The first thing he did when he arrived at Evo's apartment was snoop through his underwear drawer. He thought about messing it up, or stealing all the underwear, but figured Evo would expect something like that. Instead, Tony stopped at a woman's wear store, bought some pink ladies' underwear, and stashed them in Evo's suitcase. He packed in less than ten minutes, knowing Evo would end up buying a couple of suitcases in the States to accommodate what he bought at the outfitter stores anyway.

Proud of his subtle revenge on his brother, Tony had dinner in town, visited their mother and told her of their plans, and rolled back into his own apartment about suppertime. He made motel reservations online with Evo's credit cards, and used them to pay for the plane and the car. He made himself a peanut butter and banana sandwich and went over his notes. When he finally went to bed, he felt good; everything was falling into place. He felt even better after having spent Evo's money doing it.

Friday morning came and Tony decided he'd procrastinated long enough.

He grabbed his cell phone and looked up Dr. Fernandini's

private cell number. As he dialed, he tried to remember what time it would be in Wisconsin.

Surprisingly, she answered her cell, her voice sounding tense. "Antonio, what is wrong?"

She must have Caller Id. "Nothing, Dr. Sam, I just wanted to call and ask if the offer still stood to show me a person with their head made of cheese." He chuckled to himself and waited for the answer he knew would come.

"Oh, Antonio, a Cheesehead, not a head made of cheese. Of course, of course. Please come to Wisconsin; I would love for you to meet my friends. And call me Sami or Sam. I'm on vacation and only people from our work use formal titles."

"My brother would cringe if he heard anyone call you a man's name."

Tony could almost feel the chill. "Antonio, I do not particularly care what your egotistical, trade-principals-for-money of a brother thinks; he could jump off a cliff and I would cheer. Ooo—just *thinking* about that man makes me mad!"

Tony took a breath and held it. "Oh, oh. Does that mean he's not invited too? I kind of already told him we were both going. That's okay though, we can go to New York, or Disney World, or somewhere else."

Let her mull that over a bit. Then at the right moment I will say, "It's just that Evo is uh, let's just say he's not one hundred percent, Dr. S. Uh, his doctors say...that is...uh, I need to get him away for a while before..."

He heard a sharp intake of breath. "Oh, my God, Tony, what is it? Is it serious? I am so sorry. What can I do? By all means bring him with you—will his doctor okay him for travel? Is Wisconsin's climate good for him? Perhaps you're right and it is time we put aside our differences."

Tony chuckled to himself. *Okay, T-Man, time to check out the waters. Bait the hook and dangle it in front of her.* "Maybe

41

it is, Dr. S. You know, Evo always says how he would love to get to know you better."

She sounded skeptical. "*Hmm*, he does? Tell me, Tony, does he also call all his friends derogatory names, or am I just special?"

"Oops, you heard that, did you?"

"Which one, *Damn Sam*, *Fernameanie*, *Fern's a dingy*, or my personal favorite, the crude but clever, *Bitchthyologist*?"

Good job, Tony, you lost that one. Re-bait the hook and try again. "That Evo, ha, ha, is always joking around. Hey, I just thought it would be a cool thing if he could tell you in person about his latest discovery. He has already tried to contact you. He wanted you to be the first to know. There really is much more to Evo than you think, Dr. S."

Silence met the bombshell. *"I'll give her five seconds before....three, two, one..."*

Sam blurted, "What discovery? Come on, Tony, what did Evo find?"

Gotcha, Doc; hook, line, and sinker! Reel her in gently, now, Tony, old boy. "Evo's up near Peninsula de Paria in Venezuela and found a small lagoon full of Endler Live Bearers."

Silence. "Endlers did you say? Impossible. You are joking! Don't tease me about stuff like that, Tony. Is he sure they're not guppies or something else?"

"You may not like him, Sam, but don't insult him. If Evo said he found Endlers, he found Endlers. The problem is, however..."

Tony heard someone squeal in a definite American accent, "Wild Endlers? Send me some! Bring some with you. Don't tell anyone. Who's on the phone, Sam; is it that cute guy who works with you, or the devastatingly handsome asshole brother?"

Sam groaned and Tony chuckled. "I bet I'm the cute guy

and not the handsome asshole. Does this mean you are sufficiently humiliated so I can now blackmail you into letting me bring Evo?"

Tony could imagine Sam biting her lower lip and bouncing on the balls of her feet. He heard her sigh. "I am resigned to my fate. God is punishing me by ruining my first vacation in four years. Yes, yes, bring him if you must, but tell him to leave his corporate ego and his sarcasm in Peru. It is the only way I can tolerate him."

Tony grinned. "I'll tell him you can't wait to see him."

"You do, and they will never find your bleaching bones."

"You got yourself a deal, Doc, and don't worry about Evo. I think he has a secret crush on you. He's a different guy away from work, you'll see."

"Antonio, I have never known you to be so irreverent and underhanded."

"There's a lot you don't know, Doc, but you'll find out soon enough; and please call me Tony. I'm on vacation."

Tony hung up the phone and let out a cowboy, "*Ya-hoo*." He was happier than he'd been in months. Funny how he'd never thought about Evo and Dr. S as a couple before, probably because they fought like two male bettas in the same tank. *Hah–fish joke. Why didn't he think of it before? Sam and Evo will be perfect together.* He loved the heck out of them both, but they were so damn stubborn they would never find each other without some very devious planning. He would have to be careful because they were also wicked smart, and they would kill him if they discovered him plotting against them, or for them–whatever, a great idea is a great idea.

Tony also wondered about these Americans. Would Sam's friend conspire with him to get those two together? With a name like Fred, she had to see whimsy in life. He would charm her into helping. He could turn on the charm and the backwoods American girl would help him commit murder if he

43

so chose. He would make her see how perfect Evo and Sam are for each other.

Tony whistled the Wedding March as he threw more clothes into a suitcase. He stopped in mid-whistle and realized he had not told Dr. S that the Endlers Evo found were dead and he neglected to tell her they were coming in tomorrow night. He zipped the suitcase and smiled. She'd find out soon enough.

4

After Evo hung up from Tony, he and Luis picked up their machetes. Evo thought it would be best to send Luis back to the truck with the samples they had collected. He called Alfredo to make sure he was still back at the starting point and told him to expect his brother and make a loud scene when he arrived at the drilling site. Since Evo would arrive first and didn't want to alert anyone of his presence, he continued alone on foot. The brothers would give Evo two hours before heading to the front gates of Oil Well Site 151. Evo figured that would give him enough time to look around the backside of things before anyone discovered he was investigating the site.

Evo circled the lagoon and made his way down an animal trail toward a local village. The smell of rotting flesh pervaded the air as he neared the village. Tying a bandana around the lower half of his face, he retrieved his handgun and cautiously entered a clearing at the gates to the village. Evo noticed a small enclosure with three dead goats inside. *No wonder it smells.* He stepped around a dead chicken and neared the goat pen. The goat feed lay on the ground untouched, and the water trough was about half-full. Putting on plastic gloves, Evo took samples of the water and feed, packing them away for testing later.

Tire tracks cut deeply into the mud, but he saw no vehicles. Evo called out but no one answered. The small gathering of crude structures stood sad and silent in the morning heat.

"How the hell can I interview the locals if there are none?" He eyed the trail behind him, the grass on both sides flattened in the direction of the lagoon. He made a note in his spiral notebook, took pictures, and continued on.

A feeling of dread weighed heavily on his shoulders as he walked past the empty huts. Had Nunez crossed the line of business ethics and contaminated the food or water supplies to this village? If the lagoon poisoned the fish, could the villagers have given that same water to their livestock, or God forbid, their children?

Evo put away the notebook and pulled out his recorder. Beginning again, he documented his movements and observations as he searched the deserted village. He took pictures and gathered more samples. He rounded the last building on the street, the church, and stopped dead. Rows of freshly mounded gravesites lined the western side of the graveyard. Evo counted thirty-five in all. Many were small, and Evo's ulcer burned with the knowledge that many children had died here recently.

Evo swallowed the bile in his throat, took more pictures, and stepped to get a better look at the markers. He noted that the majority of the birth dates ranged from 1920 through 1933, and again from 2000-2011. "The children and the elderly," he murmured. "The most susceptible age groups for death by disease, and the first to succumb to ingested toxins."

Evo popped a few more antacids and turned from the graveyard. He headed out of the village toward Site 151. He stopped in the middle of the street. Turning back, he went into the church and knelt near the altar, saying a prayer for the dead. Standing, Evo stared up at the cross, tears streaming down his cheeks.

Turning abruptly, Evo marched out of the church, and out of the village.

"Children, elderly, and the livestock," he muttered as he passed the dead chickens and goats. "Flattened ground and dead fish." He took the time to record more notes before he continued on toward the drilling site. A faint trail made by the villagers made the walk down the mountain easier. By the look of the encroaching jungle, Evo estimated that no humans had passed this way for about two weeks. In another few days this trail would be obliterated by jungle vegetation.

Evo glanced at his watch, startled to find he'd spent a couple hours in the village. The light from the sun barely appeared over the horizon and he was not yet at Site 151. He trotted another twenty minutes down the mountain before he reached the site.

Evo checked out what he could of the back end of the compound, taking pictures from the high ground. He noted the drilling site quite a ways down the mountain from the village, and wrote; *Runoff does not flow uphill*, in his notebook. Collecting samples of dirt and standing water, he continued the narrative on his recorder.

Eventually, he skirted the perimeter and met up with Luis and Alfredo near the front gate. They were in the process of arguing loudly with security over permits and identification. Evo approached and ended the argument by producing the paperwork security demanded.

While the guards were engaged with Alfredo, Evo shoved the camera toward Luis. "Take a look at these pictures and hide the camera. I need to speak to the foreman. Can you and Luis talk to the men and start the initial inspection of the site?"

"But, Dr. Evo—"

"Just look professional and pretend."

"Okay, Boss." Luis nodded and the camera disappeared like magic. Evo headed into the foreman's trailer and the last he saw, Luis and Alfredo had donned lab coats and hard hats. Carrying clipboards, they headed toward the field workers. *Smart boys*.

The foreman, an affable man, didn't strike Evo as a murderer of fish or children. Ron Hansen smiled the easy smile of a man who slept well at night. An American, Ron had a

47

hearty laugh and a shrewd mind. Evo sensed brain behind Ron's brawn, and congratulated Nunez for great perception in hiring the American. Ron waited for Evo to state his business and was very forthcoming about the operation at 151. He pulled charts and retrieved graphs which told the story of ongoing soil and water samples of the surrounding area, as well as the topography of the mountain. Evo looked on, confused that the story less than an hour up the mountain should be so different from the one seen here.

"Ron, is there perhaps another mining or drilling site between here and Puerta de la Cruz?"

Ron referred to his charts and shook his head. He circled a small area at a higher elevation than the small village. "No, no," he said thoughtfully. "There's nothing between here and there." He scratched his chin. "You know, this may mean nothing, but some of the locals spoke of the 'Devil's Eye' north of their village." He marked the approximate area on the map. "I thought it was old superstition crap, but many of the men complain that they were *strongly* encouraged to go there while their women, children, and elderly stayed back in the villages. They were not more forthcoming, so I just figured it was a cut-and-burn operation, not a mine or well." He tapped the map thoughtfully. "Look at this, Dr. Castillo. Nunez owns all the land north of the village, so you or I would know of any operation up there. Must just be wives' tales and rumors: nothing more."

Evo wrote down some notes and clicked on the recorder. "Ron, have you had a lot of flooding around these parts lately?"

"We've had more rain this season than we've had in the last ten."

"Have your salt pond, or re-mix ponds overflowed?"

"Nope. We build them up with sandbags when they get too deep, but for the most part, the water treatment equipment keeps up." He lowered his reading glasses and leveled a look at

Evo. "Level with me now, what exactly are you looking for, Dr. Castillo?"

Evo thought hard about showing his cards. He figured he had to trust someone, and Hansen could be a strong ally. He let out a heavy breath. "Heavy metal contamination. Enough to kill anything it comes into contact with. I found over thirty graves in the village, dead animals–the works."

Hansen flopped back in his chair. "Wow. You don't pull any punches, do you?"

"I have to trust someone and you know your operation and the area."

"But heavy metal poisoning is more of a mining problem, not oil drilling. Does Chavez know about this yet, or Nunez?"

Evo leaned forward in his chair. "No one but you and I. I would like to finish my investigation before going off half-cocked. I have to make a report to Chavez as soon as I get back to Lima, so if you can keep this under your hat until then, I'd really appreciate it."

"Who am I going to tell? I don't want this getting out any more than you do, but have you ever met this Chavez character? I mean, since we're being honest here, what's your take on him?"

Evo thought before he answered. "To tell you the truth, the man beat me out of a promotion to get the job he's in, so I can't say I would be totally objective. Why do you ask?"

Ron cocked his head to one side. "Well, it's only my opinion, and you know what folks say about those, but think there's more to him than meets the eye."

"Oh? How so?"

Ron hesitated. "It's just a gut feeling I get when I talk to him. Some of the questions he asks have nothing to do with my business dealings with Nunez, and when I call him on it, he back peddles or becomes belligerent. Then there are the security people he hired."

"You do not hire and fire your own men?"

"Normally, yes, but six weeks ago I got a call from him telling me he was sending extra security. Those guards are real assholes, and they only take orders from Chavez. I just don't trust him."

"But you trust me after one introduction."

Ron barked out a laugh. "My friend, I could see right off, you are a stand-up guy. I hope someday we can work together on a project. Just be careful around that Chavez character, will you?"

"I'll watch my back, and you be careful, too. There is something going on here, I just have to figure it out. When I do I'll let you know."

"Good enough then."

Both men stood and shook hands. "Until next time, Dr. Castillo."

Evo grasped his hand warmly. "Call me Evo, and it was a pleasure meeting with you."

"And you as well."

Evo nodded and left the building. He spotted Alfredo taking water samples as Luis talked to the workers. Evo walked over to the men and helped finish up the interviews.

He asked Alfredo and the men about the *Devil's Eye*, but the group clammed up and dispersed.

"Wow. That certainly broke up the party fast. Come on guys, we're finished here anyway." Evo took the samples from Alfredo and led the way back to the truck.

Luis halted. "Wait one minute." He dashed around a corner.

Alfredo picked up the clipboard Luis dropped in his haste to run across the compound and Evo looked over his notes.

Luis came strolling back to the truck, followed by a guard carrying what looked like an M-13 or 16. Luis grinned at Evo and climbed into the truck. Comprehension dawned, and Evo made haste to load up and leave.

The three men packed the truck as the guard stood by, and Evo was again amazed at the dumb peasant act Luis and Alfredo put on for the guerilla. Big grins and lots of waving surrounded the three men as the vehicle sped out of the compound. Evo watched the guard pull out a cell phone before they hit the front gate. He met and held Evo's stare as he spoke into the phone.

Alfredo drove, making great time as they headed for the airport in Cumaná. It was a long trek over rough terrain, but the corporate plane was ready when they arrived.

The flight back to Lima was uneventful, and Evo made arrangements at the airport to hold the fish and the samples until the next day when their flight left for the States. He put Alfredo and Luis up at a hotel and headed for the office.

Three hours and several cups of coffee later, Evo made two copies of his written and audio notes as a matter of habit. He locked one copy in his safe and tucked the other in the side pocket of his cargo pants.

He then called Hector Chavez and gave him a verbal rundown of the trip. His description of the lagoon went without comment, but when he started on the trek through the village, Chavez stopped him cold. "What are you talking about—dead fish and dead goats? What did the villagers say?"

"There were no villagers, only a lot of graves behind the church."

"The hell you say! Castillo, did you talk to anyone else about this?"

"Only Ron Hansen, the foreman at Site 151. He's going to ask around about the village and something called 'The Devil's Eye'. I really think it's connected to the abandoned village, and the dead livestock."

"What are you blathering about, Castillo? What were you thinking, telling Hansen like that? Do those two nitwits who work for you know? Well of course they do, what am I saying? What do you think is going on here, murder? Conspiracy?"

"No, nothing like that. It's just rather odd, don't you think?"

"I think you need a vacation, Castillo."

"I'm about to take one."

"I know; your secretary called. I want that report and all your notes on my desk before you leave tomorrow."

"Okay. I have most of it on tape. I'll just have Elena–"

"No, no. Just send me the tape and your notes; I'll write the report. Don't leave it for your secretary, and don't call Nunez; I'll take care of it. You go enjoy your vacation in…"

"White Bass Lake, Wisconsin. It's near Chicago."

"Oh, right. Chicago." Chavez sounded distracted. "Uh, right. You go to Chicago and have fun. I'll take care of everything. Don't worry." There was a moment of silence and Evo tried to make sense of the strange conversation. Chavez then asked, "Your assistants; you said they are with you too?"

"Yes, but of what significance is that? Do you need reports from them or something? I guess you should know; I'm taking them with me on vacation."

"Oh, good, good. Take them with you. I can see them when you get back."

Evo scratched his chin. "If you're sure."

"I'm sure. You go and leave everything to me."

"Okay, Hector, and thank you."

Chavez rang off and Evo stared at the phone. "Well that was strange." Evo thought about what Ron Hansen had said about Chavez. Why did he want to know about Luis and Alfredo? Why did he want the report and all his notes? What was his problem with Evo's secretary? Should he call Ron and run it past him? Evo shook his head. No, why create a conspiracy theory? *Unless of course, there is one.* Evo's stomach gave a twinge and he rubbed it. *Vacation sounds pretty good about now.*

At the other end, Hector Chavez stared straight ahead. The more he thought, the tighter he squeezed his fists. His face burned and his nails bit into his palms. With one sweep of an arm, everything on his desk flew across the room, slamming against the wall and shattering onto the floor. He slicked back his hair with shaky hands, calmly picked up the phone, and dialed.

5

In a Smokey Bar Somewhere in Lima

"Are you sure you can take care of them?" The oily haired man in the dark sunglasses set his drink down on the worn table.

"Sure we can, boss. We are like chameleons. We blend in. No one will know we were even there." The filthy, rough looking man made a gesture with his hand. "Smooth as silk. Those people will never see South American soil again. You can count on us."

The man in the sunglasses looked skeptically at the second man at the table who picked his nose as he chewed a toothpick.

The picker looked up at the man with the sunglasses, said, "Smooth," and nodded his head.

"When do we leave?" The first man slid his chair back.

"Hopefully, after you two take a bath," he said under his breath. "Tonight." He cleared his throat. "The flight leaves at ten."

The first man ignored the rude comment. "We can be ready."

Sunglasses slid an envelope across the table. The other man picked it up and a key dropped into his hand. He slammed his hands on the table and leveled a glare at the boss man. "What kind of bullshit is this?" The man with the toothpick kicked back his chair and stood, reaching under his jacket.

Holding up his hands, the man with the sunglasses spoke quickly. "It's a key to a locker at the airport. Everything you need is inside. Passports, money, tickets, the works. You get paid the rest upon your successful return."

Toothpick growled, "This better be legit, *amigo*, or we're coming after you."

Mr. Sunglasses lowered his gaze and stared him down. "You'd better do the job, *amigo*, or I'm coming after *you*–both."

"We'll do the job, have no fear." The two men chugged their drinks and slammed their glasses on the table. They turned and strode out of the bar, not bothering to look back.

Sunglasses sat back, stared after them, and thoughtfully sipped his wine. He wondered if hiring cut-rate killers was such a wise choice. They seemed so rough, uncouth, and amateurish, but they were also expendable. The paltry hundred-thou it would cost him seemed like pocket change compared to what he would make on this deal. If they got nailed for murder in the States, so what? They knew nothing of his plans, nor did they know his identity. They would spend the money foolishly, and he could have them taken out at any time. He smiled and took another sip. No, it was a good idea.

Tomas and Marco made their way through the mean streets of Lima to the hovel they shared. The door to their tiny apartment slammed shut behind them and they stared at each other. Suddenly, they both let out howls that shook the rafters. "*Hooo-weee*. A hundred G's and a paid vacation in the States."

"It don't get no better than this, Tomas."

Tomas straightened and sobered. "From now on I'm Tom, and you are going to be Mark. Just like real Americans. From now on we practice using our new names."

"Tom and Mark. Mark and Tom. We do sound American." Mark turned his ball cap backward, "Yo, yo. Cool, dude. What up, dawg?"

Tom said in exasperation, "What are you trying to be, some sort of rap star?"

Mark looked at Tom over the tops of his scratched sunglasses and grabbed his crotch. "What? What? You want some-a-this, bro? You wanna piece-a-me, bee-ach?"

Tom rolled his eyes skyward as if seeking divine intervention. "You are so lame; I can't believe we're related. Did your mother drop you on your head at birth or something?" Tom sighed. "I'm going to hit the shower." He sniffed his armpits. "Do you think we overdid the dirt a little?"

"Naw, I think it made us more believable." Mark sniffed his own armpits. "*Whew*. I am kind-of ripe though. Let me shower first, dawg." He headed for the tiny bathroom.

"Hey! I called the shower first."

"Too late, bee-ach." The door slammed behind him.

Tom slumped in a chair and stared at the envelope. He picked up the key and tapped it on the table. This was their ticket out. They might have been born in the slums, but they weren't going to die there. All they had to do was knock off a couple of losers and an egghead scientist or two. Piece of cake. Murders happen all the time in the States, right? What're a couple more?

Tom slapped the key on the table. The only problem; he and Mark had never murdered anyone. Hell, the sight of blood made him heave, and Mark, what an idiot. What the heck were they thinking? They needed a plan. That's right! A bloodless plan. Poison? *Naw, we'd have to get too close.* They could drop them out of a plane, or throw them in front of a bus maybe.

Tom began to pace. *We could make it look like an accident, or suicide, or maybe a mob hit.* That would be good, a mob hit, like Al Capone. Then they could settle down and buy an ice cream shop or something. He always did want to be an ice cream salesman.

Tom shook his head to clear it. The thought of murder made him uneasy. When the little grease ball, Ernesto had propositioned them they'd seen nothing but the money. They'd said yes before they knew what the job entailed.

He thought of his mother. Crap. Mama thought they were doing fine and going on vacation. They were already a disgrace, so what the hell did it matter if he offed some people he had never met? Screw that, he thought. He'd be a rich disgrace, that's what he'd be. He just would not think about it.

Tom picked up the key then dropped it in the envelope. The shower stopped in the bathroom and the door popped open. Mark hopped into the room and jiggled his hips. "I feel good! Bop, bodama-bop! So good, bump bump, so good, Bump bump!"

Tom brushed by him on his way to the bathroom. "Save your energy, Mr. James Brown. You're going to need it."

Mark did a little dance. "Not James, not Juan, not Paco, it's Mark—Mark, uh, whatever our last name will be. Hah! Good thing we are bilingual, eh, *Tom*?"

"*Si*, Mark. That's how we got the job. That and we both have a driver's license. Who knows, we may have to run over someone." He looked at the floor and sighed. "Let me get cleaned up and we'll go." The door closed behind him.

Mark looked at the closed door. "*Humph*. What's gotten into him?"

An hour later, the new and clean Mark and Tom stood in their doorway looking at the empty apartment. "So long, old life," Tom said, and closed the door.

"Hello, new life. Mark pounded his way down the stairs and out of the building.

They threw the remainder of their belongings in a dumpster and walked fifteen blocks before they found a taxi. "The old neighborhood just ain't what it used to be," Tom said, puffing from the exertion of the walk. "Taxi drivers won't even come in here."

"What are you talking about? Taxi drivers aren't stupid. They *never* came into this neighborhood. Someday I want to live in a neighborhood where they have taxi drivers and pizza delivery."

"We play our cards right, Mark, and we will."

Finally, a taxi pulled up and they climbed in. Mark cleared his throat. "Airport," he said in his most professional voice, and off they went.

The Lima airport proved to be an adventure in controlled chaos. With the construction finished, it was much easier to navigate, but this early in the evening had commuters and vacationers vying for position at ticket counters, baggage pick-up, and rental agencies. Tom and Mark fought their way through the crowds and sat in chairs near a bank of lockers and looked around to see if they had been followed.

Thirty minutes passed before Mark leaned close to Tom's ear and whispered, "Looks clear to me, do you see anything?" Tom shook his head and they moved in.

Inside the locker, they found two tagged bags and another large envelope containing their tickets, passports, American money, and driver's licenses tucked inside nylon wallets. They also found assorted credit cards and pictures of phony kids and relatives. They gathered their duffels, and headed for the gates.

Once on the plane, they stored their bags and took their seats. They had three transfers between Lima and Chicago, and they went over how they would get from one plane to the next.

"Damn cheapskate, couldn't book us a direct flight," Mark mumbled.

"I'm sure he did it this way so we would be harder to trace. I know we have tickets, but do you think we should turn them in for others just in case the boss man has other plans, like stealing his money back?"

Mark scratched his chin. "Uh yeah, I thought of that, but I got one better. Let's ditch the credit cards when we get there so he can't trace us through them. What if he claims we stole them later just to get us arrested and rip us off the money he owes us?"

"Oh. I get it. Yeah, good idea, Mark, but the thing we really have to watch is spending too much of our cash. We may need it later, so we must to be thrifty. I hear it's expensive to live in the States."

"I read the same thing last week in a magazine. We can use the credit cards for everything until we get there. Mr. Big Boss won't be able to trace us beyond the airports." Mark settled back in his seat. "So, cousin, do we have any plans on how we are going to uh, *spend our vacation*?"

Tom looked confused and then the light went on in his head. He cleared his throat in case someone was listening. "Uh, no, Mark, but once we get there, I'm sure something will come to us. Maybe if we sleep on it now, we can think of something to do. I think I want to see the Willis Tower."

"Why yes, what a good idea. Maybe take in a museum or the art institute, too."

"Good idea, Mark. We don't have a set schedule."

"Oh, dude, I thought you had it all worked out."

"Don't worry about it. I did; or I do–or will have. Go to sleep, Mark. It's a long trip."

"Yeah, okay." Mark slept and Tom stared out the window deep in thought.

6

The aircraft ascended into the evening sky and Evo turned to watch Luis and Alfredo, their noses pressed against the window. The brothers marveled at the twinkling lights below as they left Lima behind them.

Tony yawned and stretched as the private plane soared toward Chicago. "Can you believe it, Evo? An actual vacation. When was the last time we got to do anything remotely so cool?"

Evo opened one eye. "I don't know, Disney World as kids?"

"Yeah, that was cool. We were awfully little, though."

"You cried when we took pictures of you with Mickey Mouse."

"You're the asshole who said he'd eat me."

Evo smiled sleepily. "Yeah well, you always were gullible."

"And you're still an asshole"

"Thank you. Now let me sleep."

Tony said softly, "Hey, Evo, thanks for the vacation." He slumped down in his seat, covering his eyes with his ball cap.

"Sure, Tony, no prob–Vacation?" Evo jerked upright. "Are you telling me *I* paid for this entire vacation?"

Tony smiled and crossed his arms, snoring softly. Evo threw his pillow and knocked the cap off Tony's head. Tony jumped, pretending to have been rudely awakened. "W*hat*?"

"What my ass, you cheap shit. Did you invite me along so I could pay for your trip and suffer abuse from Dr. Death on top of it? You should be paying *me* to go. Dammit, Tony…" Evo rubbed his stomach and absently searched for an antacid.

Tony sat up, concerned. "Evo, man what's up? Your secretary told me to make you get your ulcer checked out. She wasn't kidding. You really have one, don't you?"

Evo shifted uncomfortably. His stomach burned, but he refused to give in to it in front of his brother. "It's no big deal, Tony. Leave it alone."

"Look, Evo, I'm your brother, not your mother. You want to end up in the hospital playing He-man, you do what you got to do, but don't play me about not being sick. Take care of it while it's still small."

Evo exhaled and popped two tablets. He sat back, closing his eyes. "It started bothering me a few months ago. I guess part of me thought if I ignored it, it would go away. Now I'm just a little scared. I can't afford to miss work."

"Elena made me promise."

"I'll get to it."

"You got three weeks off."

"I'm on vacation."

"Not if you keel over first."

"You're worse than a wife. It's no wonder you're not married."

"Speaking of someone who should be getting married..."

"Okay, okay, I'll see a damn doctor."

"Good boy."

"*Arf.*" Evo turned his back to Tony and closed his eyes. Tony permitted himself a small smile and picked his ball cap up off the floor. He pulled it low over his eyes and drifted off to sleep.

The trip was long, but uneventful. They dozed, woke, ate, and dozed again. Luis and Alfredo continued to stare out the window. Tony and Evo played chess and cards, and Evo read while Tony played solitaire. They watched movies and Evo finally fell into a deep sleep.

When Evo woke several hours later, he noticed right off

61

Alfredo still sat with his nose pressed to the window. Luis was dead asleep next to him, drool running down onto his shoulder.

Evo whispered to Alfredo, "Why don't you ease him back into his seat? Wouldn't he be more comfortable?"

"But, *Señor* Evo, he may miss the good part."

"Uh, okay." Evo went to speak with the pilot. When he returned, he woke Tony and told him and Alfredo they were about fifteen minutes out of Milwaukee.

Alfredo tore his gaze away from the window. "All I see is the ocean, *Señor* Evo. Where is this Wisconsin?"

Tony grabbed his map and flopped in the chair next to Alfredo. He pointed and said, "Look, my friend. This is Wisconsin. This is Lake Michigan. What you are seeing is a lake. Pretty big, eh?"

Alfredo looked out the window. "*Si*, pretty big, eh. So where are we going?"

Tony again pointed. "That's Milwaukee." He slapped Alfredo on the back. "It's the beer capitol of the world."

"Is it as big as Lima?"

"There are very few places as big as Lima, my friend. Milwaukee could fit inside Lima, I'm afraid, but it is a large city by American standards."

"It looks large from up here–oh look, Luis, the airport. We are here, in America, in Milwaukee, Wisconsin. Beer Drinking Capitol in the World. I like Milwaukee already."

Tony chuckled. "Beer Capitol, Alfredo."

"*Hah*. Not after Luis and I get done drinking, *mi amigo*."

They were still laughing as they taxied down the runway. Evo took the brothers to wait for the luggage and Tony went to see about the vehicle. They met at the rental kiosk where they took a shuttle to their car. Evo took one look and thought it was a joke. "Uh, Tony? I thought you rented an SUV?"

Tony looked at the rental agent, who looked at his paperwork. "It says right here, Castillo, Antonio, one Suzuki."

"Suzuki, I didn't say Suzuki, I said SUV. I want a big, American SUV, dammit! He stomped his foot and turned to see Evo laughing at him. "What the hell are you braying like a jackass about, Evo?"

Evo clutched at his stomach, doubled over, laughing hysterically. "SUV, Su-zu-ki–must have been your accent. How the heck are we all going to fit in there?"

Tony stood by, staring at the tiny car wondering the same thing. "I don't suppose you have anything else, do you?"

The rental agent shook his head, trying hard not to smirk.

Evo grabbed the keys. "Okay, I'm driving. Let's go."

Luis grabbed the door handle on the passenger's side and jumped in, locking the door. He looked at Evo and nodded his head once. Evo smiled as Tony and Alfredo stared at the tiny back seat and the luggage piled next to the car. "Load her up boys!"

Evo popped the miniscule trunk and tried the radio. He found a country station and kept time by tapping on the steering wheel, occasionally looking in the mirror to see how Tony fared.

The car rocked back and forth as they tried to stuff the luggage in the trunk. Evo turned up the radio to cover the sounds of Tony swearing. Luis giggled and kept time to the music. Alfredo held an armful of clothes as he squeezed into the back seat, and Evo watched as Tony shook hands with the rental agent.

Tony opened the rear door and Evo heard him say to the agent, "No, my brother won't mind, I appreciate your help." Evo heard murmuring and Tony said, "No problem. Yes, sir. You're welcome."

Tony jumped into the back seat and patted Evo on the shoulder. "Let's go, Bro."

Evo put the car in gear and eased out of the parking area. He looked in the mirror and saw the agent put a suitcase in his car, and a light went on in his head. "Uh, Tony? Where did the agent get the suitcase?"

"What suitcase?"

"The suitcase he's putting into his back seat, Tony. You rotten little bastard, that's my suitcase, isn't it? I'm turning around. Now."

"Evo, wait! You can't turn around—we're on a one-way, Just keep going, and it'll be okay. It must have been his briefcase you saw."

Evo whispered, "Yeah, right. You probably didn't mess with my underwear drawer, either, did you?"

Tony smiled and pretended to doze.

Evo fell silent as he negotiated the car into Milwaukee traffic and promptly turned the wrong way. Through the spaghetti mazes of the Marquette Interchange overpasses and entrance ramps, Evo took two more wrong turns before he headed south. With Luis holding the map and Tony navigating, they finally found themselves on I-94 East, heading toward Kenosha and White Bass Lake.

With so little traffic in the wee hours of the morning, they made excellent time. The Gallegos brothers stared out the windows into the blackness, trying to see anything beyond the shoulder of the Interstate.

Their exit onto Highway 50 came up thirty miles later and because of the early hour; they decided to check into a motel by the Interstate before continuing on. Leaving everything packed in the car, Tony grabbed a small duffel bag and he and Evo dragged themselves to their room. Hearing voices behind him, Evo turned to see Luis leaning an elbow on the check-in counter, schmoozing the little night clerk into a nightcap. Alfredo sat sprawled in a high-backed chair in the lobby, snoring to beat the band. Evo smiled and shook his head as he entered their room at the end of the hall.

Claiming seniority, Evo stumbled into the bathroom first

and stepped under the hot water. The pounding spray kick-started his circulation again, and the smell of the body wash rejuvenated his senses; wiping the muzzy cloud from his brain. Not bothering with a razor, he brushed his teeth and stepped out of the bathroom. The aroma of oregano and onions filled his senses, and his stomach growled loud and long. "Wow, Tony, are you a miracle worker? How the heck did you find pizza at two in the morning?"

"Welcome to America, my boy. The clerk knew of a delivery place open 24 hours, and ordered us up some grub. Is this not fantastic?"

"Beer! You got me pizza and beer for my first night here. It's a good thing I took ulcer meds on the way here. All I can say is, 'I love you, man.' Really, Tony, you must have done something really rotten that I'll have to kill you for to go out of your way like this."

"Yes, I did."

With a mouthful of pizza, Evo asked, "What did you do, Tony? Was that *really* my suitcase the rental guy had?"

"Uh, Yes."

"Why does the rental man have my suitcase, Tony?"

Tony took a swallow of courage. "Uh, because it wouldn't fit in the trunk."

"So, we were one suitcase too many which *you* packed, in a too-small car which *you* rented, yet *your* suitcase made it into the trunk, and some rental guy has mine?"

"Uh, I guess you could look at it that way."

"And what way would you rather I look at it, oh dead brother of mine?"

"Well, I got your clothes out first, and this will give you a chance to buy new luggage."

"I didn't need new luggage, Tony, and I liked that suitcase." Evo picked up his beer and wandered to the window. He pushed the curtain out of the way and froze. He stayed like that for several seconds, and Tony walked over to see what held his fascination. Across the street stood a huge sign in front of an enormous storefront which looked to be borrowed from Paul Bunyan's cabin. The words *Gander Mountain* made Tony smile. He sighed. He would live another day. He made the sign of the cross, thankful he was off the hook.

"Don't for a minute think this lets you off the hook, Tony boy."

"I'm sure it doesn't, Evo, but it sure softens the blow, don't it?"

"Considerably." Evo put down the unfinished slice of pizza and yawned. "Well, it's going to be an early morning of shopping for me, so I'm hitting the sack. Don't wait for me, I'll find my own way to White Bass Lake."

"But, Evo, we're on vacation together."

"There's no *together* about giving away my suitcase little brother. Get lost."

"Okay. Good night. You'll see, Evo, everything will look better in the morning."

"Uh, Yeah."

7

The morning found Evo staring out the window just as Tony had left him a few hours earlier. Before he could speak, Evo said, "Hey, Tony, I have a new idea. Why don't you take the micro-car and the Brothers Gallegos and go on to White Bass Lake. I'm not sure they could find it on their own. I'll get some other form of transportation and meet you there. Write me out some directions so I don't get lost and I'll be fine."

"What if I need to talk to you?"

Evo dropped the curtain. "That's why we have satellite cell phones, *Dr. Almost*."

"That's *Almost* Doctor to you, Mister. Why can't we hang out and go together?"

"Because I'm still pissed about my clothes, I want to take my time shopping, and one way or another, I'll find a vehicle I can fit in without decapitating myself, that's why. He looked out the curtain again. "I need clothes, Tony."

Tony smiled. "So do Luis and Alfredo. We could all go over there and shop."

"I'd rather go alone."

"Shopping is no fun alone."

"Shopping is no fun, period."

"You'll probably go missing in Gander Mountain without me. I may never see you again."

"I'd rather go alone, Tony."

"That, sir, is not an option."

"Damn."

Tony smiled. "Life's a bitch."

"And so are you. Go wake the brothers; I'm going shopping now."

"I'm all over it." Tony bounded out of the room to round up Luis and Alfredo, and Evo packed up his hygiene kit.

Evo finished dressing and didn't bother shaving. He rubbed his chin and said to the mirror, "Hell, I'm on vacation."

They all met at the car, and Evo opted to walk rather than ride. Tony crossed the street with him to the entrance. They couldn't help but stare as they passed under the huge log entrance and through the front doors.

Evo felt like a kid at Christmas as he gazed in wonder across what looked like acres of outdoor gear and clothing. "Wow," was all he could say as he ran his hand over the ATV that stood next to him. "Look at this, Tony. Camo! I've *got* to get me one of these. Look, saddlebags you can pack stuff in. I could sure use this in the field. Hey, it comes with its own cooler. I could pack samples and specimens without racing against time and decay. How much?" He rummaged around looking for a price tag. "This is so cool." He rummaged around some more and flipped over a tag. "Here it is, eleven grand plus the trailer." He spun around and looked at Tony. "That's not bad, is it?"

"Depends. If I were paying for it, I'd say yeah, but since it's you, the only thing I have to say is, how are you going to get it home?"

Evo was on his back looking under the rear axles. He poked his head out from underneath and looked at Tony with a dazed expression. "I didn't think about that. It would cost a couple of grand to ship it home. Maybe it's a good you're here with me." He jumped up and brushed off his jeans. "I'm not even ten feet inside the door and about to spend thousands."

Tony laughed, clapped Evo on the shoulder, and shoved him down the aisle. "Let's get you some clothes while you're still a rich man, shall we?"

They each grabbed a cart and headed for the men's department. As they passed the front door again, they saw the brothers Gallegos standing just inside, gaping at the moose head hanging on the wall. Tony poked Evo and laughed, "They'll probably still be there when we come back." Grinning, he took off ahead of Evo.

Three hours and several thousand dollars later, four happy men exited the store. Luis was dressed like a Peruvian *Crocodile Dundee* with his khaki bush outfit and Australian hat. Alfredo looked like *Nanuk of the North,* complete with wolf-skull hat and knee-high fur boots. Tony bought a disposable camera and took pictures of them standing under the moose head.

Tony turned the camera on his brother. Evo was busy taking inventory of his purchases. Evo'd bought some killer polo shirts and chamois shirts in every color of the rainbow. He'd bought blue jeans, a *Carhart* jacket, and cargo pants. He'd also bought a fish tie and a foam rubber cheese-wedge hat.

Sunglasses, ball caps, hiking boots, sandals, tennis shoes, socks, cargo shorts, two sets of fishing gear, and a license filled two more bags. A tent, camping gear, an air mattress, and a king sized sleeping bag leaned against his leg. He'd also included beef jerky, C-rations, and freeze-dried ice cream.

As they stood out in front of the store with bags and boxes piled high around them, Tony scratched his head and said, "Sweet Mother of Jesus, Evo! Where the hell are you going to put all this? Good thing I gave away your suitcase. We'll never fit all this in the trunk…"

Pow. Tony flew backward as Evo punched him in the jaw. He landed on his butt and rolled onto the sidewalk. He looked up, rubbing his jaw. "Are you happy now?"

Evo narrowed his eyes. "My day is complete. I'm very happy, you rotten little shit. You're lucky I let you live after you gave away my suitcase and screwed up the car. So don't go razzing me about how much stuff I bought."

Tony held up his hands and scooted out of his reach.

"Hey, Evo, don't kill me yet, I'm on vacation. I knew you'd buy new stuff anyway. Heck, you're going to need a truck—"

Evo held up a hand, effectively shutting his brother up. He cocked his head, and Tony could hear a rumble in the distance. A huge black Dodge truck came slowly around the side of the store. It rolled to a stop in front of the South American "Shop-'Til-You-Drop Crew," and a tall man wearing a red polo shirt jumped out of the driver's side door. A man in a blue mechanic's uniform pulled alongside.

Tony poked Evo in the ribs and said, "*Hah*. Mr. Polo shirt looks like your kind of guy."

"Shut up or I'll hit you again." Tony shut up.

The man in the polo shirt walked up to Evo and asked, "Mr. Castillo?" Evo nodded.

"Let's step over here and we can take care of business." He led Evo to the tailgate, and retrieved a briefcase from the truck. After signing stacks of papers Evo shook the man's hand. The mechanic and the brothers had everything loaded in the back of the truck and were in the process of emptying the Suzuki and stuffing Evo's clothes into his new duffel bags.

Tony's mouth hung open and Evo clipped him on the chin, snapping it shut. "Knock it off, little brother, you look like a tourist. These gentlemen even offered to return that sardine can to Milwaukee."

Alfredo jumped in front of Evo, the fur flaps on his wolf hat flopping about his ears. "Please, Mr. Evo, could we keep the car? We can pay for it!"

Evo looked at the brothers and Luis nodded furiously. "We would like not to be an inconvenience to you, and having our own transportation is a good start."

"I don't mind if no one else does." Mr. Polo Shirt nodded his head.

Evo thanked Polo Shirt who climbed into the mechanic's truck and the two drove away. Evo turned to the eager-faced

Gallegos brothers. He handed them a credit card and said, "Gas only."

They shouted, "Yes," and hugged each other, bouncing up and down. Alfredo threw his arms around Evo, and the wolf's nose hit Evo in the chest. The impact knocked the hat off his head and it fell in the street, under a tire of Evo's new truck. They all stared at the wolf, which looked a little worse for wear. Tony bent to retrieve it.

Just then a little old lady on her way out of the store saw the wolf's head sticking out from under the tire and screamed. "You ran over that poor dog." She whacked Tony with her shopping bag. Tony stiffened then went down like a rock, landing with a splat on the sidewalk. The three pounds of wild birdseed the woman had in her bag had exploded on impact. Millet rained down on the small group like rice at a wedding.

The old woman left heel prints on Tony's back as she walked over his prone body. She grabbed the wolf hat, saying, "Oh, poor puppy."

When she saw what she held, she screamed and threw it on the sidewalk. "*Yuck*. That's no puppy. She looked over her shoulder at a bleeding Tony and bit a fingernail. "Uh, sorry. I thought you killed someone's pet."

Evo jumped to help Tony turn over. He knelt beside him as the little old lady tiptoed around Tony's inert form and patted him on the head. "Sorry, young man."

She laid the wolf hat on the sidewalk. Another little old lady in a red Crown Victoria careened around Evo's black truck, almost taking the bumper with it. People jumped out of the way as it bumped over the curb onto the sidewalk.

The car screeched to a halt and rocked wildly as she slammed it into park. The driver's door flew open, and a scrawny leg appeared in the opening.

The gathering crowd looked on while a blue-haired whirlwind carrying a pink purse the size of a small suitcase emblazoned with an enormous sequined parrot scrambled out of the huge car.

She trotted around the back of the car, elbows pumping furiously as her top speed reached about a half-mile per hour. She yelled at the top of her lungs, "Everyone back! I know CPR."

The lady with the birdseed tried to stop her by jumping in front of her. She grabbed at the pink purse "Mary, no! He's breathing. I hit him because I thought he killed a dog, Stop, Mary. S*top*!"

Mary didn't hear her (those who know her knew she was deaf as a doornail) and bowled over her friend and dragged her across the sidewalk. As she tugged, she opened her pink suitcase and rummaged inside for Lord only knew what. She headed to where Tony lie sprawled.

With her head in her purse and her legs pumping away, she never saw it coming when her feet tangled in the wolf hat her friend had dropped on the sidewalk. She tried to correct herself, but instead catapulted through the air, her purse emptying its contents in her wake.

Her head connected with Tony's chin just as he tried to sit up, and he flipped backward like he'd been hit with a baseball bat, his head making a sickening thud on the sidewalk. This time Tony didn't get up. Mary landed straddled across his chest, her purse dangling from the ball hitch on the truck.

She shook her head and her blue curls winked in the sunlight. "*Whew*. What a lucky break. She sat on Tony's chest and checked out his unconscious body. She rose and fell with the rhythm of Tony's breathing. "Just think, this boy would have been a goner without me. I saved his life. The crowd cheered and the little old lady fisted her hands over her head like the World's Extremely Light Weight Champion.

"*Whoop*. Her legs suddenly flew up in the air as Evo snatched her off Tony's inert form. She hung like a rag doll wearing cement blocks on her feet.

"Lady, he was almost a goner *because* of you! He set her on her feet.

She brushed off her sleeve and crossed her arms. "Well I never! What kind of ingrate are you?" She lifted her chin "*Humph*. Good thing I don't save lives for a living. I couldn't take the abuse."

Evo leaned over Tony, lifting his eyelids. "You're right, lady, if you did, the streets would be littered with dead bodies." He tapped Tony's cheek.

Mary sniffed and put her nose in the air. "Come, Joy, *some* people are just unappreciative of a Good Samaritan."

Joy cast a worried look at Tony from her place on the sidewalk and bit her lip. "It kind of seems to me that poor boy was just fine before we got a hold of him." She looked around at the bird seed scattered all over the sidewalk. "Wait for me, Mary. I'm going to see if I can get my birdseed replaced. There must have been a hole in the bag or something." She turned and trotted back into the store.

Mary shook her head. "Joy. What a cheapskate." She bent to pick up the items from her purse. For the first time, Evo looked at the contents of that purse, now strewn across the pavement. There were bobby pins, receipts, coupons, and a notebook. Also laying on the pavement was bubble gum, a 9/16 wrench, a shower cap, a glass doorknob, two Snickers Bars, a set of lock pick tools, some K-Y, and a .38 Smith & Wesson. Joy came tottering out of the store toting a new bag of birdseed. She was in time to watch Mary pick up the revolver. The crowd fell back screaming, and scrambled for cover.

Joy grabbed the gun away from Mary and stuffed it in the pink bag. "Mary Cromwell, I was right there when Sheriff Green told you never to carry this gun around again! Remember last time you had it? Mrs. Simmons' cat only has half a tail because of you."

"The little bastard was taking a crap on my patio. He's lucky that's all I shot off."

"Nevermind, hurry up and stash that thing before someone else gets hurt."

"Oh, alright. Geez, Joy, you're really becoming prudish in your old age."

Evo continued trying to rouse Tony, but he remained unconscious. Becoming alarmed, Evo raised his hand to interrupt the arguing seniors. "Uh, excuse me, but my brother seems to be hurt here. Can someone call for assistance, please?"

"Doctor, doctor, call 911," Mary screeched, spinning around on one foot, flapping her arms as if about to take flight.

Joy put a hand on her sternum and halted Mary in mid lift-off. "Get a grip, Cromwell."

A smooth voice from the crowd said, "I'm not a doctor, but I know first aid. What is the problem?"

The hair lifted on the back of Evo's neck. He looked up, knowing he would be staring into the startling blue eyes of Dr. Samón Fernandini. His chest tightened and he couldn't breathe as he watched her make her way through the crowd. She stared in stunned silence at Evo then followed his gaze to the unconscious body on the ground. She screeched and dropped to her knees. She reached out to touch Tony's hand.

"Tony! Oh Evo, is he all right? Tony. She fumbled with her purse and pulled out plastic gloves and snapped them on. She looked up and Evo saw tears swimming in her eyes. "Help me, Evo. Take your shirt off. Here, let me look at his head. Keep supporting his neck."

That shocked Evo back into reality. He ripped off his shirt and moved back far enough for Sam to squeeze between him and Tony. Sam felt around the back of his head and pulled back a bloody glove. She folded Evo's shirt and placed it over the wound.

74

"Where is the owner of this truck?" She felt her way down Tony's body, looking for broken bones.

"I'm the owner," Evo answered. "And before you attack me, Tony didn't get run over by a truck; he got run over by a little old lady."

"Say that again?"

"He got run over–"

"I heard that part. How can you own this truck, and what is Tony really doing on the sidewalk lying next to a dead animal? Was he trying to save it or did it attack him?"

Alfredo spoke up. "Uh, no, Dr. Sam. Evo did not run over an animal, either. That is my very wonderful new Iditarod Timber Wolf Sub-Zero hat. I guess it is not so wonderful now; it has caused much trouble." He stubbed his toe on the ground. Evo motioned for Alfredo to come toward the back of the truck where Tony lie.

Alfredo squatted next to Tony and Evo handed him his wolf hat. Evo spoke softly and patted his shoulder. "It is a wonderful hat, my friend. The lady just misunderstood." Alfredo beamed, and Sam stared at Evo as if seeing him for the first time. She shook her head to clear it and stroked Tony's cheek, looking at the bruise forming below his eye.

Tony moaned and opened his eyes. "Either I died and you're an angel, or Evo somehow found Sam and I'm in heaven anyway."

Evo snorted and Sam stared daggers at him. Tony half smiled and said, "Don't mind Evo, Sam, he's just jealous that you have your hands on me and not him." He smiled serenely and closed his eyes again.

At her sharp intake of breath, Evo looked into those devastating eyes again and stood abruptly. He noticed her eyes widen and leave his face. He heard the crowd gasp and tried to figure out what caused the commotion. Running a hand through his hair he chuckled nervously. "Man, he is out of it,

Doc. He doesn't know what he's saying. Shouldn't we call an ambulance or something?" He chuckled nervously and realized the crowd was staring at him.

Evo ran his hands up and down his thighs and walked a few paces away. The crowd's eyes followed him. He turned back and clutched his stomach as his ulcer burned anew. He noticed Sam watching him intently and tried to will the pain into submission. He forced his hand down to his pocket and shoved his fist into it, ignoring the pain ripping through his belly. He walked to the back of the truck and pulled out a new polo shirt. Pulling it over his head he heard the crowd sigh.

Evo looked at the one they called Mary and she let out a whistle. "*Hoo Baby*. It's a shame to cover up that gorgeous body. If I was only fifty years younger…"

Evo realized they were staring at his state of undress and embarrassment heated his face.

Tony picked that moment to groan dramatically and made a great show of trying to sit up. Sam helped him, and he settled back against her, his head lolling against her chest. Evo forgot his ulcer as fire seared through his veins. He pulled himself up short as he recognized jealousy. He had no time to analyze the phenomenon as a crash and a screech sounded behind him.

"*Ouch. Damn*. Wait. Here, *ow*. Hey, I can help; look what I found."

He turned in time to catch a slight body against his chest a split second after her leg banged into the trailer hitch. His arms automatically went around her as she slammed into his chest.

"*Oooff*," puffed out of her as the impact left her breathless. "Thanks, that kind-of happens a lot," she said.

"Which one, banging into things, or falling on strange men?"

She looked up at him and smiled. "The banging part."

Evo couldn't help but smile back at the endearing picture she made. Her strawberry blonde hair had flopped over her lightly freckled, pixie-pretty face, and her small, rectangular glasses hung askew. She smiled back at him nervously and pushed against his chest. He realized he hadn't let her go and stood her back on her feet.

Evo was brought rudely back to reality as a dry voice said irritably, "Excuse me, Casanova, but can you take your hands off my friend long enough to let her give me a hand here?"

Evo looked down to see Sam holding out her hand, brow raised and head tilted to the side. Evo stepped back as the pixie gave Sam a box of gauze and bandages.

"Do you keep bandages with you in case of emergency?" Evo looked a little surprised.

The pixie ripped a package open with her teeth. "I need them more often than I'd care to admit."

She stood, brushed her hands against her jeans, and held out her hand. "Dr. Castillo, I presume?"

He took her hand. "Uh, yes, and you are?"

She smiled again, animation lighting her face. "I'm Fred Miller, Sam's college roommate. May I call you Tony?"

"Not on my worst day, but you may call me Evo." At her shocked expression, Evo smiled and pointed down at Tony. "That's Tony. I'm his older brother."

"*Oh.* She jerked her hand away and stepped back, almost falling over Sam. "S-s-sorry. *Whoop.* Sam put a hand on Fred's butt and shoved her back toward Evo. She stuttered and Evo chuckled. "I guess you've heard of me. I am—how does that go, Samón? The devastatingly handsome but asshole brother'?"

Sam had the decency to blush. "Uh, something like that."

Fred practically fell apart. "I'm so sorry, Dr. Castillo. I didn't even know you were a doctor—not that it matters—but I thought…that is I heard…" She glanced nervously at Sam who just smiled. "Well, she got the handsome part right, anyway."

Evo smiled, took her hand, and kissed her knuckles. "I cannot begin to imagine the kind of words Dr. Fernandini had to say in my regard, Miss Miller, but I can assure you, I do not eat pretty American women for lunch, so please calm down. Why don't we get Tony off the sidewalk and you ladies can be on your way?"

"Oh, right. Tony. On the sidewalk–okay uh, how is he, Sam? Uh, Tony, I mean."

Sam replied coolly, "Tony will be fine, but you, my dear might need major counseling. Don't feel bad though, Evo often has that effect on people."

Evo ground teeth together, reminded once again that he had a painful burning in his stomach from the ulcer, and a pain in his ass from Sam Fernandini. "Can we just get this done so I, can get out of here, uh, I mean so everyone can be on their way?"

Tony chose that moment to pipe up, "No hospital though, please, Evo."

Fred broke in, "But you need to be looked at. That was an awful crack."

Evo asked Fred, "Do you have a local physician who could possibly see him?"

"Sure we do, we have a satellite walk-in that's open until eight tonight. If not, Mike Dudley, our local veterinarian can take a look at him." Evo searched her face for the punch line, but saw she was perfectly serious.

"Uh, veterinarian–right. Tony is not a pig, but according to Dr. Fernandini, I am." He shot Sam a smile. "With your permission, Dr. Ferna-meanie?"

Sam shot him an evil look and said very softly, "Fine with me, Dr. Evil."

Evo chuckled as he helped Tony to his feet. "Good one, Sam. I didn't know you had it in you."

"There's a lot you don't know about me, Castillo."

He raised a brow and lowered his voice. "Much of which I cannot wait to find out, Fernandini."

She spun and huffed off toward Fred's car. "I'll see you in hell first, Dr. Casanova!"

Evo stared after her, his mouth hanging open. "What did I say?"

Tony looked at a worried Fred and winked. "Round one goes to Sam, don't you think?"

Fred stared dazedly after her friend and nodded silently.

8

A much more subdued group followed Fred to White Bass Lake. Tony had a headache, Evo had a gut ache, Alfredo blamed himself for the entire mess, and Luis knew enough to keep quiet. Sam followed behind in the rental car. She had asked Luis and Alfredo if they minded, stating she wanted a little quiet time to herself. The Brothers Gallegos fell over themselves to give her that, so the little Suzuki now trailed behind Evo's new truck.

Evo told himself he was being a conscientious driver by checking the mirrors every few seconds, but in reality, he needed to reassure himself Sam didn't drive off somewhere. Why did it bother him so much? "See you in hell first," ate at him more than he cared to admit.

It took less time to drive to White Bass Lake than he'd figured. When they reached town, Fred drove straight to the walk-in clinic. Sam offered to take the Gallegos brothers to the local bed and breakfast to get them settled. She drove Evo's truck and Alfredo drove the Suzuki so Luis and Alfredo could unpack both vehicles and play with their new stuff while Sam returned to the clinic to pick up Tony and Evo.

Evo and Fred helped Tony into the clinic. Dr. Frank Beth shaved a spot and put a couple stitches in the back of Tony's head. He sent Tony home with a script and instructions. Evo and Fred had orders to watch for a concussion. By the time Sam returned, they'd eased a very groggy Tony into Evo's truck and all headed for Fred's.

Fred insisted Evo and Tony stay at her house. She claimed Tony could be watched more easily. "It's also quiet and homey," she said.

Evo protested. "What could be homier than a bed and breakfast? I understand the attraction to such an establishment is just that." He thought about Sam. He didn't think he could live under the same roof as her without making himself crazy. The thought of seeing Sam in her pajamas or God forbid in her underwear made him break out in a sweat. "We will not impose on you or Dr. Fernandini's vacation."

Fred persisted, and Evo grumbled the entire way. I'm quite sure we'll be fine elsewhere, Miss Miller."

"Fred," came a slurred voice from the back seat.

Evo looked confused. "Fred what?"

"Fred smiled. I think he means call me Fred."

"Oh. Okay, Fred, why do you insist on us coming to your house? Can't you see Sam doesn't want me there?"

Sam sighed. "Oh, Castillo, give it up. It doesn't matter where you sleep. Being in the same country with you is too close for me. Besides, Fred's right, so shut up, and say thank you to your host."

Using all the remaining dignity he could muster, Evo turned to Fred. "I do apologize. My brother and I would be delighted to stay at your home, Miss Miller."

Three voices chimed, "Fred!"

Evo turned red. "Fred."

A few minutes later, Sam pulled into the driveway of a large Victorian house. It wore the whimsical colors of the great "Painted Ladies" of San Francisco. What should have struck Evo as garish, charmed his socks right off. The peach-colored siding gave way to burgundy gingerbread on the eaves. Hues of blues and yellows outlined the windows and gingerbread, bringing the house alive and making it look almost…he sighed because he could not give the feeling a name.

"Happy."

Evo looked over his shoulder to see Sam walking up to stand beside him. She folded her arms over her ample breasts and rested on one leg. She smiled, and that always made Evo very afraid. He swallowed hard and said, "Excuse me?"

"You have the same look I did the first time I saw this house. Happy; I think the house looks happy."

Evo stared at the house again and relaxed. "Hate to admit it, Doc, but you are exactly right. The house looks happy, and very comfortable in its own skin. Kind of like your friend Fred over there." They both smiled. Tony leaned heavily on Fred as they made slow progress toward the front door. She tripped over a crack in the sidewalk and both of them almost tumbled onto the grass. Evo jumped forward and caught them. Sam chuckled behind him and he straightened. He frowned at her as a thought struck him. "And you read minds–that is very scary."

Sam put her nose in the air and sashayed toward the house. "You have no idea how scary I can be, *Doc*." He watched the gentle sway of her hips as she disappeared through the door. *Now who's messing with whom?*

Evo reached up to run his hand through his hair and found he had once again broken into a sweat. His feeble mind registered that his pants felt tight as he wiped moisture from his hand. "Crap." He went to unload the truck.

Loaded down with bags, Evo shoved his way through the front door. He froze and stared. An incredible sight greeted him. Warm, rich light bathed the room and the smell of a crackling fire filled his senses. He could do no more than stare at the beautiful fish tanks lining two walls and acting as a divider for a third. Hundreds of fish swam about, at home in natural environments, shoaling and playing among the live plants and rocks. Evo let the bags he carried slide to the wood floor as he stepped in for a closer look.

"Pretty cool, aren't they?"

Evo turned to find Fred standing next to him, her face aglow. Evo said, "Pretty cool is a good description, but I'm thinking more like amazing, or remarkable, or on a bad day, extraordinary. Did you do all this?"

"Yep; but I had a lot of help. Sam and I met a guy from New Jersey at a fish convention on the east coast in our sophomore year at UW Madison. His name is Hank MacRone, and he's the premier collector and breeder of Corydoras catfish in the country. We all e-mailed back and forth, and the more I learned from him, the more I fell in love with these little guys." She pointed to a group of eight little catfish, wiggling up the side of the tank as if they were one. They made a lazy "S" and turned to repeat the process down toward the bottom. "Those are Schwartzi's. They're endangered; and those over there–"

"Are Venezuelans, and in this tank are Robustus. You have these giants paired with Pandas and Orange Lazer–what an interesting contrast."

"You know your Corys. He smiled, and she continued. "Hanging out with Sam gave me a strong sense of conservation, and I ended up doing my master's thesis on the effects of loss of habitat on South American Corydoras catfish. When I graduated and started my pet shop, Hank sent me fish to get me going. Whenever he would discover a new species, Hank would save me a breeding group. Many of the newly discovered species I keep here for my personal enjoyment, as well as to propagate.

Between Sam and Hank, I do pretty well. I also share with friends and family. My sister, Buzz, keeps a few tanks in her basement, too."

Evo smacked his forehead. "Oh, my God, fish, basement, I forgot!" He fumbled for his cell phone and barely heard the tentative knock on the front door. Fred went to answer and the Gallegos brothers tumbled in. Luis answered his cell phone. "Hello this is Luis."

Evo had his back to the door as he shouted into his cell phone. "Luis?"

"*Hola*, Dr. Evo, it is me, Luis," Luis answered, coming up

to stand behind Evo.

Evo continued to speak into the phone. "I totally forgot–"

"That is okay, Dr. Evo, I did not." He giggled and Evo turned to see him standing there, wide-eyed and innocent.

Evo sighed and slapped the cell phone shut. "Funny, Luis, I totally forgot–"

"The fish," Luis supplied.

"You remembered?"

"*Si*, Dr. Evo. I went to the local pet store in town and bought a battery pump and air stone. The lady at the pet store, she gave me reverse osmosis water and a tank to borrow. Whatever fish survived are sluggish, but alive in the car. I knew you did not want to keep them in the poison water, but I also did not want to throw it away. I have it here." He and Alfredo each held up a large Ziploc bag filled with water, huge grins on their faces.

Evo threw an arm around Luis and grabbed Alfredo with the other. He squeezed them both. "You two are worth your weights in gold."

Fred grabbed one bag and Sam took the other. "We got a leaker here. To the laundry tub," Fred said, "Then I'm calling Ian and Mag." The two women disappeared down the hall.

With his arms still around Luis and Alfredo, Evo said, "You guys are the best. Wait, I have to show you something." As the Gallegos brothers recovered from the atypical affectionate reaction from Evo, they were steered into Fred's living room. They stood awestruck until Evo dragged them through the arched entrance and let them go. They went from tank to tank, speaking in soft tones and examining every fish they saw. They gazed reverently into the large unblinking eyes of Peruvian Altum Angelfish in one of the tanks. That's where Sam and Fred found them.

"They'll eat from your hand," Sam said softly, as they approached the two men.

Alfredo looked at Fred with watery eyes and took her hand. "This is so beautiful. Thank you for sharing it with us."

Fred shrugged. "Hey, no problem. The pleasure is in the sharing." She winked. "Wait until you see my nursery."

Alfredo threw a confused look at Evo. "Nursery?"

"Breeding room for baby fish, I think she means," Evo replied. "We'll see that later."

They all watched Sam and Fred walk into the kitchen.

Looking at Fred, Alfredo said softly to his brother, "Luis, I think I am falling in love."

Luis nodded, his eyes also following Fred. "Me too."

Evo smiled. Looking at Sam, he leaned toward the brothers and whispered, "Me too, boys, me too." Wide-eyed stares and huge smiles met his statement. Evo held an index finger to his lips and the Brothers Gallegos nodded emphatically. They followed the women into the kitchen.

Fred had five mugs on the counter and was pouring coffee into them. "Does everyone drink coffee?"

Affirmative sounds from the men had everyone gathered at the kitchen table, drinking coffee and eating cookies.

Fred leaned forward and said, "I hope you guys aren't too tired, because around here we need little excuse for a party." The men shook their heads and mumbled negative responses around the cookies. She looked at the clock. "I just wanted to warn you that in about an hour my family is going to descend upon my house, and you guys are going to be inundated with Midwestern hospitality. I hope you like Jell-O." At their collectively baffled expressions, she and Sam laughed as if they shared a great joke.

9

Fred put the men to work dragging out grills, moving tables, and filling coolers. Forty-five minutes later, the first car rolled in the driveway. After that, it seemed like the entire town followed suit until they spilled over into the neighbor's yard. Three generations of family, friends, dogs, and kids filled the yards with laughter, noise, and love. The neighbors put out tiki lights and reggae music filled the air with the rich sounds of the Caribbean.

All cars had been moved from the driveway as three more grills arrived in the backs of pick-up trucks. Men cooked brats, steaks, burgers, and hot dogs. Women bustled in and out of the house, and teenagers set up a volleyball net, Bocce balls, and horseshoes. Camp chairs went up, and the amount of food crammed on the tables made Evo, Luis, and Alfredo's mouths hang open.

Luis poked Alfredo in the ribs. "This could feed all of Honduras for a week."

Alfredo nodded. "Not after I go through there."

Introductions were made and even Tony joined the throng. Luis' eyes popped wide when someone emptied the coolers into a kiddie pool filled with ice. "I have died and gone to Heaven." He picked up a brown bottle and tried to make out the label.

Fred whispered over his shoulder. "Leinenkugle, but we call it 'Linie' with a long 'I' up here. It's made here in Wisconsin. Try it. Lots of folks like it."

Luis opened the bottle and let the beer slide down his throat. "Great. What else do you have in that pool? I'm going to test them all today."

"Good thing you're not driving, because I see Miller,

Point, Rolling Rock, Old Style, Milwaukee's Best, Moosehead—wait just a darn minute! Who put the Lone Star in the swimming pool? Get that Texas swill out of my yard!"

Everyone laughed and Fred pulled one out of the pool. "Hope this San Antonio swill doesn't give me cooties," she said loudly as she twisted off the top. She leaned into Luis and whispered, "Try one—I love this stuff, it's even good warm, but don't say you like it too loudly—you might get yourself lynched."

Luis made a great show of looking around before he snatched a Lone Star and put it in his pocket for later. He patted his pocket and followed Fred.

Luis looked for his brother and found Alfredo watching the grilling process. He held a Miller Lite in his hand. "Alfredo, why are you drinking light beer?"

"It is light, so I figure I can drink more."

He tottered off and Luis shook his head. "I am amazed that we are related sometimes."

Tony slowly made his way to the pool and Evo blocked his way. Taking his arm to steady him, Evo pulled him aside and said, "No beer for you, little brother, you're on drugs."

Tony shot him a sloppy smile and held up an orange soda. "I know, I know. I'd rather have a beer, but I'm sure I'll make up for it later. Right now, though, I'm going for the female sympathy angle. Did you see that stunning creature that arrived a minute ago?"

"Who could miss her? That's one of Fred's sisters, Alexandra. The one by the twin men is Buzz, and the one standing on the chair waving her arms around is Maggie. The one they call The Maggot."

Tony carefully nodded and felt the back of his head. "How do I look? If I don't turn my back, you can't see the bald spot, can you?" He dipped this way and that. He lost his balance and bumped into his brother.

Evo wrapped both arms around him and stood him back on his feet. "Stop the dance routine before you kill us both and try looking more like a helpless puppy. The women will bring you food and drink, little brother. You can sit by a wall and no one will see your bald spot, but by the time you get done with your sympathy act, they won't care if you are totally bald."

Tony slapped Evo on the shoulder. "Evo, you're a genius! He wandered toward the house to beg another soda, practicing his "lost puppy" look.

Evo sat in a chair and sipped his beer. He waited for the burn of his ulcer to begin, surprised when it didn't. He rubbed his belly.

"Got a bleeding ulcer there, sailor?"

Evo turned and ran smack-dab into me. He took a step back and nodded I pulled up a chair. He continued to rub his belly as he held out his other hand. "You must be Buzz, am I not correct?"

"You would be correct. Evo, is it not?"

He smiled and nodded. "It is."

"Thought so. I also know you have an ulcer; I recognize the rub. I had ulcers until I retired from police work. I patted her stomach. "Now I'm just fat and sassy." I gave him the once over, but I could tell Evo understood that I saw more than she let on. *Intuitive people must make him uncomfortable* The poor guy shifted in his chair looking around for an escape route.

I thought about being delicate, but it came out way too blunt. "Ever think about changing your job or slowing down on those wild nights on the town in Lima?"

He slid me a glance and said coolly, "My wild nights in Lima usually consist of an evening spent looking into a microscope and dining on take-out dinners."

Undaunted, I continued. "Once upon a time, back in my younger and dumber days, I almost let the job destroy me." I could see the signs in him. "Look," I said. "I only bring it up because I've walked in your shoes. My job put me in the hospital. I always thought if I went out on a stretcher, it would be because I got shot or stabbed, but a bleeding ulcer laid me low." I dug around for a business card. "Dr. Beth works down at the walk-in. He's actually an internist, but he pulls a couple of shifts a week over at the clinic to help out. He's a good man and a great doc. He saved my life; he can help you save yours."

Evo leaned forward. "I met him. He fixed up Tony this morning. Nice man."

"Great guy, Give him a call. He can see what's eating you from the inside out and give you advice on how not to let it take over your life. By the time you head back home, you can be fat and sassy like the rest of us."

Another voice intruded as one of the twins joined us. He ruffled my hair and threw an arm around my shoulders. "Sassy I'll attest to. Anything else, I'll just say she exaggerates."

He ruffled my hair again and I elbowed him in the ribs. He stuck out his free hand and smiled. "J.J. Green, Evo. Glad to meet you and your brother." He shook Evo's hand and pulled up two chairs. "I saw you talking to my girl and thought I'd better come and rescue you."

I ducked out from under his arm and slapped his butt. "His girl, my eye. He couldn't be that lucky. He is, however, my cross to bear at the moment." I got up to leave and J.J. winked.

As J.J. and I continued our bantering ritual, Evo settled into his chair with a chuckle. He looked a little envious, perhaps of my odd relationship with J.J. I supposed life in the jungle didn't offer up many opportunities to establish deep connections. I stepped away to get us another round, but I stayed within earshot.

I watched as his gaze drifted to Sam hefting a platter of burgers, which tilted precariously toward the ground. He jumped up to grab the platter, but J.J.'s handsome twin got there first. Sam looked up into his eyes and smiled back, the handsome giant touched the end of her nose as he took the platter from her.

Ahhhh, so that's how the wind blew.

Evo started from his chair and J.J. pressed on his shoulder. "Whoa, fella, she's not going anywhere. Don't mind Bob, he's otherwise occupied," J.J. said. Evo looked up and finally relaxed. His mood didn't look good as he examined the top of his beer bottle.

"Don't feel bad, it happens to all of us."

"What are you talking about?"

"You love her. It's not a terminal disease, you know." J.J. tapped the toe of Evo's shoe with his own.

"You obviously don't know Sam."

The poor guy actually tried to smile.

"Look, I'm not trying to start a male-bonding party or anything, but if I get it, don't you think other people do too? The way I see it, Bob over there is safe. Sam can play and flirt and relax around him because they both know neither one is interested."

"Is your brother blind? Sam's is gorgeous, she's more intelligent than 90 per cent of the population, she's–"

I warned them of my return with a cough. "Do you find intelligence attractive, Mr. Castillo?"

He narrowed his eyes and hesitated before he answered. "Yes, very attractive."

I smiled. "Bob doesn't. He thinks my empty-headed-but-gorgeous sister is attractive. Al is extremely intelligent, but hides it for men like FBI Bob. Part of her psychosis, I think. No one gets serious, no one gets hurt. They play and they part."

Evo watched the banter of the group consisting of Sam, Al, Tony, and Bob. "I just don't get it."

I replaced Evo's empty bottle with a fresh one. I placed a hand on his shoulder and a tidal wave of emotion washed over me. Boy-oh-boy, this man had it bad. Not wanting to frighten him, I started slowly. "I don't understand it either, but *they* do. I always thought it a frivolous waste of time, and insulting to one's intelligence."

I moved in front of him and took his hand. I stared hard into his eyes. "But let me tell you one thing, Evo. You need to let down the barriers these next few weeks. Everything is all bottled up inside you. It's tying you in knots. It's imperative you open up and let her see this side of you. Let her know the real man under the skin. Take this time and learn how to play. I have a feeling you've not played in a very long time, but if you let this opportunity pass you by, you'll look back on this vacation with nothing but regret."

Evo sucked in a breath and his eyes widened as he stared first at me and then at our hands. The slight tingle I felt when I originally took his hand strengthened, and our hands grew warm. He jerked out of my hold and broke eye contact. He looked at his hand and looked at me.

"What are you," he said, rubbing his hands on his jeans, "some kind of fortune teller?"

I raised a brow to J.J., and he patted Evo on the shoulder. "Isn't she something?"

Evo eyed me and slid back into his chair. "Yes, she is, but what I want to know is, what that...," he flapped a hand in my direction, "That uh, thing she did was."

"Just a little Irish magic, my friend. She didn't cast any spell or anything, it's just when she feels a great deal of emotion of some sort pouring off of someone, if she touches that person, most times she can understand the source, or interpret the feelings so the person can channel it in a positive manner."

J.J. blushed and looked at me. "Did I explain it right?"

I sat there stunned. I mean bowled over at how insightful that big dumb copper could be. Still a little dazed at the outpouring of emotion from Evo, I could only nod. J.J. picked me up by the armpits and plopped me in a chair. He gave me his beer and fluffed my hair. I shot him a glare and he beamed. "See? All better now." He patted my knee and took back his beer.

Evo still looked a little shell-shocked, but I figured maybe he'd never met anyone like me before. "Maybe there aren't many Irish people where he comes from, J.J. Maybe I freaked him a bit. Sorry, Evo."

He cleared his throat. "I've never met anyone with your kind of gift before. I would like to talk to you again sometime."

J.J. answered for me and my hackles rose. (I used to hate it when my ex-husband answered for me, as if I was incapable of coherent speech). "Sometime later, perhaps, but it's a little heavy for picnic conversation, don't you think?"

He winked at me.

"Why don't we get together tomorrow over at Mag and Ian's to go over those fish of yours, or we could meet at Fred's in the evening?"

I relaxed, telling myself for the seven hundredth time that J.J. was nothing like Kendrick. Ken did it because he knew everything about everything, and tried for years to beat me into submission (literally and figuratively). J.J. did it out of respect for my gift—or curse—whatever role it took at the time.

Fred came stumbling up just then, carrying a mounded plate of food and a tray table. J.J. jumped first and grabbed the table out of her hands. Fred took the paper plate in two hands just as it creased down the middle. A glop of green Jell-O plopped in Evo's lap, and Fred's face crumpled. Evo leaned forward to stand but was waylaid by a huge black monster that stuck its snout firmly into his crotch. Startled, Evo pitched back in his chair and my Jell-O sniffing dog followed straight into his lap.

"Wesley," J.J. and I both yelled, and the monster spun around in the chair, giving Evo a face full of hairy dog butt.

Evo threw his head back out of the way, and the momentum sent him and my 160-pound Newfoundland flying backward, tumbling into the yard.

With his legs still dangling in the air, Evo shoved the great ball of fur off him. He lay sprawled on his back. Wesley snuffled his face and gave him a big slurpy kiss, leaving a stripe of green consisting of bits of grass mixed with doggy/Jell-O slime across Evo's jaw. Wes then sat there expectantly, grinning and wagging his big fluffy tail, waiting for praise, or even better, more food.

Evo did a backward roll, successfully untangling himself from both chair and dog. Because he had dog slime and green Jell-O all over his hands too, he shook his head to get the hair out of his eyes and sat on his knees trying to make sense of what had just happened.

It did his ego little good to see the entire crowd howling with laughter at his predicament. He shot my black behemoth an evil glare, but Wes, oblivious to Evo's ire, basked in the attention. Grinning and wagging his tail, he lumbered over to Evo and delicately licked his fingers. This sent new gales of laughter through the crowd, and Evo gave up and joined them.

Evo stood and found himself immediately accosted by Fred holding a damp towel in her hand. She swiped at the Jell-O clinging to his jeans, and Evo yelped and jumped back when she made contact with his zipper.

Unfortunately for him, she persevered, undaunted and determined to clean the goo off his jeans, but due to the sensitive location of the green smear, Evo remained equally determined to escape with his virtue intact. Every time she lunged with the towel, he jumped back. Evo could hear her sisters yelling at her, but Fred seemed to have a one-track mind. "Hold still, I've almost got it."

The crowd roared and Evo hovered somewhere near panic. "Stop, for God's sake, Buzz, stop her! Sam, help! Get her away from me! *Saaaaam!*"

Sam wiped the tears from her eyes and she and I performed a flying tackle on Fred. We bounced along the ground and Wesley joined in the melee. Women and dog rolled over into a pile of leaves left by the kids. Fred screeched, suddenly laughing and struggled for breath while Sam and I stuffed grass and leaves down her shirt. Mag grabbed up a handful of leaves and stuffed them down the neck of Sam's shirt. Soon, ten grown-ups were whooping it up and joining in the fray. The grass and leaves flew through the crisp late autumn air, and Evo couldn't help but shake his head and laugh along with us.

Evo bent to pick up his camp chair and suddenly felt a cool breeze as Sam grabbed the back of his shirt and stuffed a handful of leaves up his back. With all the dignity of a king, Evo straightened and emptied the leaves onto the ground. He flapped the tail of his shirt a couple of times to make sure it was empty and slowly turned to watch Sam laugh. Fred stood wide-eyed.

Sam sobered when Fred poked her. Evo did not look amused.

Sam smiled. "Oh, lighten up, Castillo. You're on vacation."

"Yeah," I said. "Learn how to relax once in a while. It's good for the soul, *and* the ulcer."

Sam flicked a leaf in Evo's direction and put her hands on her hips. "Didn't you ever learn how to play? Come on, have a little fun." She narrowed her eyes. "I dare you."

10

Evo looked down at Sam and said, "Learn to play, eh? *Dare* me, Fernameanie? I'll show you who can play..."

Sam sidestepped toward Fred. Fred stepped back as Sam continued to taunt Evo. "Come on, Evo, no need to get upset. We're only having a little fun."

"Fun?" He advanced toward her.

Fred stepped back again, but Sam held her ground, a smug expression covering her features. "You don't scare me, big boy. I double dare you to do something fun. Do you even know how?"

"I know how to have fun, Sam, but can you take the heat?" Like a big cat he stalked one step closer.

The crowd "*Ooo'd*."

Sam finally had the good sense to look uncomfortable for a moment. "You don't intimidate me."

"That's your first mistake," he said, and took a step forward.

She reached out behind her for Fred and found nothing but air. She looked back and realized her friend had abandoned her. Evo took another step forward and she stepped back. Nervous, but trying valiantly to hide it, she flipped the long veil of straight black hair over her shoulder. Evo's ears flamed red and his breath caught.

Sam raised her chin and took another step back. "I can take whatever you dish out, Dr. King of the World, so stop trying to intimidate me with your macho innuendos."

The crowd bobbed their heads back and forth as if watching a ping-pong match. All eyes were back on Evo and I whispered to J.J., "Well, at least the crowd's attention is diverted from us for a while—which reminds me, buster. You and I have to talk."

J.J. ruffled my hair and said, "Wait 'til after the show, hon. I'm enjoying this."

I let out a *humph*, which made J.J. smile. I pinched the underside of his bicep and he winced and grabbed my hand, moving us forward for a better view of the action.

We moved in next to Sal, who'd closed the diner early so he could "supervise the food." This translated into catching all the latest town gossip first hand. He looked like an excited school kid. I was surprised he wasn't taking notes or pictures. My mother, bless her heart, was.

As the crowd looked on with avid interest, Evo lunged forward before Sam could scoot out of his reach. He grabbed her shirt and yanked her toward him. Their bodies crashed together. They stood frozen, nose to nose, her shirt fisted in his hand, both breathing hard, neither giving an inch. Evo slowly looked over her head into the neighbor's back yard and back at Sam. Sam narrowed her eyes and said through her teeth, "You wouldn't dare."

An evil grin spread across Evo's face, and a quiet chant of "Evo, Evo, Ee-Vo, Ee-Vo" rippled through the crowd. Quickly ducking, he grabbed her around the knees and hoisted her over his shoulder in a fireman's carry. She screeched and pounded his back as he turned away from the crowd, striding toward the in-ground pool in the neighbor's yard. The crowd went wild and followed.

Joy Broussard elbowed my mom and said, "Boy, Gerry, I didn't know you planned free entertainment. Mom ignored her and kept clicking.

Mary leaned forward and proclaimed loudly, "Joy, you're always first in line when anything is free."

"Shut up, you old bat, at least I didn't kill a dead coyote today!"

Mary sniffed. "I saved a life I'll have you know."

Joy piped up. "After you almost killed him."

"Oh, pooh," Mary exclaimed as she hitched her skirt up her scrawny legs. "Come on girls, we're missing the show. They all tottered over and elbowed their way to the front of the crowd.

The crowd roared as Evo walked with deliberate steps toward the swimming pool.

"Dump-her-in! Dump-her-in! The chant grew louder as he got closer to the pool's edge.

Sam saw what was coming and began to fight in earnest. "Evo, so help me, put me down. This is not funny anymore. Evo, I mean it, it's cold in there. Stop this macho nonsense right now!"

Evo stopped at the pool's edge. "What's the matter, Sam? Can't take the heat? I'm having fun. You dared me, remember?"

"That's not what you were talking about earlier and you know it."

"Can I help it if your mind is in the gutter? You must really be hot for me. You need some cooling off, I think." He turned so his back faced the water and leaned back a little.

She shrieked and he hesitated. "Please, Evo, that water is cold. This isn't funny." When he chuckled the crowd started up again. "Drop-that-girl! Drop-that-girl!"

He sighed mightily. "Everyone seems to think I need to lighten up and have fun. Well," he smacked her butt and she squeaked. "I'm having fun. The crowd is having fun. You really need to lighten up, Sam."

We continued to chant and Evo said to Sam, "What the crowd wants, the crowd gets." He leaned back to drop her in and Sam screeched. She grabbed him around the waist. With a snap of her back, she threw him off balance. Evo teetered on the edge of the pool and they both toppled into the water. The crowd fell silent for a second, then roared.

"Boy-oh-boy! That's the best splash I've seen in years," yelled Mom from the sideline. Evo and Sam came to the surface sputtering. Evo yelled at her, "Why the hell did you do that?"

"Because you were dumping me in the pool, you Neanderthal!"

"I wasn't really dumping you in; I only *threatened* to dump you in!"

"You were dumping me." She looked into the crowd and yelled, "He was dumping me, wasn't he?" We all laughed and nodded.

Evo ducked his head and smiled sheepishly. "Sam, I think we have created enough of a spectacle. Let me help you out." He reached out to her and she batted his hands away.

As if on cue, the crowd moaned, "*Aww*."

Sam looked indignant. She flipped the hair out of her eyes. "You're the one who helped me in, thank you very much. I'll help myself out." With as much dignity as she could muster, she slogged through the water, away from him.

Evo followed in her wake. "Aw, Sam, come on. Have a sense of humor. Besides, you're on vacation." The crowd clapped and hooted. "I have to admit though; you're a real crowd pleaser."

She whipped around, her hair slapping him in the face. "I'll give you crowd pleaser, Evo Reymundo Moronez-Castillo!" She lunged high against his chest, grabbing his head and twisting her body backward, dragging Evo under the surface with her. They surfaced together with his chin resting on her cleavage and both hands on her butt. We all sucked in a breath. He slowly looked up. She stared down into his eyes. He looked at her mouth and she nervously licked her lips. We all licked our lips as time stood still and he moved a fraction of an inch closer. I had a death grip on J.J.'s arm and he covered my hand with his. We strained forward and–

The flash of a camera startled them and us, and they both looked to the side of the pool. A woman in a skirt and pumps held a camera in her hands. Startled and now pissed, I glared as Rosie the News Whore clicked her way across the tile.

"Great, look." The camera flashed again, "Miller parties are never dull, that's for *sure.*" She leaned over the edge of the pool and held out a business card. Evo took one hand off Sam's butt long enough to take it. "Rose Hartwell White Bass Lake Review," she said. "I report the local news." She put her nose in the air. "I must say, you South Americans do interesting *in depth* research, don't you?" She chuckled and turned. Her heels beat a snappy tattoo as she quickly made her exit, her rear twitching in her too tight skirt.

Evo shook his head and muttered, "Rose Who-well?"

"That's Rosie the News Whore down at the paper," Mag supplied. "She also does a spot on local television every once in a while." Sam looked up at us. "She's not very nice, is she?"

"As a matter of fact, I don't know of a single person who can stand the sight of her. You know, once she–"We heard a wild scream and all heads turned in time to see Rosie fly through the air and make an Orca-worthy splash at the other end of the pool. A camera flashed again, this time with Mom behind the lens.

Rosie floundered a bit before she made it to the side of the pool. "Gerry Miller, you pushed me!"

Mom turned around, nose in the air in her best Rosie impersonation. "Now you can say you do *in depth* reporting." She cocked her head. "About five feet deep, I'd say." She raised the camera one more time and caught Rosie with her mouth wide open, makeup running down her face and screaming like a banshee.

Everyone roared and Mom found herself in the midst of a lot of hooting and backslapping. Evo bent low and swung Sam against his chest. He carried her to the shallow end of the pool.

"Does this mean we're engaged, Sam?"

She slapped his shoulder. "No, but it does mean we can watch our humiliation on the Six-o'clock News. Come on, the fun's over. Let me down, big boy."

"You forget, it wasn't only us who took a dip in the pool. She was still wearing her camera."

"Oh." Sam was still absorbing the news when Evo let her slide slowly down his body. He set her on her feet and her hands slid down his chest. They crawled out of the pool dripping and stood shivering in the cool afternoon air.

Fred ran up, stuffed bath sheets in their hands, and looked at Evo. She scrambled for something to say. "Uh, well, uh, at least, er, the dip got the Jell-O off those pants."

Every single person stared at Evo's crotch. Too late, he realized he wasn't wearing underwear because his were still in their packages somewhere in the truck. With his jeans plastered to his body, evidence of how much he enjoyed Sam's body smashed against his, was clearly defined in front of God and everyone. Evo's humiliation was complete. I smiled when he had the good grace to go with it.

He gave the crowd a wolfish grin, flipped his towel around Sam's neck, and yanked her forward. Her mind had just enough time to register the bulge in his jeans before his mouth closed over hers. He slid an arm around her shoulders and the crowd went wild when he dipped her low enough for her hair to touch the ground. He rested his forehead against her and said, "Now *that* was macho caveman stuff." Before she could protest he kissed her again, this time slowly rising. "That is what you do to me, Samón."

He steadied her and stepped back. To Sam's obvious disgust, she must have realized that somewhere along the way her arms had become entwined around Evo's neck. Looking dazed and confused, she stood there while he picked up her towel and wrapped it around her neck. He tapped the end of her nose with his index finger and said, "We'll continue this conversation later, baby," before he sauntered away.

The whole scene would have played out beautifully for him except his smart-assed exit line snapped her out of her stupor. Sam sprung into action. Her eyes narrowed and a sharp *Crack* resounded as Sam's towel met with Evo's butt. His eyes popped open and he stood frozen as she flipped her towel over her shoulder. She shook out her hair as she sashayed past him. "That is what you do to me, caveman *baby*."

The crowd roared.

Tony leaned back in his chair by the house and flipped the toothpick in his mouth from one side to the other. He gave himself a mental pat on the back and smiled to himself. "I'd say Round Two goes to Sam."

"Did you say something, Tony?" Al asked as she touched up her lip gloss in the mirror.

"No, nothing important." He smiled wide as he tipped his soda up and drained it.

Sam slammed through the back door and Evo headed to his truck. *Damn no clothes.* He headed back to the rear of the house. Sam stood inside the door bent over, toweling her hair. Evo barely had time to enjoy the scenery before Fred came running with clothes in her hand. Sam thanked her, ignored Evo and stepped into the bathroom.

Evo stood dripping on the tile and asked, "Has anyone seen my clothes?"

He heard laughter from the bathroom. "Should have thought of that earlier."

Fred shoved another towel into his hands and said, "I had Luis and Alfredo help Sam move everything into one of the guests rooms. I'll grab you some sweats or something and I'll be right back." With that, she took off.

Evo stripped off his shirt. It made a sopping splat as it hit the laundry tub. During the process of drying his back, he heard the bathroom door open. He turned to see Sam standing with round eyes and her mouth open. She recovered quickly and cleared her throat.

She took in his long, athletic body, a set of abs to die for and smiled. "No wonder you could sling me around like I weigh nothing." She ran a finger down the middle of his chest and patted his washboard stomach. "Not bad, Castillo, not bad at all."

She dropped her clothes on top of his shirt and went in search of a hairbrush.

Evo looked at the miniscule scrap of lace on top of her clothes. Imagining it wrapped around Sam's backside proved too much for his over-active libido and a surge of heat radiated through his body. Looking up, he realized she'd caught him staring and heat colored his face. One look at her tight little T-shirt that said, "Wisconsin, Come Smell Our Dairy Air," and he bolted for the bathroom.

Sam turned to leave the room, but her voice stopped him cold. "You know, mine still aren't as nice as yours."

Truly perplexed, Evo said, "What on Earth are you talking about?"

"Oh come on, Castillo. There're no secrets here, I saw–"

"Saw wha–?"

Evo jumped backward just as Fred careened around the corner with a set of black sweats in her hand. She hit the water that Evo dripped on the floor and skid the last couple of feet. Evo grabbed her arms and steadied her, and she triumphantly handed over the sweats. "*Whew*," she claimed happily. "That was close."

"I'll say. What would you like me to do with the towels?"

"Oh, just drop them on the floor to soak up the water for now. Someone might come in the door and slip, you know."

Evo chuckled and let her go. "Uh, yes, I can see the

possibilities."

"I'll throw everything in the washer to get the chlorine out after you're through. You go ahead and change."

"Right."

Mag and I walked through the door just as Evo turned toward us. We both stopped dead, but Mag recovered first. Always the diplomat, Mag clutched her heart and yelled. "*Hoo-Baby*. I'll take one six pack to go."

I blushed and said to Evo, "You'll have to excuse her. We only have her on loan from the insane asylum. She has to be back by seven to get her medication."

Evo smiled. "That's okay, Buzz. After the beating my ego took this afternoon, I needed that." He bowed low to both of us, crossing the arm holding the sweats across his middle. "Ladies," he said and exited into the bathroom.

I hit Mag in the arm. "You moron, you embarrassed him, besides, I think you've already had your six pack."

"You would be correct, oh sober one, but them were some mighty fine abs, Buzz. Admit it, all that bronze skin...*Whoa baby*."

I sighed. "Yes, I have to admit, he is quite beautiful. Put your tongue in your mouth now, Maggot. That's a good girl."

Evo picked that moment to come out of the bathroom. He squeezed by Mag and me and dropped his wet jeans into the laundry tub. "I can wash these later, Fred. Thank you for getting me these clothes. Now, could you please direct me to my room?

That galvanized Fred into action. "Sure I can. Right this way." We clomped through the house as Fred led Evo to a room a couple of doors down from where Sam closed door. She wore a Cheshire cat grin as she drew even with us. She leaned against the doorjamb. "Looking for these, Evo?" She swung a pair of pink lacy underwear from one finger.

"Not particularly, Sam, but if this is an invitation..."

She threw them at Evo, and they landed on his shoulder. "Those are yours, you idiot, not mine!"

"Oops," said Mag.

"Oh, oh." I said.

"What is she talking about?" Fred wondered.

I grabbed my sisters and pulled them backward around the corner by the stairs. *"Shh."* I poked my head out far enough to see the exchange, and I was jostled from behind as my sisters pushed their way in.

Evo examined the pink lace, but Sam grabbed them back and twirled the panties on her finger. She said, "Come clean, Castillo. These were in with your stuff. They're either left over from your latest conquest, or you are one kinky S.O.B."

Evo drew himself up and looked down his nose at Sam. He took the panties. "They are certainly not mine! Why would you even insinuate that I would, uh, that those things...uh, I don't know...why. There must be some explana–Tony, uh packed my...Oh my God, *Tony!*"

"Right, blame your poor brother. They were the only underwear in your entire wardrobe."

She realized what she'd said, and drew in a quick breath. Combined with our collective indrawn breaths, it sounded like a wind tunnel in that small hallway. We pulled back until we heard them speak again.

Evo allowed himself a small smile. "So, you rifled through my underwear, eh?" He took a step toward her. She had the good sense not to test him twice in one day and stepped back.

"Uh, no. That is yes. I mean...I helped Fred unpack and they fell out when I grabbed them." He advanced and she retreated. "W-what I mean is I saw them. No, wait. I felt them, uh, I mean, uh, I saw them and I...that is, I thought–"

He backed her into the wall. "You thought I had another woman's underwear in my luggage or that I wore..." He held up the tiny scrap of lace. "These?"

She looked up at him wide-eyed and swallowed. "I...I didn't really think you wore them, I thought–that is, we assumed–"

Another step brought them nose-to-nose. Sam blinked and Evo continued in a silky voice. "Sam, in the first place, these would not even fit over my foot, let alone my, ah, you know."

We snickered from our hiding place, because after the pool incident, we *all* knew.

"Second, I know this may come as a shock to you, but I do *not* make it a habit of carrying around my latest conquests' underwear." His body vibrated with suppressed emotion. "I've been in the field so long my last *conquest* probably has grandchildren by now." He leaned in and said softly, "Do we understand each other?"

She gulped and nodded silently. We let out our breath whoosh out as one. It sounded like someone let loose a giant helium balloon in the hallway. So absorbed were they in each other, the noise didn't even faze them.

Evo snatched the panties out of her hand and crumpled them. "I don't want this underwear to ever be a bone of contention between us. The only woman's underwear I've seen in the last six months is yours, approximately ten minutes ago."

We all sighed and I heard Fred whisper, "Come on, Sam don't mess this up." We leaned forward, totally captivated by the scene playing out in front of us.

Sam touched his forearm and ran her fingers lightly down to his wrist. Evo watched her fingers and didn't move a muscle. His head moved a fraction of an inch closer to her and she tilted her face up. He moved closer still, and she moved her head slightly to the right. We had hold of each other's shirts and we were all prepared for his final move when a hand tapped me on the shoulder.

We all jumped and squeaked, clutching our chests. Tony chuckled at us scattering and falling against the wall, and Mag whispered, "Geez, Tony. You scared the crap out of us."

Unaware of the scene unfolding around the corner, Tony laughed loudly. "Sorry, everyone. What are you guys doing huddled in the hallway?"

Sam and Evo jumped apart as if scalded and watched the scuffle as we tried to control Tony.

"We're watching Evo try to explain his way out of a pair of pink lady's underwear in his luggage." I said. "Now be quiet! You're going to make us miss the best part."

Tony started to laugh in earnest. We shushed him, but he only got louder. "I gotta see this."

We shushed him and pushed him behind us, but he gave a mighty shove forward and stumbled around the corner, sliding down the wall to the floor.

Still laughing, Tony looked up. Evo calmly looked down. "What the hell is so funny, Mr. Sunshine?"

Tony held his sore head and laughed. "You. Her. Them!" He pointed to the underwear on the floor.

Evo clenched and unclenched his fists. He grabbed Tony by the front of the shirt and slowly stood him on his feet. "Tony," he said slowly. "Do you know anything about how the lady's underwear came to be in my luggage?"

Tony laughed harder and slid down the wall, wiping tears from his eyes. Mag and I got the joke and we began to laugh as well. Evo dragged him up to his feet again. Still laughing helplessly, Tony held up his hands and Sam grabbed Evo's arm. "No, don't hit him!"

Evo didn't not loosen the grip he had on his brother. "I'm not going to hurt him—yet. I'll wait until his head heals, *then* I'll kill him. It seems as though my little brother pulled a little joke on me after I told him to stay out of my underwear drawer, isn't that right, Tony?"

"*Hah*. Uh, my big brother is a little anal—hah--about his underwear drawer. I packed for him because he was in the field, and decided to get back at him for giving me grief about packing his stupid underwear. So I went to the mall and bought...I bought..." He sniffed and wiped his eyes. "Those!" He collapsed in gales of laughter.

Evo got right in Tony's face. "Tony, remind me to kill you later."

Tony grinned like an idiot and gave him the thumbs up. "You got it, Bro, it'll be worth it."

Evo lowered Tony to his feet and propped him against the wall. Tony slid toward the floor again and Fred and Sam leaped forward to each grab an arm. While they fussed with Tony, Evo stared at Sam in silence. He opened the door to his room and stopped. We all stared dumbly as a red-faced Evo again started forward, then hesitated and looked as if he wanted to say something to Sam. He looked at the rest of us and decided against it. Sam froze and stared at him, letting go of Tony in the process. Fred stared at Sam and let go of the other arm.

Sam reached out to Evo and said, "Evo, I'm sor–" and he shut the door on all of us. Sam looked at the floor and bit her lip.

Tony slid to the floor holding his head, still guffawing like a jackass. Then he said something none of could understand. "Round three goes to me."

I whacked him with the pink panties.

11

With everyone dry and tucked into gender-correct underwear, life was much easier to deal with in the Fred Miller household. Luis and Alfredo packed the sample fish into Evo's truck, and the whole group of us headed out to Ian's new place. I was thankful that Fred had the foresight to send our favorite local forensic botanist samples of the dead fish so he could begin analysis before we arrived. He'd set up shop here after moving out of Milwaukee.

Dr. Ian Connor recently bought the land bordering my folk's farm and turned part of it into a forensic botany lab. He still worked for the FBI, but now he worked out of White Bass Lake instead of Milwaukee and Madison. In return for federal funding, he also did contract work for the State Crime Lab and the FBI. Sweet deal. Ian was currently in the process of transforming it into his dream. The lab was close to being finished, and one could certainly tell that plants were his passion.

As we turned into the driveway, I noticed Ian had finally gotten rid of the old *Graff's Garden Center* sign out front. What Ian planned to do with the rest of the place was cause for great speculation down at Sal's diner. I explained to Evo and Sam that "Geriatric Gossip Central" speculated that Ian was planning everything from a strip club to a Wal-Mart. Mom had asked about open auditions, and the guys down at the Moose Club wanted to book early for a Spring convention. Mag contended Ian planned to open a home for wayward plants, but Mag is an idiot.

Mom called on our way over. She told me Mary had completely gone around the bend; she needed somewhere to practice. Alright, I admit I bit. I asked what on earth Mary could be practicing, and Mom said she was practicing her pole dancing audition routine for Ian's new strip club, but Mary didn't have a pole. Mom was afraid of what Mary might do. At that, I had to turn my cell phone on speaker.

"Go on, Mom. Tell me the whole story."

Mom explained, "Mary wanted to practice on a real pole before competing with the younger crowd. She hopes to be hired as one of Ian's new girls at the strip club. I told her to use the flagpole out in front of the Sheriff's office, thinking maybe she'd get arrested for indecent exposure or excessive wrinkling or something."

"Calm down, Mom. Ian is definitely not building a strip club."

"That's what we keep telling Mary, but she remains hopeful. What do we do in the meantime?"

"Lock her up, Mom."

"Someone ought to."

We neared Ian's place. "Gotta go, Mom, I'll talk to you later. Good luck."

"What should we do about Mary?"

"Take away her boom-box."

"Easier said than done, Buzz."

"I have faith in you, Mom. Between you, Joy, and Jane, you'll figure out something. Gotta go, we're pulling in. I love you."

"Me too, honey. Give J.J. a hug for me."

"Motherrr…"

"I too, remain hopeful about some things. See you later, Buzz." She hung up before I could yell at her.

I let out an exasperated sigh and Fred said, "Matchmaking Mom again?"

"Yeah, Air Ger is at it again."

Fred sighed. "Mothers on matrimonial missions are the

best reasons for voice mail."

I raised a brow. "You got that right."

We drove around to the newly renovated building which held Ian's lab, and I was surprised at the heavy steel door with some sort of sooper-dooper locking mechanism attached. A tiny security camera and intercom sat to the left of the door, and Ian's disembodied voice said, "Yo, Buzz, come on in. Hold on a minute. On second thought, I'll come out. I want to show you something."

The heavy door cycled electronically and I pulled it open. Ian came out and led J.J, Evo, Tony, Sam, Fred, and me to the large building next door to the lab. He opened the door and we stepped inside. Ian folded his arms across his chest and grinned. "Well, what do you think? This is Maggie's work-in-progress."

We all stood there with our mouths hanging open. With a nudge from Ian, we entered the *Land of Oz*.

Fred and I said simultaneously, "We're not in Kansas anymore, Toto." Evo, Tony, and Sam just stared at us.

Mag's work-in-progress turned an ordinary pole barn into a living nature lab for grade school and high school students, as well as a science classroom and lab for college students. Live vines hung on the wall and crisscrossed rafters, also draped in moss. Background jungle noises came from hidden speakers as we passed through a make-believe tropical canopy.

We stepped into the main part of the young people's nature center, which held long tables filled with two ant farms, a bee colony ducted to the outside, a worm farm, rows of computers and microscopes. A butterfly enclosure separated the young scientist area from the advanced science labs.

Here agricultural experiments, along with alternative sources of power made from vegetables lined the long tables for the older students. Chemistry, Biology, Agronomy, Microbiology, and Botany were the main subjects of research and experimentation here. Computers, lab tables, a life-like skeleton, coolers, autoclaves, and other equipment filled the tables and cabinets. Shelves of glass vials, test tubes, Petrie dishes and other glass containers lined the walls.

Like a kid at Christmas, Mag explained that since Ian held a PhD. In Forensic Botany and she had a Master's degree in Biology, between them they could cover all the subjects easily. Mag had mentioned retiring from teaching high school, but I had no idea she meant to taking on a project as big as this.

"Ian has already contacted the local university and they're very interested in our facility. They want to hold some of their classes on site, right here. We would teach some, and visiting professors would handle others."

Stunned, I looked at her and could only say, "Beats the crap out of pole dancing."

Ian looked confused and Mag patted his arm. "I'll explain later, Honey."

I moved past her in a daze to gaze at the tropical rainforest they'd created at the far end. Enclosed in glass to keep the humidity in, the ceiling misters from the old greenhouses served as a rain source. Plant life on the interior consisted of everything from the outrageous to the bizarre. Different environmental studies would be performed as the building neared completion.

Ian said, "Everything in the enclosure is endangered or near extinction. Some had to be duplicated because we weren't allowed to export a specimen. I built it in part for public awareness, but also for research to see if we can propagate some species well enough to re-introduce them into the rainforests."

"Holy cow. This has got to be Nobel Prize stuff, Ian."

Ian blushed. "I just hope to help save the world from itself, Buzz."

I squeezed his arm. "It's a hell of a start, Ian. I'm proud of you both."

A noise to our left had us watching Evo as he poked around a native Aztec display. Evo stuck his head inside a hut and yelled, "Anybody home?"

A Banana Palm alongside the hut shook, and a rustling noise had us looking up.

Ian shook his head and sighed. "Oh, no I didn't warn you."

Evo said, "What's wrong, I was joking when I said, anyone home."

The tree shook again, and an odd voice screeched, "Nobody here but us chickens. *Cluck, clunk, clunk.*"

We all jumped back and Ian grinned. "We're in for it now."

Evo and Tony looked at each other.

"Chickens?"

"Clunk?"

"He means cluck, but he never gets it right. Dumb bird doesn't even make a good chicken."

"Dumb?"

"Bird?"

The squawk coming from the tree made me hop behind Ian. I knew what was coming.

"Dumb Bird. Pitty Bird. Pitty Dumb Bird." The banana palm shook again and out flew a giant Cockatoo. Sam and Fred came rushing out of the rain forest just in time to watch the bird come in for a crash landing. He skidded the length of a long steel table. Sliding to a stop near the two men, the bird began making "*yummy*" noises and buried his head in Evo's pocket.

Side-stepping the probing beak, Evo danced out of reach. "Hey, don't you ever feed this poor guy?"

Ian cocked an eyebrow. "Poor guy my ass. That begging thing was Mag's doing. She plays hide the treat, and now," he pointed to the cockatoo, "That little criminal has become an accomplished pickpocket."

Fred laughed. "Glad to see he's picked up some other bad habits since you took him."

Sam stepped closer. "Oh, Ian, he is so beautiful. What do you call him?"

Ian grumbled. "I try not to call him anything in his presence." His voice lowered to a whisper. "But his name is Kitty. He's very annoying about it. Go ahead, Sam, he doesn't bite, but he's such a pig he may accidentally grab some skin. That's why we can't have him in the children's section, and I've never caged him, so here he stays. We call him the local color—when I'm not cussing at him, that is."

Sam grabbed a peanut out of a dish and stepped closer. Kitty cocked his head and lifted his crown. His sharp beak opened and closed while his black tongue worked back and forth.

Sam lowered her voice and held out the peanut. She waited until Kitty moved toward her. "Hello, Kitty."

Kitty jumped a couple of inches off the table and shook his head. Ian shook his head and sighed, "Oh no, here we go."

Kitty suddenly flapped his wings and cocked a baleful eye toward Sam. He swooped in on the peanut and screeched, "Here Kitty, Kitty, *Kitty. Heeere* Kitty."

Sam wisely let go of the peanut while Kitty snatched it and hopped back toward Ian. He stuffed it into his mouth. "*Shee-it.* Them's some fiiiine vittles," he said while he spit peanut and shell across the table.

We were all staring at Ian and he held up his hands. "Uh, that's the other reason he can't be around kids. I swear I didn't teach him most of what he says."

"That's why he's back living here and not at the store with me anymore. Some of the customers found his language a bit offensive."

"He's adorable. Sam giggled as she held out a bit of mango. Kitty was suddenly her best friend, chatting away at the

113

top of his lungs as he gorged himself on the fruit.

Ian pointed to a stainless steel sink so Sam could wash up, and said to us, "Ready to see my space?"

Sam turned, "Not really, but I guess I can visit my new friend later."

We reluctantly left Kitty to his own devices and followed Ian out of the science center.

Ian headed back to his mysterious locked building, leaving the rest of us to help Mag close up the nature center Five minutes later, the heavy door cycled and we passed into a glass-enclosed vestibule. Here we donned paper coveralls, hairnets, gloves, and booties because Ian ran a clean-room which was as sterile as he could make it. I thought about getting him going by threatening to bring the dogs for a visit.

I strolled up to where he looked into a microscope and patted him on the shoulder. "Hey, Plant Boy, how's it photosynthesizing?"

Ian looked up and blinked. "It's photosynthesizing just fine in here, Buzz. How'd you like Maggie's project?"

"Awesome."

"Fantastic."

"Like another world."

Ian smiled with pride. "Mag's got the donations rolling in and can't wait to open. Do you think the old ladies are going to be very disappointed to find out they have been protesting a nature lab and not a den of iniquity?"

I laughed out loud. "They'll find something else to bitch about, rest assured, but Mary is going to awful disappointed that she can't audition on a real pole."

Ian looked startled. "What? N-never mind." He turned to J.J. "How's the bad guy business in town? All quiet down at Sal's?"

I piped up. "Crime has to stay on hold for a while because we stole the Sheriff."

Ian shook hands with J.J. "Good to know. I feel safer already."

Sam looked at the slides Ian had made from the dead Endlers. Ian had extracted the contents of the fish's bellies. He pulled one slide out of the lineup and placed it under a microscope.

Sam did the same and asked, "Ian, what exactly are you looking for over here?"

"I thought if I could identify plant matter in their digestive systems, I could test for any toxins in that plant matter. Very interesting things I'm finding. First, I'm finding heavy metal toxins such as mercury and cyanide–enough to kill a much larger animal."

He pointed to a white board listing the contents of the water as well as the plant molecules in the fish bellies. He had the toxins figured out by parts per million. The math made me dizzy, but the words cyanide and mercury were enough to convince me of cause of death.

"Are you talking enough poison to kill something such as a chicken or goat?" I remembered Evo's tale of the village.

"Or human." Ian continued, "The fish did not ingest this over a long period of time, as I did not find concentrations in the tissues. In this case, toxins would have killed off the first generation and the lake would have been completely void of fish. The toxins were most likely introduced into the lagoon by a recent run off or dumping of toxic materials."

Evo cut in. "Do you mean a runoff from a garbage dump or mining slag, or a source of natural toxins?" He looked at the floor in deep concentration.

"Cyanide and mercury, are definitely introduced from outside sources. These types of poisons do not occur in these amounts naturally. By introduction from an outside entity, the fish in that lagoon would have had no immunity built up to tolerate the poisons, even in low levels."

115

Sam held a hand over her heart. "That is why you said the F-Zero generation would have perished. They would not have lived long enough to produce first generation offspring."

Staring at the whiteboard, Evo muttered to himself, "But there aren't any garbage dumps or mines in that area, only Number 151, and that stuff doesn't leach from oil wells. Nunez owns all that land, and has only the oil operation in that area. Where the hell did it come from?"

He thought about the graves in the churchyard and asked Ian, "Are you talking about enough cyanide in the water source to kill even larger beings such as children and the elderly?"

"Larger. This is no small concentration I'm talking about. This could wipe out an entire village including their cattle."

Evo covered his eyes and muttered, "Oh, my God, I need to go back and find the source. The village, the people; good Lord, the children!"

Ian changed slides again. "But I found a very curious thing to make this case even more confusing. Some of the plant materials in their stomachs are not indigenous to that region of Venezuela."

We all stared dumbly at each other.

Ian continued. "Some of the plant material these guys ingested came from only one place known in the world. Peru."

"Peru?" we echoed.

"Peru," Ian continued. "And this might give us a great clue as to what is going on. *Platycerium andinum* is an almost extinct fern. I have one over there." He pointed to a palm-type tree which looked like it had a lion's mane growing around a large branch. "The only places it is found in the world are on the eastern slopes of the Andes Mountains in Peru. Get this. Its closest relative resides in Madagascar."

"Madagascar?"

"Western Madagascar."

There was silence in the room. Fred let out a big sigh

116

which blew the bangs off her forehead. "Boy, does that lend credence to the *Big Bang Theory* or what?"

Ian looked up at us. "Yep, but what's more curious is the fact that both of those regions are dry tropical forests. Therefore, my question is this, what would that particular plant material be doing inside a little fish in a tropical rainforest literally hundreds of miles away?"

Evo stopped his mumblings with that bit of information. "What you're saying is–"

Sam jumped in. "When we first found out Evo discovered the Endlers in the far northeastern region of Venezuela, I thought it odd they would turn up in a previously unknown and remote location. The only lake in the world where they were found was fouled by a garbage dump, so Endlers are practically extinct in the wild." She gathered her thoughts. "So you are saying that this plant is not found in the same region as these fish, let alone found in Venezuela at all."

"You win the kewpie doll. This leads me to believe–"

"Someone moved the fish there," we all intoned.

"Man, you guys are quick," Ian said.

Evo spoke up. "I know of this fern--this *andinum*. It is rare enough, but it is not listed as a 'salvageable' rare species. There's a group trying to protect a forest where these ferns grow in abundance. They grow on Quinilla trees in places like the Donut Hole Forest near San Martin. Presently, the Quinilla trees are being clear cut for fence posts and the vegetation burned off, including the *andinum*."

Sam lifted a brow and sneered. "Aren't we the conservationist all of a sudden? This from Mr. Corporate Oil Man? Isn't your only job the conservation of your huge take-home pay? How do you know so much about it, and why would you care?"

Evo drew up to his full height and looked down his nose at Sam. He said very quietly, "Because I initiated the project to

117

establish the Donut Hole as a Zone of Ecological Protection to save it. Look it up, Dr. Fernandini. I even got shot by the opposition while putting up signs for D.S. 011-96-AG." He pulled up his sleeve and she looked in horror at the angry red slash that still marred his bicep. He yanked down his sleeve, turned, and walked. When he stopped, he stood perfectly still, hands on hips and studied the plants Ian had in the corner atrium.

Stunned, Sam looked at Fred. She bit her lip. "Oh, my God, I didn't know. I didn't think. Now I vaguely remember Tony mentioning it, but not in conjunction with his brother. Why didn't he *say* something?" She looked over to where Evo gently turned over a leaf to study the backside, and took a step in that direction.

Tony caught up to her and touched her arm. "Stay here, I'll talk to him. He has strong feelings, but rarely shows this much emotion. You've obviously hurt him deeply."

Sam drew herself up. "No, Tony, I blew it, I'll fix it." She brushed by him and started toward Evo.

Tony grabbed her arm again. "Later, Sam, I mean it. He won't listen now. Approach him later. Let him stew for a while by himself."

Sam yanked her arm away, and Tony grabbed her again. Sam said, "I can admit that I've been an ass when the situation calls for it." She flipped her satin mane of hair over her shoulder. "I'll *make* him listen to me." She pulled free and stomped after Evo.

Tony looked stunned and said under his breath, "Man, you two are so much alike…"

I squeezed his shoulder. "Come on, kiddo. You can't fight their battles for them. If there's blood to be shed, J.J. and I know first aid. Let them go for now."

"It's not that, Buzz. She really *is* just like him." He suddenly grinned. "I gotta see this." He grabbed Fred's hand

and slunk off along the tree line, trying for a better view of the inevitable confrontation.

I watched as he inched closer to the quiet war going on between Evo and Sam. I saw a lot of head bobbing and large gestures. I looked over to where Tony crouched and he gave me the two-thumbs up sign–whatever that meant.

I sighed and turned back to Ian. "So, when will we be able to examine the not-so-dead fish? Can we use your place here?"

"Sure! Bring 'em on. I'd be happy to help."

Loud banging at the door stopped all noise in our building. Ian bounded toward the security camera. "May I help you, sir?" He spoke into the intercom. I looked at the monitor and saw a Grizzly Adams looking guy at the door.

"Open up here, I'm Hank MacRone." The voice boomed over the intercom.

Ian and I looked at each other. Ian recovered first. "Who the heck is Hank MacRone?"

At first I didn't connect the name. "Beats the hell out of me. Wait! I know who Hank MacRone is. Fred, Sam, come quick, you'll never guess–"

12

This is not the American dream, Tom thought as they waited in line for a rental car. If Mark didn't get them arrested before they could bump off the two morons and the scientists, Tom would be surprised. They arrived shortly after the scientist, his brother, and the two morons, but between Mark stuffing himself on Big Macs and marveling at the automatic soap dispenser in the bathroom, their targets were well on their way. They caught up with them near the car rental place, but some hassle about the car had Tom and Mark hiding behind a Ficus tree to avoid being seen.

By the time Tom and Mark followed them out the front door, the others were crammed into a small car and pulling away from the curb. Without thinking, Mark jumped into a Jeep at the curb which had its engine running. Tom hesitated then dove through the passenger window as Mark slammed it into gear and squealed the tires. They took off after the Suzuki and tried to blend in with the traffic. They followed them to a motel and waited for them to go in. They got lost on their way back to the airport, and ended up in a neighborhood much like the one they escaped. "Betcha the pizza delivery guy don't come here either, Mark."

"Betcha you're right. We gotta get out of here before someone shoots us or something."

They finally found the airport and parked the Jeep in a remote parking lot. They locked it and wiped it down. It wouldn't pay to be caught in a stolen car before they began their mission.

Tom was exhausted and really angry with the desk clerk from the car rental agency. Mark looked like he was just along for the ride. He wandered around, stared out the window, and left all the decision making to Tom. He seemed so laid back Tom almost throttled him when they were asking if they wanted luxury or fuel economy. Mark piped up for the first time all day and said, "Fuel economy," and Tom knew they would be brought a microscopic little car that would make that other car look like a freight train.

Tom wanted to give it back, but Mark convinced him that good gas economy and free miles was a good deal. The agent promised sporty, too, and when he drove up in the red hard top/convertible Cooper, Mark about flipped.

Tom said out of the side of his mouth, "We can't drive around in that thing; we'll stick out like a white guy in our old neighborhood."

The agent talked about the great the acceleration on the little Cooper, and how its maneuverability in traffic could spare them from an accident. Tom rolled his eyes.

Mark elbowed Tom. "See? It's a good get-away car too. You worry too much, little brother."

"I'm not your brother and according to my mother; you are only about five minutes older than me, so don't give me that fatherly advice crap."

Mark snatched the key from the rental agent and headed around to the driver's door. "Whatever, I'm drivin'."

Tom took off in pursuit. He dove into the driver's seat a split second before Mark got there. "No you ain't. I'm drivin'."

Mark grabbed Tom's T-shirt and tried to yank him out of the car. "Don't start with me, I'm the better driver, *and* I'm older. Besides, your mom likes me better, so move over or get out."

A scuffle ensued, but Mark succeeded in dragging Tom out of the driver's window. Tom calmly stood up. Brushing off his knees, he gathered himself up to his full height. "Okay, let's do this logically. You say you're the better driver?" Tom put his finger to his chin and rested on one hip. "Then let me see... It must have been someone else who knocked the mirror off the Jeep at the drive-up window at *Burger King,* stepped on the gas rather than the brake, jumped the curb, barely missing six pigeons and a little old lady, and ran over a garbage can?

"And it must have been someone else who drove into a ditch after we saw that girl wearing only a bra while jogging down the road."

"Yeah, good thing we stole a Jeep, huh? We would have been goners in that ditch, eh? I really thought she was Pamela Anderson; I only wanted an autograph."

"Pamela Anderson in po-dunk Wisconsin? You almost ran over your tongue."

"Yeah, well, uh...I–"

"And that poor cow in the road?"

"Okay, okay, you win. I forgot about the cow." Mark tossed the keys to Tom and stalked to the passenger's door. The rental agent staggered back into his office. He felt dizzy and plopped down into a chair. Putting his head between his knees to prevent himself from hyperventilating, he only prayed those two characters were kidding around.

Mark watched the rental agent through the window and raised a brow. He jerked his thumb toward the heaving man. "What's wrong with him, do you suppose?"

Tom slid behind the wheel and grinned. "Probably got a good look at your face, *amigo.*"

Mark pointed to his chin. "This is your *mother's* face, *Amigo.*" He jumped in the passenger's side and slid his ball cap around backward. "And I'll *amigo* your ass, bitch, get us out of here."

Tom spun the tires as he left the parking lot. The rental agent quietly passed out behind his desk.

As they sped down the expressway, Mark pressed buttons and pulled levers. He opened the glove compartment and put his window down and up several times. He fiddled with the radio. When booming bass blasted from the speakers, Mark crossed his arms over his chest and nodded his head in time with the music. "Now *that's* what I'm talking 'bout. All I need is a little blink and I'll be irresistible."

Tom hit the off button. "That's *bling,* you moron. You are such a waste of skin."

Mark lifted his hands away from his body, hands hanging, fingers pointed downward, and said, "What? What?" He put his fingers under his armpits and cocked his head. "You dissin' me dawg?"

"Knock it off, Marco, you ain't nobody's dog. Hell, you aren't even an American. You watch too much television. Americans aren't really like that anyway, so just shut up, will you?"

Mark slumped in his seat and pouted. Tom drove toward White Bass Lake as they'd been instructed and stopped at a small motel for the night. They found a local tavern and still felt the effects the next morning.

Mark sucked his coffee down and shook his head. Tom was in a little better shape and began to pack. "What a disguise we have. Most of those people thought we were Mexicans. Hey, did you dig that bar last night? 'Polka Music' they called it."

"I thought the Chicken Dance was fun."

"Those people are insane, but they got good food. What the hell was in that giant cauldron outside? You ate it and you're still alive."

Mark smiled and leaned his head back. "Fish boil, my brother. Fish boil, and everyone ate it but you. They have one every Wednesday. They cook it over a fire, man. I am not going to miss another one! They invited us back Friday for what they call a fish fry. An all-you-can-eat fish fry. Boy will they be sorry after I eat."

"Hey, *stupido*! We can't be regulars at a bar. When people start dropping like flies, they'll look at the two new guys. We have to remain in the background. Blend in. Chameleons, remember?"

"Not me, I'm family. I had fish boil and *The Beer that Made Milwaukee Famous*, and I danced the Chicken Dance." Mark smiled and closed his eyes, flapping his arms like some demented chicken. "They want to adopt me."

Tom fumbled with his cell phone. "Well they can have you, but first we work. We need to get settled in White Bass Lake and find our marks."

Mark just smiled and flapped. "*Bawk, Bawk.*"

About forty-five minutes later, sporting a mustache and a Milwaukee Brewers ball cap, Tom check into a chain motel near the Interstate under the name of Jose Gonzalez from Mexico City. He gave them cash in advance and the girl behind the counter didn't blink an eye. He took his key and she picked up her cell phone and began pushing buttons at the speed of light. *Good, just perfect.*

They drove around the building and parked. They brought all their supplies they picked up at the airport locker into the room. Mark spent the afternoon putting together a car bomb, and Tom logged the laptop they'd retrieved onto the motel Internet.

He clicked on *My Documents* and revealed a few files. One had names, pictures, and descriptions of their targets, where they were staying, background on their friends, and information about the town.

Deciding they were starving, Mark drove them down to the local diner in White Bass Lake so they could scope out the locals. Tom brought the laptop along and went over the other files while they ate. Mark made a choking sound and Tom jerked up his head in time to see the two morons they were suppose to hit, heading their direction.

124

Tom tried not to panic and looked at Mark. He had sweat pouring down his face and began reciting the Rosary. Tom kicked him hard and he almost had to peel Mark off the ceiling. As it was, Mark's chair flew backward into the path of the two morons.

Luis and Alfredo pulled up short as a chair scraped across the floor into their path. Startled, Luis said the first thing that came to mind. "Hello, may I help you?"

"Uh, no. I mean Yes." Mark looked around the diner frantically. "My uh, brother and I wanted to ask if you would like to join us." Tom shot him a murderous look and Mark frantically pulled words out of the air. "It's so crowded in here you could be uh, crushed to death by the crowd. Tom kicked him again and Mark winced. "You never know how long you got to live so you might as well make new friends for the short time you're still alive. Tom kicked him again and Mark jumped. The Gallegos brothers eyed him oddly.

"I–I mean life is short and we are on vacation *amigo*, would you care to join us?"

Luis and Alfredo looked at each other and Tom rolled his eyes. "What my *brother* is trying so clumsily to say is that we are new in town and we're wondering about the local attractions. Would you like to join us and tell us about the area?"

Luis laughed and jabbed Alfredo with his elbow. "To tell you the truth, my brother and I are also new to the town, but I think we would like to join you and get acquainted. What a coincidence that we should meet two brothers from our home country right here in White Bass Lake, eh, Alfredo?"

Mark murmured, "So much for Mexico City," and Tom blasted him again. Mark sent him a killer look, but Alfredo had already pulled up a chair. Mark rubbed his sweaty palms along his pant legs and shook Alfredo's hand. Tom addressed the Gallegos brothers and began the conversation. "So what brings you so far from home?"

"Well," Alfredo began, "My brother and I are the assistants to a wonderful scientist, Dr. Evo Castillo, and he discovered this small lagoon in Venezuela..."

Tom quietly clicked the laptop closed and slipped it back into its case as the Gallegos brothers spilled the entire story, including the doomed shopping excursion and the party at Fred Miller's.

Tom and Mark paid close attention to the details of where the scientists were staying, and made mental notes to check out the territory.

Lunch came and went with the usual fanfare at Sal's Diner, with many speculative glances thrown their way. Mark looked as if he might doze off, and Tom nudged him under the table to keep him awake.

"So, what kind of plans do you have for your vacation?" Tom eyed the brothers.

Giggling like schoolboys, Luis told them he and his brother planned to visit Great America. "Say, why do you not join us? You are on vacation, and I cannot wait to ride a rollercoaster."

Having read the brochure at the motel, Tom said, "Sure. Oh, wait! We have to visit a sick relative first, so you go on ahead, and maybe we can get together another time."

"Oh?" Alfredo looked puzzled. "I thought you had no family here?"

"*Hah*. Did I say that? Well uh, she is not really family, but just like family. She's a friend of our mother's, and we have not seen her since we were small boys. Poor Juanita."

Mark chimed in, "And her husband Carlos, who has cancer, poor fellow."

Tom gave Mark the stink-eye, but the Gallegos brothers bought the story, and Tom secretly breathed a sigh of relief. Luis told Mark and Tom that the invitation still stood, and if their visit ran short, they could meet them at Great America tomorrow before five. The party broke up after that, and Mark wished Luis and Alfredo a long life before he climbed into the Cooper.

Tom was livid. "What were you trying to prove in there, you idiot?"

"What do you mean, like when you kicked me again and again?"

"I kicked you to try to shut you up. And what was that wishing you good health and a long life bit? What kind of a smart-ass are you?"

Mark yawned large. "Oh, lighten up, Tom. I was just being polite. I don't know what happened. When we talked about the job back home it sounded like a great idea. Don't get mad at me, but I think this hit man stuff ain't all it's cracked up to be."

Tom sighed. "Don't feel bad. I figured that out back in Lima. So what are we going to do?"

Mark scratched his belly. "Don't know. Let's sleep on it and we'll figure things out in the morning."

They made the rest of the trip to the motel in silence. Once in their room, Tom flopped into the only chair and saw Mark slide into his swim trunks. Tom furrowed his brow and asked, "*Now* what are you doing?"

"I'm taking a dip. Did you see all those beautiful women down by the pool? I'm gonna get me some-o'-that!"

"Like hell you are! You're going to stay right here and help me plan."

"Not now, little brother, I am going trolling. Maybe I'll get the catch of the week." He slipped out the door before Tom could grab him.

Tom sighed and pulled out the laptop. He hooked up to the Internet again and began to surf. He Googled some of the names mentioned by Luis and Alfredo. "Hmm," he said out loud. "Great America. The two morons–geez, I can't even call them that anymore." Angrily he punched more keys.

"Luis and Alfredo are going to Great America tomorrow. Roller coasters, water rides, fun for the whole family. Crowded. Daytime. Perfect. That's where we'll get 'em." He retrieved directions and wrote everything down.

Satisfied, he took a shower and crawled into bed. Lacing his fingers behind his head he thought about Luis and Alfredo Gallegos. It was stupid to meet them. They were actually pretty decent guys. Tom hated the fact that they had names; it made them real people, not just anonymous targets. The two morons thought they'd met new friends. Little did they know they'd invited a couple of murderers into their lives with open arms. Humph. They were Morons; didn't they know never to trust strangers? Maybe they deserved to be knocked off.

It was especially hard to cry off the Great America trip. Good thing he'd made up that sick relative story. They promised to meet them later if they were available. Available? *Hell. I'll be available to watch as we blow you to smithereens.*

Tom rubbed his fists into his eyes, trying to block the picture of flying body parts and spraying blood. It was no use. What a poor excuse for a hit man. He turned off his light and pulled the covers over his head. Tears leaked from his eyes as he thought of innocence lost and what people would do for a little money.

Mark crept into the room about three hours later; still dry because he'd never gone to the pool. He hoped Tom didn't find out he'd gone back to the tavern to visit with his new "family." He drank soda so his tongue wouldn't slip up; he kicked back with some new acquaintances, shot some pool, and threw a few darts. He changed clothes in the car and sat in the parking lot for a while, thinking about their job.

I hope that Tom has more of a killer instinct than I do, because right now I want to walk away from the whole thing.

Mark dropped his clothes on the floor. He brushed his teeth and crawled into bed. He hoped for a miracle, like on TV. Maybe they wouldn't have to murder the two morons and the Big Boss wouldn't find them. *Maybe we can live happily ever after right here in Wisconsin.*

Now who's the moron, Mark? Fat chance. He figured they commit murder, get caught, fry in the electric chair, never getting to spend the money for which they'd thrown away their lives. We're dead men either way. Good things never happened to guys like us. He closed his eyes and dreamed of Big Macs doing the chicken dance in Wisconsin.

Waking with new resolve, Tom threw a pillow at Mark. "Wake up, you party animal, we have a job to do. We can grab breakfast in White Bass Lake before the two morons leave for Illinois. We'll stop back here, pick up the car bomb, and then go to Great America. I found it on MapQuest it last night and it looks easy enough to find. If the two morons are as dumb as I think they are, they suspect nothing and won't have found the homing device we put on their car last night."

Stretching, Mark tried for nonchalance. "Sounds good to me. I hope we finish by supper. I'm going to 'throw some shoes' tonight with my new family. They said it is great fun." He grabbed a towel and ducked into the bathroom.

Tom scratched his head and waited for Mark to reappear. "What does that mean, throw your shoes? Who are you throwing shoes at?"

Mark looked at his new Vans. "I don't know, but I hope they give mine back, I just bought these yesterday."

They grabbed some breakfast at McDonald's because it was quick and close, and zipped back to the room to pick up the bomb. Mark grabbed some motel brochures for Great America and other local destinations, and they waited by the Interstate for the Gallegos brothers to arrive.

Alfredo and Luis were not long in coming, and spotted the red Cooper right away. They pulled off the road to see if Mark and Tom needed help.

"You guys okay? If your little car broke we can help. We're going to Great America so we can ride you that far."

Mark ducked and started putting on like he was a bad ass, hoping to discourage the brothers from taking them with them. "You muthas ain't ridin' me nowhere. Chumps."

Tom biffed him in the chest, fumbled with the key, and the cooper suddenly came to life. "Thanks anyway, we're okay—overheated a little, I guess. We were just checking the map to make sure we were going the correct way to the hospital. We're visiting Aunt Juanita today. She's scheduled for chemotherapy later, so we're going early."

Luis furrowed his brow. "I thought you said your Uncle Carlos had cancer?"

Alfredo said, "No, I distinctly heard a family friend had cancer, not an uncle."

Mark barked, "It was. Uh, I mean we just call her Aunt Jemimah."

Tom poked him. "Juanita."

"Juanita, that's right." Mark lowered his head and shook it slowly, sounding sad. "Poor Juanita."

Tom mentally scrambled for the lie from the night before. "Yes, that's correct, but Aunt Juanita almost had a heart attack last night worrying over Uncle Diego—I mean Carlos. Carlos Diego. Cancer. Poor Uncle Carlos. Poor Aunt Juanita. Tom wiped his eyes with his T-shirt.

Luis looked from one to the other. "Well, good luck. Sorry to hear about your aunt. Catch up with us later if you can."

The Gallegos brothers waved them as they pulled around the Cooper. Mark waved back, then fell back when Tom backhanded him in the chest. "What are you doing? Can't you get a simple story straight? Aunt Jemimah?"

Mark looked sheepish. "I was remembering breakfast. Sorry. Anyway, I was being friendly. What was I supposed to do? Besides, they aren't bad guys, just dead guys. It's not like they'd rob us or nothin'."

"If people around here will take your shoes, they might try to take our car. Don't forget, those guys are strangers too. We need our car."

"Do you think I can buy another pair of shoes in case I don't get mine back after I throw them? I liked the mall. We could get some kick-ass shoes at the mall. Look!" Mark pointed to the map. "There is a mall near Great America. Let's go, what do you say?"

Tom blew out an exasperated sigh. "Maybe we can just steal a pair of shoes and you won't have to worry about them anymore."

Mark looked slyly at Tom. "Hmm. I don't know; I sure had fun at the mall. They had an ice cream store right there inside! I'd like to go to a mall again sometime."

Tom was thoughtful. "Hmm, ice cream is always a plus. Yes, I'd like to go again, too."

Mark smiled contently and settled into his seat. He could get through this. He would finish the job and then say goodbye to Tom. He would stay here with his new family and friends. Today would be a piece of cake. "I'm glad you agree."

13

Ian undid the locks and a large smiling man lumbered through the door of his lab.

"*Hank,*" both Sam and Fred screeched. Racing to the changing room, they grabbed him from opposite sides. They bounced up and down, hugging him and talking at the same time.

"What are you doing here?"

"Did you hear about Evo's fish?"

"It's so good to see you."

"Did you bring us new fish?"

"When did you get in?"

"Have you spawned any C-3383s yet?"

"When did you get back from Venezuela?"

"Have you named your new babies yet?"

"We're so glad you're here!"

Hank hugged them both at the same time. He stepped back and laughed. "Whoa girls, let me get a word in. Let's see if I can answer your questions. Ian called me in, yes, it's great to see you too, no, today, yes, today again, yes, and I'm happy to be here too." He hugged them both again.

He looked at me and pointed. "You are definitely one of Freddie's sisters. Hmm, Buzz or Mag? I know you're not Alexandra, because you're not wearing high heels."

We laughed and I replied, "Buzz, Mr. MacRone. I have a few of your fish."

"Now there's a good girl." Hank held out his hand and I took it. My world immediately closed in and I tried to ignore feeling of vertigo that came over me when his hand touched mine. A dark wave of nausea swooped through me and I grabbed for something to hold onto. Hank must have let go of me because the air cleared and my vision returned to normal.

I found myself sitting in a chair with everyone looking at me. J.J. stood next to me and had a hand on my shoulder, kneading it gently. I blinked and shook my head. The last thing I remembered was shaking hands with—

I would have shot out of the chair, but J.J. held me down. Voices mumbled around me, and I focused on them. J.J.'s rich tones filled my head and I zeroed in on him.

"...all the excitement. I'm sure she'll be okay in a minute. Why don't you go on and show Hank around. We'll catch up later."

The voices faded and I heard Fred say, "I still have a bunch of offspring from your fish, Hank, and I've enjoyed them immensely. I'd love for you to come and see what I've done with them."

J.J. knelt in front of me. Taking my hands in his, he looked back at Hank, and then at me. "What happened, Buzz? You came apart after you took MacRone's hand. Is he a bad guy?"

Still a little disoriented, I simply nodded. "I don't know why or how, but foul energy poured off him, J.J. It knocked me over."

"Should I toss him now?"

"No, let's see what he wants first, okay?"

J.J. nodded stiffly. I could see he was tense, but he didn't go after Hank.

Almost back to normal (whatever *that* means), I put on a genial face and watched the little group approach. "Take a lesson in gentlemanly manners, Connor," Mag said out of the corner of her mouth and strolled into the lab.

Ian opened his mouth to say something, but was interrupted once again by banging on the outer door. "Is the whole damn town going to show up today?"

133

The smiling faces of Jack Bordy and Jack Jr. greeted Ian as they hauled two large coolers through the door. "Specimens," they echoed each other.

Sr. continued, "They arrived Fed Ex a few minutes ago and we saw all the cars so we brought them down. Thought you'd want them quick."

Ian hefted one of the coolers. "Thanks guys. Suit up and come on in."

Sr. grabbed a gown. "Thanks, Ian, don't mind if we do."

Jr. poked his father. "This don't look like no strip joint I ever seen, Dad."

Sr. calmly stood on Jr.'s toes. "Shut up and listen, boy. Shut up and learn."

Ian was about to close the door when it jerked open again and my sister, Al slipped through.

Crap. Just what I need.

She took in the entire room. "Boy, Ian, did you invite the whole town over today?"

"Shut up, Al," Fred said. "Why'd you let her in, Ian?"

Ian stepped forward. "I asked her to come out."

Our gazes flew to Mag who laughed. "Don't get your undies in a bundle, little Freddie. Ian has a computer glitch and Al is going to fix it."

Fred stared with an incredulous look on her face. "You mean Al actually knows something useful?"

"There's a lot about me you don't know, dweeb child." She turned her back on Fred, and Fred stuck out her tongue.

Al swept by me with her nose in the air and I swatted at the fumes she left in her wake. "*Whew.* I sure know who's wearing too much perfume.'"

"You're so lame, Buzz, you're almost as immature as Fred."

I grabbed Fred when her hands turned into claws and she went for Al's throat. "Whoa, Trigger. Not here, and not now.

Ian asked for her help."

"Then I'm leaving. I refuse to breathe the same stinking air as that evil bitch."

I still had a hold of her and she began to squirm. "Come on, Fred, don't be a baby. Why you let her get to you like that, I don't know."

"Leave me alone, Buzz." She struggled to get out of my grasp. "Let me just kick her ass and I'll be happy."

"Take a 'lude, baby girl or she'll impale you on a stiletto." I didn't want to hurt Fred, and my reluctance to do so gave her a distinct advantage. The little shit slipped out of my grasp and had an arm around my neck before I knew it. I struggled but my airway was becoming smaller by the second. I wrestled with her for a few more seconds and heard J.J. laugh. I finally got pissed off enough that I raised my elbow to jam it in her side when Sam came over. She touched Fred's arm and said, "Take a breath, my friend. Come and talk with me."

Sam gently took Fred's arm from around my throat. The half-nelson Fred had on me eased and I sucked in a much needed breath. I rubbed my neck. "Shit head," I muttered irritably, "I was only trying to keep her from getting killed by Al. I'll remember next time to let Al have her for lunch." Sam ignored me and took Fred across the room, speaking softly.

J.J leaned over, ruffled my hair, and whispered, "Al sure brings out the best in people, doesn't she?"

I jerked my head out of the way. "Al's mostly a pain in the ass. She's just a bitch the rest of the time. What's up with Fred? Makes me wonder about the advantages of being an only child."

He chuckled and ruffled my hair again. "It's not half as much fun as you guys have–believe me."

Ignoring my crabby attitude, he threw an arm around my neck and we walked to where Ian and Hank stood in deep conversation over a particular slide. I poked J.J. in the ribs, and he danced back, rubbing his side. "Yo, woman, that smarts."

"Yep, and don't you forget it."

He gave me an injured look. "If you ask me, all you Millers are a pain in the ass."

"Yes we are, and don't you forget that either, Green."

Hank chuckled. "How long have you two been married?"

I choked and J.J. chuckled. We answered simultaneously. It sounded something like, "*Hah*. Uh...We're not, uh...Married...*Hah*. Marry into a family of lunatics?...I wouldn't marry him on a...Horse's ass. She and I have known each other too...naked...Since childhood...Did you say naked? She won't have...A prayer...Gone to hell in a hand basket...I said, did you say naked?"

"Stop! Please stop! Hank held up his hands. "May I take that as a we're not married yet?"

My hand bit into J.J.'s arm and we nodded.

"Well, you sure sound like you are." I took a large breath and Hank held up his hand. "Please spare us all and don't start again."

"Okay," I said meekly.

Hank let out a hearty laugh and turned back to Ian. "Well, boyo, what have we got here?"

"Excuse the stupid joke, Hank, but I'm literally a fish out of water. I'm hoping that between you, Sam, Evo, and Fred I might be able to make sense of all this. Step over to the whiteboard for a minute. I think I can bring you up-to-date more quickly this way."

While the men spoke, I sidled over to Al, who tapped away at Ian's computer. "Got it figured out yet, Al?"

She looked at me over her half glasses and said, "Almost. Ian is definitely a genius when it comes to plants, but I think he slept through *Computers 101*."

We shared a chuckle and Al turned back to the computer. I sobered as I tried to remember how long it had been since I'd shared a joke–or anything but animosity–with Al.

It had become a habit to snap on every little thing with her. She was such a pain most of the time, always adopting a 'holier than thou' attitude with the rest of us. As I watched her, I wondered if she'd developed an attitude as a defense mechanism to deal with whatever crap ate at her.

"You ain't no shrink, Buzz, so stay out of her head," I muttered, mostly to myself.

"It's about time you realized that," Al said, gaze glued to the computer screen.

"What the hell does that mean? Geez, just when I thought maybe you weren't as big a pain in the ass as I thought..."

"No, I admit I'm a pain in the ass, but the ten million dollar question is...why?" She smiled mysteriously and went back to typing.

I left and went to sulk by J.J. "Bonding with Al, are you?"

I shot him an evil look and he ruffed up my hair again.

He leaned in close and whispered, "I'm proud of you, Buzz. It's about time you guys stopped bickering and got to know each other."

He kissed my ear and I got that mushy-kind-of-warm thing going again. *Oh, no, not again. Stop it, Buzz, it's only J.J.. Don't go stupid, girl, hold it together. It's Only J.J.*

I pretended great interest in the slides in front of me until my breathing returned to normal. I felt my cheeks to see if they were within normal temperature range before returning to the crowd. I needed to think about something that didn't remind me of J.J., or sex, or of sex and J.J. in the same sentence. "Oh, my God, I'm in trouble."

"Whatcha thinkin' oh-mastermind-detective-sister-o-mine?" Fred looked amused.

"Don't laugh, but I was thinking the people in this room represent about a hundred years of schooling."

"Wow, should I feel intimidated or something?"

"Funny you should say that. I was feeling really undereducated until I realized that we all have our special talents."

"Such as?"

"Oh, I figured we could probably take most of them in a loogie launching contest, or spoon-hanging, cow pie tossing, beer chugging, or something equally worthwhile, so what the hell, they're only people, right?"

Fred laughed, "You are so right, Buzzard, with talents like ours, we have the world by the ass!"

"Right you are, oh belching champion of 1974. C'mon, sis; let's make those eggheads put those doctorates to work, shall we?"

"I'm with you, detective."

I walked over to the whiteboard and pushed the button to forward the screen (leave it to Ian not to have the standard flip-over kind like mine). I picked up a marker and began to draw. Now when I say draw I mean it in the most elementary fashion. Lakes are circles, mountains are lumps, people are sticks—you get the idea.

I drew a big Venezuela, and marked the lake with the dead fish, the village, the jungle, and Drilling Site 151. With Ian's help, I drew in the mountains and proximity of where the *andidum* is found in Peru. I marked in the only known lake where they'd found the endangered Endlers. "So, sports fans, what adds up here, and what does not?"

"What do you mean?" J.J. walked to the board.

"Instead of continuing with a science project that results in more questions than answers, let's put this on paper like an investigation. Now what are the facts as we know them?"

J.J. grinned. "I love it when you speak police."

"Shut up and help, J.J." I poked him in the chest and he sat.

Ian said, "We know plants are in the wrong spot."

138

I drew a line from the Venezuelan Rainforest Lake to the dry tropical forest in the Andes.

Sam added, "We know the Endlers have never before been found in that area."

I drew a line from the lake near 151 to the lake where Endlers were found by Evo and Luis.

Evo said, "We know the poison couldn't have come from 151."

Sam corrected him. "We *think* the poison could not come from 151."

"No," Evo corrected, "We *know* it. I called my lab this morning and the tests I took show no indication of any leaks or accidental runoffs in that direction, which would have been *uphill*. Soil and water samples yielded no signs of heavy metal content, and the drilling site is forty minutes on foot downhill from the lagoon. I tried to call Ron Hansen, the foreman at 151, but he must be in the field because there's no answer at his office."

Sam dropped her head. "Wow. I uh, that's good to know."

I drew an "X" through Site 151. "Okay, so what does all this mean?"

Fred jumped in. "We know Endlers aren't found in the same spot as the ferns, and the ferns can't grow where the Endlers were found."

"Ergo?" Hank shifted his weight forward.

"Ergo," I said smugly, "I believe the fish were transported to that lagoon from the region where the *andinum* is found."

Evo spoke up. "I don't know if this will help, but there has been an extraordinary amount of rainfall in the area where we found the fish."

I looked at Evo. "How do you know this?"

Evo barked out a laugh. "Hell, Luis and I slogged through it. The rainfall is almost double the norm for this time of year. I also confirmed this by way of Foreman Hansen at the Site. He said their pumps were working overtime, but everything is keeping up–no spillage. What does that have to do with anything?"

"Maybe nothing," I said. "But it lends credence to our theory that the fish were transported in, because that plant material in their bellies could never have survived in that amount of rainfall. Also, the runoff, if there was one, had to come from further up the mountain, where you and Ron Hansen claim Maldonado has no drilling or mining interests."

Hank spoke up. "So in essence you're saying?"

Making checks and slashes on the whiteboard to prove a point, continued. "I am saying *someone* stocked the lagoon, and someone *else*–I presume someone else–poisoned the fish and the village water supply, and it was not Maldonado Oil."

"But why? Those villagers represented a workforce, and it was their personal water supply."

Hank looked confused. "What's this about a village disappearing?"

Evo took up the explanation. "There was a village uphill from the lagoon. I found dead livestock and many new graves in the churchyard.

"The rest of the people must have fled before whatever killed their kin struck them. I believe it was the same toxins in their water supply as what killed the fish in the lagoon. Buzz thinks perhaps the rains washed something down the mountain–I don't know, but we need to find out."

I couldn't believe Hank didn't get it. "Hank, the villagers didn't poison themselves. I think it came from further up the mountain."

Evo chimed in. "But there is no evidence there is anything up there."

Fred asked, "What about this Devil's Eye the oil guys spoke of?"

"Maybe there was another natural pool up the mountain

from which the rain overflowed to transport the poison into the lagoon." J.J. added.

I nodded. "That's my guess, but it has to be manmade, as toxins in large amounts such as Evo found don't normally exist in the wild. Evo, were you able to confirm there was nothing further up the mountain?"

Evo's shoulder slumped. "I didn't have time to check, but Hansen said the Nunez oil site is the only operation on that mountain." He sat up. "Maybe there is something illegal going on further up the mountain. A couple of locals were very afraid when they told Luis and Alfredo something about the Devil's Eye—"

Hank's bellowing laugh startled us into silence. "*Devil's Eye*? *My* eye! What kind of crap is this displaced plant business? Transporting plants? Transporting large quantities of fish? Poisoning a pond? How ridiculous."

The hair on the back of my neck stood up. "I beg your pardon?"

Fred cut in before I could behead him with words. "Whoa, Buzz, I think he means that it doesn't make sense for someone to stock such a remote lagoon with little fish no one cares much about, and then poison them."

Hank continued. "What are the chances someone filled up a lagoon with fish, and then someone else presumably created a separate toxic water source that accidentally or intentionally killed off those fish?"

Evo said, "Uh, slim to none?"

"Exactly," Hank blustered. "Naught but an idiot would think someone took the trouble to use expendable fish to stock an out-of-the-way location and then poison it. To what end? What would be the point? I think that Maldonado Oil Company needs another look. They're the only ones with a motive. Money talks, you know."

I was really pissed now, and took a step toward Hank. I

pointed to myself. "Well, this idiot thinks the answers lie with the fish. Without seeing the site, how can we make a determination on motive?"

Hank would not be cowed and took a step toward me. "Assuming, of course that criminal intent is actually involved?"

I advanced on him again, ticking the facts off on my fingers. "There is nothing in the region to warrant toxic waste entering the lagoon naturally. Fish that don't live there were found mostly dead in said same lagoon. A rare plant which cannot survive in that climate is found to have been ingested by those same fish. An entire village has disappeared, and you, sir, do not find probable cause to look into the situation?"

I felt J.J. grab the back of my shirt before I could bump chests with Hank. He hauled me back. "I think that wraps it up for now. Maybe we can get together later and run over some of the finer points. Evo, why don't you make a couple of calls to your boss so we can clear up any questions regarding anything being uphill from the village? Ian, Mag, and Sam will continue to look at the specimens Evo brought here, and the rest of us can take time to sort out our different theories. We can meet at Buzz's or Fred's tomorrow or the next day to sort things out. How does that sound to everyone?"

We concurred, and our group began to take its leave.

On the way home, I called Sam at the lab and asked if she, Ian, and Mag would meet us at my house in about three hours to discuss how to proceed.

"Sounds like a road trip is in order," Sam said.

"Road Trip? I'm not talking about a road trip. I can't just take off to Venezuela! We–"

"Peru."

"What? Oh. Peru, *then* Venezuela. Out of the question. We'll discuss this at my house later. See you then."

Hanging up the phone, I stared straight ahead until Fred screeched in my ear. "Road Trip!" Excited, she began to babble. "Plans! We need plans. Passports. When do we go? Luis and Alfredo can run the pet shop. I'd bet they'd love to. Buzz, take the dogs out to Mom's. She'd love to have them."

"Fred." J.J. put his arm around my neck and spoke up.

"Hell, Honey. I'll just stay at your place so the dogs don't get too traumatized. Wes, Hill, and I will be fine. They love me."

I'm sure I looked horrified. "Honey who? Stay at my place? Are you insane? Don't answer that. Let me think. I can't go anywhere. I shook my finger at him. There'll be talk, James Joseph Green!"

"There's always talk. It'll just be our turn again, but think of it this way. You won't have to be around to hear it."

Fred rambled the rest of the way to my house and thirty minutes later the rest of the gang arrived. "So much for three hours," I grumbled.

The minute they clambered through my front door, plans for *the great trip* were being hammered out loudly.

I could think of no further arguments against the trip, as they had just about everything figured out. I looked helplessly at J.J., Evo, Sam, Ian, and Fred. "I uh, don't have bug spray."

Evo chuckled. "But you do have a passport?"

"Y-yes, of course."

"Then it is settled. I can see what kind of a flight we can get out. Our pilot is staying at a hotel near the airport, and if he is sober, we'll get out tonight."

"Tonight? I can't leave tonight!"

Evo took Sam's arm and led her a short distance away. They spoke in low tones, and I could see they were making personal plans.

"Fred," I said while the others were occupied. If we leave tonight Mom will kill us. You're hosting Thanksgiving this Thursday, remember?"

"Oh, crap, I forgot. I'm sure Evo and Sam won't mind

waiting until after the holiday, and if they do, we'll just follow later on Friday. Sound good to you?"

"No, but it sounds better than the alternative."

Evo was on his cell phone. He hung up and came back to the group. "Tony will stay here. Alexandra said she will keep an eye on him. For medical reasons, I think he would best serve us investigating the live fish at Fred's house—if she does not mind."

Fred waved him off. "Heck no! *Mi casa* is *su casa* or however it goes. My house is your house. He can work down stairs, and Luis and Alfredo can assist. My only request is that we put the trip off a couple of days, after the Thanksgiving holiday."

Evo slapped his forehead. "I'm sorry; your American Thanksgiving holiday is at the end of this week, is it not? That might be to our favor. It will give me time to contact my pilot and make sure he is sober, as well as finalize the arrangements in Lima. It will give us all time to prepare; you need to pack for the jungle. I'll make you a list."

I swallowed hard. "Jungle?"

Fred elbowed me in the ribs then threw an arm around my neck and bumped my hip in rhythm. "Wee-de-de-de-de-de-de-de-do the lion sleeps toniiight. Yes, Buzz, we'll be two cheeseheads in the Jungle."

I jabbed her back and she sucked in a breath. "Uh, make that one cheesehead and one shithead."

Fred grimaced and I smiled, feeling much better.

Sam looked around at the group with misty eyes. "Thank you all. I cannot believe you would all put your lives on hold to come with me to check out some stupid little fish." She looked up at Evo and took his hand. "Your first vacation in forever and you're going back for me." She swiped at a tear.

"For the villagers, the fish, and for science, Samón." Evo kissed her temple and walked away, leaving her staring and stunned.

"*What* was that all about?" She stared wide-eyed at Fred and me.

Still irritable, I said, "I don't know. It's these men; I think they're all whacking out."

Fred stared after them. "Yep. Maybe it's a full moon or something."

A shiver crawled up my neck and I nodded toward the dead fish. "Whatever it is, I have a feeling whatever we find in Venezuela, will make our little discovery here seem mild in comparison."

14

The following morning, Tom and Mark followed the Suzuki carrying the Gallegos brothers into Illinois to the Great America exit. Mark was rubbernecking at the Gurnee Mills Shopping Center. "Holy Cow, Tom, did you see that? We *gotta* go back there! There must be a thousand stores in that place!"

Tom yanked the Cooper right and caught the ramp in time. "That's Bass Pro Shops and they also have a 120,000 gallon aquarium in there with live native fish. I read the advertisement. They have a shooting range and about a mile long shopping mall attached to it."

At Mark's eager expression, Tom became adamant. "No, we are *not* going there. We have a job to do." He thought about it and softened. "Maybe we'll go afterwards, okay? Maybe they have an ice cream store. I'll need ice cream by then."

Mark smiled and sat back.

Tom let a few cars get in front of them. As they turned right into the Great America parking lot, they could not help but be awed by the size of the place. They had to scramble to keep track of where Luis and Alfredo parked the Suzuki. They parked about ten rows away and waited.

The Gallegos brothers gamboled like puppies to the front gate and went in. Mark grabbed a brochure, sat back, and grumbled. "Don't see why we can't go have fun while we wait to murder 'em."

"Shut up and wait. Let's see how quickly the parking lot fills up, and then we'll see how much time is left. If we have to wait for dark, it'll be a long day."

Mark stopped flipping through the brochure and looked up. "Then we could go shopping until then. Look at this brochure. They've got a sports store the size of that Wal-Mart by our motel."

"You'd better find a suitcase outlet too, Mark. You're going to need it."

"Maybe I won't go home. We have papers that say we're citizens. Why not just stay here? Think about it. You could get a job, raise a family, and buy ice cream every day."

Tom smiled. "Hmm, ice cream every day?" He shook his head. "Knock it off, we can't do that, we're about to become wanted men. We can't stay here and do the chicken dance for the rest of our lives. What is your new family going to say when they see your face on the Six o'clock News?"

"I don't know...probably something like, 'Where did we go wrong?'"

"Oh, shut up, Mark. You are so lame."

"I'm lame? And you say *I* watch too much American TV?"

They sat in silence. Tom was amazed at how fast the parking lot around them filled up. By 1:00 in the afternoon, cars sat wall-to-wall for what seemed like miles. The Gallagos brothers had parked away from the crowds, but no one could tell, as their car was sardined in tight.

Mark had taken the top off the Cooper hours before, but now the afternoon sun beat down on their heads. Tom was asleep, so Mark quietly set the top back up, only locking one latch for fear of waking his cranky cousin. Their section of the parking lot was in direct sunlight, and the day marched on. Mark fiddled with the seatbelt, and then proceeded to make animal figures out of duct tape.

Hot, bored, and having no more fingernails to chew, Mark crept quietly from the car with the car bomb in a backpack. He inched along the rows, stopping whenever he heard a scrape or bump. Finding the Suzuki proved harder when creeping along bumpers, but Mark knew how to count and made it with only a couple of glitches.

147

He poked his head up and saw a police car cruising his direction. Rolling under a minivan, he held his breath. If Mark were Irish, he would have known that according to Murphy's Law, the owners of the van hiding him would choose that moment to return to their vehicle for lunch. But as Mark listened to the clatter and slamming of doors, he prayed some snot-nosed kid wouldn't drop a ball or chase a cat, or take a whiz on the tire and spot him under their vehicle.

Sure enough, the van rocked as a family arrived and the doors slid open. He heard dragging sounds as they pulled out a cooler filled with food. He rolled his eyes at the loud whiny noises, as spoiled American children made demands. Mark settled in to wait. "Snot-nosed American kids. They should see where I grew up then they'd have a reason to complain," he muttered.

The smell of peanut butter filled his nostrils and his stomach growled as the family ate lunch. Crap. That's all he needed. He had to get out of here and back to the Cooper. Mark inched toward the front bumper. He heard sounds of the lunch being packed up and let out a breath. Thanks be to God they were going back into the park.

At the sound of, "Okay kids, let's go," Mark smiled.

More sounds of closing lids and the van rocked. Oh, no, they were getting in, not out! Visions of the family driving out of the parking space exposing Mark smiling a toothy grin and holding a car bomb flashed through his mind. He was about to make a break for the car in front of him when he spotted a pair of extra small feet next to his shoulder.

The sound of a zipper made Mark blanch. He scuttled across the width of the van just as the sound of liquid hitting pavement reached his ears. A stream of tinkle made its way around the tire and Mark watched with morbid curiosity as it filled in the cracks in the asphalt and wound its way around pebbles and garbage. The trickle of urine became a stream and

Mark eyed it warily. "Wow. Good thing he's a little guy. The kid will run out any second."

He waited as the stream continued. Mark began to panic as it crept closer to him. How the heck much water could one small kid hold? The trickle now looked like a raging torrent, crashing against rocks and breaking up into whitewater rapids. *What the hell, hasn't this kid taken a whiz since last year?*

Mark inched away until he plastered himself against the opposite tire, and realized with irony that not only was he pissed off, he was about to be pissed on!

In his deepest voice, Mark growled, "Okay kid, pinch it off now or I'll break it off!"

The stream cut off immediately. The kid screamed like someone had stabbed him. All hell broke loose as the mommy jumped out of the driver's door. This gave Mark the opportunity to scoot across the aisle and dive under the car next to him. He crabbed forward and slid under the next car in line. Thankfully, the surrounding cars sat far enough off the ground that he could squeeze under. He kept it up in a zigzag pattern until he was far enough away not to be noticed. He got up and pretended to tie his shoes as he discretely brushed off his clothes. He grinned when he heard a little voice cry.

"*Mommy*! Mommy! The Pee-Pee Monster yelled at me. Come look. It's the Pee-Pee Monster! He said he'd bite it off!"

"That'll teach the little bastard not to piss in public." Mark tucked in his shirt and strolled casually to the Cooper.

Tom was awake when he slid into the passenger's seat. He opened one eye, took a deep breath, and calmly asked, "Any chance that screaming over there has anything to do with you?"

"Naw, some kid screaming about a monster. Probably pissed his nappies in the fun house."

Tom sniffed the air. "Smells like that Pee-Pee Monster got you too."

Mark took a whiff and felt his pants. He inspected his

jeans and saw a wet splotch down by his boots. He grabbed for the door handle. "Why, that rotten little pisser..."

Tom grabbed his arm. "Hold on, *amigo*." Between chuckles, Tom said, "Fine bad guy you are. You went from being the Terminator to being the Urinator. Hah-ha-ha! The Urinator who does a chicken dance. Oh how far the mighty have fallen. Ha-ha!"

Mark shoved. Tom flew out his door and lay howling on his back in the parking lot. His legs still inside the car, he clutched his middle as he guffawed at his own jokes. Mark slammed out of the car and took off across the parking lot.

Tom wiped the tears from his eyes and stood. He could see Mark heading in the direction of the Suzuki. He sobered, grabbed his backpack of tools, and headed after him, chuckling every time he thought of Mark getting peed on.

As he approached the car, Tom decided there was no reasoning with Mark. Tom had messed with his delicate ego, and Mark now had something to prove. He already had the car open from the passenger's side and wired the bomb to the driver's door.

"Why the door, Mark? I thought we agreed on the ignition."

"Because it's how I want it done. Quick, easy, done. You got a problem with that? Let's just get this out of the way. Then we can take care of the others and get out of this godforsaken country!"

Tom looked around and took a deep breath. Hands on hips, he observed, "I don't know, Mark. I kind-of like it here. I think you had the right of it. This might be somewhere we want to settle."

"Naw, I'd probably kill some little pisser and that would be that." Mark finished in the car and carefully set the small bomb between the seat and the door. He backed out toward Tom, who had his nose wrinkled against the smell that emanated from Mark's pant leg. Mark locked and carefully closed the car door. "Let's go shopping, I'm still pissed off." He wiped the door handle clean and walked briskly away.

Tom leaned down to pick up both back packs and burst out laughing again. "Better to be pissed off than pissed on, I say." He stumbled back toward the Cooper and threw the backpacks into the car. Still chuckling, he crawled into the driver's seat.

"Would you just shut up and drive, you moron? At the rate you're going, we'll never make it back."

Tom wiped his eyes and started the car. "Bladder late than never."

Mark scowled. "Knock it off with the piss jokes, Tom. Turn on the radio or something."

"Maybe I can find some 'Urethra' Franklin. Ha-ha-ha! I kill me."

Mark punched Tom in the arm. "*I'm* going to kill you in a minute."

"Okay, okay I'll stop! The mall is right over here, we can take a leak…I mean a peek inside and buy you some new pants. Sound good *amigo*?"

"Sounds good to me. There's a sign for blue jeans. Let's go."

After four pairs of jeans, three CD's, three paperbacks, a new pair of tennis shoes, some new socks, a couple of Cinnabons, a personalized keychain, and some Cold Stone ice cream, they headed to the car.

Back in the parking lot of Great America, they found a parking space about thirty rows away from the rigged Suzuki, right on the end. Mark wiggled into his new jeans and said, "Now this is what I call a front row seat."

"Yeah, if I had binoculars."

"Which I just happen to have." Mark pulled a pair of bird

watching binoculars out of a bag and settled back. He said to Tom, "Quit whining and read a book. We still might have a long time to wait."

Tom slurped his ice cream and belched. "Shoulda let me buy that portable DVD player. I could be watching *Shrek* by now."

Mark ignored him and slipped a CD in the player. "The Beach Boys, man I love surfer music."

Tom mumbled, "All that talk about water just makes me want to pee."

"I heard that. Just suck it in; you just went at the mall."

"Oh, yeah, I remember."

Tom looked out the windshield. He suddenly hit Mark with the back of his hand. "Hey, Mark, look at that! Aren't those our guys? What's with the duck hat? And those balloons. He chuckled. "Do they look like the demented tourists from hell or what?"

"They are tourists." Mark came close to a smile as he took in the sight before him. Luis and Alfredo looked like an advertisement for souvenir sales. One could barely see them under the funky sunglasses, glow necklaces, T-shirts, funny hats, sippy cups, a giant stuffed Scooby-Doo, and Mylar balloons. They weaved like a couple of drunks trying to balance their booty. "No wonder they're leaving early. They'd need a trailer to get anything else back."

Tom brightened. "Think we could steal their Twickets before we blow them up? They won't need them to get back in free tomorrow, they'll be dead."

Mark rolled his eyes and Tom looked away across the parking lot. He spotted a man in a sweatshirt looking like he was holding something in his sleeve. He looked around and dodged behind a car. "Hey, Mark? Look over there."

"Never mind the damn Twicket," Mark said through gritted teeth. "Just keep an eye on those guys."

The man in the sweatshirt skirted the parked cars quickly, looking in windows as he passed each vehicle. Tom watched as he weaved quickly through the aisles. "Mark, look over there. There's a guy–"

"Shut up, Tom. They're coming."

The man in the sweatshirt was now three rows away from the Suzuki, still ducking and weaving. Tom knew a carjacker when he saw one. "Mark, that guy! He's headed for the Suzuki. I think he's going to break in!"

"What?"

"Oh, my God! Tom threw open his door and tried to bolt. Mark caught his T-shirt and dragged him back in the car. "Where the hell are you going? The brothers are headed toward the car now."

Tom scrambled to sit up. "The guy, the guy in the sweatshirt. That guy over there is going to steal the damn car. We gotta stop him or he'll get blown to bits! We gotta tell him– *Ohhh, Shit.*"

A fireball blew skyward as the would-be carjacker popped open the driver's door of the Suzuki. Luis and Alfredo were close enough to be thrown back from the blast and land in a heap in the parking lot. The barely latched roof of the Cooper flew off and landed on the hood of an SUV behind it. Windows shattered on surrounding cars, and alarms went off by the dozens. Bits of engine, rubber, and car-jacker rained down on the parking lot as Mark and Tom slowly stood on the seats of the roofless Cooper, watching open-mouthed as the scene in front of them played out in slow motion. Tom jerked open an umbrella and held it over their heads as they stood staring at the ball of fire across the parking lot. Bits and pieces of *whatever* plinked softly off the umbrella and fell to the ground. Mark held out his hand to catch some debris, and a pinkie finger plopped into his palm. They both stared at it.

"Shhhit." Mark dropped the finger.

"Oops," Tom said.

They looked at each other and slowly lowered themselves down into the car. They sat in stunned silence as chaos reigned (or rained) around them. The scream of fire trucks and squad cars shook them out of their stupor and as one, they exited the car.

As if by unspoken agreement, Tom and Mark calmly walked back to the SUV and retrieved the roof of the Cooper. After some hand pounding and Tom jumping on one corner, they got the roof fastened down. They leaned against their car and crossed their arms.

Tom broke the silence first. "What now?"

Mark shook his head. "Don't know. Plan B I guess."

"And what exactly is 'Plan B'?"

"We'll think of something." He stiffened. "Oh, no, that's all we need. Here they come. They've spotted us!"

Mark spazzed and spun to face the Cooper. He said out of the corner of his mouth, "Act casual. Look surprised. Pretend like we followed the fire trucks or heard the blast, but *we just got here*."

"Casual, right." Tom leaned against the Cooper and plastered a smile on his face.

Mark faced forward again and tried to look calm. He arranged his face in what he thought looked relaxed, and Tom thought he looked rather constipated. Not knowing what to do with his hands, Mark raised a hand to lean on the Cooper. Forgetting the window was down, he hit open space instead and fell through. Mark let out a high-pitched screech as he landed head first on the passenger side floor with his feet dangling out the window.

Tom grabbed his feet and yanked him out. "You idiot. He mimicked Mark in a girlie voice. "'Look casual,' he says. You look like a constipated moron. Now shut up, here they are."

They both feigned surprise when Luis and Alfredo came

stumbling over, wearing blackened T-shirts and dragging a one-legged Scooby-Doo.

Luis waved with a sippy cup. "*Hola.* Hey, you broken car guys. Hallo. Disaster has struck our vacation, and Scooby saved our lives. They both collapsed against the Cooper, dropping their packages and breathing hard.

Tom blurted, "Uh, we'd just gotten here when we heard the blast and then the fire trucks. So someone tried to steal your car, ch?" Mark elbowed him hard. Tom flinched.

Alfredo and Luis stared wide-eyed at Tom and Mark. Alfredo said, "How did you know? The fireman just told us this."

Tom opened his mouth and Mark stomped on his foot. As Tom inhaled, Mark stepped forward and put an arm around Alfredo. "We heard people talking as they passed by us. Is it true a man tried to break in and got blown up?"

Tom rubbed his sore foot on the back of his other leg. "Heck of a security system they have on those rentals these days."

Luis and Alfredo blinked.

Mark threw an arm around Tom's neck and squeezed. Hard. "My brother, he is always joking. Even in the time of a crisis. Ha ha. Well, we have been shopping as you can see." He indicated the shopping bags in the back seat. "But we are finished now. If you would like a lift back to White Bass Lake, we would be pleased to help you out."

The brothers both smiled. Luis wiped a tear from his eye. "Oh, thank you, *Senór*. We would like that very much. We would normally not impose, but we are in dire need. We only need to tell the police and call Evo, our friend."

"*Police?*"

"Yes, they were going to contact our friends in White Bass Lake to come and pick us up, but if you are going that way, it would be most convenient."

Mark wiped at the sweat that had popped out on his brow. "Oh, sure. Go ahead. We'll load your stuff so we can leave right away."

"Thank you both. We will return in a moment."

Tom held up the one legged Scooby-Doo. "Do you want to keep the casualty of war here?"

Luis hit Mark on the shoulder. "*Hah-ha*. Casualty of war. You guys kill me." He and Alfredo walked to the squad car.

Mark stared after them and said under his breath, "You have no idea, *amigo*." they stuffed the dog in the car, and minutes later, bundled Luis and Alfredo in after, and sped off toward Wisconsin.

15

I walked into Fred's kitchen the next morning to find Evo staring at a cup of coffee. I leaned against the sink and folded my arms across my chest. "Wishing it was brandy?"

His head snapped up. "Huh? I'm sorry, you said brandy? At nine o'clock in the morning? I think not, thank you very much. Do you drink this early in the morning up here?"

"Don't put it past a cheesehead, Evo. Some folks put beer in their cornflakes up here." At his horrified expression I relented. "I'm just kidding about the brandy, you look very preoccupied."

He rubbed the back of his neck. "I did notice wherever we go someone is drinking brandy in something else. Is that normal up here too?"

"We are known as The Dairy State, but we could be called The Brandy State, The Beer State, or just The State of Inebriation. Some folks just drink a lot."

"So I gathered. I was thinking of Luis and Alfredo. I dragged them up here and they almost got blown up yesterday. I'm not much for coincidence, but I see no motive to hurt them. What's your take?"

"The police are investigating. I do find it interesting that their two new friends just happened to be there when the Suzuki blew up."

"Yes. It seems curious to me that the car would explode for any reason."

"Sounds more like a car bomb than a curious coincidence to me, Evo."

"Luis explained that they invited them, but the new friends had business to attend to in the morning hours, and went down later in the day. I'm more troubled about my hasty decision to bring Luis and Alfredo to Wisconsin."

"If they're in any kind of danger, they're much safer here with us, than alone in Lima, don't you think?"

"Yes, I know you're right. Another thought I just had was that they are on a vacation of sorts and I never thought about money. I even told them they were on vacation, so they don't expect to be paid. Their pride will keep them from accepting money from me."

"Then tell them it is a working vacation. If you want, we can have them do some running or odd jobs, and you can pay them."

"Great idea, but I don't have a local bank account."

I told Evo it was just as easy for him to give me the money and I would write a check that the Gallegos brothers could cash at the local bank. Evo was thrilled and we worked out the details.

Later, Evo handed Luis and Alfredo each a check and told them they were still on the payroll, even in America. The brothers could not believe what luck had befallen them. They clutched their checks in both hands. After many thanks they scuttled out the door and piled into their newly rented car. This time they'd rented a Jeep. They zoomed out onto the street and headed for downtown.

I watched as an unfamiliar car followed them down the street and a funny feeling tickled the back of my neck. I caught Evo by the arm, pointed to the dented red Cooper and asked, "Hey, do you recognize those guys?"

Evo squinted after the small red car. "No, why do you ask?"

"They don't look familiar, but that Cooper does," and almost to myself, "Where have I seen that car before?"

Fred looked up from the couch. "Car? What car?"

Sam walked into the room brushing her hair. She stopped

next to Evo and I. "Are we looking for a car? Do you mean that little red one?"

We answered as one, "Yes."

We stood for a moment watching the vehicles as they turned left at the end of the block and disappeared.

Evo shook his head. "I don't recognize the car or the men."

"Hmm," I said. "It'll make me crazy until I think of it. It might be my imagination, but it looked like they pulled out behind the Gallegos brothers."

Evo scanned the street. "From where?"

"I don't know from where. I didn't actually *see* it pull out, it's just a feeling I had when they drove past."

Fred looked up from her book. "Oh, oh. Don't discount those 'feelings' Buzz gets. I did once and was almost run over by a train and consumed by fire ants." She picked up her book and thumbed through to her bookmark.

Silence. Everyone stared at her.

She looked up again and sounding ominous held up a hand. "Don't ask. Just trust Buzz's instincts, or it'll be fire ant city for you." She went back to reading.

Tony shook his head in wonder, leaned forward, and said softly, "She sure is cute, but definitely a little odd." *Pow*. A pillow hit him in the back of the head.

"*Ow*. Hey, I've got stitches here!"

Fred smiled her Mona Lisa smile. "Oops, must have slipped out of my hand."

"And catapulted across the room by itself? Don't you find *that* a little odd?" Tony poked at the bald area on the back of his head.

Round innocent eyes blinked at him. She stood and said over her shoulder, "Odd, like me, perhaps?" She laughed as she sashayed out of the room.

Tony stared after her. "Wow, behind that innocent façade, she is lee-thal!"

"And don't you forget it," she shot back from the kitchen.

Tony looked at me and I said, "She hears well too."

"I guess she does." He touched the back of his head and looked at his fingers. "At least I'm not bleeding."

"Waaah, you baby," came from the kitchen.

I yelled to her, "Yo, Fred, let's take a drive."

"Where to?"

"Coffee."

Fred poked her head out of the kitchen and said, "I'll get my shoes."

I smiled. "I'll get my dogs."

Evo cocked his head. "Coffee? We have coffee here. Why do we need more coffee?"

Sam leaned over the back of his chair and spoke quietly into his ear, "Coffee doesn't necessarily mean *coffee* to the Miller sisters. *Coffee* can mean anything from *you're in trouble now*, or *I need to talk*. Let them go. Let's you and I test that water Alfredo and Luis brought over. We can talk science for a while."

The hairs at Evo's nape stood up as her breath caressed his neck. *Oh, crap. That isn't the only thing standing up*. What the hell was he going to do now? He cleared his throat. "Uh, yeah. Okay, let's test the water." Whoa, what the heck was he thinking? Testing water would mean that he'd be alone with Sam. "No, wait. We can't do that!"

She straightened. "Why ever not? Don't you want to test the water?"

Evo hoped she had no idea how much he wanted to not only test the waters, but to dive right in. "Uh yes, but no, that's not I, uh, just not now. Uh, I um." He gave her a brilliant smile, "I want ice cream. And if the Millers are going down town, why don't we tag along and get some?"

She looked skeptical. "Well, all right, if you're sure…"

"I'm sure." Public place, lots of people; he'd be safer there than he would be alone with her here. Timing was everything, and he had just begun to set the stage. He didn't want to jump her before she was ready–or before he was ready for that matter.

I wanted to talk to Fred alone, but that chance flew out the window when Evo announced that they would come too. I wasn't sure how it happened, but suddenly everyone had business downtown and piled into my car. Let me qualify the term "car," it's actually a huge SUV, so the dogs and five people fit relatively easily. So it's a car, but not a car. See?

I sent the Gallegos brothers by way of an easier, but longer route to the bank. I took the shortcut and hoped to beat them downtown.

I stepped on the gas and Hillary passed some of her own. All the windows went down and Wes hung his huge furry face over Evo's shoulder. I looked in the mirror and saw Wes drip doggy slime onto Evo's shoulder. I opened my mouth to say something and I caught Sam's twinkling eyes in the mirror. She held a finger to her lips, and I held my tongue.

The bank sat on a corner a couple of blocks away from Sal's Diner, otherwise known as "Gossip Central." Actually, Sal's Diner is a couple of blocks away from anything in town. Anything about anyone at any time can be heard at Sal's. That's because everyone in town (and those passing through) stop in at Sal's for the best food and gossip this side of the Mississippi–probably the other side too, but I've yet to conquer the Wild West.

I slowed down outside the bank entrance. I saw the new Jeep pull around the corner on the opposite side of the road and park. Luis and Alfredo were so excited they tumbled out of the car and immediately crossed the street. At that moment a red Cooper came squealing and accelerating around the opposite corner on two wheels and headed directly for the Gallegos brothers.

"Oh, my God," I yelled.

In that instance I saw a blur off to my left. I hit the brakes just in time to avoid Mrs. Simmons' cat, Crapper, who at the moment was fleeing from a bat-wielding and livid Mel Brooster. "You damn crapper! He screamed at the cat as they both charged into the intersection.

"Oops," Fred chirped as she flopped back onto the seat, "The 'Creeping Crapper' must have laid a bomb on Mel's brand new patio furniture."

Luis and Alfredo stopped in the middle of the road to view the spectacle, and the Cooper picked up speed. I laid on the horn. Jumping out of the car I only had time to yell, "*Look Out,*" before Luis and Alfredo noticed the Cooper bearing down on them only a half a block away.

Luis and Alfredo dove for the curb as the cat streaked past them heading in the opposite direction. It ran right into the path of the speeding Cooper. The cat zigged when it should have zagged and launched itself into the air toward our side of the street. The Cooper didn't recover fast enough and I heard a loud *thunk* when car met cat. Crapper bounced off the front bumper and sailed through the air in our direction.

Mrs. Simmons flew out of Peabody's hedgerow like Bubba Smith on a pass play and yelled, "I got him!" As she screened left, her plump little legs pumped mightily and her arms stretched out to catch the cat.

Crapper came in for a landing about three feet in front of Mrs. Simmons and I mentally drew a line through another myth of the animal kingdom. Cats definitely do *not* always land on their feet.

The driver of the Cooper must have been startled when he popped the cat, because he skidded out of control and I instantly saw another disaster in the making. A man wearing a winter face mask darted into the street and had that "deer-in-the-headlights" look as he dropped his Nike duffel bag at his feet. The outside alarms on the bank added to the cacophony of us screaming, dogs barking, and sirens blaring.

In slow motion, we watched as the driver of the Cooper wildly spun the wheel trying to avoid the guy in the street. The guy took a step and remembered his gym bag. He turned to pick it up and the Cooper blasted him into the air. He rocketed over the back of the Cooper and landed with a sickening thud on the street. The Cooper slowed and jumped the far curb, stuttering to a stop against a tree. Moe the Deputy slid sideways to a stop in the intersection, burst out of the squad, weapon drawn, and ran toward the guy with the duffel bag, who lie frighteningly still in the street.

"Pooh." Mrs. Simmons exclaimed as she knelt to examine the cat's inert form.

Startled out of our stupor, Fred and I looked at each other and said, "Poo? As in poo-poo?"

Mrs. Simmons knelt beside the cat. "As in Pooh Bear, but because of his, uh, little quirk , I thought "Poo" rather apropos. Don't you?" She looked up at us through watery eyes.

Fred quipped, "Apro-*pooh*, you mean. *Hah*, I kill myself."

"Shut up Fred or I'll do it for you."

But Fred was on a roll. "As in curiosity killed the, uh, you know. Only, this was 'Cooperosity' killed the Crap."

"Not funny, Fred Miller," Mrs. Simmons said.

Fred and Mr. Brooster chuckled while Evo and Sam just stared at all three of us.

"Is it d-dead?" Luis and his brother came puffing over to my car.

Mr. Brooster nudged Pooh with his baseball bat. "As a doornail, I'd say, and good riddance!"

The voice of reason broke in on the conversation. I said, "Hey guys, what about the dead looking guy in the street?" Most of us turned to where the guy with the duffel bag was being attended to by EMS personnel.

"When did they get here?" I took in the whole scene.

"Do they work on cats, do you think?" Mrs. Simmons sounded hopeful.

The abandoned duffel bag looked ragged and forgotten with the zipper open and the tire track cleaving through the middle. Money hung out of the hole in the bag, and I realized the Cooper had foiled a would-be bank robbery.

Sam stepped up to a stricken Mrs. Simmons and put an arm around her slumped shoulders. She looked down her nose at Mr. Brooster. "Sir, saying 'good riddance' is an unkind and insensitive thing to say about this lady's cat!"

Brooster opened his mouth to point out Fred's tasteless jokes, but Mrs. Simmons patted Sam's hand. "No, it wasn't. He's right. Everyone hated that cat. He wasn't even really mine. I think he hung out at my house because I'm the only one in town who hasn't tried to murder him at one time or another." She sighed heavily and looked around at the gathering crowd.

I admitted, "She's right, Sam. I know I tried to off him once or twice myself. I even tried to convince Wesley to sit on him one time, but don't you guys think we should maybe check on the guy lying in the street?"

Fred acted as if she didn't even hear me. "Yep, I'm guilty too. He crapped on my patio furniture more than once. I turned the garden hose on him and half drowned him one time."

Mrs. Simmons looked up at Fred. "The man in the street crapped on your patio too?"

"No, no! The cat. I was talking about the cat." A murmur went through the small crowd. Like Saturday night confessions, the people in the crowd admitted how much they hated Crapper the cat, and shared the various methods they used to attempt to rid the world of his crapping ways.

Stanley Thorpe said, "Yep that damn cat cost me a new lounger, a-hundred-thirty-seven dollar ticket, and a night in jail because I tried loading his ass full of buckshot within city limits."

I yelled in my best outside voice, "People, the cat is dead! Should we try to see if that guy the Cooper ran over suffered the same fate?"

"Yeah, and who was it that shot off the end of his tail?" I tried to single out the voice in the crowd, but couldn't.

"Someone shot the dead guy in the ass?"

"No, you idiot! The cat! Crapper the cat got his ass plugged by Stan Thorpe."

Someone else yelled, "No, no, no. It wasn't Stan; Mary Cromwell shot off the cat's tail. I was there and saw the whole thing. Sheriff Green took away her gun."

Stan took off his ball cap. "I'm going to kind-of miss that damn cat."

Sounds of sympathy rippled through the crowd, and I almost smiled because I knew the disappointment wasn't because the cat croaked, it was because they no longer had a common enemy. I figured it was okay though, being a small town, they'd find someone else to hate before long.

Evo brought an empty box from the back of my car to Mrs. Simmons, and placed her cat inside.

I spotted our medical examiner coming out of the bank and waved. Shouts of, "Hey, Malcolm! We got you a customer over here," came from Stew Brenner and his big dumb brother, Lou.

Malcolm immediately changed course and hustled over to where we stood. Mrs. Simmons held out the box and said, "Crapper got croaked, Malcolm. Could you take care of him for me?"

"Uh…well…Uh, I don't usually do cats, Elda. I'm here to look at an, um, accident victim." He consulted his ever-present clipboard. "Car versus man, not car versus cat. Maybe we should call Mike Dudley. He would be the one–"

"No, no. It has to be you, Malcolm." Mrs. Simmons began

to sob.

I, of course interfered once again. Pulling Malcolm aside, I spoke softly. "C'mon, Mal, you're her brother. Do the brotherly thing and take the damn cat. Stick him in the cooler and call her later. I'm sure she'll figure out what she wants to do by then. Ivan and the paramedics are still loading the body into the meat wagon over there."

The crowd backed me up and Malcolm, clearly under duress, and blushing a bright pink, snatched the box containing the dead cat and stomped off to his car. The crowd sighed and began to break up, heading toward the ambulance.

I watched as Deputies Larry and Curly took pictures of the spot where the Cooper hit the guy, and Shemp headed toward the tree where the Cooper still rested.

The Cooper! I grabbed Luis' arm. "Luis, I think that car was headed right at you guys. It looked like it was going to mow you down until it swerved and hit the cat; and well, that dead guy with the duffel bag."

"Dead guy?" The word drifted through the crowd.

Alfredo tugged on Luis's sleeve. "Hey, my brother, did that not look like the car our new friends, Mark and Tom drive? It was small and had a stripe just like that."

"Yes it did. Maybe they were trying to say hello and did not realize they were traveling so fast." Luis stopped and his eyes popped open wide. "That is it! They swerved to avoid hitting us and instead ran over the cat, and uh, well, that guy over there. I wonder where they are now."

"Oh, they probably feel very bad about the cat and, uh, that guy over there, and will be by in a minute." Alfredo tried to see over Evo's shoulder. "We should wait for them."

"Wait! I see their car by the tree. Maybe they're hurt. Let's go check on them."

I didn't want to scare them, but I also didn't want them standing on the street like sitting ducks. "Uh, why don't you run over to the bank before it closes and cash your check? We can check on your friends for you. Then we can all meet at Sal's for coffee and you can tell us how you met up with your new friends."

The Gallegos brothers brightened. "Okay," they said and once again trotted off toward the bank.

I spun back to Fred, Sam, and Evo. "That car was bent on mowing down your boys. I'd bet money on it, Evo. What's up with that?"

"How should I know? The only place they've been without me is Great Ameri–"

"*The car bomb*," we all said at once.

16

"The car bomb?" Mrs. Simmons seemed confused.

"*The car bomb*," Fred screeched.

"Car bomb," rippled through the crowd.

Evo ran a hand over his face. "Oh, my God! If that bomb was meant for them...if this incident was no mistake..." He fisted his hands in my shirt. "Buzz, when you picked them up at Great America, did you see any Hispanic men nearby?"

"Evo, there are Hispanic men living all over the Midwest. Of course there would be some at Great America, but if you remember correctly, I didn't drive down to get them." I thought hard. "The boys did mention, however that their friends drove them home. I brushed it off at the time, but maybe I should have questioned them."

Sam sucked in a breath. "What if the car bomb was planted on the Suzuki and the car-thief man was blown up by accident? What if those guys in the Cooper were the 'friends' Luis and Alfredo were talking about? What if, oh my God, what if they rode home with the killers? The car thief could have set off a bomb meant for Luis and Alfredo!"

Evo narrowed his eyes. "The fish. It has to be the fish."

"The fish?" I didn't make the connection.

"He nodded. The dead fish." He looked down at Sam and took her hand. "The ones from Venezuela. I've been so busy enjoying myself that I almost forgot the original reason for dragging Luis and Alfredo along." He turned to me. "I didn't want them badgered or questioned by the media about the site or the fish until I had Sam check them out. I'm an environmentalist, not a fish specialist. I thought the easiest way to avoid problems would be to remove the brothers from South

America altogether–at least until we sorted everything out. What if whoever killed those fish and the people in the village found out we were here? But why Luis and Alfredo, why not me?"

Fred looked across the street at the bank. "Looks like someone might want to remove them permanently. Maybe they want to eliminate all witnesses, and began with the easy targets. Wait, here they come now."

We all watched as the Gallegos brothers exit the bank, exclaiming over their cash. They gamboled like puppies and I felt that old feeling of anger for innocent victims wash over me. The questions were already formulating in my mind. *Why would anyone try to kill someone over dead fish? What could be worth following and murdering someone in a foreign country? Who are they and why are they here?* The matter bore looking into.

Alfredo and Luis were stopped by Larry and Curly. Larry gestured to the blood smear on the street and to the Cooper. Alfredo stared with big eyes and Luis shook his head and talked animatedly to the deputy. They both looked at the Cooper and their shoulders slumped. Then Luis looked toward us and pointed.

Larry moseyed across the street to where we stood. He hitched his pants and leveled a look at me. "Hey, Buzz, Mr. Gallegos here tells me he and his brothers are guests of yours and your sister Fred."

I eyed him closely and felt the hair stand up on the back of my neck. "That's right."

"He also tells me those are his friends over in the Cooper talking to Moe."

"I believe they met when they went to Great America the other day. Is there something wrong?"

"I don't know as of yet, Buzz. I need to run a few things past J.J."

I began to speak, but Larry held up his hand. "Now, Buzz, I know you think J.J. will let you in on the investigation, but I have things well in hand. You're not a cop any more, but it seems pretty odd that you always seem to be one step away from the action. You elbow your way in and push me out. This time you may be a little *too* close to the situation. Besides, how am I ever going to get anywhere when I never get to investigate? J.J. is going to call us by the Three Stooges names forever if we don't get rid of you, so if you will excuse me..."

"Get rid of me? Just how are you going to rid the world of me, stooge number two?"

Larry (or whatever his real name was) suddenly began backpedaling, and with fervor. "Wait! Stop! I didn't mean that the way it sounded. Buzz, call her off!"

Fred shoved me aside and stomped up to Larry. She poked him in the chest with two fingers hard enough that Larry took a stumbling step back. "Phillip Knight, you are such moron. The reason J.J. calls Buzz in to help is because you four idiots spend more time drooling over tight-assed little co-eds than you do practicing police work."

"Now, Fred," Mr. Stupid continued, "You know it's just because Buzz is the Sheriff's girlfriend that—*Ooof.*" He bent in half when Fred punched him in the belly.

"Fred," I snapped, "Why the hell did you do that?"

"One, because I couldn't take any more stupid stuff coming out of his mouth, and two, because I couldn't reach his testicles."

The crowd gasped. *"Ooo."*

Out of nowhere, Mrs. Simmons jumped into the fray and blasted Larry in the nose with her fist. He gave a muffled yelp as he grabbed his nose.

She yelled right in his face. "Before you ask, that was for talking bad about Gerry Miller's girl! The idea, being jealous of Buzz. And this," she stomped on his foot and he howled like a scalded cat, "Is for being just plain dumb. Now you go on home to your momma, Phillip Joseph Knight, and tell her what happened here before she hears it down at Sal's."

Fred picked her jaw off the pavement and exclaimed, "Wow, Mrs. Simmons, you really gave him what for. You go, woman!"

Mrs. Simmons demure personality belied a backbone of steel. Interesting, and good to know. I patted her arm. "Thank you, Mrs. Simmons, but you didn't have to hit him for me." I steered her toward her home. "Are you going to be okay now?"

She shook off my hand. "Of course I'll be okay. I'm going down to Sal's. I think your momma is having coffee with Jane Knight and the girls, and I think I'll join them."

"And thank you for clearing up the boyfriend thing with him too."

Mrs. Simmons tossed her head back and shook her short grey curls. "I should say. Just because you and J.J. are affianced, Phillip should know you would never compromise an investigation."

Before I could speak, she hitched her purse to the crook of her elbow and tottered off in the direction of the diner, looking to all the world like a plump little penguin on her way to a fish feast.

Belatedly, I shouted after her, "Just for the record, J.J. is *not* my..." I sighed. "Aw, forget it."

I shook with exasperation. Then I turned back to Fred. "Yo Fred, why don't you grab Alfredo and Luis. Take my car and I'll meet you at Sal's."

"Sure, Buzz. Hey, are you going to let me help with the investigation like you let Mag help with Carole Graff?"

"What investigation?"

"Don't forget, big sister, I *know* you. Show me your right hand. I'd bet money you have your cell phone out and your finger on J.J.'s number."

I rolled my eyes while Sam picked up my right hand. "You win the prize, Fred, but why is she calling J.J.?"

I could see the light come on. "Wait! I remember. He is Sheriff Green from the party, right? Buzz's fiancé, I think your mother said."

Fred's and my mouths dropped open. "Fiancé!"

"Oh, *no*."

Fred giggled. "She said that?"

I fumed. "Where did she get that idea?"

Fred giggled again. "*Hoo-wee*. The Geriatric Gossip Central is probably having a field day with this one. The females in town will be out for your blood now, Buzz, not just your hair."

Sam added, "No wonder Mrs. Simmons said what she did."

I paled. "Oh, my God, does J.J. know?"

Fred giggled. "You'd better hope not."

"I'm *sooo* humiliated."

"You must be *sooo* humiliated."

I stopped, breathing hard. "Shut up, Fred, I gotta think." I leaned forward and put my hands on my knees. "Oh, man, this is bad."

Fred patted me on the back. "Don't make such a big deal out of it. We gotta go. Here come Luis and Alfredo." I guess I just sat there on the curb. Fred snapped her fingers in front of my face. "Come on, Miller, priorities. Coffee first, death and marriage second." She smacked the back of my head. "Snap out of it, Miller, we have bigger fish to fry here."

Wallowing in self pity I wailed, "I guess I really should call J.J. Oh hell, how can I do that now?"

"By remembering this isn't all about you, Buzz, that's how."

Startled, I looked up again. Fred grinned. "I knew that would bring you back. Call J.J., Sam, Evo, and I will get the

Gallegos brothers over to Sal's. We'll meet you there."

I called J.J. The phone rang once. "Hey, Buzz, miss me already?"

"What are you talking about Green? I just saw you yesterday."

"Hey, don't be so touchy, pal. I was just teasing you. What's up?"

He couldn't have been more reassuring. I instantly relaxed. "Oh, J.J., I'm sorry. I'm a little frazzled. I'm over at Main and Elm. Do you have time to stop at Sal's?"

"Just so happens I'm at Elm and Ash. I'm coming to the burglary scene, so I'll swing by."

"Wait–eh…uh…uh." But J.J. had already hung up.

I snapped the phone closed and stuffed it in my pocket. I looked at the blood smear as the fire department hosed down the street. "Oh crap." I'd forgotten about the burglary. I handed Fred the keys. "J.J. is coming by about the burglary."

"Okay?"

"He's only two blocks away, so he's going to grab me too."

She flashed me an evil grin. "Boy, I wish someone who looked like James Green would grab me."

"Shut up, Fred. He's just around the corner–there he is now. I'll fill him in on the way over. You just get the brothers over to Sal's. They can follow in the Jeep."

I gave Fred's shoulder a pat, and she stepped backward. She teetered on the curb, lost her balance, and screeched. Her arms swung in giant arcs, but her center of balance was somewhere south of where we were standing. She slipped off the curb and stumbled into the street in front of J.J.'s squad. Brakes locked and tires squealed as J.J. slid to a stop inches from Fred. She collapsed on the hood of the squad.

A smiling J.J. stuck his head out the window. "Uh, nice to see you too, Fred. Decide to just drop in today?"

"Oh. Um, well, I have to go now. Uh, we'll see you later.

Sam, Evo? Let's go." She grabbed an arm apiece and yanked them toward the car.

"What was that all about?" J.J. glanced at me as we pulled away from the curb.

"You know Fred, she trips."

"Yeah, like the time she tripped over the dog and landed in the Jell-O surprise my mom made last year for the Fourth of July picnic."

"Yeah, sort of. Listen, J.J., this may be nothing, but let me run it by you."

I explained what had happened and J.J. listened intently. He told me that the guy with the duffel bag had just robbed the bank and the Cooper kept him from getting away. Unfortunately, J.J. had just heard from the hospital and it didn't look like the bad guy was going to make it.

"Those two guys in the Cooper are heroes, Buzz."

"I think they might be murderers, James. They were aiming for Luis and Alfredo, J.J. The burglar just got in the way; kind-of like the cat."

"You know this as fact?"

I sat back in the seat. "No, I don't. Between the flying cat and the flying Gallegos brothers, and the flying burglar, I'm not sure what I think. I do know that your deputy Phil–no wait! Darryl, I think, is in a world of trouble though."

"Who is Daryl?"

"Uh, Stooge Number One, Moe."

"Oh, Moe. Moe isn't so bad. He can handle the initial."

I hesitated. "I uh, also had a little altercation of sorts with Stooge Number Two."

"Which one is Two?"

"Larry, or Phil maybe."

"Oh right, Larry the Moron. Tell me what happened."

I began the story and worked my way up to the boyfriend line as we pulled up to a stop sign behind my SUV. I had a horrible thought. "I can't be here!" I grabbed for the door handle.

"Geez, Buzz, what are you squawking about now?"

"We can't arrive together in your car! What will Gossip Central do with that little tidbit? I gotta go—just, uh, follow us."

"Us who? Buzz?"

"J.J., you don't understand. We'll never explain our way out of the boyfriend thing if we arrive together—especially now! Do you want to get married next week? That's what those conniving little old ladies are up to! Let me out."

"Wha-a-a?"

He slowed to a crawl and I jumped out of the squad and J.J. stared after me in mute surprise. I barely caught Fred as she pulled away from the stop sign. I banged on the door and she slammed on the brakes. I heard a *thunk* as Wesley hit the back of the driver's seat. I yanked the driver's door open and shoved Fred over.

She drew a breath to let me have it and I snapped, "*Don't* say a word," and she wisely stayed quiet. We drove the rest of the way to Sal's in silence, and Luis and Alfredo, and J.J. followed behind.

17

The drive to Sal's took less than five minutes. As we neared the diner, I became aware of loud music and a lot of yelling. Crowds of people gathered at the entrance to Sal's Diner and spilled out onto the sidewalk. Their shouting was indiscernible above the clamor of a boom box blaring music across the street.

We watched as Sal ran out of his diner, still holding two eggs in his left hand and a spatula in his right. He waved the spatula toward the street and we heard him yelling in Spanish. As we pulled into a parking place on the street, Sal scuttled over toward us and switched to English. "What the hell is that crazy Mary Cromwell doing over there by the parking meter? Is she pole dancing? Oh my God. Call J.J. Call the cops! Get that crazy lady away from my place! Oh, no, this is bad for business; she's going to drive away the customers. Help, police! She's cuckoo! She's *loco*! Help, *help*!"

He ran over to my window and yelled in my ear. "Buzz, arrest that woman! She's going to cause a riot! People will revolt. People will riot. It will be Clark Kent all over again!" I suppressed a grin.

"That's Kent State, Sal." We slowly climbed out of the SUV and watched the spectacle before our eyes. Even my dogs looked shell-shocked and could only stare. A boom-box sat on the curb near Mary and hip-hop music blasted from its speakers. One scrawny, fish netted leg wrapped around the parking meter she shimmied up and down. It looked like Lawrence Welk meets the Disco Hoochie Grandmama from Hell. Whatever the hell it was, it hurt my teeth.

Trying hard to keep a straight face, I said to Sal, "Yep!

You're right about one thing, Sal. That's Mary all right, but what the heck is she doing?" I blinked against the glare. "Oh, my God; what the heck is she *wearing?*"

"I don't know," Sal said, scratching his head with the spatula, "but it's got to be illegal. You better shoot her quick."

Fred appeared at my side and let out a whistle. "*Hoo-wee.* That is just wrong. No eighty-year-old woman should be allowed to dress like that. How the hell did she come up with that outfit?" Mary let go with a couple of hip thrusts. "Oh, my God!" Fred choked. "No eighty-year-old woman should be allowed to do that. I agree with Sal, we'd better shoot her quick or get J.J., fast! Didn't he follow us over?"

I felt a little queasy as I gaped like a mouth-breather at the odd scene in front of me. There was my mom's eighty-year-old friend Mary Cromwell in all her glory, ruby red lips smacking kisses at the crowd, pink feather boa flapping in the cool autumn air. She hacked as she spit out the feathers which kept sticking to the red blobby stuff that covered her lips and the acreage around them. She looked like a Botox reject from Hollywood. For a second, I didn't know if she was having a seizure or she attempted to pole dance on the parking meter.

"What the hell is *that?*" Evo's bewildered voice filtered through the haze of my brain.

"I don't know, but it sure is gruesome," Sam said.

Fred giggled. "Gruesome doesn't quite cover it, Sam; Ghastly, frightening, appalling, horrific."

Sam and I turned to Fred and said, "Shut up, Fred."

I was distracted from further comment when I heard my mother's voice shouting from the diner, "Mary Lou Cromwell, you get your skinny butt off the streets! Ian is *not* opening a strip club, and if he was, he sure as hell wouldn't hire you!"

Wolf whistles and hoots from other diners now on the street interrupted Mom's tirade. Pennies and nickels flew across the street as people threw change. It seemed to incite Mary, as she shook her booty to "*Shake your Booty.*"

Mom gathered steam. "Mary, I mean it! You're going to catch your death in that stupid dress. I just may be the one to kill you."

Mary wore a blue sparkly mini dress, reminiscent of the disco era with a halter neckline and no defined waist. It barely covered her butt and when she dropped the boa and bent to pick it up, it didn't. The crowd got an eyeful of Mary's black lace thong. *"Ohh Noo."*

Black fishnet stockings covered her scrawny legs and her orthopedic shoes looked like cement blocks on her feet. Her tight blue curls were topped with a plastic tiara, and her faded grey eyes twinkled from somewhere under the sky blue smears she had troweled across her eyelids.

J.J.'s cruiser crept up the street until it pulled even with us. Sal immediately ran around the front of the squad and began yelling in J.J.'s ear.

"How're you gonna stop this, eh? Arrest her, or...or shoot her, or call the *loco* loony police. You gotta get rid of her, J.J. She's gonna have an accident!"

"Sal, slow down. I think you mean *cause* an acci–"

No, no! She's gonna have an accident right there in the street. J.J. ducked as Sal gestured wildly with his left hand. One of the eggs he held popped out of his grasp when he gestured toward Mary. We watched in stunned disbelief as it sailed through the air in slow motion. The crowd "*oood.*"

The egg made a perfect arc, which by all the laws of physics should have dropped about five feet in front of Mary. Whether the wind caught it or my mother willed it, that egg had a mind of its own as it hitched in mid air, and shot another four-and-a half feet. The egg splatted squarely on Mary's gyrating butt.

"Aw, man. What a shot! That egg would have missed had her rear-end not been hanging out into the street." Fred hooted.

The crowd stood momentarily shocked into silence as Mary continued to undulate to the Beach Boys on the boom box. She suddenly became aware that she had egg on her butt.

Several things happened at once.

The adults, "*ooo'd*."

The kids, "awwed."

J.J. slapped a hand over his eyes.

Fred and I slapped hands over our mouths.

Sal squeaked.

Mary squawked.

Egg dripped onto the boom box.

The Beach Boys groaned and died.

Silence descended. Wesley calmly stepped around the squad and crossed the street. He grinned and wagged his tail as he slowly sashayed to where Mary stood. He looked at the egg dripping off Mary's butt and looked at the boom box. He looked at Mary's butt again.

Now people insist that dogs are not decision makers, but I could almost smell the rubber burning as Wes pondered his options. Obviously realizing that discretion was the better part of valor, Wes dropped his head and licked the boom box. As egg dripped off Mary's butt onto Wesley's head, Mary snapped out of her stupor.

"*Saaalll*!" Mary rounded on the owner of the diner.

"*Jay Jaaay,*" Sal yelled as he beat it back into the diner.

"Wes-leee!" My egg-sucking dog looked at me after hearing his name.

"*Maaa-rrry,*" Mom, Jane, and Joy all chorused from the door of the diner.

The crowd suddenly came to life and roared; applause and shouts filled the air. Coins flew in Mary's direction. One would think the Packers had just won home field advantage with such a hullabaloo. A tail wagging Wes looked up and grinned, egg dripping off one ear.

Mom and Jane intercepted Mary as she charged across the street bent on revenge. Wes must have thought the boa was some strange molting bird, because he gave chase and grabbed the end. A minor tug-o-war broke out which Wes won, and he came trotting back to the car with his prize.

Mom and Jane hustled Mary through the diner parking lot and stuffed her into Mom's truck. Last seen, Mary left a red blob on Mom's back window where she kissed it, and she waved to the crowd as they sped down the street.

J.J. spoke first. Hands on hips, he turned to us. "Well, it's going to be a zoo in there, so we might as well forget it." He consulted his watch and added, "Besides, Sal's going to be closing in a half hour. I'll call what's-his-name, Curly, to take the reports, so let's get out of here while we still can."

"It's going to take longer than that to fill you in on everything," I said.

Evo looked at his watch. "What time do you end your work day, Sheriff?"

"Call me, J.J. Tell you what, let me just call Edie and tell her I'll be on my cell phone if anything comes through Dispatch."

J.J headed back to the squad and we closed in as a group. Fred said, "Why don't we have Luis and Alfredo retrieve the live fish from Ian's, and meet us back at my house? We can call Hank, Ian, and Mag and make it a party."

"Great idea, Fred, I've been dying to show Hank your fish." Sam slipped an arm around Evo and rubbed his back. "Are you agreeable?" He looked like he just swallowed his tongue. He looked down at her and could only nod. I chuckled to myself. *That man had it bad.*

Sam patted him on the waist. "Evo, why don't we go with Luis and Alfredo? We can take your truck and the boys the Jeep. We can meet Buzz and Fred back at the house later." She rubbed his back again and the man broke out into a sweat.

He tried for coherency and failed miserably. "Uh, I…That is, I don't think…Uh, is it wise, uh, shouldn't we, uh…Buzz?" Evo looked at me with *save me* written all over his face.

I looked at Sam and she winked. She knows, I thought. That little crapper knows Evo can barely be in the same room with her without exploding into a blithering idiot. I should help him out. He may not make it back alive if I don't rescue him. It was a lovely thought.

I flashed Evo an evil grin. "Sounds great, Sam. Luis and Alfredo, are you sure you're okay?"

They looked at each other. "Of course we are. We were not hurt. It was the poor cat and the man with the bag of money who had all the trouble."

I felt myself grin. "Okay. We can all meet back at Fred's, eat pizza, and look at fish."

Evo closed his eyes and swallowed hard. "Thanks, Buzz."

Evo gained enough composure to grab Sam's hand as she moved away. He pulled her close and said in a quiet, rumbling voice, "You are playing with fire, my dear."

She turned her startling blue eyes on him. She raised her hand between their bodies, deliberately running it up the zipper of his jeans, and laying it lightly over his pounding heart.

His entire body jerked, and she smiled slowly. "I know. I can feel the heat. We still need to have that talk, you know."

"Talk," he croaked as he spun her away from him and nudged her toward my SUV. "Like hell we'll talk."

I heard Sam giggle as Evo practically picked her up and threw her into the truck.

As our little group began to disburse, the chugging and sputtering sound of a vehicle on its last leg made us all turn. The little Cooper came to a stuttering halt behind Luis and Alfredo's Jeep. Two men climbed out and started toward us.

Luis and Alfredo were the first to react. They leapt forward and each grabbed a body. "Mark! Tom! Our friends!"

181

They shouted greetings as they pounded their friends on the back. Mark and Tom did the same. Suddenly, remembering they had an audience they stepped back. An awkward silence descended upon our group.

Alfredo shouted, "You are our heroes!"

Mark shifted uncomfortably. "Right. Heroes. We are not heroes, my friend."

Tom scuffed the ground. "No, we are not heroes, but we are your friends. Whatever happens, know that we treasure your friendship."

Luis clapped a hand on Tom's shoulder. "What is this? What are you talking about? You act as if you are going somewhere. We can all hang out together like friends do,"

Tom dropped his head and sighed. "Yeah, friends. Uh, we just stopped by to make sure that you are not hurt."

"No, my friend, we are okay. Would you like pizza? We are going to have pizza at our friend Fred's house."

"Good idea," I said. "Why don't you join us?"

Mark looked like he might cry and Tom looked sick. "I'm afraid we can't. We have to visit our sick Aunt Maria tonight. We have to go now. Thank you." They scuttled over to what was left of the Cooper and chugged down the street.

Luis looked at us and said sadly, "Those poor men; so many sick people in their family."

I asked, "What do you mean, Luis?"

"Every time we see them another relative is sick."

J.J. looked at me. He raised a brow and I winked. I put an arm around Luis and steered him toward the car. "That's too bad. Tell me, who exactly is sick in their family?"

18

The large man paced back and forth, wondering if he needed to go to Wisconsin and do the deed himself. His amateur hit squad had not been in contact with him, nor had he read anything online about the three South American scientists being murdered. He could find no trail of credit card receipts to even tell him where they were. What were those morons doing up there, drinking beer and eating cheese in Milwaukee? What must he have been thinking when he hired those two anyway? He ran a hand through his hair. Should he send Reymundo? It would leave him without a bodyguard, but which was the bigger risk?

"Damn," he muttered as his secure phone rang. "What is it?"

"It is Mark and Tom calling from America," Tom said in a small voice.

"Well, did you kill anyone yet?"

"Uh yes, we did, but not exactly the people we were supposed to kill."

The man could feel his blood pressure rising. "What do you mean, you idiot? Who the hell are you killing up there?"

"Well, sir, a car thief, a bank robber, and a cat, to be exact."

"A cat? A goddamn *cat*. I didn't send you up there to murder a cat. You're fired, both of you, and you are dead men when I get my hands on you. Do you hear me? *Dead!*"

"Yes, sir, we hear you. We have already decided we do not make good assassins. We will not be coming back to South America then. You can understand that, I am sure. We will get jobs and pay you back the money we have spent. Think of it this way; you have saved money by not having to pay us the second installment."

"Second installment! What are you, some kind of smart ass? Your second installment is going to be a bullet in your miniscule brain, you imbecile."

"Sir, we wish to ask that you not hurt these people. They are not bad people. If you were to meet with them you would see for yourself that they are–"

"Don't tell me you spoke with them. I suppose you told them about the hit too, didn't you?"

"No, sir, we mind our…"

"Liars! What do you know about the mine? Did you say anything to them about the mine? You keep your mouths shut, do you hear me? Or I will personally make sure it takes days for you to die! He slammed the phone down so hard it rattled in the base.

Tom pocketed the cell phone and blew out a shaky breath. Mark clicked off the small recorder. They both sat in silence a moment and Mark said, "Now what?"

"Now we find the Sheriff and hope he can protect us when the assassin comes to get us, that's what."

"Do you really think he will do that?"

"Let us hope this Sheriff Green is an honest man and does not sell us out to the real assassin. American police make deals all the time. Dirty cops. The Mob, don't you watch CSI?"

Mark stood and pocketed the recorder. "Let us go and find Sheriff Green now. How much time do you think we have?"

Tom thought a minute. "Probably no more than forty-eight hours. If he is rich enough, he could hire a private plane, but that would draw attention. I believe they will fly commercial, and they will fly as soon as possible."

"Yeah, and we have drawn enough attention to ourselves already. Maybe since we killed only bad guys we will not be executed. Or deported." Mark thought a moment. "Maybe we can tell them we came to protect Luis and Alfredo, and Mr. Bad Guy is coming for them as well as the scientists."

"We can try, but we will be lucky if the Americans don't kill us first."

"They won't."

"How do you know?"

"There is no death penalty in Wisconsin, I checked."

Tom thought for a moment. He put his hand on Mark's arm. "We have to tell the truth. You know, my almost brother, we are dead men no matter what happens?"

"Yes, I know, but we need to make sure the doctors, Luis, and Alfredo are safe. They are good people and do not deserve their fate. We will die as men of honor, instead of the greedy snail slime we were paid to be."

Mark held out his hand. "Then we are together on this, *amigo*?"

Tom grabbed his hand and dragged him close to hug Mark tight. "We are together, my American brother. Let us go now, and try to stop a very bad man."

Reymundo was irritable and cold by the time he hit Chicago. The rental agency screwed up his car reservation, but in keeping with the low-profile persona he adopted, he made no complaint. The rental company offered limo service to wherever he wanted to go. He thought about it and figured he would allow the limo driver to take him. By the time Reymundo finished business in Wisconsin; he would eliminate the driver, ditch the car, and return to South America before the rental agency knew anything was amiss.

The agency retrieved his overnight bag and Reymundo retrieved the handgun and map left for him in an airport locker. The bouncy little girl behind the counter ordered a limousine and asked Reymundo where he wanted to go. He replied, "Joliet," after consulting a map. Within minutes, they had him whisked off on a golf cart, and in no time, he climbed in to a silver limousine parked at the curb.

Perfect, he thought as he settled in the back seat. The car is full of gas and the windows are blacked out. *Hah.* Americans are so stupid. They pulled away from the curb and continued around the circle to the Interstate. Heading south on I-294, the chatty limo driver bought into Reymundo's feigned interest in Chicago and lowered the partition. He began a monologue about all the famous people who had ridden in his limo, and threw in tidbits about Chicago history as well. Reymundo listened with half an ear as he looked for an opportunity to begin his work.

As traffic slowed for yet another tollbooth, he asked the driver if he would pull off the Interstate so Reymundo could take a picture of the skyline. Being an affable guy, the driver did as asked. He pulled off the Interstate and looked over his right shoulder, prepared to begin his narrative on Al Capone.

He looked Reymundo up and down and said, "Hey buddy, where's your camera?"

Reymundo just smiled and calmly leaned forward. With his right hand he brought the 9mm up and popped the driver in the forehead.

Wiping the blood and grey matter off the end of the silencer, Reymundo said, "You forgot to smile, Mr. Limo Driver." Chuckling at his own joke, Reymundo crammed the driver's hat on his own head.

After stuffing the driver onto the passenger side floor, he climbed in behind the wheel.

Throwing his overnight bag on top of the body, he pulled back onto the Interstate. He got off at the next exit and pulled into a truck stop. Other limousines were parked in the lot, so Reymundo figured he wouldn't attract much attention. He drove behind the last row of trucks slowly, opened the passenger door, and shoved the body out into the weeds with his foot.

Reymundo closed the door and proceeded to the truck stop exit. He pushed the hat forward at a cocky angle over his brow and smiled arrogantly in the mirror. "How was that, Mr. Capone?" He smiled as he drove away.

He got back on the Interstate, heading the opposite direction. He reset the GPS and found a radio station he liked. He hummed along to a tune his mother had sung to him in a different life. He realized what he was doing and smashed the off button. "Where did that come from?" He growled, as he pulled off his glove to suck on his bloody knuckle. "Focus, Reymundo, focus." He put his glove back on and drove the rest of the way north in silence.

19

Thanksgiving is always an ordeal at the Miller household. This year with all the extra guests, it promised to beat all previous records. Al, Mag, me, Mom, Dad, and Sam sat around Mom's kitchen table and discussed plans for the big day. We decided to have it at Fred's this year because she had a formal dining room, a huge kitchen, and five of the guests were housed there. We took a vote (as this *is* a Democracy), and then we made Sam tell Fred.

I was glad it wasn't at my house. It's rather small and it would take an Act of Congress to remove all the hidden dog hair so it didn't end up in the eggnog. Al's house was a bitch because of the white carpet and it looked like normal sized people would break the uncomfortable and spindly antique chairs–and since we live in Wisconsin, *normal* to us is plus-size in California. I hate Al's house. Al hates my dogs. It's a mutual thing we handle most maturely; it usually involves a lot of yelling and name calling, then deciding the party would be held at Mom's or Fred's.

Fred's house is beautiful, big, and roomy; with huge comfy leather chairs and old polished pine floors which seem to invite clamoring feet and doggy toenails. Fred's house seems busy-cum-chaotic on a peaceful day, perfect for the mayhem we expected on Thanksgiving.

I picked up J.J. and his deep fried turkey on my way over. Because his mom's quilting circle had volunteered to serve turkey dinner at the old folk's home in town, she wouldn't make it to Fred's until after dinner. Sylvia called me and asked (ordered) me to pick up J.J., and she would be over later with his car. I did as I told, and soon J.J. sat next to me, babbling on about his wonderful turkey fryer, and I nodded and smiled, while inside the idea of fried turkey made me rather queasy.

I didn't want to hurt Green's feelings, so I didn't tell him I had a cooked and sliced a turkey hid under the far back seat. I triple wrapped it in hopes Wesley wouldn't give it away, because if that dog knew it was there, it would be history. When we arrived at Fred's, we saw Mag bundled up and standing in the driveway, cooking yet another turkey on the grill–looked to me like she's a little afraid of fried turkey too. We yelled, "Hi," as J.J., Wes, Hill, and I piled in the back door, arms loaded with turkey, beer, and buns.

I let J.J. deal with Mom and the unpacking while I snuck out the back door with a couple of beers and said to Mag, "Here, Master Baster, have some anti-freeze."

She took the beer and looked over her shoulder. "Thanks. I heard that J.J. was, of all things, *frying* a turkey?" I nodded and took a swig. She said, "The thought made me very afraid, so I'm cooking an extra one in case his tastes like turkey jerky, or turkey poopie, or something equally obnoxious."

I threw back my head and we laughed. I held up my brewski and we clinked bottles. "So did I. We shared a good laugh over the fact that with three turkeys and we'd have leftovers for everyone. She took the turkey off the grill and we hustled it into the house.

The kitchen overflowed with the wonderful smells of baking holiday pies and breads, brewing coffee, and roasting sage. Roasting sage? "Hey, Mom," I yelled over the din, "You're not cooking a turkey, are you?"

She bustled over to where I stood and yanked me down to her five-foot-two level and whispered, "Don't you tell, J.J. or you'll hurt his feelings. This is just in case J.J.'s turkey sucks. Now out of my way, shoo! She flapped the dishtowel she held at me and I skedaddled, wondering if the soup kitchen would need a couple of extra turkeys–maybe we could pawn off the fried one on them.

Pasting a serene smile on my face, I went back to taking in the ambience of Thanksgiving. One of my favorite things when growing up was to run outside, take a deep breath, and run in the back door just to inhale those smells. I opened my eyes to see Mag with hers closed, absorbing the smells like we were both kids again. She looked at me and smiled. I grabbed her, hugged her close, and said softly, "You still do that too?" She nodded; her eyes suspiciously damp.

"By the way," I said out of the corner of my mouth. "Mom's making a turkey too."

"For real?"

"Yeah, for real."

Still snickering, we walked into the controlled chaos. It was a beehive of activity as Luis pulled pies out of the oven, and Fred and Sam sliced a ham at the sideboard. Mom stood whipping potatoes, and Dad leaned against a counter, eating Doritos. The back door banged open. Al struggled through, loaded down with bags and boxes, and dressed like she was going to a Broadway opening. She teetered on her high heels as her packages hung off her body in a delicate balance.

She would have made it to the counter unscathed except for the fact that 160 pounds of happy Newfoundland chose that particular moment to check out the newcomer in the kitchen and show her the love. Wesley whooshed past me through the kitchen door from the living room like a runaway freight train. He slammed on his brakes, but as Physics 101 teaches us, 160 pounds of mass times velocity makes it impossible to stop a furry, runaway train skidding along a newly waxed wood floor in ten feet or less.

We all watched in frozen fascination as imminent doom hung over Al's teetering body. One of her stiletto heels caught in Fred's rag rug by the back door. Oblivious to the peril she faced, Al continued to lift her foot up and down, trying to rid her heel of the string. It was like watching a Hitchcock movie camera as it panned in on a clueless Al (coincidentally looking, today, like Janet Lee from *Psycho*), the screen suddenly flashed to Wesley "Bates" Miller as he barreled his way toward his victim swooping in for the kill.

At the last second, Al looked up to see Wesley's black hairy face bearing down on her. She took in the lolling tongue hanging from his grinning maw and screamed like she was being hacked to pieces in a shower stall. She scared the beegeezes out of Wes, who tried desperately to slam on the brakes.

His huge hairy paws backpedaling on the slippery floor, poor Wes looked for, all the, world like Scooby-doo when he saw a ghost. Some smart-ass must have thought the same thing, because large hands grabbed my shoulders from behind, and I heard "Rutt–Roe, he-he-he-he-he-he," right before the crash.

How Wes avoided a full frontal, I don't know, because Al stood there like six feet worth of limp lettuce as the dog sideswiped her legs. With the proficiency of a skilled gigolo, Wes used the last of his forward momentum to slide his wet cold nose up Al's legs, landing it directly into her crotch. Now I don't know what that gesture says about Wesley's choice between Al's cooch and Al's cooking, but I do know what it said about the load of food she carried.

Letting out a howl that could shatter glass, Al whacked Wes with a bag of dinner rolls, which promptly blew up and shot into the air. Wes abandoned his quest of imparting his special hello to Al, and tried instead to catch a dinner roll on the fly.

As I stood in the doorway, powerless to stop the chain of events that unfolded at warp speed, I had an inspirational thought of the true meaning of Thanksgiving. I looked reverently skyward and said, "Thank you Lord, for I am not carrying the sweet potatoes or the cranberries."

Scooby (or J.J., as it turned out) lifted a hand off my shoulder and popped me in the back of the head. "Shame on you, Buzz. Poor Al is covered in a rainbow of side dishes, and you're laughing."

"Poor Al, my butt! That'll teach her to wear stilettos while carrying half of a feast." I grinned as he moved to stand next to me, leaving his other arm around my shoulders. Just then, Mom came in from the dining room carrying a bowl of mashed potatoes, and I saw through the open door, Hilary trotted close on her heels, and both were looking down. "Buzz, these potatoes need butter on top. Would you—"

Wes heard Grandma Gerry's voice and scrambled for footing in the yuck displayed in colorful patches all over the kitchen floor with Al as the centerpiece. Tears of laughter ran down my face at the sight of Al draped in Kazan and deviled eggs. She lifted a dripping hand out of the bowl of cranberries and tried to yank her skirt down. She must have been in Aunt Minerva's recipe box, because if I was not mistaken, she had Jell-O salad with cottage cheese and cabbage dripping off her head and onto her collar.

With a mouthful of cornbread and applesauce dressing, Wes sprayed Al with the remaining foodstuffs on the floor as he skedaddled in one place trying to find footing on the now slick floor. He took off at a high lope as Hilary looked up to see the treasure trove of food across the room. She trotted behind Mom and hit her from behind. I looked at Wesley in Mom's flight path, and panned in on Mom gabbing away about potatoes; totally clueless that she too, headed toward certain disaster. I opened my mouth to yell, but nothing came out. I flapped my hands ineffectually at Wes, which alerted J.J. to the danger Mom walked blithely toward.

She was about two steps away and I still felt like Charlie Tuna with my mouth moving, hands flapping, and nothing but bubbles coming out. Wes must have gotten a cranberry stuffed up his nose, because he chose that moment to throw his head back and sneeze, expelling said cranberry, and at the same time, startling Mom so she hit the brakes inches from the river of dog spit and dressing on the floor.

"Whoop–*Eeeahhhhh.*" She squeaked as she bobbled the bowl of mashed potatoes in her hands and spun toward me. The bowl teetered, but Mom was able to hold on and also miss the sea of side dishes on the floor. She stood clutching the bowl to her chest with one hand on the cooking island, trying to catch her breath.

Now, I'm pretty sure Mom would have made a full recovery had Fred not chosen that moment to exit the bathroom and scream, but scream she did. I guess Mom hadn't quite recovered as much as I had hoped. Fred not only startled Mom, she scared Wes and Hilary too. Wes jumped backward toward Al, and Hillary scrambled for footing, passing gas as she followed Wes.

As Hill jumped away from Fred's caterwauling, she hit Mom in the back of the legs. Fred jumped forward to grab Mom, and I jumped forward to grab the flying potatoes (I do have my priorities). Fred caught Mom and I almost caught the potatoes. I snatched the bowl from mid-air and clasped it to my breast in my best imitation of Franco Harris's "*Immaculate Reception.*" Fortunately (or unfortunately if you were me), the open end of the bowl raced toward me and we ended up with booby-potatoes that night, but on the bright side, at least the potatoes hadn't been buttered yet. On the other hand, the damn Jell-O salad made it to the table practically unscathed. I keep trying to train Wes to eat Jell-O salad, but he is too afraid (or too smart), I think. Hilary treats Jell-O salad like a box of Cracker Jacks. She digs around in it until she finds the surprise inside.

Dad calmly watched the entire episode from the cheap seats, still leaning against the counter by the stove with a

Dorito poised at his mouth. He calmly laid the bag on the counter and brushed his hands on his jeans. He looked over at J.J. and said, "Hey J.J., would you mind calling for that plant doctor fellow–what's his name again?"

"His name is Ian, Bill."

"Yeah, that's right, Dave. Call Dave and I'll get a manure shovel to get this crap cleaned up out of the kitchen." He hitched a suspender as he tip toed through the mess on the floor, and grabbed his barn coat on his way out the back door.

We all stared after him long after the door closed behind him.

20

A ruckus in the front of the house drew the attention of those of us waiting for any excuse to get out of kitchen cleanup detail. It looked to me like the boys had things well in hand, so Sam and I snuck out the kitchen door and ran like hell. We were equally surprised to see old, hearty Hank MacRone introducing himself around the room. Puzzled, I turned to Sam. "I didn't know Hank was coming."

Sam raised her eyebrows at me. "I didn't know he was even invited."

"It's not a big deal, but a little odd. He made a point of telling us he had a previous engagement elsewhere tonight..."

My mind immediately began to think of nefarious reasons why Hank would suddenly show up here out of the blue, and what kind of appointment could he have possibly had in a town where he didn't know anyone, half-way across the country? One of those prickly feelings that Hank had ulterior motives for being here shimmied up my spine. *Shut up, Buzz, There's a perfectly good explanation why Hank would show up at a family dinner on a holiday two thousand miles from where he lives....Not!*

"Very odd indeed," I said. "But let's not ask him about it right now, Sam. We'll tell the boys not to mention it and see what Hank has to say. Would that be okay with you?"

Sam clinked her beer bottle against mine. "Okay by me. I'm just curious." Her smile faded as she looked at me. "Buzz, you don't actually think there actually is something wrong, do you?"

I observed Hank as he worked the room like an Illinois politician on the campaign trail. I stood by and nursed my beer as I watched him watch everyone else.

J.J. strolled in from the kitchen and I sidled up to him. I spoke so only he could hear. "What's up with that guy? I mean, what's your take on him?"

"I'm trying to figure his angle," he answered. "How much do you guys really know about him?"

"I only know what Fred and Sam told me. I just have this odd feeling about him that I can't explain. I keep thinking it's because I don't like him, but I have this gut feeling..."

J.J. grabbed my elbow and pushed me back toward the wall. I slapped at his hands.

He eased back. "I know, I know. It's just that I think there is more to him than he's saying. Combine that with your 'uneasiness' and it becomes more sinister by the minute."

I kept that in mind as I studied Hank. He stood next to Sam, admiring the stunning display of Marlboro Discus swimming through a cloud of Cardinal Tetras in front of them.

Hank suddenly turned and rubbed his hands together. Without preamble he said, "So where are these fish you brought with you?"

J.J. and I whipped around and together whispered, *"The fish."*

Sam looked startled. "I didn't actually bring them. Evo found them if you recall. I have not examined them yet." She checked her watch. "Buzz, do we have time to fetch Evo and Fred and go down to take a look at our survivors? Alfredo and Luis moved them to Fred's breeding room."

I told her I would check and returned with both Fred and Evo. I gave them a quick heads up on my suspicions along the way. Fred told me I was full of crap and Evo muttered, "I never did like that guy." We trooped downstairs to Fred's fish room.

There were four five-gallon tanks set up for the surviving Endlers, and I could see the flashes of metallic silver, green, and orange as the busy little fellows zipped back and forth chasing females.

Hank bent close to the tank and exclaimed, "*Ha*. There you are my little beauties."

Sam stood beside him. "Ian has finished examining the dead fish, and according to the toxin numbers, he cannot understand how these little fellows could have survived."

J.J. and I stood in front of the last tank. I squinted to make my viewing better. There was a sand substrate in the tank, and I could barely make out movement in the far corner. "Uh, Sam?"

She turned. "Yes?"

"Uh, would you come over here? I think I see a Cory in the back of this tank."

"Impossible. These tanks are newly set up, and there were no Cory catfish in them. I also don't remember seeing any when Luis and Alfredo brought them in, but I only glanced at the bags; Luis and Alfredo did most of the acclimating of the fish."

Hank stepped in front of her and strode across the room. He squeezed between J.J. and me, and efficiently shoved me out of the way. "That's impossible. Let me see."

My blouse was becoming itchy and I looked down in horror to discover I still had mashed potatoes smeared across my chest. I excused myself to change out of my potato boobie blouse, and Sam went to check on the boys in the kitchen, leaving Hank with J.J., Evo, Fred, and the fish.

Once upstairs in Fred's room, I rifled through her drawers and couldn't find a thing that would work. Her style is more like trendy chic and mine is more like *Where's the beer and pretzels?* casual wear. Fred's clothes on me would have looked like Paris Hilton meets Erma Bombeck.

Frustrated, I slammed the drawer and noticed I sprinkled dried mashed potatoes on the floor. "Serves her right," I said, slamming the door on my way out.

I headed for the stairs and ran right into Evo, who exited

his room. "*Ompf.* Sorry, Evo, I was preoccupied. Are you okay?"

"I'm okay. I guess you didn't find anything to wear. Either that or you are rehearsing to be your dog's new chew toy."

"Very funny. I have to run home to get something to change into, because aside from the fact that Fred is a size 10 and I'm a 14, Fred's idea of style and mine are poles apart."

"Buzz, this could be your luck day. I think my idea of style and yours might just be alike. Comfortable."

"If you have an old sweatshirt, I'm your woman." Another idea sparked in my mind. "Say, I may be able to help you with your love life, and help myself to your clothes at the same time. *Wow.* This could be *both* our lucky days."

"What do you mean by 'lucky', Buzz, and whose love life are you helping?"

I hooked an arm through his. "Come on, cowboy; let's get a load of them thar fancy new duds-o-yers, and I'll tell ya how yer gonna catch that purty little South American filly downstairs." His brow lifted, his mouth quirked, he opened his door, and bowed low as I lead the way in.

"Holy cow," I said as I walked into an outdoorsman's paradise. "Hell, Boy, did you buy out Gander Mountain or what?"

"I bought jeans, polo shirts, sweat shirts, tank tops, and over shirts…" As he ran down the list as he threw an example of each on the bed.

"Evo, stop! This is more clothes than I own, and you're only here on vacation. Let me grab a sweatshirt and I'll be fine. Thank–"

"No, no. Wait a minute; I have the perfect thing, I think." He rummaged through the clothes and came up with a pink T-shirt and a black and pink plaid flannel shirt. "Here, Buzz. This is more your color. It's also plenty big enough to go over your…uh, your…your…you know…" He dropped a flannel shirt on a chair and made lifting gestures around the pectoral area of his chest.

I laughed and Evo turned a dark shade of red. I thought he was going to pass out. He spun around to the mountain of clothes in the chair. He yanked out the pink T-shirt and shoved it at me. "I hate pink. The lady at the store, she said it would be sexy with my black hair, and Tony grabbed it. I think she just wanted a date. I was going to change the oil in the truck while wearing it, but here, you take it." He shoved the offending shirt under my nose.

I snatched it out of his hand "It so happens that I love pink. Turn around so my sports bra doesn't offend your delicate sensibilities." He did. I ripped off the potato blouse and slid the T-shirt over my head. I tied the soft flannel shirt at my waist and Evo surveyed the handiwork.

"Gee, Buzz, you look great. You look a hell of a lot better in pink than I would have. You look like–"

"Mine?"

I spun toward the door and saw J.J. lounging against the jamb. I realized he'd been standing there watching me and I narrowed my eyes at him. "Yours, my sweet patootie, you butt head. We're not in public, Green, so you can knock off the silly stuff. How long have you been standing there?"

Evo took that moment to back away from the sparks.

J.J. just stood against the jamb with a thumb hooked in his belt, and smiling that small smile that shows off his dimples. *Does he do that on purpose?*

"Long enough," was all he said.

Evo looked panic-stricken and he blurted, "Doesn't she look great in that shirt? She was full of potatoes and she going to go home to change. I had this shirt I didn't like and..."

J.J. stepped into the room and closed the door behind him. He slowly reached up and took the Silver-Belly off his head. He set it on a dresser and folded his arms over his chest. "And where exactly did she change into your clothes, Castillo?"

"Sir, I would never."

I decided to let Evo off the hook, and worked on becoming crankier by the minute. "Knock it off J.J., you big bluffer, you got Evo all upset for nothing. I was going to go home rather than try to wear Fred's 'Tooth Fairy' clothes, so Evo offered me these shirts. Stop trying to intimidate him. He's traumatized enough already."

I took a breath and geared up for the next verbal assault when I noticed J.J.'s shoulders were jumping up and down. He stood there pinching his upper lip trying to keep a straight face. I looked closely and realized the idiot was laughing.

"Green, if you're laughing at Evo, he's going to kick your butt. If you're laughing at me, I'm going to uh, well, I'm going to make-uh-Evo kick your butt anyway. I'll even hold you down."

J.J. laughed harder and Evo was saved from answering when his door was shoved open and a dripping Al wearing nothing but two towels came blundering into the room. "Oops, sorry. I heard Buzz's voice and thought this was Fred's room. I'll just go–" She began to back out.

"Wait, Al," I yelled. "Fred won't have anything to fit your six foot frame, but Evo just bought a brand new wardrobe. I fingered the soft flannel of my shirt. It ain't Armani, but it sure is comfortable."

Al looked doubtful and the men looked pole-axed. I must have looked pissed because after J.J. picked his tongue up off the floor his gaze flew to me, then to Al, then back to me. He picked up his hat and he and Evo slid over near the door.

What could I say to that? "Gee, Green, enjoying the view?" I gave a choking laugh.

"Buzz…"

I stepped up nose-to-nose, glared at him, and said through my teeth, "Don't *Buzz* me, pal. Like I said; 'mine' my ass–you're welcome to her; just wait until I get out of here."

"Buzz wait…"

I looked in the mirror and saw his eyes flick back to mine. He at least had the decency to blush, but I'd had enough. *Damn. That's what I get for wishing on a star.* I felt my eyes burn as I said quietly, "Just go, J.J."

I heard the door click and I took a deep breath. I turned to Al and held up a lavender T-shirt with a matching flannel shirt. I took a fortifying breath and said, "How about this?"

I watched her eyes as they slid from the closed door to me. They visibly widened, and she wisely pretended the incident with the men never happened. I went along out of habit.

"Oh! This is pretty. And look, we kind-of match."

I rolled my eyes and wondered to myself for the hundredth time in our lives if she really was that clueless. *Naw, she did it on purpose,* I thought as I bit the bullet and blasted her. "Al, you have been in this house a hundred times. You knew this wasn't Fred's room."

She sighed and looked away from me. "Yeah, I did."

"Why do you *do* stuff like that? You wonder why I have a problem with you."

"Oh lighten up, I was just experimenting."

My mouth hung open. "And those two men you just embarrassed the crap out of were what? The Guinea pigs in your little experiment?"

"Oh, get over yourself, Buzz; you act like I committed a personal crime against you." She looked at me and I just sat there like a stupid sheep.

Her smug expression turned horrified as she ran the scene over in her sleazy pea-brain. "Oh my God, Buzz, I am so sorry! J.J.–ah, I didn't know. Oh my–I would never had–I didn't mean–"

"Forget it. You proved your point so just–"

"Buzz, honest, I didn't mean–"

"Bullshit, Al. What exactly *did* you mean? What were you trying to prove? That you are still beautiful? That you can still turn a head, and make men drool? Embarrass childhood friends and turn them into blithering idiots? What could *possibly* be behind the motive for a stunt like that? And it *was* a stunt, wasn't it?"

A tear rolled silently down her face as she nodded, and the fight went out of me. Then I got pissed. *Really pee-ahssssssed.* I jumped on the bed, got right in her face and grabbed her arms. "Al, listen to me! You are way too old to be acting like this. You were a pretty girl, and you are a beautiful woman. God gifted you with a wonderful brain, so use it! Grow up and get with the program, for God's sake. You're worth so much more than this. Aren't you embarrassed that Rosie the News Whore is your only friend anymore?"

Her eyes welled and I sighed in exasperation. "Do you even realize what you are missing in life, wasting it on stupid shit like this?"

I held up my hand when she opened her mouth. "And don't give me any crap because I'll let you in on a great secret. Do you remember Mom telling us over and over about beauty being only skin deep? Hate to be the one to tell you, but every word was true, pal, and I feel so sorry for you if you think your only gift is your face. What are you going to have left when the face goes? Because it will and don't you think for a second this is jealousy talking. You are worth so much more than you give yourself credit. Use it. Use your damn brain!"

She stared at me for a long moment and her eyes narrowed. "You are incredible; you know that, don't you?"

Okay, here it comes, "Yes," I deadpanned. "I am."

"No really, I mean it. You aren't the least bit jealous of me. You are just really pissed for me and at me, aren't you?"

"Yes, Al." I sighed, "I am."

"Well, I'll be darned, that's great."

"Huh? What do you mean? *What's* great? Al? Are you okay? I am pissed! If you think you can play whacko space cadet and I'll let it go, you're sadly mistaken, so straighten up or I'll blast you, I swear."

She smiled calmly and patted my arm. "No, I'm okay, Buzz. I sure am glad we talked. I'll apologize to Evo and J.J. Hey, do you want me to fix it with–"

"*Don't* fix a thing! Pretend nothing happened. Please."

"Okay," she said, and babbled on and on as if nothing happened. She began to fold Evo's clothes. What the hell am I supposed to do now? Can't hold a grudge, can't take back what she did. Slapping her was out of the question. She seems sincere enough. Staying pissed was only going to make my ulcer hurt. I sighed and went with the moment. Again. It was easy to pick up on the conversation Al was having with herself.

"…because we haven't done the matching shirt thing since we printed all those *Miller Sisters* T-Shirts at the fair and gave them to all our friends–well actually, they were your friends, and Fred's, and Mag's but it sure was fun. Remember that, Buzz?" I sat there in a trance, the nodding sheep all over again.

Al prattled on and I wondered where those young girls went. I thought back to all those kids we hung out with. We were more family than, well, family.

She laughed at a long ago memory and the out-of-body feeling I'd been experiencing faded. A picture of us all laughing came to mind. Geez, that was a long time ago.

She continued, as if I was an active participant in the conversation. "Remember Mag with the mud dripping off her nose? Remember us all paying our fifty cents just so we could squirt the water race man at the carnival?"

She belly-laughed at that, and I'd have had to have been dead not to remember. I allowed myself a small chuckle at the sight of the water race guy running for cover.

She rolled on the bed, kicking her legs in the air and

laughed gleefully: either not knowing or not caring that I was not taking a sweet stroll down memory lane with her. "Remember when we toilet papered the squad car outside the commercial building? And then they got a call and had to jump in it and take off?"

I had to chuckle at that one, because we were under suspicion but never got caught. Totally at ease, Al dropped her towel and slid on the lavender T-shirt, babbling about God knows what.

Damn. Buzz, you have to quit cussing like this all the time. Al looked stunning with all her clothes on, but I had to grudgingly admit she was a goddess in just her skin. Well, I thought with nasty satisfaction; at least I got it all over you in the bazoomba department you little home wrecker! Well, not exactly a home wrecker because we didn't have a home, or anything to wreck for that matter, but it was like she now knows my deepest, darkest secret and I was really pissed about that. I wasn't kidding when I said her best friend was none other than Rosie the News Whore. *Shit.*

What if she told Rosie? Or worse, what if she told J.J.? What if J.J. found out in the classifieds next week? Crap, I'll think about that later–back to Al. Maybe I could croak her and dump the body…no, Mom would worry. For some reason she liked Al. But I forgive her because Mom likes everyone.

The flannel shirt hung on Al, but it would work. It didn't matter anyway. *Who would care but Al?* She grabbed up a pair of black sweats and pulled them on. She cranked the waist smaller with the attached strings, yanked the towel off her head, and helped herself to Evo's round brush. I grabbed a couple pair of extra-thick wooly socks, and we were stylin'.

Finished, she looked sideways in the mirror. She patted her hips. "Good thing I have the big ole Miller butt, or these babies would never stay up." She giggled. I sat stunned that my pain in the ass sister even knew *how* to giggle, let alone make fun of her own butt. *I gotta get out of here.*

She tied the flannel above her sweat pants and giggled again. I laughed at her giggle. She laughed because I did. We looked at each other and fell on the bed laughing until it hurt.

The bedroom door swung open and again, Evo, J.J. and Bob stood staring at us as if we were escapees from the cuckoo's nest.

We sat up and I pushed my wispy brown hair out of my eyes. "J.J. Evo. You're back. Bob, hey, how are you?"

"Good, Buzz, good. It's great to see you guys. I almost didn't make it—"

He froze and stared at the bed. I sighed. *Here we go again.*

I heard a muffled, "Bob?" from beside me. Al took about ten pounds of long strawberry blonde curls and whipped them over her shoulder in her best Rita Hayworth impersonation. The men all stared and no one said a word. All three men just stared and swallowed.

Oh hell, someone had better throw some cold water on them, but it wasn't going to be me this time. I got up and re-piled the clothes. "Thanks for the clothes, Evo; you're a lifesaver."

"Uh, er, yeah, okay. Any time."

I squared my shoulders and squeezed out the door. I wasn't quite ready for prime time, so I ducked into Fred's room and flopped into a chair at her vanity. Yes, Fred had a real live old fashioned vanity; complete with an antique brush set and a million little colorful perfume bottles. I sat staring at the woman in the mirror and thought.

J.J. once told me he hung out with me because I was the only girl he knew who wouldn't get crazy on him. He told me I was "comfortable, like family," that he felt safe with me. *Safe! The story of my life. I don't want to be safe, for God's sake. I want to be devastating for once. Sexy.* I looked in the mirror, and what looked back at me? Safe. *Crap.* I sighed. Oh well, at least I was something. I stuck my tongue out at my reflection in the mirror and gave me a razz-berry.

I listened as Al worked her crowd next door; directing all that raw sex at Bob.

I felt a little sad because all signs of Al the giggler were gone, and the cool, arrogant bitch was back, except her hair was a rat's nest and she wore (God forbid) flannel, wool, and no makeup. Even with puffy wool feet, she hid behind the cool princess façade she had worked so many years to perfect. Poor, FBI Bob. He tries so hard to be indifferent. She's going to have him for lunch. I just had to eavesdrop at the door.

"What brings you back, Bob? Come to play with the small town girls again?"

Bob answered, "The viper speaketh. Don't give me that crap, Alexandra; you've never been small town in your life."

"Tell me my sweet." I almost gagged. "Have you spent these weeks I've been away sharpening that nasty tongue of yours?"

"You know, you should wear no makeup more often. It gives you an almost human quality."

I peeked out the door and saw Al's face change in the mirror. I was just in time to see Al suddenly realize she wore flannel and wool, and no war paint.

Damn if I didn't feel sorry for her and ran across the hall to save face. I grabbed Al's hand and yanked her off the bed. We stood side-by-side, shoulders back. Nose in the air, I addressed J.J., Evo, and Bob. "Come, Al, we will away to where we are appreciated for our *inner* beauty."

I shoved Al out before me and glided across the room and struck a pose in the doorway, sliding along the jamb. "Later, dahlings." I slipped out the door. It must have worked because all we could hear as we clattered down the stairs was loud, loud laughter coming from Evo's room. *Figures, Al left them spellbound and I made 'em laugh... Shit.*

206

21

A whirlwind of activity followed the Thanksgiving holiday. Being a consummate traveler, Evo orchestrated an almost hassle-free trip. I was one of the snags when I showed up at the rendezvous carrying two suitcases and wearing a pith helmet with a mosquito net, sunglasses, a tank top, a windbreaker, rain gear, gauntlet gloves, cargo pants, snake boots, and carrying a backpack filled with enough outdoor gear, toilet paper, freeze-dried food and bug spray to take a third world country on a camping trip to the Wisconsin Dells during monsoon season.

Evo explained that wearing a pith helmet for traveling was like wearing a cheese wedge hat to a wedding. Mag wanted to know the problem with either scenario, and I was thankful she wasn't coming, but I did give her the pith helmet. She would be attending Roger Ettleson's wedding next week. One needed a pith helmet around the Ettleson clan when they were drinking, which was most of the time.

Tony helped strip me down to the bare bones, but I wrestled my bug spray away from him and stuck it in a side pocket of my cargo pants. They allowed me a change of underwear and socks, a shirt, raingear, and deodorant. They told me I could bring a comb or a ball cap so after careful consideration, I chose my trusty University of Wisconsin Bucky Badger ball cap. I figured if I got lost in the damn jungle, someone might see my bright red hat, but I could wave my little black comb in the air until the cows came home and twenty years later some researcher would find that comb in petrified alligator poop.

I managed to stash a bunch of Caribou Coffee bars and

some coffee teabags in my duffel bag before the men commandeered the luggage. I didn't want to take too much food because they stole my toilet paper. I smiled to myself because I also managed to steal Mag's iPod. . I secretly stashed it in my other cargo pocket. I walked like I had a full diaper, but I was happy in the knowledge that at least my belly and my brain would be taken care of. I'd worry about the mechanics of the other end later.

Evo evidentially found his pilot sober because Esteban was in great form by the time we boarded. The plane itself was a study in luxury. Seating along the sides of the plane and behind the cockpit were roomy and a soft leather. Air Force One should look so good. Wet bar, food, no dog hair–it made me very nervous.

I settled in the plush seat and shuffled my cargo pockets around until nothing stabbed me in the legs. I dug around for the earphones and slid them into my ears. The sounds of a Strauss waltz danced through my senses. The Dramamine I took must have done its job because I barely noticed the passage of time.

I was rudely awakened by the sound of Led Zeppelin screaming *Black Dog,* and somewhere in my muddled brain I realized Mag's iPod must have changed venues automatically. I wiped the drool off the corner of my mouth and checked my shoulder for any wayward slime. I took stock of my surroundings. Thank God no one had noticed. I missed my dogs. I missed having coffee with my sisters at Sal's Diner. I even missed J.J. I wanted to call my mom to tell her I was still alive and I looked at my watch to see if it was too late to call her. It wasn't even noon yet.

"Oh crap," I said aloud.

"What?" Fred, Evo, and Sam all looked at me.

"What?"

Fred sighed. "Buzz, did you forget something?"

"Yeah, my head; but don't worry, I found it up my butt. What was I thinking by making this trip? You guys are the PhD's. I'm just a dumb ex-flat foot who hates bugs. And here I am, going to the bug capitol of the world to do, what? Haul my happy ass through the rainforest so I can be some anaconda's afternoon snack? I hate snakes worse than bugs. No offense guys, but I hate things that want to kill me, four legged, two legged, or no legged."

"Now, Buzz," Fred said in the condescending *mom* tone I so loathe, "Maybe we'll find you a bad guy to shoot or something. You'll feel much better then. Just take another Dramamine and you'll wake up somewhere over Central America."

"Shut up, Fred. I saw *Romancing the Stone*. I know what it's like down there! Have you ever seen those pictures of the one lane mountain roads in Bolivia? No guard rails! Parts are crumbling off–the road just suddenly isn't there! They cut goat trails on the side of a mountain and expect you to drive on them stuck with Velcro or something!"

"Buzz, you're working yourself up for no reason. Bolivia is not Venezuela. Tell her, Evo."

"Actually, she's correct about the mountain roads in Bolivia–"

Sam jumped out of her seat. "Shut up, Evo, you're not helping." A phone rang and Evo moved to pick it up. Sam came to sit next to me and explained, "We're all in this together, Buzz. We all are going to be slapping the same bugs, and hiking the same trails."

I tried for nonchalance and it came out snotty. "Yeah, but I'm about twenty years older and about an axe handle wider than you, little girl."

A chorus of "Shut up, Buzz." echoed off the fuselage.

I gotta stop trying for nonchalance. "Okay, I'm cool. But I don't see why you brought me along. There's no murder to investigate, and I'll just be in the way."

Evo hung up the phone he and said, "That's where you are wrong, my friend. That was the second in command at Site 151. They just found the foreman, Ron Hansen, with his throat slit and his office ransacked."

22

Evo made several phone calls after that and I began to compile notes from the information he'd gathered from his visit to Site 151. The rest of the trip sped by as we kept busy formulating plans of action.

Upon arrival, we were rushed through customs, hesitating only long enough to get our passports stamped. "Nunez's money at work," Sam whispered snidely.

"Whatever greases our way through this mess, I'll take it," I replied.

"Me too." Fred puffed as we pushed and shoved our way toward the exit and a waiting Limo.

Once inside, we all let out our collective breaths. Evo was the first to recover and said, "It's only a ten minute drive to my place, and Armand," he gestured toward the driver, "Will then take you guys to Sam's. I'll meet you there in the morning."

Sam sighed. "I don't know why you won't just come with us, Evo. I have plenty of room, and it will keep us together. You're already packed."

Evo held up his hands. "Okay, okay, I don't want to argue. Just let me go up and pick up my messages, and I'll come with you." Sam gave him a smug smile, and Evo shook his head.

Armand pulled up to the curb in front of Evo's apartment complex and Sam jumped out with him.

"Hey," he said when Fred piled out after Sam. "I thought you were going to wait down here for me."

"Uh, I want to see where you live," Fred said.

"I'm curious, too. I want to see the royal palace," Sam admitted.

I climbed out of the limo. "I guess I'm coming, too." I bent to the window. Tongue-in-cheek I said, "Hey, Armand, want to come see the rich guy's bachelor pad with us?"

I about dropped my teeth when Armand answered in English, "No thanks, pretty mama; I be chillin' right here with Bob Marley." He plugged headphones into his ears and as the window rose, I saw him close his eyes and bob his head to the music.

I ran to catch up with the others, and we took the glass elevator to the top floor. I opened my mouth to comment on Evo's digs and the words froze in my throat. The doors slowly opened upon the chaotic disaster which used to be Evo's apartment. Other than a collective indrawn breath, the room was eerily silent.

Sam broke the quiet as she laid a hand on Evo's arm. "Oh, my God, Evo. What could have happened?"

"Get Tony on the phone!" Evo went directly to the bedroom safe. The door hung off its hinges and black powder outlined the blast area. Evo rifled through a drawer and came out with a small flashlight. Shining a strange blue light into the empty safe Evo sighed and said, "They didn't get anything."

"What do you mean they didn't get anything? The safe is empty."

"Ah, but that wasn't the real safe. This is the safe where I keep my expired credit cards and money. I also have a couple of knock-off Rolexes, a few warranties for stuff that doesn't belong to me, and a deed to a piece of property under a garbage dump. This safe is for someone who wants to rob me. It looks like the real thing, and by the time they realize there must be more, the cops are crawling all over. Watch and learn ladies; watch and learn…"

Evo shined the blue light into the safe again and I saw a patch of lighter blue on the bottom toward the rear. Evo ripped a strip of something like dull duct tape off the bottom of the safe. He then pulled a card from his pocket and ran it over the uncovered space. We heard a click and a panel dropped out of the wall next to the closet.

Evo shifted so he stood in front of the panel, and pressed his thumb on the pad. A sexy female voice said, "Hello, Dr. Castillo, you're home."

Evo smiled and said, "Hello Ava, it's been too long."

The sexy disembodied voice laughed softly and the panel rose by itself and once again blended in with the woodwork. Suddenly, the closet doorjamb moved toward us and the panel across the back wall swung open. A large steel door lies before us. Evo stepped up to the door and pressed a button. A keypad slid out and he punched in several letters. He then grabbed the wheel on the front of the safe and turned it to the right. With a whoosh of air the huge door swung open.

Evo turned to us wearing a large smile which melted when he saw us staring at him, dumbfounded. "What's wrong?"

I recovered long enough to point at the safe and say, "Uh, er...I uh, what the hell *is* that, Fort Knox?"

"No, just some things I don't want stolen."

"Holy cow," Fred said as we all stepped inside. "Is all this yours?"

"Yes, except the family jewels, they belong to Tony's future wife."

"Tony's wife?"

"Yes, it does not look as if I will marry, so they will go to the next in line."

Being the diplomat I am, I said, "Geez, Evo, you should be embarrassed to be this wealthy. What do you spend it on— other than this place and a new truck in America?"

"Well, this place is paid for, as I own the building, and the rest, I don't get much chance to spend anything because all I do is work."

"Well you're buying lunch tomorrow, that's for sure." We all laughed and it broke the ice. Evo closed up, the police were called, and Evo ended up spending the evening with us anyway. We hung out until the last cop left and the alarm system was repaired. Evo called in some sort of clean-up company to take care of the apartment, and we finally had Armand dive us to Sam's.

It was a tired and subdued group that gathered at Sam's kitchen table after we settled in.

Sam carried mugs of coffee to the table and began the conversation. "Evo, why would someone ransack your home and blow up your safe? What could they possibly expect to find?"

"I've been thinking about nothing else the entire evening." He sipped from his mug. "The police said someone ransacked Ron Hansen's office as well. I can't help thinking the two are linked. The timing is just too coincidental."

I spoke up. "Evo, where are your notes from the interview with Hansen?"

Evo looked at me like I was from Mars. "Notes?"

"Yes, notes, reports, audio tapes–whatever you had at the interview. I've been racking my brain and that interview is the only thing you and Ron had in common other than a trashed place. I think the killers were looking for those notes or information from the interview."

"Then why didn't they trash my–"

"*Office*," we said together. Evo grabbed the phone and called the police again. He told them he had cause to believe someone might try to break into his office.

He hung up the phone. "I gotta go."

"Not without me," I said as I grabbed my jacket.

"Not without me either," echoed Fred.

Sam came running from the direction of the bathroom. "I'm coming too, Castillo!"

Evo's cell rang and he barked a hello into it. He said thanks and hung it up. "Armand heard on his police scanner that they were going to my office and he is headed back here to get us right now." We all grabbed our jackets and Sam turned off the coffee. She locked the front door and Armand came screeching to a halt in front of the house.

"How sweet," Fred said.

Evo sighed. "It's his job, Fred."

"I still think it's sweet."

"I'll tell Armand you said that."

"No, I–"

The passenger window rolled down and he said, "Ready to go?"

Fred opened the front door and climbed in. She looked into Armand's startled eyes and said, "You know, Armand, it's really very sweet of you to come back for us."

Armand had that deer-in-the-headlights look. "Ahhh, I, well, it's kind-of my job, Miss Miller."

"Your job does not include coming back after hours to tote us across town." She patted his knee and I thought he was going to go through the roof.

"Just drive," Evo barked and Armand hit the gas.

Fred didn't let him off the hook, however. "So what's a nice Italian boy from uh, Queens, right?" At Armand's wide-eyed, slow nod she continued. "From Queens doing driving a Limo in Lima, Peru, in South America, listening to Reggae music and a police scanner?"

Armand swallowed. He stared out the windshield and mumbled. "How did you figure that? Man, I thought I had it goin' on with the South American thing." He looked in the mirror. I smiled. Armand winced. Evo rubbed his face and Sam looked perplexed.

Fred just stared at Armand.

Armand gulped. "Evo?"

Evo looked ill. "Can we discuss this later, please?"

Fred narrowed her eyes and leaned closer to Armand.

"No," she said slowly. "I think I want to talk about Armand now."

I thought I had better say something to my big mouthed sister. "Uh, just drop it, Fred. Maybe he's shy."

Evo gave me a grateful look and said, "Uh, yes. Let's talk about our plans once we get downtown."

Fred moved even closer to Armand. "Are you really shy, Armand? Or do you just not want to be the one who tells us you are a cop?"

"A cop," Sam squeaked.

I sighed and agreed. "A cop. A Fed, I'd bet. CIA?"

Armand winced and then sighed. "ATF," and then, "Damn."

Fred's eyes widened and quickly narrowed. "What is Alcohol Tobacco and Firearms doing down here? And why are you driving us around in a Limo?"

I butted in. "If he told us he'd have to kill us. *Right,* Armand?"

"Uh, yeah. Right."

Fred persisted. She inched toward Armand and he began to squirm in earnest. I reached through the divider and grabbed Fred by the hair. I gave it a good yank and was rewarded with a loud screech and her full attention being diverted to the back seat.

I got in her face and said through clenched teeth, "Shut *up,* Fred, and leave him alone. Evo and Armand will tell us what is going on in good time." She opened her mouth and I held up a hand. "*Eh.*" She stopped. "If you want to stay in this limo, if you want to continue on with the grownups, you will cease and desist right now. Do you understand?"

She lowered her head, but I could still see the green smoke coming out of her ears. "Okay," she mumbled, and flopped back on her side of the car. I saw Armand wipe sweat off his forehead and chuckled to myself. *Poor Armand, little Fred is a lethal weapon when she turns on the charm and starts pumping for information.*

Armand drove up to the main entrance of Evo's building and wove his way around the police and emergency vehicles. He stopped as close as he could to the front doors and let us out. The security guard on the door recognized Evo and with some pretty slick fast talk, we headed up to his office.

We exited the elevator and had to step around a garbage can. An officer rushed up and Evo had to do the song-and-dance-routine once again to get us down the hall. The door to Evo's office hung by one hinge, and the hallway was littered with papers and bits of wood and plastic. Evo stepped up to a man taking photos and introduced himself. A South American version of *Colombo*, complete with wrinkled trench coat and cigar (sans the Peter Faulk squint), stepped in front of him.

Running short on sleep and even shorter on temper, Evo barked, "What is it now?" as he tried to see around the cop.

The policeman raised a brow and slowly took the cigar from his mouth. In English he said, "You, Dr. Castillo?"

"Yes. Please, I need to get to my office."

"One moment, Dr. Castillo." He eyed us around the cigar smoke, and held up a badge. I am Inspector Vargas. "Were you aware of anyone in the building earlier this evening, maintenance workers, office personnel, anyone?"

"No, I just flew in from the States. You can check with the airport."

"Yes, I already did. I take it these are your traveling companions."

"Yes. What is this about? Was someone hurt or something?"

"As a matter of fact, two people were killed in a blast in which your office was virtually destroyed. Step over here with me please."

Evo moved to follow the policeman and we all took a step

forward. Vargas halted and held up a hand. "Dr. Castillo only, if you please." We all backed up as one and stood against the wall.

"Someone died I'll bet," Fred whispered.

"Duh," I said.

Just then Evo's voice choked out, "Sam, It's Elena." Sam shoved her way past the many bodies blocking her way and hurried to Evo's side.

She grabbed his arm and he turned to gather her close. We followed in Sam's wake, and moved like a battering ram to where the two of them stood gazing down at a gurney. Peeking around Evo, I could see a sheet drawn back and the mutilated body of a dark haired woman lying beneath.

At Fred's indrawn breath, I shoved her behind me and said, "If you're going to be sick, get the hell out of here."

I could hear her swallow several times. "No, no, I'm okay. Sam may need me. It's just a shock, that's all. This body doesn't look as bad as Carol Graff did when we pulled her out from under Mom's house a couple of months ago, and I promise not to trip and fall on top of this one, okay?"

I almost smiled when I remembered how Fred and Al fell on top of a dead body in Mom's back yard, making everyone including the dogs gag.

Turning my attention back to the present, I asked Evo, "Who is Elena?"

Sam answered, "Evo's secretary. I know her mother. Nice woman."

Stepping closer, I asked the cop, "Does it look like she died in the blast, or has any determination of that nature been established?"

Vargas sent me a shrewd glance and asked, "Law enforcement?"

"Retired."

"Step over here, I would like to show you something."

218

We walked to where the door hung off the hinges. "The evidence has been collected and the pictures taken, but if you would like to walk through with me, I would consider it a favor."

"Of course," I said. *Duh. Like I'm going to pass an opportunity like this up?*

I looked around and tagged the EMS worker for some plastic gloves. I pulled out my camera phone to take some general pictures we could look at later. I immediately saw the origin of the blast, and as I suspected, Evo's safe had been blasted. The lingering odor and the way the door was blown off the safe had me asking, "C-4, remote detonator?"

"You're good."

"Pretty obvious. That was a big blast for such a small safe. They either wanted to make sure destruction of the office was complete, or they weren't as professional as we first thought." I moved to the desk. The overturned chair lay off to the right. I looked at the bottom and examined the armrests. I went to pick it up and asked Vargas, "May I?"

"Of course, we are through here."

I turned the chair over and pulled the leather seat away from the armrest. "Inspector?"

Vargas leaned over my back.

"Do you see here where the armrest meets the seat? It seems there are fibers here that have no connection to the leather or the metal. I think they're rope fibers. Your medical examiner can tell us if Elena had rope burns on her wrists or not." I knew damn well the fibers were rope. They'd be finding a murder victim instead of an accidental death in Elena.

Vargas stared at the remnants of the burned rope. Still bent over, he calmly spoke into his radio. In a matter of seconds, a tech showed up with tweezers and a glass vial. He plucked the fibers from the chair and deposited them into the vial. Vargas stepped forward and whispered in his ear. The tech was shaking in his boots by the time Vargas finished reading him the riot act. He glanced up at me on his way out of the room and said something I didn't understand. As he passed through the office door, he ran into a brick wall. I watched as his feet lifted off the floor and he floated backward into the room on the end of Evo's arm; his scrawny neck stuck in Evo's large hand.

"I think you have something to say to the lady."

The tech choked. "I say nothing. He spit on the floor. "Vargas, call him off!"

Vargas lifted an eyebrow. He sucked on his stogie and let the smoke out slowly. As he contemplated the burning end of his cigar, he said quietly, "I think perhaps not. One, you owe this esteemed lady an apology for degrading her because she knows your job better than you do, and you owe her a thank you for maybe saving this investigation. Two, I haven't decided whether to let Dr. Castillo choke you before I fire you, or vice-versa."

The tech gasped, and his eyes bugged out of his head. Vargas rolled the cigar between his fingers and tapped the ash into an empty garbage can. The tech wheezed and began to turn blue, and I thought I'd better say something quick before we had another body. "Hey, Evo, you'd better put him down because he doesn't look too good. Besides, where are we going to hide the body if you kill him?"

At that, both Evo and Vargas laughed and Evo dropped the tech and watched as he collapsed in a heap. The tech gasped, choked, and did the tuna flop on the floor. His arms flew out to the side, and Evo stood on his palm so he couldn't slither out of reach.

The tech made a sorry sight and swallowed hard. "I sorry, American lady, so sorry. I did not know you a police woman and I am *stupido*."

"That's alright, young man, thank you," I said before

anyone did him more bodily harm. "Let him up, Evo. We have bigger fish to fry. Inspector Vargas, thank you so much for allowing us into your crime scene." I all but yanked Evo out of the room and back into the hall.

I hustled him past Sam and Fred and began to pull off the latex gloves. "Let's get out of here, I've seen enough–oh, crap." I suddenly put on the brakes. Fred and Sam ran into me. I stumbled forward and because my head was down, I ran into a wall. Feeling a little woozy, I backed away and searched for what stopped me. *Ah, there it is.* With the gloved hand I picked up what appeared to be a severed finger. Turning the glove inside-out when I took it off, I tucked it into the tech's hand whispering, "The other person in the room. Elena had all her fingers. This one probably belonged to the bomber."

I turned back toward my sister and friends and said, "Let's get out of here."

We turned tail and bolted.

23

After leaving Evo's office, Armand took us straight to the airport. Our bags were already loaded and we took off for Venezuela. A Land Rover awaited us at the other end, and we loaded our gear. There were several places to stay, and I registered as a vacationer in Cumanná at a large chain hotel. We'd caught about two hours of sleep before my phone rang for a wake-up call. Evo was already up and had bags full of food-like substances when I dragged my jet-lagged butt down the stairs.

Fred laughed when she saw me. "How can you be jet-lagged when we went from Lima to Venezuela?"

"Shut up, Fred. Give me coffee."

Fred snickered and said in a stage whisper, "Rule Number One, never try to converse with Buzz before morning coffee." After Sam and Evo gave her an odd look, Fred said behind her hand, "She has a drinking problem and an addiction."

Okay, I admit it; I might have been a little cranky from lack of sleep, food deprivation, lack of caffeine, and respect at this point, but I was not about to take crap from Suzie Snowflake over there. She stood between me and my first cup of coffee, and I wanted to say, *"Feel lucky, punk?"* before I shot her.

I bulldozed my way right through Fred's smirking countenance, looking like Mike Singletary going for the opposing quarterback unabated. I grabbed a cup of thick steaming coffee out of Evo's hand and plopped down in a lounger to savor the moment. "Ahh, Heaven," I said and sighed. The aroma alone would have knocked your socks off.

When I came up for air, I stared at the group who stared at

me. With my nose arrogantly pointed skyward, I held up my cup. "My drinking habit is coffee, and my drug of choice is caffeine."

The looks on Evo and Sam's faces were priceless as they sagged in relief, and Fred grabbed her middle and laughed like a fool. "Bozo," I said into my cup as I sucked down more life-blood.

Funny how I needed only one cup to feel human again, but back home I'd have already been through a half-a-pot. I stood and refilled my cup. Turning to my two *amigos* (plus Bozo the Sister), I cleared my throat. "Is the tour bus ready?"

Armand joined us wearing a Hawaiian shirt and a Red Sox ball cap, flowered shorts, and Roman sandals. "Jungle tour, this way." He pointed to the Land Rover parked outside the entrance, sporting an *Armand's Jungle Tours* magnetic sign on the door.

I patted my cargo pocket to make sure I still had my bug spray and climbed in beside Armand. He looked a little disappointed and I patted his arm. "We decided that Fred has to sit in the back this time. We don't want you to drive off a mountain or anything."

"Oh yeah," he said. "Uh, probably a good idea." Turning a deep shade of red, Armand kicked the SUV into gear and it gave us all whiplash as he tore away from the curb.

We decided we would begin at Site 151, and work our way up the mountain. The gates were locked, but Evo's master key got us in. There was a filthy Jeep parked by Ron Hansen's office, and Armand pulled quietly up to the other side of the building. We all got out and I eyeballed Sam and Fred. "You stay."

"No way!"

"I'm coming, too!"

"Shut up, both of you, and listen. Fred, you get behind the wheel in case we have to get out of here fast. Sam, you face backward so you can watch her back. I have a feeling this might not go as smoothly as we had hoped."

"Oh, oh, I get it. You have one of your feelings, Buzz. I am not moving a muscle, and neither are you, Sam."

Evo raised a brow. "That went better than expected."

Fred had a grip on the wheel and a hand on the key. "*Never* blow off any *feeling* Buzz gets. If she has a feeling something bad is going to happen, watch your butt because it is definitely going to happen. Remember fire ant city? Be careful, you guys."

Armand came around the back of the SUV. "Here," he said as he shoved a 9mm into my hand.

I checked the clip and turned to see him give an AK47 to Evo. I looked at my hand gun and decided it was a good time to whine. "How come Evo gets a cool gun and I get a pea shooter?"

Evo ruffled my hair and my eyes stung thinking about J.J. "Because I'm trained in warfare and you're an ex-cop."

"Oh." I looked at my weapon and sighed. *Damn, I hate it when they're right.* I chucked a shell into the chamber and nodded. Armand led point, then me, and Evo brought up the rear as we approached the foreman's office. By silent agreement, we entered through the back door, hoping to avoid a shoot-out as well as scare the crap out of whoever was in there into running away without trying to kill us.

Armand halted and reached for the door knob. It turned, and Armand signaled that it was open. My feeling of uneasiness increased as the door opened and Armand snuck a peek low and around the corner. He signaled with a nod and I came in high. Evo brought up the rear, crouched and facing backward. When Armand stopped I touched Evo's belt. He stopped, but kept an eye on the back door. We were in a kitchenette which subbed as a sleeping area. It held a small fridge, a stove, a cot, and a sink. Cabinets without doors lined one wall, and a miniscule bathroom next to Evo. I suddenly had the urge to go–bad.

"Must have been all that coffee," I mumbled to myself.

"Why, do you have to pee?" Great timing detective," Evo whispered. "Didn't your mama teach you to go before you went out to play?"

"You picked a fine time to become a comedian."

"Shh," Armand said.

Then we heard it. A soft scraping against the wood floors from the other room. A shadow crossed the doorway in front of us and Armand moved like a whisper on the wind. He took one side of the doorway and Evo and I had the other. Armand pointed in the direction he looked and held up his index finger. In the direction Evo and I were facing no one visible, so I held up a fist.

Armand whipped around the corner and yelled, "ATF! Drop to the floor!"

Evo and I came around the corner just in time to watch a white guy in a pith helmet dive through a front window. Armand rushed to the window in time to see the guy jump into a running vehicle. He peeled off a few hundred rounds from his assault rifle in our direction as the car sped away.

Armand turned to us and said, "Well, that was a useless endeavor. Let's see if he left anything worthwhile." We began to look around the ransacked office.

Evo took the kitchen and I took the desk. Opening each drawer and glancing over company paperwork didn't shed any light on who the guys were and what they were doing here. From the looks of the office, they trashed it in search of something. We could only hope they didn't find it. I flopped in Ron Hansen's chair and looked around. I rested my hands on the backs of the arm rests and they suddenly flew forward. I ran my fingers underneath and found an indentation. Sliding it forward, the bottom of the right armrest shot forward to reveal a compartment. In it, a folded paper popped up and in a sing-song voice I chirped, "Look-ee what I found."

The sweet feeling of discovery suffused my body and a little tingle raced up my spine. I pulled plastic gloves from my cargo pants and carefully extracted the papers from the armrest. "Think this might have been what they were after?"

The roar of an engine answered my question as Armand yelled, "Oh crap, they're back. Get out! Go, go, *go*!"

Bullets riddled the desk and I dove to the floor with a thud. "I think they brought their friends." I checked the magazine on my weapon and risked a peek around the desk. Armand returned fire from a window, but Evo lie on the floor by the bathroom. I felt my blood drain down to my feet as I took in the dark puddle pooling next to his body. "Bloody hell, Armand, Evo's down!"

"Throw me his weapon!" Armand's voice barely carried over the noise of the ricocheting bullets. I watched Lassie enough as a kid, and between that and police training, I knew how to crawl under gunfire.

Using my elbows to inch across the floor, I made it to Evo's side and kicked his weapon toward Armand. He scooped it up in one hand, flipped the strap around his huge forearm, and began firing with both hands. Flipping Evo over I muttered, "Thank God we have Rambo along for the ride."

Between bursts of gunfire, Armand yelled, "Get him out, and get ready to move."

Now, I'm by no means a petite miss, but Evo is a very large man. With bullets spraying over head, and smoke beginning to fill the rooms, my options were becoming more limited by the second. Looking around desperately, I remembered the bathroom. I Lassie-crawled to the door and jumped inside. I ripped the shower curtain from the rod and prayed it would hold. Inching back toward Evo, I saw his eyes, not open, but at least fluttering.

"Hold still, pal." I spread the curtain from his shoulders down to his feet, and rolled him onto his side. He grunted, but didn't move. I stuffed the curtain under his body as far as I could and rolled him back over. It was then I saw the blood seeping from a wound by the AC joint of his left shoulder. Ripping off the bandana I had around my neck, I stuffed it under his T-shirt. I took his right hand and pressed it to the wound. "Hold that." He winced and grunted, but obeyed.

I grabbed the shower curtain and inched backward toward the rear door. Nothing can prepare one for dragging the dead weight of a six-foot-three, solidly muscled man. I might as well have been dragging a Mack Truck. Step, yank, inch. Step, yank. The fire play continued from the other room, and I feared it wouldn't be much longer before they burst through the front, or made their way around to the back.

I was about half-way through the kitchen and puffing like a steam engine when manic footfalls, stumbling, and shouting sounded behind me. In a split second, I recognized Fred's graceful entrance and heard Sam let out a screech. "Evo!"

"Help." I gasped for air and the two of them moved like they were shot out of a cannon. Sam had one side of the curtain and Fred grabbed Evo's good arm. We yanked, and tugged, and finally wrestled him around the corner and out the door.

We got him to the Land Rover and Fred opened the rear door. Standing bent over and sucking in air, I said, "We can't pick him up, so we'll have to get him in the car in increments. Head and shoulders first since they're heaviest."

Running around to the opposite side, Fred got into the SUV. I ran the curtain under Evo's armpits, which made him howl like a wounded bear. Sam and I heaved, lifted, and shoved him through the door. Fred grabbed him by the T-shirt and shower curtain and pulled with all she had. We were still doing the heave-ho thing when Armand burst through the back door.

"What the hell?" He stuffed his weapons in my hand and lifted Evo's butt in the air. It's a good thing Fred had closed the other door or she and Evo would have flown out the other side of the SUV. As it was, Evo's body sprawled across Fred, and Sam kicked his legs off the seat and jumped in beside him.

Armand snatched back the weapons and jumped in the passenger's seat. "You drive," he yelled at me. I slammed the Land Rover in reverse and spun the tires in the dirt. Armand shoved an AK47 in Sam's hands and yelled, "Point and shoot." He grabbed a hand and slammed it on top of the weapon. "Hand stays here—it'll climb up on you. Spray it back and forth if you can!" He looked over at me. *"Drive, Drive!"*

I slammed the SUV in gear and tromped on the accelerator. The tires sprayed dirt and rocks all over the building, just as some bad guys burst out the back door. Caught momentarily by surprise, they held up a hand to protect their faces from the flying rocks. That's all the opening Armand needed. He let fly with his automatic weapon, which kick started Sam. I looked in the mirror just in time to see her grit her teeth and take a deep breath. She popped up behind the luggage like a pro and let fly a barrage of gunfire over the heads of the hapless bad guys.

"Lower," Armand yelled as he turned forward. In the side view mirror I saw the three men at the door drop, and I saw Sam spin around and bite on a knuckle. Tears spilled over her cheeks as she brushed a lock of hair off Evo's forehead. Fred had her head down and her hand pressed to the bandana.

I peeled around the corner of the building on two tires and the men at the front of the building turned to shoot. Armand picked off three of them like ducks at a shooting gallery, and Sam caught another running from the building. I roared out of parking lot and yelled for everyone to hold on. I had to make one more pass across the entrance to the building, and spun the Land Rover in a donut that would have made my old Evasive

Driver Training Sergeant smile. I spun the wheel and the Rover barely fishtailed as it bolted forward. One lone man ran madly from the front door, and there was barely recognition in his eyes before Armand popped him. I veered away from the building and headed toward the front gate. A couple more guys ran from the building and jumped into a Jeep. I tore across the parking lot and sped through the compound.

I didn't remember so much equipment being in the way on our way in, and had to weave around the land movers, derricks, piles of sludge pipes, forklifts, and a sundry of other oil drilling stuff which I had no clue of their purpose. The Jeep stayed back, firing half-heartedly at the back of the Rover. Damn, they will probably shoot holes in my underwear. I heard a pop and a hiss. Damn, there goes my spare bug spray. Now if they shoot holes in my underwear, I won't have to worry about the biting mosquitoes, because my underwear will be covered in repellent.

Finally, the gate came into view. I fully expected a full complement of artillery, but unless they had a battalion hiding in the jungle, one lone guy with a big smile on his face was the only person on the gate. Armand hesitated a second, and the man on the gate brought a rocket launcher to his shoulder.

"*Oh, shit*. The guy took aim on the Rover. I cranked the wheel right and shot down a side road. The rocket launcher went off as we made it to the end of the road, and I cranked the wheel to the left again. We all screamed as I took another right. The Rover went up on two wheels again and banged off a stack of long pipes. The strap snapped and the pipes rolled into the road behind us just as the Jeep following us came around the corner.

Consecutive blasts shook the earth as the Jeep ran into the pile of pipes and the rocket ran into the Jeep. The explosion sent a fireball into the sky and bite sized pieces of metal and men raining down on the compound. I skidded around another corner and once again found myself bearing down on the gateman. He seemed surprised to see us, and reached forward to grab something. I calmly lifted my left hand and fired. I smiled as the bullet went through the top of his skull. *You still got it, kid.* We tore past his slumped body, through the gate, and up the jungle path.

I glanced sideways at Armand, to see his mouth hanging open as he stared at me. "Wow. *That* was like the sexiest thing I ever saw. Will you marry me?"

In the aftermath of the near-death adrenalin rush, I found that statement particularly funny, and laughed. Now I don't mean the tee-hee titters. I mean belly-laugh-had-to-stop-the-Land Rover or drive into a palm tree guffaws. Tears ran down my face and I held my side. Fred started laughing and even Sam guffawed. Armand looked at us like we'd come from outer space, and gave it up to have a good chuckle himself.

"Oh, Armand, you are so fickle. You wanted to run off with my sister earlier and now you want to marry me because...why?"

"Man, I haven't seen anyone drive and shoot like that in my life, only in the movies and they weren't women."

I got myself under control and found a place in the shade where we could doctor Evo. I pulled off the path and noticed that Sam had her make-up kit out and rifled through it. Armand jumped out of the rover and brought a first aid kit, the likes I've never seen before. It opened like a tackle box, but also had drawers in the side. He pulled out sterile bundles complete with autoclave tape and set up on a portable stand. We set up a cot and helped Armand move Evo to it. It looked like a mini surgical ward in the middle of the jungle.

In comparison, Sam looked kind of dumb standing by the Land Rover holding her eyebrow tweezers. Briskly, she said, "Uh, I'll take it from here," and shoved the tweezers in her pocket.

Fred careened around the side of the vehicle with a fifth of Jamison's she had stashed for a celebration and a first aid kit we packed before we left the states. If it wasn't so absurd, it would have been funny. We all looked down on Evo's ashen face and each of us wondered if he was going to make it through the next hour.

24

Sam took the Irish whiskey from Fred. Armand split Evo's shirt up the middle. He cut the sleeves and eased the armholes to the side. Sam took a healthy swig of the whiskey. "His breathing is shallow." She felt his pulse. "Heart is strong and steady though." She took another swig and handed the bottle to Fred.

Armand stepped forward. "I can take it from here, ladies."

Sam stepped nose to nose with him. "Ah, no you don't. I have it covered. You can help hold him down. Let me see what you have in your trusty toolkit."

She pushed past him and knelt before the box. "Oh look! Lidocaine. Evo, my dear, you are in luck."

Sam laid out a syringe and bottle. She washed her hands in alcohol and dried them with gauze. She opened the sterile pack and perused its contents. Gloves on, she strung catgut through a needle and made a spare. The scalpel lay next to the forceps. Gauze sponges were piled on the end of her *table*. All looked ready, and she pulled on another pair of sterile gloves.

"Okay," she sighed. "I'm set." She picked up the bottle of Lidocaine and pulled the numbing agent into the syringe. Carefully pulling the bandana away from the wound, she inspected the jagged edges. Starting at the top of the wound; she worked her way around the site. Next, she poured green soap on a sponge and swabbed out the wound, using bottled water to irrigate. Fred turned green as the blood oozed forth and quietly turned to throw up among the ferns.

Armand pulled a magnifier from somewhere and held it close to the wound. With the forceps Sam poked around inside and pulled out a couple of wood splinters and a bullet. The blood flowed freely now and Sam cleansed and irrigated the wound one more time. Evo was with us now as Sam worked to sew him up. He watched her intently as she worked and occasionally winced when she hit a tender spot. When she finished, she covered the tidy row of black stitches with gauze and tape. Sam picked up the scalpel and tapped it against her other palm. "Now all I have to do is carve my initials in and I'm done."

"S-s-s-sam," Evo groaned. "Not f-f-f-funny."

"Don't be a baby, I'm kidding," she said, and kissed his forehead. "Lie still and don't open your wound."

She turned to clean up and his eyes followed her movements. Armand distracted him by stuffing a couple of pills in his mouth and gave him a bottle of water to chase them down. He helped Evo to sit and after his head stopped spinning he took the pills. "What were those?"

"Just a couple of 'Oxies'. It'll take away the worst of it for now, but they may knock a rookie like you out for a couple of hours."

Evo gave him a crooked smile. "Then you'd better get me back into the Rover, because I really am a baby with pain drugs."

Sam stepped up, took the water bottle, and shoved it back toward Evo. "Okay, but drink more water before you go bed-ee-bye, big boy. You need to hydrate."

"Yes, ma'am," he said and slowly leaned forward until his head rested against her chest. Her arms automatically circled his good shoulder and stroked the back of his neck.

Evo opened an eye and winked in my direction. I smiled. He waggled his eyebrows and snuggled into Sam. Armand spoiled the moment by banging the table back into place on the back of the Rover. "Okay, boys and girls, let's get a move on before the bad guys find us."

Sam disengaged herself and helped Evo into the Rover.

Fred sat on his bad side and Sam on his good. Evo slipped an arm around Sam and pretended to fall asleep. He leaned over her and crammed her arm against him until she had to slip it around him to keep him from smothering her. He fell asleep with a small smile on his lips.

I bumped along the primitive road until the village came into view. Carbon based objects decayed quickly in the rainforest and except for a couple of piles of feathers and hair, there were no signs of dead animals. I drove past the church and further up the mountain. The road narrowed until it disappeared.

I pulled off to the side as far as I dared and looked at Armand. "Don't tell me, we walk from here?"

"Yep."

"What about Evo?" Sam looked concerned. "Do we just leave him here?"

"Yep."

Fred climbed out of the Rover "We can't do that. Shouldn't Sam stay with him?"

"Yep."

"Good," I said. "Fred, you should probably stay too, don't you agree, Armand?"

"Yep." He hefted a backpack out of the Rover and onto his back. He handed me Evo's backpack and turned back to the track leading up the mountain. I guessed I wasn't going to stay at the Rover with Evo and the girls.

Walking at a brisk pace, he disappeared quickly into the undergrowth. We all stared after him. I struggled with the straps to the backpack and told Fred, "If Armand doesn't kill me with the pace, I'll see you when we get back. Call J.J. on Evo's satellite phone and tell him what's going on."

"Okay." She hugged me close. "Take care, Buzz. Watch out for those anacondas."

"Thanks, Bitch." We both laughed and I started off after

234

Armand.

The trek through the jungle was slow going and uphill all the way. We followed a trail of sorts, but it must have been an old one because the jungle had taken back most of it. We'd walked about forty minutes when Armand stopped and jumped off trail. I followed and tumbled to my knees, breathing hard. "Did you hear that?"

At first all I heard was the quiet. Then I realized it was the first time since we set out that it really *was* quiet. No rustle, squeak, shriek, or rumble could be heard. I adjusted my focus and heard a low and continuous rumble in the far distance. Not the rumble of an animal, but of a diesel engine. The mosquitoes began a Buzz-fest on the back of my neck, and I scrambled for the spare repellant. Armand started to gag from the fumes and moved back onto the trail.

Fifteen more minutes of walking brought us to a clear-cut area filled with mounds of mud, rock, logs, and other debris. Mud was everywhere. The men working in the yard were covered with it. Off to the left was a holding pond of some sort, and Armand took off in that direction. I stumbled after him and saw a massive pile of rubble ahead. A huge machine stood off to one side and pummeled the pile of rock with jets of water. The water ran off the pile and into a holding pond.

I lifted my camera phone to take pictures and Armand whispered, "We need to get closer. I have to get a sample of that water. The testing equipment is in your backpack." He backed us into the jungle and dropped his pack. He had to take mine off because I couldn't bend that way anymore.

"Stay here. If I'm caught, get back to civilization as fast as you can." He unzipped Evo's backpack and I was happy to find a real digital camera on top. I snatched it up and uncapped it.

Armand slipped into the jungle and as the vegetation closed behind him, I suddenly felt very alone. A shiver ran up my spine, and my throat tightened. I could feel myself hyperventilating. I recognized the beginnings of a panic attack and forced myself to slow my breathing. Thinking of anacondas, I knelt on the damp earth and closed my eyes. Breathe two, three, four, out two, three, four. Breathe, two, three, four, out… Suddenly, at the edge of the jungle a large man carrying a machine gun strolled past less than ten feet in front of me. I watched as he hesitated a few steps beyond my position. I raised my hands, ready to shoot when I realized he'd stopped to light a cigarette. He moved silently away, and I let out the breath I had been holding.

Thinking of how close I came to killing the man made me start hyperventilating again. *Focus, Buzz.* I choked my panic down and took another steadying breath. *Snap out of it, Miller.* I took a swig of water and wished for the whiskey we'd left back at the Rover. Hefting the backpack, I moved in the opposite direction Armand had gone, and eventually came to what I figured must be the front door. I knew a mining operation when I saw one and knew this must be the *Devil's Eye*. I zoomed in on the entrance and snapped picture after picture. I moved as close as I dared to the main road and wondered why the heck I slogged through the jungle when there was the equivalent of a two lane highway leading away from the entrance down this side of the mountain. The camera clicked and clicked as I took pictures of the operation, the road, and the license plates of every vehicle I saw.

Sliding in place behind some earth-moving equipment, I got a better view of the main road. Mammoth tractors piggybacking multiple trailers chugged down the mountain as empty ones arrived. Men in hard hats came out of an office trailer across the road and I snapped their pictures, too.

Figuring I'd better get back before someone spotted me, I retraced my steps through the jungle and after checking the area for snakes and carnivores, I settled in to wait for Armand. Time passed slowly and I moved a little closer to the cleared area so I could watch the operation.

My knee felt wet and I pawed through the vegetation to see on what I had knelt. A small trickle of water made its way past where I sat. I walked a couple of yards down the mountain and dug to the ground. More water. I contemplated the significance of the trickling when I heard movement to my left. Silently drawing my weapon, I crouched at the ready.

"Buzz."

"Yep. Ready?"

"Let's get out of here."

"I'm right behind you, Armand."

We slipped and slid down the mountain toward the Rover. Twice we stopped because we heard noises, but Armand let it pass and we continued downhill. No wonder I'd thought death inevitable on the way up. That was a steep hike.

Nearing the spot where the Land Rover should have been, I thought I heard music. *What the hell was Fred up to now?* Armand signaled me to stop. We listened to Queen singing "Fat Bottom Girls" and Armand gestured that we circle the site going in opposite directions.

I drew my weapon and moved off to my left. I looked behind me, but Armand had already disappeared into the foliage. I couldn't stop myself from moving closer to the Land Rover, and I had gone about fifty feet when I reached a break in the vegetation.

What I saw turned my blood to ice. Evo sat slumped, half out of the Land Rover. A man dressed in fatigues and carrying a machine gun sat on the hood of the vehicle, smoking a cigarette and watching the path Armand and I took up the mountain. A clone of the man on the hood had Sam backed against the passenger side door. He held a long pointed knife at her throat, speaking softly. Queen blared from a portable boom box in the vehicle and Fred danced with a third man on the same side of the Rover. I thought that odd until I saw that he held a revolver pointed at her middle. A fourth guy sat in the driver's seat smoking a cigarette.

I didn't breathe. I had a death grip on my gun. Sweat poured off me as I crouched, ready to spring the second the guerilla turned his back to me. I was so intent on the scene before me Armand walked right up and slid a hand over my mouth. Good thing he did, because I have to admit, he scared the crap out of me. I squeaked and jumped as Armand pulled me to the ground.

"Don't lose it now, kid," he whispered in my ear.

"My sister."

Armand pulled me back into the jungle and we settled down about twenty feet in. "Look," he began. "Fred can hold her own—believe me, I was caught under her spell when you first arrived, remember? Thank God she's on our side or the U.S. would be in trouble. Old boy won't stand a chance unless they run out of music."

I took in a long, slow breath. "Okay. What do you want me to do?"

"That's my girl."

"Don't be patronizing, pal."

"Sorry. First we see if we can sit them out. Sooner or later someone is going to pee or look through our luggage or something. As soon as they split, we take them out. If I can lure one into the jungle, I can get him with no gunfire. If we have to shoot, we'll draw attention from those guys up the mountain. I'll get Evo, which means you'll have to drive like hell down this mountain. Can you do it?"

"Yes."

"Okay, let's split up."

I nodded. "I want to move toward the passenger's side so I can squeeze off a good shot on Fred Astaire over there."

"Good. Walk no further than the front of the Rover. We don't want to create crossfire. I'll go no further than this side of the back. Wait for the scuffle; that will be my signal."

I nodded and we separated. And I waited...and waited. The guy with the knife continued to tease Sam. Fred was getting tired, Evo looked dead, and the guy on the hood kept dozing off. *Enough of this bullshit. Where the hell did Armand go, anyway?* I sat there as my butt grew numb thinking that even if something happened, I'd be too crippled up to do anything. I was about to shift my position when I spotted a tarantula the size of Cincinnati crawling across my boot. *Anaconda. Worse than anaconda, fucking Godzilla the spider! Shoo spider, go home now.* He didn't move, but I saw his eight little eyeballs staring malevolently at me. I began to hyperventilate. I waved my gun over its head trying to scare it back to Spider hell. Apparently, Mr. Tarantula hadn't seen that movie because the gun didn't faze him a bit. I flapped my hands at it. I blew in its direction. I wiggled my foot, but it only made him climb toward my leg. *Oh No! Here he comes! Woman Eaten By Giant Tarantula. Details at Ten.* I shook all over, I felt sweat run like water down my back, and reached blindly for a stick to poke him. I must have been noisier than I thought because a booted foot stepped on my groping hand. I heard a click and felt the cold steel of a gun barrel as it rested gently against my temple.

"Oops."

"Oops is correct *senorita*, now move slowly to the car."

"Er, sir, if could you please get King Kong the tarantula off my leg, I would walk on my hands to the car."

"Is the *senorita* afraid of the little spider?" I felt him shift and heard a sound like a softball slapping into a catcher's mitt as he punted the tarantula, and saw a large hairy brown body sail over my head and land somewhere down the trail. I felt giddy and queasy at the same time, but scrambled to my feet, shaking like a hound dog pooping peach pits. I took a couple of deep breaths and focused instead on the rather smelly little man who wanted to kill me.

I realized the man hadn't seen the gun in my right hand while I flopped around on the ground, as it was buried in vegetation. I must have been really preoccupied with the tarantula not to hear him approach me. Even if I didn't hear him, I should have smelled him coming. He was as ripe as an old garbage dump, and I had to choke back to keep from gagging. He smiled and grabbed my left arm. He tried to pull me forward so he could position himself to shove me from behind.

I staggered to my feet; leaning heavily on Mr. Smelly's arm. While he supported most of my weight, I swung my right hand up and shoved my gun into his ribs. "Thanks for getting rid of the spider, pal."

His eyes grew huge as I ducked and pulled the trigger.

As soon as the gun went off I was already crouched and moving toward the back of the vehicle. More shots echoed out. I took advantage of the distraction, popped up, and fired a shot at Fred's dancing partner. He flew backward, slamming against the SUV and slithered to the ground. Fred dove under the Land Rover.

Breathing hard and scrambling, I kept my eye on the guy who now held Sam by the hair. He dragged her down and slammed her hair in the door of the Rover. Sam couldn't reach far enough to free her hair, so she crouched near the ground to stay out of gunshot range. *Where the hell is Armand?* With only one guy left, I moved back toward my original position and saw Fred with the boom box in her hand, creeping up on the idiot who held Sam captive.

With one eye on the guy on the ground and one eye on the guy who'd jumped out of the driver's seat, I moved closer to the guy holding Sam by the hair. I slithered out of the jungle and Lassie-crawled on my elbows (I was getting really good at crawling) toward the front of the truck.

I raised my weapon just as Fred brought the boom box down on the smoking guy. I grabbed the hanging cord off the radio and ripped the other end out of the cigarette lighter. I rolled over to the bad guy and grabbed his hands. I tied him up all nice and tight and signaled Fred to give me her belt. She thought I meant take off her pants and refused. I ripped the guy's belt out of the loops and shackled his legs to the electric winch on the front of the Rover.

By mutual consent, Fred crawled into the front of the Rover and came up behind Sam. I pointed to the boom box still clutched in Fred's hand and to the guy who held Sam. I circled back into the jungle and made a lot of noise as I grabbed vegetation and hid my gun. When I came out directly in front of the hair puller, his attention focused squarely on me. I stumbled into the clearing carrying palm fronds and small flowers. "Hey guys, look what I found! Palm trees and orchids and *oooh,* Sam, did you find yourself one of them South American hotties? Well let's break out the party music before we go back to town. I'll do a little hula with my palm fronds."

I danced away and swayed the fronds back and forth. The bad guy was so stunned he stood frozen and focused. While I did the fat butt rumba, Fred slowly moved across the front seats and opened the door enough to free Sam's hair. She then moved up behind knife boy and lifted the boom box high. The bad guy had just gotten to the "Who the hell are you and what the hell are you doing?" part, when slugger Freddie hauled back and cracked his head open with the boom box. He dropped like a stone and I wasn't sure if the odd expression on his face came from being caught unaware, or reaction to a middle-aged American prancing through the jungle wearing palm fronds. Sam skittered around collecting weapons of all kinds and I tied the last guy up.

Sam checked on the guy I'd shot. "Uh, Buzz? You did a nice job of trussing this guy up, but I think Fred can have her belt back."

I turned toward her. "What do you mean? Oh." The guy had a bullet hole in the middle of his forehead. "Oops."

I checked on Evo. "Thank God those Oxycontins worked on him like that, or he would have messed up the whole works; bullet hole or not."

I let out a breath and peered into the dense jungle. "But I still have one question, what in Sam Hill happened to Armand?"

25

Fred furrowed her brow and her nose wrinkled. "Yeah, where is dear old Armand anyway? Wasn't he with you? Did you lose him or did he chicken out? Don't tell me we have to go into the jungle and look for his sorry butt now." She was still shaking and stuffed her hands in her pockets.

Sam's eyes grew big. "What if the bad guys got him? Won't we have to rescue him or something?"

I grunted as I tied a granny knot on my makeshift shackles. "No way in hell I'm going back up that mountain! He has to be somewhere near because we came down together. I wonder if the bad guys got him. If we can't find him, that boy is on his own until we can get a hold of the Feds. We need to get Evo out of here, and we need Armand's backpack with all the water samples, so let's make a quick perimeter search where he told me he'd be."

Sam tied her hair up on top of her head. She grabbed my lucky Bucky Badger baseball cap from the Rover and stuffed it on top of the pile. "You don't think he's been captured or something, do you, Buzz?"

"No, I don't. There were only four guys. Boy, I hope he's not hurt. He was supposed to be the hero and save the day, and I can't think of a thing that would have changed his mind. In all seriousness though, we need to find him, so grab what weapons you can carry and put a gun in Evo's good hand. Let's try to camouflage him a little so he's not such easy pickings."

We did what we could with Evo and the three of us met for a final briefing. I explained how Armand and I came through the jungle and how we saw them before we were caught. "Armand and I made a pact to stay around ten feet inside the jungle and never go in back or front of the Rover. So," I spread my arms wide, "He has to be within the length of the vehicle in the jungle. Let's go as a group so no one gets shot or lost, okay?" Fred and Sam both nodded.

We slipped back into the jungle with Fred closest to the vehicle so one of us had an eye on Evo at all times. We'd gone about half way down the length of the Rover and a shiver ran up my spine. The three of us stopped, and something told me to look up.

Upside down and hanging by one foot, hung our Italian-American limo driver-cum-ATF Agent Armand Spaghettios or whatever his name. Arms folded, swinging in the breeze, he seemed in good spirits, despite his unfortunate predicament. At least he wasn't dead–yet.

Armand smiled widely and spread his arms wide as he swung gently back and forth. "Ah, what lights from yonder palm tree? Why, 'tis a bee. Or is it just the Buzz?" He eyeballed our un-amused expressions. "*Hmm*, or maybe 'tis just the sting?"

Hands on my hips, I stared back. "Har-har, Mr. Hero. You cut up pretty good for a man hanging upside down. You're lucky some hungry anaconda or South American guerrilla didn't find your Italian badass."

He narrowed his eyes. "Could you find it in your hearts, fair ladies, to cut me down, please?"

"I guess so, Shakespeare." I looked at Sam and Fred. "Fair Ladies? What do you think? Should we cut him down so I can shoot him or should we leave him as tarantula fodder?" Sam and Fred looked at each other and nodded. They turned to me and made snipping gestures with their fingers.

We pulled Armand down by the arms until we could reach his feet. Fred and I held him while Sam sawed at the rope. When the rope broke, Armand came loose like a whip shot. He sent us all sprawling into a heap. Bruised and breathing hard. I was not amused. "Dammit, Armand," I choked as I tried to shove him off me. "You're supposed to be the professional here. You were supposed to save the day. I thought you walked off or something worse!"

"*Ahhh, ow*. He cracked his elbow on a rock trying to stand up. His knees looked watery and he had no feeling in his legs. He stumbled and Fred caught hold of him. "No, I've just been hangin' around here since I left you. I figured if I called out, they'd hear me and we'd both be dead." He wobbled where he stood. "I take it you got them?"

"I nailed two of them with a boom box," Fred said.

I nodded. "We even left one alive, I think."

Armand stumbled forward. "Good. Let's get out of this God-forsaken hell hole. We half dragged Armand back to the Rover, and had to bend his legs to get him into the vehicle.

Evo was awake, but groggy when we returned. That could have been because our prisoner was trying to hoist Evo onto his back so he could carry him away. Evo grunted as the bad man jostled his injured shoulder.

Fred looked at the guy and then at the Rover. She looked at me and said, "How do you suppose he got loose from the winch, I wonder?"

Sam yelled, "Who cares, let's get Evo."

We ran to the opposite side of the Land Rover where the still partially tied up little bad guy struggled to balance Evo across his shoulders. We watched him waver and sag beneath Evo's large frame.

I stopped dead and laughed. "Consider this equation," I said. "Man, five-feet-one-inch and 100 pounds soaking wet, hoists dead weight of six-foot-three, two hundred and thirty pounds. How many feet can five-feet-one-inch travel, and at what speed?" I began to hum the *Jeopardy!* tune.

We finally took pity on the little man and the three of us lifted Evo off him and maneuvered him back into the Rover.

Armand clipped the bad guy on the chin and strapped him and one other to the luggage rack. We all clambered into the Rover and took off the way we'd come.

At the crossroad leading to the lagoon or Site 151, I stopped the Rover. "I think we should check out the lagoon."

Sam piped up. "Thank you, Buzz. I so wanted to take a look, but I didn't want to put you all in greater danger. Can we see how far we can make it in the Rover? Evo said the track ahead leads directly to it."

Armand shrugged. "I don't have a problem with it, thought we might be walking into more trouble. I'd rather continue on and get these guys to the local police." He gestured to the men tied to the luggage rack.

"But we may never get back here. I really need to at least take a look around."

Armand sighed. "I don't want you three walking into danger. We'd better just go."

The three of us stopped and looked over our shoulders. I said, "So Sayeth the maneth hanging in the treeeth?"

Armand had the grace to blush. "Okay, I get-eth it. Quick stop, then back to civilization, okay? I'll stay here and stand guard. Take weapons with you."

"It's a deal!"

I put the vehicle in low and continued forward. It wasn't as bad going as I thought. In no time we were at the lagoon. It was just as Evo described it. The smell of rotting flesh and vegetation was almost overpowering, but Sam didn't seem to notice. She and Fred donned plastic gloves, grabbed a bunch of vials, and headed toward the shore with fishnets. I gave myself an extra dose of Deet and told Armand we wouldn't be long.

I stumbled over roots and slogged through mud, trying to breathe through my mouth. I had to stop and gag twice, but finally made it to the small beach. Holding my nose I waded over to Sam and Fred. "Find anything?"

246

Sam lifted a brow at me then studied the contents of her net. "Lots of dead fish."

"Very scientific. Anything at all alive?"

Fred's head shot up. "Sam, over here–you won't believe this!"

Sam waded through the water to where Fred held out her net. We peered at a small miracle. Inside the net flopped a *Corydoras* catfish–the little bewhiskered cat wiggled energetically in the net. The miracle was not the fish itself, but the fact he lived.

"Holy catfish, Batman! Where did this little fella come from?" I grabbed a jar with fresh water and opened the top.

Sam dumped the Cory in. She held him up to the sun and examined his squirming little body. She looked almost startled as she turned back to us. "Fred, Buzz, where I cannot be sure without positive identification, I don't recognize this specie of Corydoras. I'd swear it is a match to the one at Fred's house. They are not exact, but it might be a gender or age difference. See that purple over green shimmer? See that black circle around the eye? It looks like he has freckles, but no other spotting."

I poked Fred in the side. "Yo, fisher woman, find us some more of these."

We hunted and netted until the sun took a downward turn.

Finally, Armand yelled from the Land Rover, "Hey, Evo is up and the sun is going down. We have to get off this mountain now!"

Exhausted, we dragged ourselves back to the SUV and carefully packed away our new babies. Armand insisted on driving, and we used clothes and duffle bags to cushion Evo. Armand gave him another painkiller so the jouncing wouldn't kill him.

As we passed Site 151, we went the opposite way around the perimeter. As we neared the front gate, Armand killed the engine and went to reconnoiter the way past. He came up behind us and scared the crap out of everyone—including the bad guys strapped on the back.

"Looks clear. Let's hope I'm right. Hang on, Evo. He started the engine and gunned it down the main road.

We made the airport in Cumanná in record time and Evo insisted we not stop at the hospital—too much hassle and too many questions. Sam checked his wound and declared him to be holding up. Evo gritted his teeth as we all but dragged him onto the plane. I left Sam and Fred to fuss over him and Armand made several phone calls to his people. He'd barely hung up when a black Navigator screeched to a halt near the Rover.

I poked my head into the plane and called Fred and Sam over to look. "Hey, are those guys we tied up aliens? 'Cuz it sure looks like the *Men in Black* have arrived."

They snickered and agreed. We watched as the unsmiling men in black suits untied our prisoner as if it was a sight they saw every day. In silence and with micro-precision moves, the black suits threw the prisoner into the back of the Navigator. Two suits got in the front and one got in the back. The doors slammed behind them and they disappeared in a flash.

"*Hoo-wee*. That was kind-of creepy. Hey, Armand, are you sure you knew those guys? No one said a word."

"Company men. I used to try to fit in like them, but I bleed real blood, so they kicked me out of their fraternity and made me do undercover work, thank God."

I shook my head in wonder. "No kidding. Well, let's get the rest of our stuff in here. The pilot says he's ready to go. I guess this means you won't be involving the local police?"

Armand grunted as he hefted Fred's large duffel. "You guessed correctly, Buzz. Now get going, we don't have much time."

The plane took off and we all breathed a little easier. We

made plans to return to Sam's house, rest, clean up, and take the samples of the new Corys to Sam's lab in the Tambopata Reserve in Peru. Evo made a call to the owner of Site 151. President and CEO Ramon Enrique Maldonado-Nunez himself answered the phone.

We tried to listen in on the conversation, but couldn't understand much. I became bored and pulled out the digital camera to look at the pictures I'd taken at the mine. When I got to those of the entrance, I brought the camera to where Evo sat talking with his boss. He distractedly looked my way and I held up a finger. He asked Nunez to hold on and said, "Not now, Buzz, let me finish this conversation."

"But Evo, look at these men. Do you know any of them?"

"In a minute."

"No, now! Evo looked at the screen." He glanced at the camera and stopped talking. He hit the zoom and his eyes widened. If his quick indrawn breath wasn't a dead giveaway, when he snatched the camera out of my hand told me I'd hit the nail on the head.

He barked into the phone, "Mr. Nunez. The mine I told you about. According to the American federal agent, the coordinates put it on land you own. I have in my hand a picture taken of the entrance to the mine, and Hector Chavez is standing in a hard hat issuing orders. Yes, sir, I am sure. Yes, sir, I'll meet you when we touchdown in–" Evo looked up at Armand who held up two fingers and a fist. "In twenty minutes, sir." Yes, sir, I understand. You be careful as well. Good bye."

Evo dropped the phone and leaned his head back on the cushion, exhausted from his efforts. "Everyone, listen. I think I figured out part of the story here. Let me see if you agree. It looks as though my immediate boss, Hector Chavez is running an illegal mining operation on land owned by Nunez Oil. It would seem to me that if Nunez knows nothing of this mine,

Chavez must have been pocketing the profits as well." He absently clicked through the pictures in the camera. "What I don't understand is why, and on what is he spending his money?"

Evo froze and stared at the screen on the camera. He held out a hand toward Sam and whispered, "Samón, look at this."

Sam took his hand. "Evo, what could possibly induce you to call me by my real name?" She smiled as she sat next to him.

Evo held up the camera, and in only a split second, Sam cried, "Oh, my God! Fred, look–what do you see?" Sam held out the camera to Fred.

"I see a bunch of guys in hard hats–holy cow, is that Hank?"

"Hank MacRone?" I knew the answer before I asked the question.

"Hank MacRone," Evo sighed.

Armand took the camera out of Sam's hands. "Who is Hank MacRone?"

"A fish expert from America," I said. "The kind of fish we just took out of the poisoned lagoon." I studied the picture. "Mines, fish, money, poison. How are they connected?"

Evo suddenly made a grab for the phone. He winced when his stitches pulled. "Oh my God! I have to call Tony. He might be in danger!

I picked up my phone and punched in the number to Fred's house. "Oh Lord, Alfredo and Luis might be in danger too. Wait! Oh my God, I think–they already are! Their car blew up at Great America, they were almost run over at the bank, and Lord knows what else has happened since we left. I have to call J.J."

Fred shook her head. "But, Buzz, those were accidents, weren't they?"

"I'm not so sure." I clicked off and punched in J.J.'s number.

"Sheriff Green."

"J.J. Buzz."

"Hey, how's my baby? Boy do I miss you."

"Yeah, I know, I miss you too, and I'm not your baby. Listen, Green, it's not going so well down here. Evo's shot and his boss is corrupt." I heard him moan, but I forged ahead. "Hank the fish guy is in cahoots with Evo's corrupt boss. We don't know the connection yet, but it sure looks fishy."

"I think this whole thing is totally fishy if you ask me. Come home, Buzz, let the Feds take care of them. Being an American down there in the middle of something like this is not a good idea. Think about Fred. Do you want her in the middle of everything?"

"Don't play that card, Green; you know I can't get out now. As to Fred, she's holding her own, and there's no way she'd come home now except kicking and screaming. Work with me here, pal."

"Okay, but tell me everything, and then I want to talk to Evo."

"Listen J.J., I'm putting you on speakerphone so we can all talk. You need to put one of your guys on Alfredo, Luis, and Tony. Just park Moe, or you, or FBI Bob in Fred's house and inform those guys they're probably in danger, and by all means, don't let those new friends Tom and Mark near them."

"You think maybe those guys are involved in this?"

I explained my theory about the alleged "accidents" happening to Luis and Alfredo and how their new friends were always around when someone died.

"Wow."

"Yeah, not only that, what if they send the big guns to finish the job?"

"Yeah, okay I'll get Bob to cover the house and I'll get one of my other guys to cover Fred's pet shop. I'll personally drive them to and from the shop. Can any of you think of anything else I can do at this time?"

Evo leaned forward so he could be heard. "Yeah, J.J. would you see if Al can hack into some government records down here and check out a man named Hector Chavez? I would, except they blew up my computer." He gave J.J. Chavez's pertinent information.

Fred piped up. "She can use my computer in the den. That way she'll be right there at my house the next time we call."

I added, "Got all that J.J.?"

"Sure, Buzz, but I want you home soon. Now would be good, but I'll settle for as soon as you can."

My cheeks burned and a pool of warmth settled somewhere beneath my rib cage. *Slow down, Miller, he didn't mean you as an individual, he meant all of us.* "Deal. It seems pretty weird that Hank would be involved with a guy like Chavez, but if he is, and those Endlers have oddball plant material not endemic to that area, I want to know how we can pin-point the location. It looks as though Hank might have discovered a new species of Cory catfish and used the Endlers as a cover crop. We might have a case of 'The Fishy Fishologist Finagling the Find.'"

"Aside from the lousy alliteration, Buzz, are you saying Hank might have *placed* those fish in the lagoon? What the heck is he doing up by the illegal mine?"

"In all likelihood, the same thing as us, following the poison. Maybe Hank is pissed that Chavez killed off his fish. Maybe they're in cahoots over the ore from the mine. Maybe he just stumbled on the mine and got caught."

The plane. "Listen, J.J., we're approaching Lima's airport. I'll call you later."

"Is everyone still listening?"

I looked at Sam, Evo, Armand, and Fred gathered around the open mike all shaking their heads.

I folded my arms and said smugly, "Why? Did you have

something else to say to me?"

"Yeah, Miller. Come home to me." At my sharp indrawn breath, he added, "And I, uh, I also wanted to tell you that..."

"*Stop!* I lied. Everyone is still listening." I grabbed for the phone, but before I could get my hands on it, Fred snatched it up and held it out of my reach.

"I was just going to tell you the dogs are doing fine, but Wes knocked over the clothes hamper and made mincemeat out of your potato shirt. What's up? What did you think I was going to say with all those people listening in?"

"How did you–?"

"I *know* you, remember?"

"I remember. See you later, Turkey Butt." I rang off.

I made a show of stuffing the phone in my pants and hooking my seatbelt. My face glowed red-hot and I could feel the gaze of Fred's beady little eyes boring into the back of my head. No one said a word as they buckled in, and landed with no mishaps. We gathered up the duffel and our equipment. Armand must have made another phone call, because another black SUV complete with silent men in black suits boarded the plane and off-loaded Evo, who complained about everything from his stitches to his empty belly. Sam shoved a pretzel rod in his mouth and told him to stop whining. His eyes bugged out of his head, but he shut his mouth long enough to be carried off the plane.

A limo pulled up and Armand dismissed the driver, who joined the Men in Black as they sped off to parts unknown. We stared at Armand as he dragged himself to the limo, but he shrugged his shoulders. "I might as well drive; we don't want any people we do not know added into our already complex equation. Who knows who they could be working for." Whistling, he proceeded to sling gear into the back.

The drive to Sam's house lulled all but Armand and me to sleep. When he pulled quietly to the curb, he signaled that I come with him to check out the house. "Want to help me make sure no uninvited guests are in there drinkin' our Kool-Aid? They left a light on for us."

"The lights were out when we left, Armand."

"I hear you, pal. We going in together, or do you want to take coverage on the rear of the house?"

"Together," I said. "That way if someone crashed our party, we'll run his ass out the back door. At this point, I don't care who it is, I just want them gone."

"Let's go then, Buzz."

Drawing my weapon, I moved in close behind him. He tried the front door, but it was locked. He used Sam's key and I heard a soft *snick* as the lock slid open. I stayed low and we entered quickly, checking the corners, and anything with a door. We got to the kitchen door and saw the light under the jamb. I jumped across to the other side of the doorway and waited for a signal from Armand.

He rose to his feet and I stayed low. He made eye contact with me and held up one finger. I began to sweat and my stomach tightened. He held up the second finger and we both took deep breaths and focused. My muscles bunched as I prepared to jump through the door. Armand began to raise the third finger and I couldn't believe what happened next.

26

The kitchen door flew open and smacked Armand full in the face. Blood spurted out of his nose and he howled in pain. I jumped up just as a tall figure rushed through the door right into my gun. I grabbed a fistful of shirt collar and jammed the barrel under his chin. Yanking his face down to about an inch from mine I growled, "*Breathe* wrong, asshole, and I'll blow your tongue through the top of your head." I twisted and the man flipped over my hip and landed with a whoosh face up with the muzzle of my weapon in his throat.

"*Gawk, aaack–mumph.*" The intruder's eyes rolled back and his head slowly sunk to the floor. I followed him down, still holding his collar and pressing the gun against his lower jaw. He was either really, really scared or I held him a bit too tight, because he quietly passed out at my feet. I stuffed the gun into the back of my jeans and flipped him over. I tore the shoelace out of my left tennis shoe. I made a loop in one end and cranked his wrists together before wrapping the lace around both.

Sam must have heard the commotion and jumped through the front door holding one of the machine guns we'd taken from the bad guys in the jungle. Her eyes were like saucers and she bared her teeth.

She yelled in a voice about two octaves above middle-C, "Don't anybody move or I'll shoot!"

Standing with my foot between the shoulder blades of the passed out guy on the floor I asked, "Wasn't that a line from an old James Cagney movie?"

Sam lowered the weapon and shrugged. "It was the only thing I could think of at the time."

"Good job, Sam. Uh, would you mind giving me a hand here?"

She placed the gun on the floor and scraped the hair out of her eyes. "Sure, what do you need? Say, Buzz, who is that under your foot?"

I looked down and realized I still had my foot between the shoulder blades of the guy on the floor. "I don't know, but Armand needs an ice pack and I need rope or something so I can tie him up right." I gestured with my gun to the now moaning man on the floor.

"By doze isss broke," Armand wailed.

Sam sprang into action and hopped over my prisoner into the kitchen. I took that moment to pat down our new bad guy for weapons. I pulled him into a sitting position and dragged him out of the doorway by the collar. I propped him against the wall and held the gun on him.

I noticed he was at least a well-dressed bad guy. He had on and a nice yellow golf shirt tucked into a new pair of straight-legged jeans. His western boots were gator and his watch a Rolex. I began to get an uneasy feeling about the identity of our perpetrator when Sam rushed through the kitchen door with a bag of frozen peas, a towel, and an extension cord.

She tossed me the extension cord and tended to poor broken-nose Armand. Fred came staggering through the door under the arm of Evo. He leaned heavily on her and never said a word. Pain etched heavily on his face, my heart went out to him. Fred lowered him into a leather recliner and turned to face me. She stood there puffing like a racehorse.

I struggled to tie up our bad guy and yelled, "Hey, Fred, give me a hand with this guy, would you?"

She looked behind her hoping, I guess, that I was talking to someone else. Seeing no one, she stumbled over to the kitchen door. We lifted our prisoner onto a spindle-backed chair and I ripped off the shoelace and pulled his hands through the slats. I tied his hands off the best I could with the extension cord, and then ran it around the front of the chair and Fred tied his feet to the legs. He seemed to be coming around, but he took his sweet time doing it. *What a pansy.*

Fred rushed over to help Sam with Armand, so I checked on Evo. His eyes were still closed but his breathing was slowing to normal. I picked up throw pillows and tucked them around his bad side. Fred and Sam took Armand into the kitchen to clean him up, and I sat across from Evo and waited for him to get past the pain.

He finally opened his eyes and took in his surroundings. "Are we at Sam's? Where is everyone?"

"We're at Sam's, but uh, Armand had a slight mishap. Sam and Fred are patching him up in the kitchen. On the brighter side, we caught ourselves a bad guy." I pointed to the man in the chair.

Evo looked over toward the man in the chair. If he could have paled further, he would have. He became agitated and is mouth dropped open. "Oh-oh-n-no! Noo...n-n-noon...noon, was all that came out.

I looked at my watch. "Boy, you have been out of it, Evo. It's way past noon. It's almost seven p.m.!"

Sweat beaded on his forehead, and I began to become alarmed as Evo began hyperventilating and struggled to get up. "No! No! Noon (pant, pant) noo...noo (pant) Nez!"

At this point I knew I needed help holding him down. A blood spot appeared on his bandage. "Sam, could you come out here please? Evo is ranting and I don't understand."

Sam walked into the room, followed by Fred and Armand sporting a bag of frozen peas on his nose. "Ranting?"

"What was he saying?"

"The last thing he said was no, no, noo, nez."

Evo struggled to pull the pillows from under his injured

arm. The man in the chair began to come to. I tried to calm Evo, and Sam took his face into her hands. "Evo, what is no, no, noo-nez?"

She straightened and looked at the guy in the chair. "No, no, noo-nez. No no noonez Oh my God, Buzz! He's saying Nunez. The guy you almost killed over there must be Evo's boss, Ramon Enrique Maldonado Nunez."

Evo rolled his eyes and flopped back in the recliner. He winced as his wound sang.

Sam and I stared in silence as Mr. Nunez, owner of half of Peru or something equally big, opened his eyes. We scrambled over to the chair and clawed at the extension cord, untying the knots currently cutting off the circulation above Nunez's gold Rolex.

"Take anything you want, but please don't hurt me," he mumbled.

I had a great idea. "Sam," I whispered. "Maybe he won't remember that I was the one with the gun to his head. Maybe he'll think we saved him from burglars."

Sam looked skeptical as she used her teeth on a particularly obstinate knot. "I on't oh." She spit out the extension cord. "I don't know, Buzz. He probably saw you. We should just fess up and apologize. He'll understand. Right?"

I dropped the cord. "I think I just got Evo fired and I'm going to spend the rest of my short life in a dirt floor prison cell with tarantulas and an anaconda for company, that's what I think! I'll never see my dogs again. Maybe if I hide, you can say you didn't know me. I ran in and ran out."

"Oh, just shut up and get the man untied," Fred said.

I looked up and Mr. Nunez's face was inches from mine. His eyes were wide open and he said, "Al Capone, I presume?"

I freed his wrists and he rubbed them vigorously. "Buzz Miller, sir. I would like to say that I am truly sorry for mistaking you for a burglar, but we've not had much luck with good will from our fellow man lately."

Maldonado-Nunez raised a brow. "I could see that when I caught a glimpse of Evo's office. I then went to his apartment and saw the same type of damage. I came here next. The back door wasn't locked so I made myself at home and brewed a pot of coffee. My decision to wait for Dr. Fernandini seems not to be one of my better ideas. Never once did I think I would cause so much mayhem. Please accept my apologies, Ms. Miller, Dr. Fernandini, and you as well, Dr. Castillo. I only wanted to help in any way I could."

Fred stood in the kitchen doorway and patted him on the shoulder. "You made coffee, Mr. Nunez. That helps a lot. Thank you." She brought out mugs for everyone and we settled on the sofas and chairs. Sam sat on the arm of Evo's recliner, fussing with his shoulder.

"Now, first things first. My name is Ramon, and that is what I expect to be called." He looked at Fred. "And the Angel of Mercy?"

"Fred Miller, sir. I'm pleased to meet you." She handed him a mug and his eyes followed her across the room.

As he caught himself, he jerked his eyes back to Sam. "Dr. Fernandini, or may I have the honor of calling you Samón?"

"I am just plain old Sam to my friends, sir." She clasped his hand warmly in hers.

"Never plain and certainly not old, my dear, but I will call you, Sam." He raised her hand and kissed it.

I thought Evo felt bad pain or something, as he made a sound like a steam engine bleeding its lines, and almost came up out of his recliner. Sam pulled him back down and sat on his hand. Oh. I thought. I get it now. Evo was jealous. He was marking his territory, and Sam somehow knew it.

"Mr. Nun–Ramon," I said. "We've just returned from Venezuela where we made a few startling discoveries. Would you like to see the pictures I took of an operation called the

259

Devil's Eye Mine? They're still in the camera at the moment, but the screen is large enough to see them clearly."

"I would, of course. Evo and I will view them together." He got up and dragged the oak chair next to Evo's recliner.

Evo signaled for his backpack. "Sir, before we begin, may I?" He dug through the backpack for an envelope addressed to Ramon Nunez. Evo tore it open and handed it to him.

Evo explained. "While I was in and out of the drug haze my colleagues kept me in, I realized that the contents of this envelope are what got my apartment, my office, and an innocent bystander blown up." He poured the contents on his lap. "This," he held up a grey rectangle, "Is my digital recorder. This," he held up a sheaf of paper, "Is my full report to you, along with the research our friends in the States performed before we flew back here." He placed the pictures and lab reports from the water and the village in Nunez's lap.

Nunez went through the pictures. When he came to the churchyard with all the newly dug graves, he dropped the picture in his lap and covered his eyes with his hands. "Evo, tell me we did not do this. Please tell me my corporation did not harm these villagers or their children."

Evo put a hand on Nunez's shoulder. "Sir, I have never known you to disregard people or the environment. The pictures I'm about to show you should explain what happened to that village." He handed the camera to Nunez. "Armand over there with the peas on his nose is a United States government agent, working undercover on a parallel case with ours."

I saw what was coming and made chopping motions at my throat to get Evo to shut up. The pain medication he took must have given him a bad case of motor-mouth, because he ignored my pleas and continued. He pointed in my direction, and I slipped behind Sam. Evo didn't seem to notice. "Buzz, the lady over there who knocked you down and tied you up is a retired police official also from the States and a personal friend. She

260

and Armand hiked another couple of kilometers up the mountain and discovered this mining operation."

Nunez clicked through the pictures. "What is this place, Evo? If it is only a couple of kilometers up from the village, would that not place it on my land? I know of no such mining operation in that area." He looked at the next picture and froze, and sighed. "So this is what you wanted me to see. The peasant who would be king; Hector Chavez."

"I am sorry, sir."

"Don't be sorry, it was my own arrogance which caused this. I promoted him over you because you are such a vital element to my success. I could not bear to pull you from the field and risk sending a lesser man in my name. I tried to ease my conscious by granting you a raise in pay."

Evo started. "Another raise? I don't want another raise."

"Well, you got one. Don't you ever check your finances?" He looked at all of us and continued. "Now because of that one poor decision to promote Chavez, I have put all your lives in jeopardy." He looked at Evo. "I almost had you killed."

Evo shifted in the recliner. "Begging your pardon, sir, but that mine is not a new operation."

He looked through more of the pictures and stopped. "Yes, but that is why your apartment was destroyed and your office blown up isn't it? Because of this mine?"

Evo nodded. "I believe when I reported to Chavez about the lagoon and the village, he thought I was too close to finding out the truth about the mine. That's why the snipers shot at Luis and me. My initial investigation of the lagoon with the dead fish and the deserted village left me with many questions and no answers. I took my work with me when I went on vacation to the States. I also have a habit of copying my field notes and locking them in my safe at work until an investigation is complete. Chavez knows this, and probably sent someone to retrieve them. No record, no Evo, business as usual."

Evo dug in the side pocket of his cargo pants and pulled out a plastic bag. "This time however, I didn't put copies in my safe; I put them in this bag and took them with me. My theory is that when Chavez had his men blow my safe at work and found no papers, he ordered my house safe to be 'checked' as well. My guess is, when they again found no reports, Chavez figured if he eliminated the source," Evo pointed to himself, "he eliminated any further problems."

Evo's story exhausted him, so I took up the tale. "After Evo checked out the village, he went to Site 151 to speak with your foreman, Ron Hansen." Evo nodded and closed his eyes. "A good man and they murdered him."

I continued. "Close as we can figure, when Chavez found out, he had no way of knowing what Evo had told Hansen. We think Chavez subsequently had Hansen murdered and his office ransacked. This is where we came in. Had we been later, we might have been able to avoid getting shot at, but as it was, sooner or later an altercation with the bad guys proved inevitable."

I sat back and let Nunez digest the information. Fred came through with the coffee pot and Nunez absently held out his mug for a refill. He set it down and steepled his hands at his mouth. After a few minutes, he nodded slowly as if he had come to some decision. When he looked up, his eyes bore into Armand's. "Now young man, where do you fit in with all this crazy business?"

Armand took the bag of peas from his nose and said, "Now *that*, sir; is another tale entirely."

27

"My name is Armand Sargetti," He sent me an evil look, "*Not* Spaghettios." I blushed and pointed at Sam and Fred. They tried for innocent looks and pointed back at me.

Armand continued. "I'm an agent with Alcohol, Tobacco, and Firearms in the United States. I was sent here to investigate arms dealing. I followed a trail, which began in New York, and it took me through Mexico and Central America down here to your neck of the woods and specifically to your corporation. I met up with Dr. Castillo while posing as an environmentalist on sabbatical, and I just happened to be on hand to help out when Evo here got himself in a little hot water over some ferns that grow on trees."

Evo snorted. "Hot water? The truth is I'd have bled to death if Armand hadn't carried me out of that forest after I got myself shot by that maniacal crazy man."

Armand shrugged, "Whatever. I didn't think pounding a sign in the ground warranted shooting someone, but to each his own. Anyway, I found myself liking Dr. Do-Gooder over there, and after the agency did a background investigation, they brought Evo in on the perimeter, sort-of like a civilian inside man. Neither of us thought you or your companies were involved in the arms trading, but the trail kept leading back to your door."

Armand made a small sound, which could have been a laugh or a belch. "I thought my best cover would be as Evo's personal limousine driver, so I was set.

"Then came the promotion of Chavez, and I had my doubts about you again, Mr. Nunez. I bugged rooms, tapped phones, tailed vehicles, crashed parties–you name it, I showed up. In your circles, the limo blended right in, and since Evo is almost always out of town, I had all the time in the world to check things out. Word on the streets was that someone big tried to hire a hit man to go to Wisconsin to take out, and I quote, 'A couple of morons and a couple of scientists,' but I couldn't get close enough to be granted an interview so I could find out the details. I connected the dots when Evo called to arrange a ride from the airport.

"Talk about lame; it wasn't until then I realized the scientists on the hit list were Sam, Evo, and his brother Tony."

Evo leaned forward and winced. "*Ahhh.* So when Armand and I exchanged information over the phone, we put two and two together and–"

Whack. Sam's hand left a red mark on Evo's cheek. "And you decided the women involved were not worthy of knowing the truth? That maybe somewhere in that six-foot-three hunk of *macho stupid,* you would shelter us from the cold hard world? Well look again, Capitan Courageous, bullets know no gender! We could have avoided a lot of anguish if you had been straight with us from the start. That hole in your shoulder matches the hole in your head."

Evo looked helplessly around the room, and landed somewhere to the left of me. "Sorry, but I didn't want Sam involved and I didn't even know you then, Buzz."

Fred yelled, "Yeah? Well look who got shot!"

I glared daggers at him. "You'd best be glad Sam hit you and not me. I'd paste you to the wall, macho man. Did you at least let J.J. in on your fishy little tale? Because if you didn't and I find that he or anyone in White Bass Lake has suffered because you withheld this information, I'll shoot your ass myself."

I tore my cell phone off my belt and dialed J.J. I knew he'd be in bed by now, but I needed to hear from him. He picked up on the first ring. "Hey, gorgeous, I was just thinking about you.

I'm in your bed."

"Knock off the malarkey, James J. Green. Is everyone okay up there? Anyone get say, killed or maimed in the last twenty-four hours?"

I had his full attention now. "No one croaking except the horny toads up here. Which reminds me, sugar, when are you coming home, anyway?"

"Eh, eh-uh, just as soon as I can make arrangements, J.J. Now think. Has anyone new come into town in the past day or so? Male, Hispanic?"

"Not that I know of; are you going to let me in on why you think I should be up to my ass in corpses, or is it your little secret?"

"I'm sorry, J.J. I just found out a South American hit man-or-woman might be headed into town to take out Evo, Sam, Tony, Alfredo, Luis, and if I'm correct, those two new friends of the Gallegos brothers. If he hasn't shown up yet, then he'll probably come in tonight or tomorrow. I'm coming home, J.J." I glared again at Evo. Tonight if I can get a flight out."

"That's great," he said. "I'll pick you up at the airport."

"No need; I think Evo's truck is still in long-term parking at Mitchell Field. I'll let you know when I get into town."

"How? Will you sneak in here and put your tongue in my ear?"

"You, Green, are a warped man. Just do me a favor and make sure Tony, Alfredo, and Luis are okay. Now listen, there's something I have to tell you." I told J.J. the whole story, as I knew it. I honestly believed he would have beaten the crap out of Evo at that point; stitches or not. I put J.J. on speakerphone while he cussed a blue streak.

He wound down by pointing out that the two alleged big strong men sent to watch over the women ended up being one who caught a bullet and one with a broken nose—who might also still be hanging upside down in the jungle had it not been for the three helpless women. "Man, I don't know what century you knuckleheads are from, but Buzz is more than capable of taking care of all of your sorry asses! I haven't seen more intelligence and spunk come behind the letters PhD than I have in Sam, and Fred is a Miller Sister; I need not say more. Damn it, I knew I should have been there!"

"Water under the bridge, J.J. Slow down a minute or I won't tell you the rest."

"Don't even insinuate that there's more…"

I heard him breathing on the other end. "We have bigger fish to fry now—a-ha. Fish to fry."

"I am not amused, Buzz. Get on with the story."

"Uh, ahem, okay. Anyway, Hank MacRone was in the pictures I took at the mine along with Hector Chavez. Can you get FBI Bob to check out Hank's possible connection to Chavez on the home front? Hank's an importer of tropical fish and not involved in mining. Chavez works for an oil conglomerate. There's got to be a connection, but I can't see one now."

"I'll get Bob right on it. Actually, I'll get Al and Bob on it. Hurry up down there. I uh, well, I want you home, and uh, the dogs miss you too."

"They won't even recognize me after you get done spoiling them. You're not letting Wesley eat ice cream at night, are you?" From the silence on the other end I gathered Wes had gained another ten pounds. "J.J., you can't let those two dogs walk all over you."

"They don't walk all over me. We have a good time, don't we guys?" I heard enthusiastic woofing in the background, and my eyes misted. I really did miss those three idiots.

"I'll be home before you know it, J.J. Hug the dogs for me, and I'll call you from the airport."

"I'll clean out my ears to make room for your tongue."

"You, James Green, are a disgusting individual."

"It's part of my charm. Bye, babe." He hung up the phone

before I could yell at him again.

I stared at the phone for a second and shook my head to clear it.

Nunez chuckled and I looked up. "Your husband, no?"

I sighed. "No, sir, an old friend."

Nunez looked at the floor, smiling and shaking his head. "Friendship is a strong foundation." He looked me in the eyes and shook his finger at me. "Do not waste an opportunity for happiness, my dear."

"I, uh, no…well–"

There was no use being embarrassed, as Nunez silently rubbing his wrists, trying to get the circulation going again, Armand kept touching his tender nose, Fred fell asleep standing up, and Sam stared at a wall. Evo pointed out smugly he was the only one awake, and I pointed out that he had slept most of the last twenty-four hours.

Evo straightened in his chair and cleared his throat. "Why don't we call it a night and get back at this tomorrow morning? Maybe we can wind this up and get back to the States."

Sam's head snapped around. "You're going back? I mean, I wanted to go back, but I didn't think you would."

"Why not? We're on vacation. What would I do here with no place to live, a bullet hole in me, and no office to go to? I'd rather be in Fred's house, watching the fish swim."

Nunez spoke up. "You're not going anywhere until I have you checked out at the hospital. No offense ladies, but this way he can get some legal," he narrowed his eyes at Armand, "Non-narcotic pain medication. I also want to have his shoulder x-rayed to make sure the bullet didn't nick a bone. Then you go back to the States and you will take off another four weeks or so to recuperate."

Evo muttered about doctors and bosses while Fred went into the kitchen to turn off the coffee. She decided to wait at Sam's house with Nunez while I took Evo and Armand to the hospital. Fred said she would have everything set up by the time we got back.

We all jumped as we heard a scream from the bathroom. Sam exited with a smug smile on her face. Armand followed, whimpering about his poor nose. Sam spun on him. "Oh shut up, you baby. At least it's straight again."

She grabbed her jacket and came over to help me lift Evo from the chair. Evo struggled to stand on his own. He saw Sam bearing down on him and held up his good hand to ward her off. "Don't hurt me, Sam! I'll never call you Fernameanie again. I swear—just don't hurt me!"

"What are you talking about, Castillo? We're taking you to the hospital. Let's go."

Between Nunez, Sam, and me, we gave Evo the heave-ho and helped him to the limo. Nunez murmured something about making phone calls. With Armand at the wheel, we made it to the hospital in record time.

Ramon had called ahead and briefed the hospital staff of our arrival and an entourage met us at the Emergency Room entrance. They whisked Evo away in a wheelchair while Sam and I were escorted to a private waiting room.

Armand was waylaid by a team of nurses when he walked into the ER They must have known him by the size of his nose. Sam and I had a chuckle when we heard him hollering down the hall, but they returned him to us with watery eyes and a pristine bandage across his swollen proboscis.

Evo arrived outside our waiting area about an hour later, and we were treated like royalty all the way out to the limo. I drove back to Sam's because Armand was on drugs and currently lolling in the passenger seat. Evo lie in the back seat draped across Sam's lap, a small secret smile on his lips. He reminded me of Wesley sprawled across me on the big wooden swing in our backyard. Evo looked perfectly content as Sam stared out the window and absently ran a hand through his hair.

My eyes stung thinking about home. *What a wienie I am.*

Back at Sam's, I was surprised to see Ramon Nunez still at the house. He drank tea with Fred and laughed at something she'd just said. He jumped to his feet and helped us get Evo through the front door. "Welcome home, everyone. Freddie and I have been conversing on many subjects. I have alerted the proper authorities and have procured what you Americans would call a search warrant, which will permit government officials to seize any and all records, personnel, or items related to the mine. They will call me when they leave for the mine."

"Wow," I said. "How the heck did you get justice's wheels to turn so fast?"

"Simple, really. For one, the mine is on my property and what is the purpose of having money if one cannot, say, grease the wheels of justice so they turn faster?"

"That's one hell of a lube job, *Señor*."

Nunez raised his eyebrows and smiled. "Fascinating, is it not?"

Fred grabbed my hand and dragged me across the room. "Look, Buzz. Ramon went out and bought a whiteboard."

"Why on earth for, I wonder?"

"While we are waiting for the plane to get ready, we can put what we know together. That way, we can help with the police investigation down here." She pointed to the writing on the board. "The black writing is what we've been able to piece together so far. The red off shoots are the possible theories we discussed, the green notations are the variables and probabilities, and the blue squares are pieces that are still missing from the equation. That's how you do it at home, right?"

Fred's eager expression reminded me of my dogs when I took them to Dairy Queen. "Fred, you did a wonderful job, and probably saved many man hours of work on this investigation."

Fred sent a smile in Nunez's direction. "I couldn't have

done it without Ramon."

"Ramon, is it?" Fred and Nunez both blushed. "Tell you what," I pointed to Evo and Armand. "Let's get our guys on injured reserve situated and we'll go over everything we have so far."

Nunez sat up. "Did you not want to sleep when you returned here?"

I took the coffee mug Fred offered and drank deeply. "Not quite yet, I'm buzzing on caffeine right now."

One would have thought it would be an easy task to make Evo lie down for a while, but he resisted Sam's attempts to lead him to her bedroom. He hung on to the doorjamb with his good arm while she propelled him from the rear. "Evo, you are not cooperating! Just lie down for a while and let the medication work for you."

"I don't want to lie down alone, Sam." In an unexpected move, Evo spun and grabbed Sam around the waist. He pressed her against the bedroom door and his lips hovered inches from hers. He looked directly into her eyes and said, "Samón, my love, normally I would fight the Devil himself for a chance to crawl into your bed, but between the drugs, the investigation, and the fact that your house is full of company, I am forced at this time to decline such a lovely invitation." He moved a fraction closer and smiled slowly. "I will however, take a rain check." He bent and kissed her.

Sam recovered from her shock and her eyes narrowed. She shoved away from him and spoke softly, venom dripping from her words. "You arrogant clod! You think that with one crook of your finger I would be ready and willing to jump into bed with you? What was your major in college again, Penis 101? Good thing you have the excuse of being on drugs, or I'd–"

"Sam, wait! I didn't mean–"

"Right. What part did you not mean? The jumping into my bed now, or jumping into it later? Perhaps when you grow up

270

you will come to the realization that some women have more to do with their lives than to line up to become another notch on your bedpost!"

She spun and left him leaning against the door to the bedroom. He pinched the bridge of his nose and shook his head as if trying to clear his muzzy brain. Fred went over and helped Evo back into the living room. She said through her teeth, "Evo, what the heck were you thinking? You confused and embarrassed her."

Evo gave her a drug-induced lopsided smile. "Sorry, Fred. Is that what I did? Maybe the doc gave me truth serum instead of pain drugs. I mean, how the hell else could I have been so stupid? At least I didn't totally lose it and tell her I love her, she'd probably hold that against me until I die." He snorted and didn't hear Sam's indrawn breath. She backed farther behind Fred and shamelessly eavesdropped along with the rest of us.

I could see Fred smiling wickedly and thought, oh, oh. She's really going to give poor Evo the business now.

Fred made soothing noises as she directed him to a chair. "Why can't you tell Sam you're in love with her?"

Evo's speech became a little slurred and I had to turn to hide my smile. Little did the big man know, but he had an audience of five avid listeners. He clasped Fred's hand in his good one and spilled his guts. "I can't tell her until she likes me better. You know whatsh really *shhh*-ad, Freddie?"

"No, Evo, what is really sad?"

He looked left and then right. He blinked slowly and raised his dilated eyes to Fred's. "I'm really, really shhhad becaushh not only am I shtupid enough to fall in love with a woman who hates me, I really like her a lot too." Fred was about to say something, but he cut her off. "No, really, Fred. Ever shinsh I met her when Tony—you know my brother Tony, isn't he the best? Anyway, I meet Sam and whammie! I'm in love with Sammic. Ha-ha, good joke on me, eh? So what do I do? Do you know what the shuave and debonair Dr. Evo Raymundo Moronez Castillo does?"

"No, Evo," Fred said gently, "What did you do?" Sam poked her from behind and Fred ignored her.

His head dropped foreword and I thought he had blessedly passed out. Suddenly, it popped up and he continued like nothing happened. "I inshulted her, and I propositioned her, That'sh what I did. Boy did I make her mad."

"You insulted her? How did you do that?"

"Oh," he sighed, "I don't know. After listening to Tony expound on her virtues non-stop every time I talked to him, I had it in my thick head that he had a think for her–I–I mean a *thing* for her. When I first laid eyes on her it was like being hit in the head with a log. Like being run over by a shhteamroller. Like fireworks in my brain–"

Fred interrupted. "I get it, Evo. I certainly agree that Sam is stunningly beautiful."

Evo gave Fred a pleading look and grabbed for her sleeve. He missed. "No, no; that'sh just it, Freddie. She's so much more than beauty, but did I say that? Nnnot me. I made some shtupid remark about what kind of research she did with Tony."

Sam turned red and Fred was aghast. "You didn't! No wonder she reacted like she did. And you. That's not like you, Evo. What were you thinking?"

"About weddings, and babies, and happily ever after. By the time I pulled my head out of my ass I'd destroyed any hope of a civil conversation, let alone a relashionship. I blew up like, instant and insanely jealous or I had temporary inshanity. I don't know what it was, but it certainly blew away my happily ever after."

"Your, er, happily ever after?"

His head flopped sideways and he winked at Fred. He stumbled forward and Fred guided him to the bed. "Let me tell you a she-cret." His whisper could have been heard in the next town. We all crammed in the doorway to listen. "Since that day almost two years ago when I met Sam? I have not been on so much as a shingle date, let alone knocked...nuttted...notched my damn bedpost. He clucked his tongue and winked again. "But you jusht wait and shee, Freddie old girl. I'm going to marry that woman and make about five or six little Sammonies of our own." He brightened. "And fish tanks. We'll have lots of fish so Sam has something to do while she's spawning." He laughed drunkenly at his own joke. Suddenly, he sobered and made a grab for Fred's sleeve. He missed again. "But you have to promise you won't shay any...anything to Sam. She's lessh than enamored with me at the moment." He let his head drop back on the pillow. He muttered to himself about his six little Sammies and a dog before fading into oblivion.

Another one bites the dust.

Fred propped up his bad arm and said softly, "Don't worry; your secrets are safe with me." Evo smiled and drifted off to sleep. Fred turned to all of us and giggled. "Well, that was enlightening, wasn't it?"

We all turned and stared at Sam. She stood in the kitchen door, red faced and teary eyed. She blushed furiously and tossed her hair over her shoulder. She said with feigned disdain, "Huh. Can you believe that guy?"

We all stood there like sheep, nodding in the affirmative.

Ramon said, "He sounded sincere to me."

28

Hours later, Ramon checked his watch and said, "I hate to break up such a lovely moment, but I am meeting with police officials regarding the mine. If you would excuse me, your plane will be ready after six o'clock tomorrow morning to take you home." His cell phone rang. He spoke in rapid, short sentences and hung up. "I leave in fifty minutes for the mines. The paperwork has come through and all is well."

Armand spoke up. "Please, sir, if you don't mind, I'd like to accompany you to the mines. I'm so close to the end of a very long assignment, I'd hate to miss out on the finale."

Nunez nodded. "I hoped you would suggest just that, young man." He looked at Fred and nodded, and then at me. "Ms. Miller, if you would also honor me by coming, you would be most welcome. Please do not feel obliged, but I understand from your sister that you might want to see this through."

I could only stare and nod. What the heck did Fred say while we were gone? I didn't really want to know, but I wasn't going to miss this opportunity. "Thank you," I choked out.

Fred sidled up to listen. Sam said, "We'll stay back and take care of our resident invalid. The helicopter only seats so many. I'm a fish doctor, not a cowboy—sorry, Buzz, I didn't mean you. I'm a survivor, but not cut out for a shoot out at the not-so OK Corral. I leave that to you law enforcement types. I'll stay and work on identifying the fish we picked up at the lagoon."

She turned to Fred. "You can take care of 'What's His Name' over there. You're more the nurturing type. I'm not." Sam spun on her heel to leave the room.

"But he wants you."

"Uh, yes, I think that has been established, but I also think that it would be better if you took the first watch."

Fred shrugged. "I guess that's it then." She raced across the room and caught me up in a strangle hold. I hugged her back and when she finally backed off I noticed she had tears in her eyes. "Be careful, Buzz. Mom would kill me if I didn't bring you back home."

I laughed. "You be careful as well. You might want to call J.J. and tell him we'll be delayed. Remember, those bad guys are still trying to take out Evo. If they find out he's here, you three might be in greater danger than us. Don't go out, lock the doors, and make sure one of you keeps an eye out for trouble."

Nunez came in from the kitchen. "I have arranged for four men to watch the house. Two will be in front, and two in back. This should keep you safe."

Fred bounced across the room and grabbed Nunez up in a tight hug. He raised his brows, and then gently patted her on the back. A weepy Fred finally let him go. "Thank you, Ramon. For all you've done."

"You are welcome, little one." She hugged him again and he blushed. "You Americans are very affectionate. Not that I am complaining my dear, it's just, I am not used to so much exuberance. Most people are a little intimidated by me."

Fred looked at him questioningly. "Why would anyone be intimidated by you? You're a caring person and a good man. Your mother raised you right, and that's what impresses me, Ramon."

Nunez gently lifted Fred's chin with his index finger and gazed down at her. "And you, my dear are one in a hundred million; and I thank you." He pressed his lips to hers in an achingly sweet kiss that had us all whistling.

Evo poked his head around the corner just in time to see Sam and I each hug Ramon. Even in his groggy state, I could see his eyes grow big with recognition, then narrow in jealously.

Evo cast a sardonic look our way. "Ahem. Now that the hug fest is over, could we get on with the business at hand, please?"

Sam lifted her nose in the air. "Mr. Castillo, your sarcasm is not only unbecoming, your unwarranted jealousy indicates a certain lack of maturity which I find extremely undesirable in a grown man. Why don't you just go back to bed?" She turned tail and made a grand exit into the kitchen.

"What's up with her?" Evo muttered to himself. We couldn't help but giggle. Evidently, Evo had no recollection of his earlier romantic confessions.

About twenty minutes later, Armand, Ramon, and I piled into the car waiting in front of Sam's house and headed for the airfield. A team of silent-but-deadly looking men met us at the plane. One of them yanked my backpack from my hand and threw it into the cargo area. We boarded a helicopter, which to me looked as big as a 747, and I sat crammed between two stone-faced, surly giants wearing bandoliers over camouflaged flak jackets. I felt as out of place as a cowboy in a rock-n-roll bar in my stylish outdoor wear from Gander Mountain. At least I wasn't wearing fluorescent orange or my red *Lucky Bucky* ball cap. I'd have really looked dumb then.

Since I didn't understand the language, they pretty much ignored me. Armand, who sat a couple of giants down from me occasionally leaned forward and gave me the abbreviated version of what was being said. I could barely hear him over the roar of the blades and the yelling of the other men, but I understood that we were taking the helicopter to the base of the mountain, where anyone coming down the mountain or attempting to go up would have already been waylaid by a National Police Special Forces Unit and American ATF agents.

I also learned that the men in the helicopter wanted to dump Armand and me at the bottom of the mountain before they continued on their way to the mine. Armand protested hotly and Ramon stepped in and sided with Armand. I sat back, safe in the knowledge that everything would be all right and relaxed for the first time in two days. I must have been exhausted because I woke up sometime later sprawled across the guy next to me. I sat up, pushed the hair out of my eyes, and wiped the drool from the corner of my mouth. Humiliated at being found in such a predicament, I turned to apologize to him. He looked down at me, grinning from ear to ear. His gold front tooth glinted in the meager light.

Not knowing what to do, I patted his knee and said, "*Gracias.*"

He nodded enthusiastically and patted me on the head. "Is okay," he said.

From then on, camaraderie of sorts sprang between us. I thought maybe I should have drooled on someone earlier, we'd practically be family by now. Armand told me we were nearing the bottom of the mountain. He said we wouldn't be stopping there, but continuing up by truck so as not to arouse suspicion.

We landed with a thump, and as the guys on either side of me stood. Sandwiched between them like I was, they just picked me up with them. Ramon asked me once more if I wanted to stay at the bottom of the mountain, but I guess my face gave me away and he waved me off. I had a bad moment when I saw the men piling into the back of the huge six-by-six ore trucks, but one of my new buddies grabbed my hand and dragged me to the cab of one of the trucks. He boosted me up and I became once again, a Buzz sandwich as we lumbered up the mountain.

I'd lost track of Armand when we exited the helicopter, but I knew he rode in one of the trucks behind us. The guy on my right rifled through a side compartment and came up with a dirty camouflage hat and crammed the smelly thing on my head. I could barely see over the dashboard, but I had little

277

interest in the local scenery. I patted his arm in thanks and he flashed a toothy grin.

The long bumpy trip gave me plenty of time to think. What could a tropical fish importer have in common with an illegal mine operator? The whole scenario was totally fishy in my book. Back up, Buzz, and take things one at a time.

Mining operation; mining ore on someone else's property, chiseling ore out of the ground, moving it to a site where the precious metals could be extracted, getting it out of the country, and either financing something of magnificent proportions or laundering it in some other fashion. And don't get caught doing it. No way could it be done, but this arrogant jerk had pulled it off, until now.

Tropical fish, a billion dollar industry. Most exports go to the United States, Great Britain, and Asia. Many new species are still being discovered in oxbow lake regions in Venezuela, Columbia, and Peru. A man could make a lot of money if he were the only person to possess a new species of Corydoras and no one else could locate them. Where's the motive? It seemed a lot of trouble to go through to me. Ian had said the fish in the lagoon were not indigenous to that area by the plant material they ingested. They must have been transported in from somewhere else. Why would someone do that?

It hit me like a ton of bricks. Power. Notoriety. Hank. Hank loved his place in the spotlight in the fish world. He gloried in discovering new species. He had access to the area, and was very persistent in his questioning Ian about the Endler Live Bearers in Ian's lab. What if Hank discovered a new species of Cory and didn't want the rest of the world to know their origin until he'd pocketed millions of dollars and the fame for himself? He could mislead the rest of the world by making them think the new species of Corydoras were found in the lagoon here. The fish would spawn in small quantities, or be fished out by the competition, and Hank would be the only source in the world. What if the Endlers were just a cover crop to hide the new species of Corydoras from the rest of the world? He could cash in twice, as the Endlers were endangered but very prolific. Television time, articles to write, books to publish; now we're talking Hank MacRone! Maybe that was the source of the black smog that enveloped me when I took his hand. But how was Hank's connected to Chavez and the mine? Think, Buzz.

The diesel engine was so loud I could barely hear myself think. How could drivers stand it day in and day out? *How does Armand fit into this equation?* Something still didn't add up.

I watched a truck rumble past us on its way down the mountain. I wondered how long of a trip it would be to transport the ore to its final destination. They probably transported it by ship, or turned it into paper money and transported it by plane...

Plane! Holy cow, how could I have missed it? Fish are transported by plane. Paper money could be transported by plane. Fish could not go through customs, because x-rays render fish sterile. Armand was looking for an arms dealer. If the fish were transported disguising the illegal arms, the weapons wouldn't be detected because they wouldn't be x-rayed.

I grabbed my cell phone and called Armand.

"Buzz?"

"Armand, I got it figured out! I just don't have the *how* yet."

"Well spit it out for God's sake!"

I ran through my theory and he added to it. "If the ore can be extracted on-site, then couldn't they transport a higher volume of product; in this case, probably gold? I'll ask Nunez how to go about exchanging large amounts of gold into paper money, but I'd bet much of it is going to finance the purchase of the arms you're after."

279

Armand thought a second. "Hank probably gets a piece of the pie and therefore keeps his mouth shut. Chavez might even be behind the transportation of the fish to the phony locations."

"But, Armand, where do those dead fish and the abandoned village come into play? I can't believe it's all part of a grand plan."

"I don't know, but you'd better call Sam and Fred right now."

"You're right, See you." I hung up and dialed Sam's house.

"Hello?

"Sam, it's Buzz."

"Hi, Buzz, how is it going? Where are you?"

"Going well, and on our way up the mountain. Look, I need you to check something. Would you check the world registry for Corydoras catfish and see if Hank recently discovered a new species in Venezuela?"

"Sure, Buzz, but why? He would have said something to us had he made a new discovery, wouldn't he? Wait! Are you talking about our new little guys from the poisoned lagoon?"

"Yes I am."

"Hold on and let me fire up the computer." As she turned on her laptop I proceeded to explain my theory on speakerphone. Fred and Sam went from disbelief to skepticism, to outrage as I ticked off the circumstantial evidence against their long time friend.

"Here it is," Sam exclaimed, as she pulled up an obscure ichthyologic website. Corydoras MacRoni."

"Macaroni?" I hooted. "As in elbow macaroni? As in 'and called it Macaroni?' As in macaroni and cheese? What was he thinking?"

Sam sighed. "I think Hank probably wanted his new fish pronounced Macrone-eye to make it sound more Latin. The "a" is probably a typo."

"You and I both know everyone will call them Macaroni.

Hank will be a laughingstock."

"I agree. Now we only have to figure out what the heck he's up to."

"That's what I hope to do at the top of this mountain. How's our patient?"

"A pain in the butt."

"Good. That means he's feeling better. Got to go, I'll call you later. Could you keep puttering away at the computer and see if you can find any more recent 'discoveries' made by Hank?"

"Will do, and thanks. Bye, Buzz."

"See you later." I slapped my phone shut and stuffed it into a pocket. I pulled out a topographical map of the mountain, and pointed to where I thought we were. My companions both pointed to a spot much closer to the top. I gave them thumbs up, and they did the same back to me. The driver downshifted as the incline grew steeper and just when I became apprehensive about falling off the mountain we leveled off and drove into a large clearing at the opening of the mine.

Our driver pulled to the far left of the lot, followed by truck after truck until a rumbling diesel barrier formed across the only exit off the mountain. My companions and I scrambled down from the cab, and the rest of the small army exited the other semis. I had an assault rifle stuffed into my hands as they pushed and shoved me along with them. I hunched my shoulders and tried to look bigger as we stood shoulder to shoulder (in my case, shoulder to hip) across the front of the trucks, weapons at the ready.

One by one, the workers noticed us standing there, and one of them rushed into the trailer, probably Chavez's office. I looked for a security force around the mine, and felt a bit surprised to discover that the only men who held weapons were those patrolling the perimeter. This Chavez guy was way overconfident he wouldn't be caught.

281

I watched as Ramon Nunez led a group of men toward the trailer. I slipped out of line and a hand snaked out and grabbed my collar. I twisted around and freed myself-scurrying along to catch up with Nunez. I peeled off like a Blue Angel when they neared the trailer, and ran around the other side of the entrance where a crude road carved a path out of the jungle and ran along the north end of the mine.

I inched along, watching for guys with guns and large hungry reticulating snakes. My foot caught on something and I looked down. I almost gave myself a heart attack when I saw a three-inch diameter monster hovering over the toe of my boot. I almost shot the damn thing until I realized it wasn't an anaconda, but a muddy fire hose. When my blood pressure finally dropped and my breathing returned to almost normal, I took one final shaky breath and followed the fire hose.

What I found at the end of that hose put the final piece of the puzzle in place.

29

I heard it before I saw it. The sound of water cascading over a waterfall drowned out much of the noise around me. I scrambled, slipped, slid, clawed, and slithered my way up a huge mountain of mud and remembered to check for snakes before I lay on my belly watching the mining operation from above. Behind a monstrous glass enclosure, the waterfall poured over a mountain of stone. I was so confused by what I saw; I yanked out my cell phone and called Sam back.

"Buzz?"

"Yeah, Sam, it's me again. Say, how coherent is Evo? I need to talk to him."

"He's a grouchy old coot because he's refusing pain meds, and unfortunately for us, he's very coherent. Hold on."

I smiled at the affectionate tone in Sam's complaints.

"Buzz? Evo. What's up?"

"Evo, explain to me about how gold mines pollute the environment. I didn't retain all of our conversation, but you said something about acid and ores and heavy metals."

"Sure. A relatively cheap way of extracting gold from ore is called heap leaching. The crushed ore is piled up and a cyanide solution is sprayed into it. The cyanide reacts with the gold and is collected in leach beds and in overflow ponds. They re-circulate the ore and through a process 'cyanidation' the gold is extracted."

"That would make the product more pure for transport."

"And a lot less heavy."

"Evo, I'm sure I just found the source of our poison. I'm looking at a pile of rock being bombarded by what looks like water from a huge fire hoses. The water falls through the rock into a trough leading to collection ponds."

"It sounds like you hit the mother lode. You're with the cops, right?"

"Well, sort of. So cyanide is our poison? Didn't Ian find traces of more than one heavy metal in the fish and the water?"

"Yes, and that could be because when cyanide breaks down heavy metals it can form other poisons. When cyanide combines with other chemicals it can create substances which are even more toxic than the cyanide itself."

Sam yelled from the background, "Freshwater fish are especially sensitive to exposure to cyanide."

"Wow," I said. "Do you think that with the heavy rainfalls this season, those ponds overflowed and ran down hill to the village, into the water supply, and ultimately into the lagoon? That would explain why Ian couldn't find heavy metal toxins embedded in the tissues of the fish–only in their stomachs. If the fish weren't native to the area, they would have absolutely no immunity to a fouled water supply. Those dirt bags at the mine poisoned the people of the village and anything that came into contact with the water."

Evo was on a roll. "Right you are. The cyanide actually blocks the absorption of oxygen by the cells, and ultimately causes suffocation…" I listened with half an ear to Evo when I heard a round chuck into a chamber, and felt cold steel on the back of my neck.

"Uh, Evo? I think I have to go."

"…Parts per million, whereas sixty to seventy micrograms per liter of cyanide…"

The gunman pressed hard against my neck and his other hand pressed down on my shoulder. I tried to interrupt Evo. The gunman flopped me forward onto the ground and gently placed a foot between my shoulder blades.

"Uh, Evo, there's a bad guy with a big gun pointed at my head. I have to hang up now."

"But when you are talking about a contained water source like the lagoon…"

"*Evo!* I'm hanging up! No offense man, but there's a guy here who wants to shoot me!"

The man holding the gun nudged me and fired off orders, none of which I understood. He pressed his foot across my shoulders and exerted enough pressure to make it hard to breathe. I didn't have to be bilingual to know he wasn't inviting me to luncheon al fresco. He was trying to crunch-in my el-chest-o. I heard Evo still firing off statistics and ignored him.

"Two-hundred micrograms per liter would pretty much decimate anything which ingested–what did you say? Shoot you? Buzz, Buzz! Are you there?"

I puffed pretty hard, and couldn't get enough breath to answer. I remember some grunting and wheezing going on, but as the guy with the gun practically stood on me. "Evo, (*puff*) they got me. If I die, (*wheeze*) get these bastards!"

I dropped my phone without hanging up and someone booted me in the ribs and flipped me onto my back. Gasping for air, I found myself staring down the barrel of a very large rifle. Crap. I stayed perfectly still while two guys argued back and forth. My eyes were watering, but I could make out a total of three bodies–all of whom were armed and assuredly dangerous. Crap again. I was definitely in deep doo-doo. I heard the tinny voices of Evo and the girls coming from my cell phone. I didn't dare move to pick it up, but one of my captors must have heard the yelling and picked up my phone.

"Allo?"

I heard Evo on the other end and prayed he would distract these morons until I got a head start. The guy on the phone laughed and gave the phone to one of the others. Already on speaker, they carried on a four-way conversation with Evo. I started to squirm away, but the only way to go was downhill. I didn't want to risk falling into the leach pond, so I scooted back the way I came. Head first, I inched my way over the crest and began to slither down the hill.

One of the men threw back his head to laugh at something Evo said and happened to look to where I should have been lying on the ground. He spun around and looked around the immediate area and down toward the cyanide pond. I tried to squirm faster about the time the man spotted me sliding through the mud backward on my way down the opposite side of the hill. He shouted and shoved the others. I thought I'd better exit fast, stage left.

I flipped over onto my stomach and gave a mighty shove with my feet. I hit a slick spot and surged forward. Water from the leaking fire hose slicked the hill like an old Slip-n-Slide. I began picking up speed as the guys at the top dropped my cell phone and fumbled for their weapons. I positively flew down that hill. Paddling with my hands, I shot like greased lightning over a hump and caught some good air before I hit ground and scooped up a mouth full of mud. I heard gunfire, but felt nothing as I accelerated to warp speed. I swiped at my eyes and realized my new buddies from the plane and truck ride were firing on the guys at the top of the hill who were firing on me.

The bottom of the hill rushed up at me and I remember thinking that Dad always joked that a fall off a cliff wouldn't kill you, it was the stop at the *end* of the fall. I saw my doom approaching at breakneck speed and wondered fleetingly if death by anaconda would have been less painful than death by mudslide. Over my screams I heard a colossal *boom* and wondered briefly if I'd broken the sound barrier.

I hit the bottom of the hill and catapulted into the air. Lord knows how far I flew before I crash landed. I curled into a ball and hit the ground with tooth-jarring impact. Though I'd prepared myself for the stop, the collision knocked me into tomorrow. When I finally came to, I thought my eyeballs must have blown up because my head hurt like hell and I was stone blind. I soon realized that mud packed every orifice of my body and not only could I not see, I couldn't hear and could barely breathe. I shook my head like a wet dog.

Noise exploded all around me, and a stabbing pain in my chest made me suck in a much-needed breath. I clawed at my eyes to remove handfuls of mud. I reached down to wipe my face with my shirt and found only mud covered skin. Oh no! I was blind and deaf, and somehow my shirt burned off on my way down that hill. I felt someone wiping the mud out of my eyes, and when I could see again, I couldn't do anything but laugh, and it hurt like hell.

Surrounded by a battalion of grinning South Americans, I shook my head and sent mud flying like a retriever shedding water. Uproarious laughter followed and I wondered why they were so entertained by my predicament. I became decidedly uncomfortable and happened to look down to make sure my sport bra was still in place. What met my eyes was a bust that would have made Dolly Parton jealous. It seemed my sport bra had collected mud all the way down the slope and packed it into my bra, from below my chin half way to my navel. I saw Armand, among the crowd, snap a picture with his cell phone and laugh. I realized something else in that moment; I really did hurt like hell.

The pain was so sharp it turned my knees to rubber. I grabbed my ribs, and mud squirted out of my bra and onto my laughing audience. "Armand," I yelled as blackness swept over me. Then nothing.

When I came to we were the a helicopter heading back to Lima. I noticed several things at once. I could see, I was clean, no longer half naked, and my bust had shrunk back to regulation size (sigh). I looked up into Armand's smiling eyes and said the first thing that came to mind, "Do I have you to thank for this?" He nodded his head and I said, "Does this mean we're engaged?"

He laughed and patted my hand. "Unfortunately no, Buzz." He put the back of his hand against his forehead. "Alas, I am just the beast of burden who toted you and your mongo mud bazoombas back to the trucks. I had to fight off your new buddies for that right. They also insisted on slinging a hammock in the back of a truck so you wouldn't be jostled around on the way down. We got you off the mountain, but to my regret I didn't have the pleasure of being on the cleanup crew. The hospital staff did it."

I swung at him and the pain in my side took my breath away.

"Hold on old girl, you have broken ribs. I don't want to be responsible for one going through your lung."

"Crap, it must have broke when that Bozo kicked me, or from the ride down that mudslide Whatever, it sure stings."

"Stings? Right. I've had broken ribs. Bees sting. Broken ribs take your breath away."

I laughed, but the pain had me grabbing my side again. "Wait! What about the mine, Armand? Tell me what happened! Where's Nunez? Where's Chavez?"

"*Whoa.* Let me see. Chavez is in custody of the National Police. The U.S. wants his ass, too, but frankly I'd be surprised if he made it through the judicial system down here alive."

"Why do we want him?"

"Arms, baby. Arms! That's what he did with the gold. He bought up arms and smuggled them through Port of Miami, New Jersey, New Orleans, and Seattle. From those places he distributed them world-wide. Quite the operation."

"Evo. I said. Call Evo."

"Already did, and he told me what you thought about the fish and the toxins. When I confronted Hank, he broke down and spilled his guts. Chavez caught him stocking the lagoon with the Corys and the Endlers, and in return for not announcing Hank to the world as a fraud, he blackmailed Hank into shipping arms along with the fish. Hank also made some damn good money off the deal. It was a great set up for a couple of unscrupulous, and might I add arrogant characters, like MacRone and Chavez. They've been flying under the radar since they began. That is, until one lone scientist threw a monkey wrench into the works."

"And the aftermath, Armand? Do they have an EPA down here that will do the cleanup of the waters and the jungle?"

Armand ruffled his hair. "My agency is sending people. They'll work with the Venezuelans to neutralize the toxins and clean up the mess around here. Nunez is footing most of the bill. He's going to use the profits from the mine for the cleanup and to rebuild the village at a different location."

"So you're finished down here as well? What now Armand? Do you go home or what?"

"I have some time off coming to me, Buzz." He sighed and looked out the window. "I thought I might take a trip to the upper Midwest, maybe Wisconsin. Who knows? I might make it over to White Bass Lake. Got an extra cot for a good old Italian boy from Queens?"

I squeezed his hand. "You bet. One with your name on it."

Armand dug around in his pockets. "Wait! I almost forgot, I have something for you."

"A present? Oh, I love presents."

"Uh, not exactly," he muttered and patted his pockets. "Where the heck did I put it?" He grabbed his jacket and rummaged around in the pockets. "*Aha.* Here it is!"

With a flourish Armand presented me with the ultimate souvenir, my mud-caked cell phone.

30

Between Armand, Evo, and me, I think we had enough pain medication in us to anesthetize a small third world country. Thank the heavens we were traveling by private plane, otherwise we would have been detained at customs as drug dealers.

It was a beat up party of five that arrived in the wee hours of the following morning at Mitchell Field in Milwaukee. Though not physically injured, an exhausted Fred and Sam ran themselves ragged trying to take care of three invalids. Well, make that two invalids and a faker. Armand's nose looked just fine, but he basked in the attention he received and swore his broken nose was a debilitating injury.

Airport Security took one look at us and dispatched someone to retrieve Evo's truck from long-term parking. They even helped load our gear into the back. Sam drove and Fred navigated. It was clear sailing at that hour of the morning on the expressway, so we made good time getting to White Bass Lake. Sam stopped first at my house and she, Armand, and Fred helped me to the porch. My porch doesn't have a rail, so we were discussing the best way to get me up the stairs when the door flew open.

"Damn it, Buzz." We all looked up at the wild man who burst through the door, and I'd never felt anything that close to a sense of *home* than I did at that moment. The stress melted away, the picture of J.J. mad as hell standing with his fists balled on his hips blurred around the edges until I saw only him. I felt warm and safe and a little muzzy Tears filled my eyes and ran down my face–probably side effects from the drugs.

I was so busy soaking in the ambience; I never thought to warn Armand about Wesley. Armand stood directly opposite the door when J.J. threw it open and in the direct line of fire when a one-hundred-and-sixty-pound ball of black fire came roaring through the air. Wesley's paws caught Armand squarely in the chest and knocked him off his feet and onto his butt. Wes was so happy everyone had come just to see him, he did the doggy dance on Armand's body while Armand sucked air like a vacuum cleaner and yelled about his nose.

Fred ran to Armand's rescue and hauled Wes off to the side. He treated Fred to big slurpy doggy kisses, which splashed off her and onto Armand. Fred let go of his collar, and Wes turned back to Armand. Hilary chose that moment to come through the door and stand patiently until Wesley finished sliming Armand. I noticed her when she leaned against my leg, and I grabbed hold of J.J.'s belt so I could lean down and rub her ears without falling on my butt.

Wes finally realized he was licking a stranger and abandoned Armand and started back on Fred. "Wes, no. Down. Off. Off!" Fred stumbled over Armand and fell backward, her hand connecting with Armand's nose. Armand wailed and Wes treated it like a new game. Wes crouched on his forelegs and lifted his butt high in the air, tail wagging, and mouth grinning.

I knew that stance as Wes's version of the "tiger pounce" and figured I'd better distract him. I still held onto J.J.'s belt and said out of the corner of my mouth, "Protect me, Green." I turned to Wes. "Wesley, I'm home."

Wesley's head shot up and he spun in circles. He finally saw me standing next to J.J. and bounded forward to greet me properly. A split second before take-off, J.J. yelled, "*Down!*" I dropped my teeth when Wes hit turf. King Wesley, Doggie School Dropout obeyed a command for the first time in his four years on earth.

"Holy crap," I said

"Holy Crap," Fred echoed.

"Wow," said Sam

"Wow," echoed Evo.

"Did someone get the plate number of that bus?" Armand, lay horizontal on the front lawn.

A very smug J.J. leaned over and scratched Wesley's ears. "Good boy." Wesley leaned on his leg, grinning back and wagging his tail.

J.J. hoisted me up the stairs and waited until I got situated on the reclining love seat before he started yelling at me again. "Damn it, Buzz."

My head hurt. My ribs hurt. I wanted more drugs. Annoyed, I said, "Didn't we already do this part?"

J.J. blew out a sigh and ran a hand through his hair. He skulked back and forth and I mentally braced myself for the tirade of the century. He took a deep breath and turned to Fred, Armand, Evo, and Sam.

"Thank God you all made it back in uh, sort of one piece. Anyone want coffee? It's morning, we might as well."

Evo relaxed and smiled, "I'm in. Sam? Fred?"

Fred looked up from rubbing Wesley's belly. "Okay with me, Armand?"

"I'd rather have a beer if you have one. I've had a rough couple of years the last few days."

J.J. gave him a perplexed look. "Years?"

I poked J.J. in the butt. "We'll tell you all about it. Get your coffee and come sit." I patted the love seat next to me and Wes came flying through the air.

"*Down*," J.J. yelled and Wes hit the floor inches in front of the love seat. He gave J.J. an injured look and laid his head on my knee. Hilary put her paws on the love seat and J.J. boosted her up. She crawled in my lap and quietly passed gas.

I sighed and fanned the air. "There's no place like home."

The odor finally wafted past Armand and he choked.

"*Whew*. What the heck *is* that?" When he saw me pointing at Hilary he shook his head. "Don't you all be feeding me that *the dog did it* crap." Hilary promptly fizzed again.

We all laughed and Fred fanned the air around him. "Welcome to the family; you've just been officially initiated by Hilary, *The Canine Source for Natural Gas*." As if on cue, poor Hill cracked off another one for good measure.

A bit concerned over Hill's overabundance of odiferous emissions, I wondered aloud if I should take her over to Dr. Mike's and have her checked out. J.J. said, "Uh, don't worry about Hill. She, uh, had a little ice cream and sauerkraut last night and has been farting up a storm ever since."

I rolled my eyes and sighed. I patted poor flatulent Hilary and J.J. grabbed me and ruffled my hair. "*Ow*." I winced from the pain and he pulled back.

"Gee, Buzz, are you okay? You know, come to think of it, you really do look like death warmed over."

"I've been through hell, so leave me alone. My ribs are broke, I have a headache, my entire body feels like it was run over by a Mack truck–"

"Yo, Miller, slow down. You're starting to whine." My face heated and I turned a lovely shade of pink. He kissed the top of my head and looked over at Armand. "Hey, you with the broken nose, want to give me a hand? It'll get you away from the stench for a bit."

Armand practically lunged across the room. Evo said, "I'll help too," and followed them to the kitchen.

I narrowed my eyes at J.J. "Don't you dare grill them to death James J. Green. I know how you operate. Watch him, Armand; he'll have you spilling the family secrets in less than five minutes."

"I'll be on my guard, Buzz. Don't forget I'm tough, I'm from Queens."

"Whatever the heck that means," I muttered. "Okay."

Five minutes later, Sam went into the kitchen and brought back coffee. "They're talking about maybe trying to work with the government to get Hank back to the States. What I want to know is why Hank would jeopardize everything in his life just to put his name on a fish?"

"Money," I said.

"Fame," Fred said.

Sam sighed. "I wonder what will happen to him now."

I took a sip of coffee and wondered how much of Hank's fate I should reveal to Sam and Fred. According to Ramon Nunez, Hank would go away for the rest of his life, if he lived that long.

Knock, knock, knock, bang, bang.

"Hey, Green, see who's at the front door?"

J.J. mumbled, "Probably the Geriatric S.W.A.T. Team. How would they know you're even home yet? I sure as heck hope Edie didn't say anything over the police radio; all those little old ladies have scanners. Oh my God, just the thought makes me queasy. Jell-O salads at five-in-the-morning. Brats, noodles. *Uhh.* He clawed at my good arm, sliding down to his knees as if in prayer. "I couldn't choke down one of your Mom's infamous hockey pucks if I tried. Please don't let them in!"

"Green, you are an evil man."

"Yep, and if I can avoid your mother's hockey puck hamburgers, I'll live to be an evil *old* man!"

"Just get the door."

J.J. wiped his nose on his sleeve, dabbed at his eyes and sobered. "Okay, but you'd better come clean up the mess."

"What mess?"

"After I get stampeded by four little old ladies, my body will be imprinted with orthopedic shoe prints. My flat remains will have to be delivered to my mother—wait! My mother will probably be among them. I can't win."

J.J. chuckled as he swung open the front door. "Uh, Buzz, I think it's for you."

I leaned over to greet my mom. "Yo Ger–" No further words came out as Luis and Alfredo were shoved through the door followed by a very large man with an equally large gun.

"Tell me where they are," the giant demanded.

I struggled forward and J.J. tried to hold onto my shirt. "May I help you, sir? I believe you are in the employ of Hector Chavez, am I correct?"

He raised the gun to my face. "What would you know about it? I'm here for the two docs and these two pieces of dead meat." He gestured to Luis and Alfredo as they huddled together on the floor. Alfredo had blood seeping from his lower lip and Luis had a black eye.

I figured the bruises were part of the persuasion the hit man had used on the Gallegos brothers to find us. I tried for negotiation tactics, but it came out bitch. "Hey, Buddy, your boss is in jail, and your mission has been cancelled. Call him if you don't believe me. We just got back from making sure he went away, so lose the gun before you rack up murder charges, eh?"

He leveled a look at me and said in a dead voice, "Where are the scientists, Big Mouth?"

J.J. took a step forward and the giant shot the floor at his feet. Splinters flew up from the wood floor and the giant's face split into an evil grin. "Don't move law man." At J.J.'s frown the giant said, "Yeah, I know all about you crazy people. You and the big mouthed Bitch must be the cops."

He gestured off to the side toward Sam and Fred. "One of them is the girl doc, so the other doc has to be close by."

Fred held out her cell phone. "Call your boss, sir. Call South America and you'll see that this mission is over. Use my phone. Please, just do it."

I looked over at the house phone and saw that it was off

the hook. Fred must have dialed 911. I hoped Edie would understand the danger as she sent J.J.'s deputies, Moe, Larry, Curly, and Shemp over here.

I instantly had another thought, *Ted!* It meant that our bumbling, incompetent constable, Dead Butz would hear the call, and if he heard it, so would his mom. Mary would call Mom, and Mom would call Jane and Joy.

I barely had time to finish the thought when I heard the roar of an engine coming down my road. A red Crown Victoria with blue hair at the wheel could barely be seen over the dash. The Crown Vic's tires squealed as the huge car skidded sideways at the entrance to my driveway.

"What the hell is this?" The hit man stared out the window.

A scrawny leg kicked the driver's door open and Mary Cromwell hopped out of her car. She held a basket and the smell of bread wafted through the front door. The passenger door and the two back doors also popped open and the rest of the Senior Women's Action Team followed Mary to the front door. Mom carried a large salad bowl and Jan had a big grocery bag. Joy dragged a cooler behind her and Dad stepped out eating a brownie. *Oh crap, they were listening to the scanner!*

"Welcome home, Buzz," Mary squawked. "Time for a party!"

The giant grumbled and tucked his gun under his jacket as the little old ladies bustled past him on their way to the kitchen. He leaned toward me. "One word and I'll waste the old girls where they stand."

Mary winked as she passed me. "We'll get the food set up, Buzz. You just entertain your guests."

"Ah I, uh what..." I said as I watched my mom wink at Fred before she disappeared into the kitchen. *They know, but they sure aren't very subtle.*

The giant squared his shoulders. "Now just a damn

minute; I got business here to tend to." He reached for his gun as another car pulled into the driveway.

Mark and Tom tumbled out of the beat-up Cooper and Tom addressed the giant. "Hey, Reymundo, looking for us?"

Mark added, "Didn't anyone tell you the war is over?"

The giant we now knew as Reymundo turned toward Tom and Mark. "I knew I'd find you incompetent little bastards sooner or later, but how do you know me?" He raised his gun.

Tom stepped forward. "I called my friend at our local newspaper office when I learned the name of your boss. He gave me the names and descriptions of his known murder-for-hire guys. You answered to the name I picked. Not bad for a moron, eh?" Reymundo was so confused, he forgot to keep his weapon raised.

Behind us the kitchen door blew open and the Blue Hairs rushed out armed and hilarious. They stood abreast like a showdown from the old west, trying for menacing and achieving comical. Dressed in muumuus and combat boots, clutching .44s in their hands, it was truly a Kodak moment. Reymundo froze, stunned. He stood gaping at the spectacle before him.

From behind me came a rumble which grew into a roar. I barely opened my mouth to yell when a black rocket flew past J.J. and me, and blasted Reymundo from the rear with 160 pounds of enraged Wesley. Hill followed and grabbed his upper thigh in her famous Bulldog Chomp.

A squad car bumped over the curb and skidded to a stop in the front yard as chunks of mud and sod flew in all directions. Moe and Larry tumbled out behind the squad doors, shotguns resting on the open windows. J.J. joined Wes on top of the bad guy and wrestled the gun away from him. I dropped to my knees between his shoulder blades and when I looked up, I stared down the shaking barrels of four .44 caliber revolvers. Mom, Jan, Joy, and Mary stood over us with their weapons drawn and their eyes narrowed. It was truly a frightening sight. I understood why Reymundo stared.

Moe and Larry jumped from behind the squad doors and cuffed the screaming Reymundo. "Dirty Harry Mary" kept booting him in the side, yelling, *"Go ahead, punk, make my day."* Armand finally grabbed her around the middle and carried her kicking and screaming back into the kitchen.

Hilary drew blood, and Wesley's jaws had to be pried off the back of Reymundo's neck. The deputies carted the sobbing hit man off to jail. I was so proud of my puppies I gathered them close and cried into their fur. Hill blinked up at me and Wes grinned and wagged his tail.

Luis and Alfredo's friends, Tom and Mark, stood off to the side, scuffing the sidewalk with their shoes. I looked up at J.J., who stared intently at them. Tom noticed and hit Mark on the arm. They put their heads close together to say something and as one straightened and moved forward toward J.J.

Mark bit his lip and looked up at J.J. Tom cleared his throat and stepped forward. "Sir, um, we are under arrest."

I didn't realize I had grabbed Fred's arm until she winced. I let her go.

J.J. eyed the two men coolly. "I beg your pardon?"

Mark pulled at his collar and spoke this time. "We would like to be under arrest, please."

J.J. looked at me and calmly opened the rear door of the squad. With a flourish, he bowed and said, "Gentlemen, step into my office. Could you at least give me a hint as to why I should be arresting you?"

Tom cleared his throat again and turned toward J.J. "Yes, sir, we can...It is murder."

Everyone gasped.

J.J. sighed and looked skyward. He leveled a look at the two men and opened the rear door of the squad. "Gentlemen, you have the right to remain silent..."

31

I tossed my keys to Fred and climbed into the squad next to J.J. We drove in silence, and I was surprised when we passed the Sheriff's office. I must have looked confused, because J.J. patted my knee and said, "I'll tell you in a minute."

He pulled into the parking lot of Sal's Diner. Now I *was* confused. J.J. said in a low voice over the roof of the squad, "Calm down, Buzz, they're not going anywhere; they came to us–remember?"

He met me at the rear of the squad. "I haven't decided if I have to arrest anyone yet, and I think they'll be more comfortable talking in here rather than the office, don't you?" He placed a friendly arm around my shoulders and turned me toward Sal's. "Besides, I really need a cup of coffee, don't you? Sal will want to be in on the gossip anyway."

He left me standing with my mouth hanging open as he opened the door of the squad so Mark and Tom could get out.

J.J. made a show of dusting off his hands and smiled. "Let's have some coffee and talk, shall we gentlemen?" He gestured toward the diner with a sweep of his hand.

Tom and Mark looked at each other, and then at me. They looked as if they should have had those little cartoon bubbles over their heads that said, "*Huh?*" Wearing matching bewildered expressions, they followed J.J. like sheep to the slaughter. I walked last through the door. Looking around the crowded room I spotted several people who would call my mom and J.J.'s in about thirty seconds. Lovely, I thought again; the special at Sal's today is going to be mutton.

J.J. weaved his way through the dining area toward a booth in the far corner. Mark and Tom sat restlessly in their seats, each looking a little grey. They sat across from J.J. and me, and two more forlorn individuals I had never seen. By mutual consent, they told us they decided they could no longer pretend to be paid assassins because, as Mark put it, "We really suck at it."

Tom agreed, his head bobbing. "We suck for sure. How can people kill for a living? I killed one bad guy for sure, maybe even two, and I cannot eat or sleep! Luis and Alfredo are our friends, and poor little kitty..." He sniffed and wiped his nose on his sleeve, "What are we going to do?"

They sat in silence for a moment as Donna approached their table and filled their coffee mugs. She smiled and said in a booming voice, "I know what you can do."

Mark and Tom stiffened. Wide eyed, they slowly looked up at the smiling waitress as they waited for the other shoe to drop. Donna plopped the coffee pot on the table and put her hands on her hips. "When you go back to South America, take Sal with you. That way he'll be out of my hair for a while. He needs a really *looong* vacation." She laughed heartily at her own joke, and a few customers joined in.

"Why does he need a vacation?" Tom stared at us blankly. I rolled my eyes, because I'd heard about Thursday Night Football the night before, and knew what was coming.

Donna slid a glance toward Sal and quipped, "The Chicago Bears lost again last night and the quarterback broke his ankle. Sal has been crying into the eggs all morning. He's in desperate need of long-term 'The-Bears-Blew-Another-Season' counseling."

The diners guffawed and Sal threw his arms into the air in obvious distress. Bits of egg and ham flew off the end of the spatula as Sal muttered to himself. Doug Ryan calmly placed his hand over his coffee cup as the egg flew in his direction. He never broke stride in his conversation as the fluffy projectile plopped onto the back of his hand. He tipped it sideways and dumped the egg onto the table.

Donna snatched up her coffee pot and chirped, "See what I mean?" She spun on her heel and called, "Enjoy," over her shoulder as she continued her one-woman stand-up routine, all the while pouring coffee and taking orders.

Mark smiled after Donna and sighed softly. "This is a really nice place, Tom. These are nice people. We have new friends and I have a new family and a horseshoe tournament next Friday. For the first time in our lives, we almost belong to something good."

"Not for long, though. We're going to die soon," Tom said and sighed morosely. "If the Bad Guy Boss does not kill us first, we will rot in jail here then be deported and killed later in South America."

"Chavez is in jail, gentlemen." At the look of bewilderment, he explained that Hector Chavez, their "boss" was finished in South America. The looks of confusion turned to elation and I felt sorry for them.

J.J. pushed the hat back on his head and scratched his forehead. "I'm sorry, gentlemen, but murder is still illegal, even if you knock off a bad guy. You recklessly endangered the lives of two innocent men, and inadvertently killed a criminal. One act does not justify the other."

I picked up the conversation. "The town sees you as heroes for the stunt at the bank. Between the dead cat and the dead burglar, everyone in town has something to be happy about, but once again, you jeopardized the lives of–"

J.J.'s cell phone rang. "Green, here. Phil? Phil who? Oh, Larry, the deputy–good. Yeah, go ahead, Larry, what's up? No kidding, the bank guy? I did not know that. He what? Well, that's good news. No, no, shackle him to the bed anyway, and you take the first watch since you're already there. Can you get a hold of Moe, Shemp, and Curly and work out a schedule for the watch between the four of you? I'll check in later. Yeah, thanks, Moe. Bye now."

He clicked the phone shut and stared at it for a moment. When he looked up I saw it in his wry expression. Before he could speak I said, "The burglar didn't die, did he?"

J.J. looked at me and shook his head. "How *do* you do that?"

"I read you like a book, Green. Geez, who else would you have been talking to the deputy on the bank caper about, the damn crapper cat? And by the way, you were talking to Larry, not Moe."

"I was talking about the cat."

Tom perked up. "The cat, he is alive?"

Mark said, "The cat crapped?"

"No, the burglar," J.J. replied.

"The burglar crapped?"

"No! The burglar didn't crap, and the cat is still dead. The burglar is alive."

"Oh, Crapper the Cat died–the burglar didn't. I thought you had good news." Tom sighed.

"I do. The guy you hit last week just came out of surgery alive. He had a blockage and they were able to save him." J.J. sighed.

Mark added, "We did not kill him? How could that be?"

"My deputy tells me they revived him on the way to the hospital, and the doctors just now finished patching him up. He survived the surgery, but he's in serious condition."

"So we only have two murders on our heads and not three. Boy, I feel better, only two life terms." Tom stared at his coffee.

"No," I said, "Only one. The cat doesn't count."

J.J.'s cell phone rang again. "Green here–oh hi, Edie, what's going on at the office? They did? When?" J.J. checked his watch. "Okay, yes, I know we still have to prosecute, but still, that's better than a poke in the eye with a sharp stick any

302

day. Yep, thanks, Edie, I sure will–bye now."

J.J. looked up at Tom and Mark. Tears welled in their eyes as Mark said, "Did the death toll just rise?"

J.J. shook his head in wonder. "That was my dispatcher Edie. She said she just got off the phone with the State of Illinois. Seems like they were able to get a fingerprint and DNA from pieces of the guy you blew up at Great America. Turns out he was on the FBI's *Most Wanted List.* They confirmed that he's an escaped serial killer from Joliet Prison, and the Feds have been following a trail of dead bodies for three months through six states trying to catch him. You two did in one afternoon by accident what top agents in the FBI have been trying to do for months. According to the Feds, you two idiots are national heroes."

A cheer went up from the now-standing-room-only diner. Sal himself slapped a couple of plates on the table and fired off something I couldn't understand. Tom and Mark thanked him and Tom leaned forward. "He said thank you and no charge for lunch because we are heroes twice in one day!"

The two men basked in the adoration of the crowd. J.J. looked around in amazement. "I never got a free lunch, and I've caught more criminals than you could shake a stick at!"

I smiled. "Get over yourself, Green–you never blew up a notorious serial killer before."

"This is White Bass Lake, Buzz, not New York City for God's sake! We're not exactly overrun with serial killers, in case you haven't noticed."

I leaned close. "Don't get your Superman cape in a bundle, James Joseph Green. Just because your nose is out of joint there is no reason to take it out on the rest of us."

J.J. stared broodingly into his coffee mug, searching for answers. I was just about to feel sorry for the crybaby when his gaze snapped up to mine. He gave me a sly look. "So, uh, Buzz, you think I wear a red cape, eh? You think I'm

Superman?" He waggled his eyebrows at me.

I humiliated myself by blushing. "I think *you* think you're Superman, you lunatic. I took a huge gulp of hot coffee and nearly knocked myself out as the fire burned a path down my throat. I grabbed for napkins and slapped them over my mouth as coffee squirted out my nose. J.J.'s eyes twinkled in merriment as mine watered in pain. I snatched up my ice water and slugged down half the glass.

I discretely (as one can be in front of half the town) inspected my tongue in a spoon for damage when that jerk wearing a star said, "That's what I love about you, Lois Lane. Always at my phone booth when I need you."

"Thcrew yoo an yer thone booth, Thooper Jerk." I said around my sore tongue.

J.J. had the temerity to laugh at me, and I poked him in the ribs—hard. He threw an arm around my shoulders, clamped my neck in the crook of his arm, and gave me a giant noogie. I made choking sounds and pinched the tender skin of his triceps. He yelped and let me go. I held my broken ribs and gasped, tongue hanging out of my mouth.

Tom and Mark looked on like amused little old ladies watching their favorite grandchildren gambol in the backyard. They looked as likely to murder someone as Bozo the Clown.

"Green, focus here! What are you doing? We have an interview to finish."

"Lighten up, Miller, I have pie to finish. Here, taste this." He popped his fork into my open mouth. An explosion of blackberries tantalized my scorched taste buds. I began to file away the tart/sweet sensation when I heard a titter behind me.

I swung around to see the brave soul laughing at me. I rolled my eyes and sighed loudly as I gazed upon the collection of geriatric gossip mongers listening to the entire exchange. *Damn, they followed us.* Beaming smiles wreathed their beloved, but conniving faces. My mother, J.J.'s mom Silvia, their friends, Jane, Mary, and Joy, and my dad, who brought Jake, Elmer, and Old Bob Buford from the assisted living facility all crowded around a four-person table.

"Oh, no," I breathed as they closed in on our table. Chairs scraped, tables slid together, and I was painfully sandwiched between Mary's boney ass and J.J. I elbowed him again. "Didn't you just lock her up?"

"I never got that far because Ted came in and bailed her out. She has a court date on Tuesday."

"But why write her a ticket at all?" My mother shot J.J. a dirty look, "Geez J.J., I can't believe you did that! Shame on you."

"But, I–"

"James Joseph, you should be ashamed of yourself! Why, in my day–"

"B-but Mom…" J.J. stammered.

Mary grinned from ear-to-ear. J.J. leaned toward me and said, "Tell them or I will."

"Tell them what?" I stared at him innocently.

Mary gave him an evil grin. "Yes, J.J., tell them what?"

Dad said, "Come on, Mary, who wrote you the tickets for Indecent Exposure and Disturbing the Peace if J.J. didn't?"

As if a light bulb blinked on over the entire crowd, the word "Ted" rippled through the diner.

"That incompetent, sawed-off, doughnut eating constable wrote up his own mother?" My dad sounded flabbergasted.

Mary's dabbed her dry eyes with her napkin, playing it up big. "He surely did, Bill." She sniffed. "When I asked that little rat why he cited his own poor mother just for practicing for an audition, he called me a, a…" She sniffed and dabbed at her eyes for effect. "You tell them J.J." She sighed heavily and placed the back of her hand against her forehead. She leaned on my shoulder and her damn plastic tiara stabbed me in the neck.

J.J. drew a breath. "He told her she was–"

Mary jumped up, kneeled in my lap, and said in a stage whisper, "He told me I was a stinking cow and I had flat boobies!"

She moved forward, and my legs felt like they were impaled by those boney knees of hers. "Mary, my ribs!"

Mary backed off. "Oops! Sorry."

She continued her tirade without breaking stride. "Then he said something about bats and crows and he said I had a hairy butt!"

The bell over the door tinkled. The diner went silent for a split second, and then a booming voice said, "I did not call you a stinking cow, you crazy old bat! I told you that you wouldn't be *slinking* off *now* and that you needed to learn a lesson. I did not say you had, uh…flat, uh, you know, boobies, but that you are *flat* out *loopy,* mother!"

The crowd gasped. The senior women stood and started moving toward the hapless, brainless constable as he took one more stab at talking them out of a lynching.

"And another thing," he yelped, shaking his index finger. Scuttling backward, he tripped over a chair. "I was talking about that lousy hairy *mutt* of Buzz Miller's! I didn't say you had a hairy butt!"

Totally irritated and still dumb as a box of rocks, Dead Butz scuffed a toe on the floor, muttering to himself. "She's as kooky as she is deaf. I shoulda put her in a home a long time ago."

Realizing he'd just belittled his mother again, he jerked his head up, afraid to see if anyone else heard him. He figured correctly (for once) when he saw the other seniors closing in on him. Canes were raised and chairs thrown aside, Dead Butz backed slowly toward the door of the diner. He looked toward Mary for help, who now sat quietly beside me, arms folded and a smug little smile on her face. "That'll teach the little son-of-a-bitch to write *me* a ticket," she said out of the side of her mouth. I snorted coffee while Ted ran out the door and onto the sidewalk followed by Mom, Dad, and four or five others. J.J.'s mom threw the latch. My mom threw a bagel.

"Why, Mary Cromwell, you are positively evil!"

"Yes, Buzz dear, I am, but Teddy is too stupid to realize it. As long as he continues to treat me like a dotty old woman, I'll continue to act like a loony old lady, and he'll continue to threaten to commit me. It's the only thing he's good at anyway. Lord knows he stinks as Constable. We all shared a laugh.

"Oh look, there goes Bill and Gerry now."

I looked out the front window and saw my folks drive by in the one-ton dually. "That's funny," I said almost to myself.

"What's funny, Lois?" J.J. smiled at me.

"Knock it off, Clark Kent. Mom and Dad just drove by, and I swear I saw people in the back seat."

J.J. peered out the window. "People in the back sec–oh, no! We looked at the empty seats across the table with a wide-eyed stare.

"Oh, *no*! They escaped! I tried to wiggle out the front door.

"Wha...what?" Mary looked at us blankly.

"Mark and Tom," we both yelled again, and took off out the back door of Sal's.

We jumped into the squad (J.J. jumped and I crawled, complaining the entire time) and tore down the street after my parents and the two escaped South American-wannabe-hit men. We scanned the streets looking for the truck, and I finally spotted it at the Pick-N-Save at the edge of town.

We threw equally puzzled looks at each other and pulled into the parking lot. We parked the squad a couple of spaces down from the truck, snuck up, and pulled open a door. Empty. No Mom, no Dad, no bad guys, *nada*.

We decided to look inside the store, so we split up at the door and took opposite aisles. I had to fight myself not to stop at the coupon machine. I spotted Luis and Mom making their way toward the registers with a loaded cart, and altered my direction in order to intercept them before they hit the doors.

I hailed J.J. on the way to the checkout line, and he headed through the crowds in my direction.

We met them as Mom almost finished unloading the cart, and Mark bagged the groceries, calmly as you please. J.J. went ballistic. "Where the heck did you guys think you were going? You were under arrest."

Mark's shoulders slumped and he bit his lower lip. Tom moved to stand next to him and I poked J.J. in the side. "Uh, J.J.? They weren't really under arrest yet, remember? We were just talking to them in the diner."

Tom spoke up. "Did you not want us to leave, Sheriff Green? Your mother kindly asked if we could help her shop. She wanted to buy the big bag of dog food, but she cannot lift it easily. She asked if we could um," He thought a moment. "Give her a hand, I think she said. My cousin and I will give her many hands. She is a nice lady."

Mark piped up. "She bought us ice cream for helping. Moosetracks."

I looked at Mom. She gave me a wide-eyed innocent stare and I shook my head. "Sounds like her. Well, you guys have to come back with us now, okay?"

Tom and Mark bounded to where we stood. Mark saluted J.J. "We are ready to face the song, yes?"

J.J. lifted his ball cap and scratched his head. "Music." At their confused expressions he said, "Face the music. I guess so, boys. Come on, let's go."

Tom tapped me on the shoulder. "So what happens to us, now?"

Mark looked longingly at Mom's groceries. "Will we be done before the ice cream melts?"

I opened my mouth to try to explain when a deep, heavily

accented voice said from behind me, "You want to know what happens now? Now *amigo*, you will die."

It was like E.F. Hutton had entered the grocery store. No one spoke, no one breathed. Tom and Mark were shaking and had their hands in the air. J.J. stared over my shoulder, and I dared not move.

With arms held away from his body and palms facing whoever stood behind me, J.J. broke the silence. He spoke softly and his eyes never wavered from whoever was back there.

It was as if he and the foreign man were the only ones in the room. "Sir, whatever your business is with these men, it can be worked out. Please lower your weapon and step outside with me. We can discuss anything you want, but let's step outside and speak."

The rumbling voice again spoke. "They come, too. Are any of you the scientists from Lima?"

Mark blurted, "Reymundo, they are not here but what are you doing out of the hospi–"

I automatically reached out to touch Mark's arm, and in doing so turned to my right. I was about to shush him when I saw movement out of the corner of my eye and felt cold steel rest against my temple. I moved only my eyeballs and wished I hadn't when I stared into the flat black eyes of a man who was obviously very comfortable with the thought of murdering strangers.

I didn't dare speak, and J.J. tried again to convince the huge assassin to put down the weapon and follow him outside. My Mom made a small noise and the assassin's attention swung in her direction.

All hell broke loose. As the gun lifted away from my head, I pushed off of Mark and spun toward Mom. I focused on her panic-stricken face as she dropped the mayo jar she held in her hands. As my momentum lifted me off the ground I stupidly thought, Thank God that jar is plastic or I'll look like shredded cheese when we both hit the floor. I jumped for Mom and felt heat sear the arm on my bad side.

I saw Mark move in my peripheral vision and I hoped he was smart enough to drop to the floor and crawl out the door. With all my attention focused on Mom, I had no other thought but to put me between her and that gun.

I caught Mom around the waist in a flying tackle. I knocked her off her feet and she flew backward into the cart, and the man behind it. He hit the woman behind him, and the domino effect took out three more people. I wish I could say it was a neat and tidy scene straight from a heroic novel, but the ugly truth about reality is that when I dove for Mom, I took out the candy stand and the magazine rack, and the man behind us took out the sign and the end cap behind him. *The Beer That Made Milwaukee Famous* suddenly exploded into a series of fountains that would have made Tommy Bartlett cry.

I simultaneously crushed my poor mother and felt a flash of heat across my temple. I looked up to see the man behind us still holding the top half of a bag of dog food; which now emptied onto my blazing head.

I heard people screaming and metal clanking as I attempted to see if I had flattened poor Mom into a pancake. My vision went fuzzy and my ears rang. I thought I heard another shot, and people screamed and scrambled for cover. I tried to see through the pain, and the feel of warm wetness rolling off my head registered faintly in my fogged up brain.

I sank into a bottomless pit. With the last vestige of consciousness, I shoved at the candy rack with my feet and felt it give way. Shaking the dog food from my eyes made the lights dim and my head swim. I still had a hand on Mom, and scooted backward, dragging her behind the rack.

Blood from my head wound seeped into my eyes and I blinked to clear them. When I opened them, all I saw was a fuzzy 400-pound woman in a bikini. It scared me almost as much as dying from a bullet wound. I thought I'd died and gone to Jenny Craig hell until I read *Aliens Made Me Fat!* and realized I stared at the headlines of a tabloid.

I heard more yelling and the report of a gun. The acrid sting of smoke and human sweat mingled with crushed lettuce and dog food. I knew I had to do something, but the hundred-pound weights that were my hands dragged me to the floor. I dropped behind the magazine rack once more.

The world ran in slow motion, but I couldn't do anything to speed it up. I felt like I was wading through one of Mom's Jell-O and cottage cheese salads and prayed this would not be my final thought before my demise. I struggled to stay conscious and felt an electric current shoot through my body when I saw J.J wrestling with the hit man.

Mark had hold of the hit man's gun hand and pointed it to the ceiling, squeezing off shot after shot, trying to empty the weapon. Panic ensued as people screamed and ran everywhere.

Suddenly, out of the chaos skulked Tom, creeping around Cash Register Number Three, behind Mark. When he stood, I noticed the plastic grocery bag in his right hand. Determination etched on his face, he gave the bag a mighty windmill swing straight toward the assassin's head.

The bag blasted into the hit man's nose, and the crunch of bone and cartilage as his nose collapsed echoed across the store. Reymundo stood stiff as an arrow.

J.J. slid off Reymundo's back landed on his feet. He pasted the guy right on his broken and bleeding nose. The hit man toppled like a mighty oak, and I figured the end of the mêlée drew near. I couldn't be sure because pain blasted through my head and traveled past my shoulders and out the bottoms of my feet. Blessed blackness gently wrapped its comforting blanket around me as I passed out among the Mounds Bars and Puppy Chow, waiting for the fat lady on the magazine cover to sing.

* * *

I came to minutes or hours later, the pain a roiling caldron in my head. I chanced a peek over the fat lady's ass and saw that the coast was clear. Mom stood with her arms around Mark as he sobbed onto her shoulder. J.J. had cuffs on the bad guy, who looked to me like he was still unconscious, lying face down on the floor. I tried to get my limbs to move, but even blinking took an Act of Congress.

Mary Cromwell stood next to Mom, gesturing largely and speaking with Rosie the News Whore. Rosie, dressed in nothing more than sweat pants and a sports bra, stood sweating and scribbling notes on an in-store coupon for deli meats. *Figures.*

Tom held a can of canned pears in his hand and he grinned and pointed, his mouth moving, but I heard no sound.

Mom's voice blasted like a train whistle in my left ear. That's when I realized Mom sat on the floor with my head in her lap. "Tom, are you okay? What are you doing yelling about that can?"

Tom held up the can and said, "This is what I hit the bad guy with! I did much damage to his face with this one small can." He tossed the can into the air and caught it. He read the label. "It is a can of pears in h-heavy syrup. Can you believe one little can did so much damage?" He suddenly brightened and pointed to the label. "It must have been the heavy syrup."

My eyes rolled to the back of my head and I passed out.

32

It was a miracle that "Hard Case" Judge James Avery allowed Defense Attorney Tess Bannigan to talk him into a low-cash/ROR bond for Mark and Tom. It probably helped that it was an election year and they were local celebrities. It also helped that Evo hired the best Defense Attorney in the tri-county area to defend them.

At this time of year, most people are worried about Christmas shopping. Normal pastimes revolved around watching football, drinking beer, and complaining about the weather. The people of White Bass Lake could talk about nothing but the upcoming trial of Mark and Tom. Mark's new family even showed up to lend moral support–even Mark's first pair of tennis shoes showed up.

When interviewed by Rosie and her staff, Eli Moore claimed he and the missus were passing by a horseshoe tournament when someone threw a pair of shoes into the road, but they landed in the back of his cart instead. When he asked the folks at the tournament who they belonged to, they just laughed and laughed. By the time he sorted through all the misinformation, the owner of the shoes could not be found. He was here to return them to their rightful owner.

I don't remember much of my hospital stay, but I was told I had it pretty tough going for a couple of days. Now, two weeks later, I sat staring at one of Fred's fish tanks, watching the new Cory cat fish skitter up and down the glass. "So it ended up being the new strain of Cory catfish that were moved, Hank just added the Endlers as a cover crop. Good thinking on Hank's part, because the Endlers reproduce at such a rapid rate, it kept the Corys hidden. Later on he could claim he'd found the Endlers in the lagoon. Double payday."

Sam jumped in. "And that was a smart move because the real location of the Macroni would be kept secret so Hank would be the only one in the world to have them. Ian traced the Macroni to a remote oxbow lake in a dry tropical forest about a hundred kilometers away. Without Ian, I don't know if we would have figured out the fish angle."

Fred brought in more snacks. She shook her head. "The whole project went up in smoke when Chavez decided he wanted a cut of the action and blackmailed MacRone into transporting money from the illegal mining operation. Only Chavez didn't count on the heavy rains overflowing his leaching ponds and killing all those villagers, their animals and the fish in the lagoon."

Sam added, "Chavez also did not count on anyone discovering the mining operation. When Evo and Luis stumbled across that lagoon, they opened a huge can of worms."

Evo shrugged. "Worms? Better to fish with, I suppose."

Sam elbowed Evo in the side. "Ha-ha, very funny. Hey, I heard Nunez offered you a vice presidency in his conglomerate and an even more insane salary than you already have." Sam turned to him and grabbed his tie. "I also heard that you had a major malfunction and turned him down. Why on earth would you do that?"

"Oh, I didn't exactly turn him down; I told him I'd have to think on it, as I would be very busy for the next few months."

"Busy? What could keep you so busy?"

"Well, I told him I planned on getting married, and then there would be an extended honeymoon, and then my new wife and I would have to decide in which direction life would take us. Then, depending on what we decided, I'd let him know."

Sam blanched. "You're getting *married?*"

"Why yes, we are."

She gulped. *"We?"*

"Us? The Gallegos brothers hugged each other. Alfredo said, "I always wanted to see Niagara Falls."

Tony laughed. "I'll take you to the Wisconsin Dells. I hear it's pretty cool."

"Do they have ice cream?"

Tony placed an arm across the shoulders of the brothers and quietly led them from the room. "A lot of ice cream, as a matter of fact. Some come in 31 flavors, some come in dots, and some freeze dried. I have some upstairs, why don't we check it out?"

The courtroom was standing room only as the sentencing hearing began.

Tom and Mark stood in front of Judge Avery. He furrowed his bushy white eyebrows and cleared his throat. He looked sternly at Tom and Mark before he.

"Ladies and gentlemen, at the request of the defense, the defendants chose not to go with a jury trial, which is their right under the Sixth Amendment. The defendants opted instead to enter into a plea bargain, to which the District Attorney and the Defense Counsel has agreed upon, am I correct Counsel?"

The D.A., Andy Doolittle nodded. "Yes, your honor."

Judge Avery scowled at Tess Bannigan, seated at the defense table. She nodded and said, "Yes, your honor."

Avery leveled a look at Mark and Tom. "And you gentlemen? Do you understand your rights, your crimes, and the consequences thereof?"

They answered in unison, "Yes, your honor."

We held our breaths. Judge Avery sat back. He blew out a long sigh and steepled his fingers. "Well then, by the power vested in me by the State of Wisconsin, I do hereby hand down my findings. On count one, reckless endangerment by usc of a motor vehicle; the defendants plead guilty. The recommendations by the State are for one year in prison and three years stayed upon successful completion of three years of parole. Upon violation, parole will be revoked, and the three years in prison will be re-instated." He looked at Tess, Tom, and Mark. "Is this the agreement as you understand it?" They nodded, and Tess said, "Yes, your honor."

Judge Avery took off his half-glasses and leaned on both elbows. "Now, I find myself with a little problem with this agreement." He waved a piece of paper in the air. "Would counsel approach the bench please?"

Tess looked stricken. She glanced at us before she squeezed Tom and Mark's hands and approached the bench.

"Ahem, that means you too, Andy." The prosecutor started, tucked his tie in his jacket, and followed Tess to the bench.

"Oh no, I can't stand this," I whispered as I gripped J.J.'s arm. He patted my hand and held on to it. "It ain't over 'til it's over, Buzz. We did all we could for them."

Judge Avery seemed to talk for a half hour before he sat back and shooed Tess and Andy back to their tables. Andy stayed a few more seconds, and Judge Avery murmured to him in low tones.

Tess turned back to the table with a stunned expression on her face, not looking anyone in the eye. She walked stiff-legged back to the Defense table and sat between Mark and Tom. The three heads bent together and I could hear Tess's voice murmuring to Mark and Tom. They suddenly sprang back from Tess and sat ramrod straight in their chairs. They both stared straight ahead–not moving a muscle.

"Oh crap. J.J., this is not good. He's going to slam them, I just know it."

"Shhh. Are you getting a feeling about this?" He patted my knee.

I blinked, surprised. "No. That's gotta be a good sign, right?"

The crowd murmured and Judge Avery pounded his gavel.

District Attorney Andy Doolittle spun away from Judge Avery and walked back to his table. He picked up the papers on the table and stacked them in a neat pile front of him. He folded his hands on top and stared forward. I felt like throwing up.

The courtroom was silent as Judge Avery's voice rang out from the bench. "I have an unusual case before me today. The defendants have admittedly committed crimes against the State. They have entered into a plea agreement, of which I no longer agree. I have received in writing from the Governor of the State of Illinois a dismissal of all charges of murder one."

The room sucked in a collective breath. Judge Avery continued as he read. "In lieu of the acts of heroism and the extenuating circumstances surrounding the accidental death of serial killer Buddy Ray Levi, The State of Illinois and the Federal Government no longer see fit to proceed with charges against the defendants."

There was another collective gasp and all fell silent again.

Judge Avery looked up and took off his glasses. "It is hereby ordered by this court and agreed upon by both the state and the defense that the aforementioned agreement between the prosecution and the defense be quashed and sentencing ordered herein. Will the defendants please rise?"

The three of them slowly stood as one.

"By the power vested in me by the State of Wisconsin, I hereby order that a three year prison sentence be withheld, and that three years of probation be instated. It is further ordered that the defendants are each assigned 300 hours of community service, 100 hours per year per defendant. Counseling and schooling shall be completed as recommended by Probation and Parole, and upon successful completion of all programs and probation, the felonies shall then be expunged and the defendants shall be eligible to apply for citizenship to the United States of America if they so choose."

Two silent heartbeats were followed by pandemonium in the courtroom.

Tess became a South American sandwich as Mark and Tom hugged her from both sides. I jumped on J.J. and Fred jumped on me. Luis and Alfredo jumped over the divider and jumped on Mark and Tom. Judge Avery sat back with a self-satisfied smiled and even Andy Doolittle nodded his head and shook Tess's hand.

The bailiff didn't even try to maintain order as he walked Judge Avery out of the courtroom.

I watched Rosie the News Whore jump over chairs and elbow bodies aside in order to be the first to interview Tom and Mark. I couldn't hear much over the roar of the crowd, but I did hear Mark say, "...No, Ma'am. This is the Christmas present of a lifetime. For the first time in our lives, we are free men." And I heard Tom say, "...A Green Bay Packer jersey and lots of ice cream. That's what I want for Christmas!"

We walked out of the courthouse and started down the steps. I heard a high-pitched "Oops!" and braced myself. Fred flew by J.J. and me on her butt, sliding down the slippery courthouse steps. Armand followed in her wake, trying to grab her collar to slow her down. "It'll be good to get back to normal," I said as I took J.J.'s arm.

We passed Fred as she came to a bumpy halt at the bottom of the stairs. Armand had her by the arm and Fred rubbed her butt. J.J. raised a brow. "Uh, yeah. Normal. I don't think that word is in the Miller Sister dictionary."

I elbowed him in the ribs. "Watch it, buster. Our parameters of 'normal' might be slightly wider than some people, but we mean well."

J.J. laughed, threw an arm around my neck, and ruffled

my hair. "That you do, Buzz, that you do."

"Hey, pal, watch out for the bullet hole."

"Oops." he kissed my temple. "Sorry."

I caught a flicker of movement out of the corner of my eye and dragged J.J. to a halt. "Oh no, it can't be!"

Half the town slid to a stop at my outburst, and all heads turned north just as a motley looking cat streaked across the parking lot, followed by a bellowing Rick Glass. "Come back here you little turd."

I registered a voice yelling, "Oh my God, it's Crapper the Cat come back from the dead."

Many other voices joined in. "It can't be!"

"That damn cat is supposed to be dead!"

"How many lives does that cat have?"

"Someone shoot it before it craps again!"

"I just bought new patio furniture for my wife for Christmas!"

"Hah! It ain't gonna be new for long."

Just then I saw our ME slink around the corner of the courthouse. "Malcolm, did you save that damn cat?"

He stopped and nervously crushed his hat in his hands. "Well, I noticed it wasn't quite dead when I got him back to the office, so I nursed him back to health. I couldn't help it, Buzz, honest! My sister told me she'd keep him out of sight, but he must have escaped."

The cat zipped around a car and made a flying leap into the air. He landed claws out on Mark's chest. "*Ow*. Oh! It's Kitty! Look, Tom, he's not dead. We are not murderers after all. Hooray for Kitty!"

He danced around the parking lot with that stupid cat under his jacket.

Malcolm called out, "Do you want to keep the cat? He needs a home."

Tom and Mark both looked hopeful. Mark kept a

protective hand over his jacket. "You are not joking? We may keep this wonderful animal?"

Some smart ass in the crowd yelled, "Yeah, keep the damn thing and take it back to South America! Let it take a dump on someone else's patio furniture!"

I heard Ian say, "Mag, that's enough," and I smiled.

Mark and Tom waved excitedly to the crowd. Tom yelled, "Thank you, my friends. Thank you for your support and for this wonderful cat." They turned and hustled down the street.

I sighed as we walked toward my SUV. I saw my mom talking to Jan and Joy. My dad wore the long-suffering expression men get when waiting for their wives to quit gabbing. The majority of the crowd headed toward Sal's for coffee. Mary danced a shimmy for Ian, still delusional, but hopeful. Fred tripped through the parking lot, and walking at a good clip next to her was my youngest sister, Al, who wore stilettos in winter and looked sleek as a cat.

Mag opened the door to my SUV and Wes came barreling out, excited that so many people came just to see him. Grin, wag, grin. I looked for Hill and saw her peeking out the door. Smart dog, saves her energy.

"Yep, everything looks normal."

"Normal to you, maybe." J.J. squeezed my shoulders as we neared the SUV. He steered me toward the passenger's side. "Hop in, old girl."

I shot him an evil look and climbed in. "Hey, buddy, I resemble that remark."

We laughed as we headed out of the parking lot. J.J. slammed on the brakes to avoid hitting Mark as he ran in front of us. J.J. yelled, "What the–"

Crapper the cat was about a half a block in front of Mark as he streaked through downtown. I looked at J.J. "Yep. Normal."

He just smiled, shook his head and we headed for home.

33

"You may kiss the bride."

Mary Cromwell blew her nose loudly. *"Whaaa.* I love weddings."

The bride and groom turned around at the distraction–the fifth so far–and the priest cleared his throat. "Ahem, may we continue, please?"

Evo chuckled, shook his head, and turned back to Father Matthew. "Please, Father; do continue." He smiled down into Sam's eyes and said gently, "Where were we again?"

Standing under the flowering arbor in Fred's backyard, Evo and Sam exchanged vows in a lovely ceremony on an even lovelier spring day. I helped Fred plant the bulbs which now lined both sides of the seating area. I swear I must be the worst gardener in the entire world. No wonder they say I have a black thumb.

Fred's side bloomed with a profusion of color and scents. My side had five tulips and one hyacinth with five flowers on the stalk. My crocus did just that. I figured I had better start listening and learning from all the people trying to help me overcome my black thumb syndrome. This was becoming embarrassing.

J.J. and I sat near the back, as he was also supervising the roasting of the pig. I somehow got hooked into organizing the food tables and it looked like we were going to set a new record for the diverse selection of Jell-O salads consumed in one afternoon. Sal made the cake; a stunning three-tiered affair complete with a blue waterfall in the center and cavorting dolphins diving in and out of swirling waves around each layer.

Someone (my money was on Tony) had removed the bride

and groom from the top tier and replaced them with two plastic cartoon *Nemo* clown fish; one with a veil and one in a white tuxedo. It was a definite winner.

I tore myself away from my musings just in time to hear Sam say, "I think we're at the kissing part."

A loud voice from the back yelled, "Just kiss her, Evo, but hurry up about it 'cuz I want a beer!"

The crowd laughed good naturedly as Evo slowly lifted the veil and folded it behind Sam's head. She lifted her startling blue eyes to his and he looked as though his heart would burst. Wrapping his arms around Sam's shoulders, his head slowly descended. Her lips parted. What must have been only a few seconds seemed like a lifetime.

I hadn't realized I had a death grip on J.J.'s arm until he pried my fingers off and said, "Whoa there, Buzz, you're cutting off the circulation to my gun hand."

With the thrill of the moment passing, my heart rate returned to almost normal.

J.J. flexed his hand and looked around. "Hey, do you think we might get through this without another mishap?"

"Don't say that. Remember Murphy's Law; whatever can happen, will. We aren't out of the woods yet. Keep an eye out— uh, I hate to tell you, but I have one of those feelings coming on."

J.J. went on immediate alert. "Oh, no, I'm definitely afraid." He scanned the crowd again, focusing on Mary Cromwell. "I put my money on Mary."

Meanwhile, Evo lifted his head from the scorching kiss, tears stinging his eyes. "I love you, Mrs. Castillo." Sam smiled back. "Same here, Mr. Castillo." She dabbed at his eyes with the lace hankie she'd borrowed from Fred.

The smiling newlyweds turned to the crowd and Father Matthew introduced them as Mr. and Mrs. Evo Castillo. Fred stepped forward to give Sam her flowers and tripped over her train. Tony leapt forward and caught Fred on the way down. He held on to her and whispered something in her ear. They both laughed and Evo looked into Tony's smiling face. "What are you grinning like an idiot about, little brother?"

"Oh, I was just thinking. Since the 'Bitchthyologist' married 'The Evil One', will you name your firstborn *Evil Fernameanie*?"

Sam winked at her new brother in-law. "Of course; unless it's a girl, that is. Then we'll call her Toni."

Tony jumped forward and threw his arms around both of them. "*Aww,* I love you guys."

The crowd went wild. Evo and Sam fought their way down the makeshift aisle through back slappers, kids, hand shakers, dogs, and other well wishers.

Then it happened. Mary flew out of her chair and attached herself to Evo's side blubbering about beautiful brides and lovely weddings. The huge pink purse hanging off her arm swung around his back and knocked Sam into the crowd. Evo stumbled and almost took Tony down trying to shake off Mary and grabbed for Sam. He tried his best to extricate himself, but Mary stuck like glue and wouldn't let go. Her purse swung wildly and Tony had to duck to avoid being clocked. Understandable since the Gander Mountain incident, he'd been a little purse-shy.

Dragging the leg to which Mary was still attached, Evo slowly inched down the aisle. The blue sequined stripper dress Mary wore for the wedding rode up her scrawny fishnet covered legs. The higher it inched, the more nervous I became. The thought of Mary's bum exposed to the entire town was enough to make the strongest man queasy, but when I heard my dad and Dead Butz yell, *"Oh, My God, Mary, nooo!* I feared the worst. I took a fortifying breath before I had the courage to peek around J.J. to see what the commotion was about.

A sobbing Mary still clung to Evo's side. A large black

323

smear of mascara marred his pristine white tuxedo. She had one leg slung around his hip and the other around his thigh. Evo had to do the step-and-drag walk in order to continue to move in a forward motion. He dragged Mary while maintaining a hold on Sam. I watched in horror as Mary's dress hiked higher. Up over the tops of her garters it crept and a feeling of foreboding came over me that made me hyperventilate. The dress slid up until Mary did the one-cheek-sneak-peek, and I had to jump out of the way when Mrs. Waller squeaked and passed out next to me.

J.J. scooted forward and placed his western hat over Mary's 80-year-old thong-clad bum. Fred came out of nowhere and grabbed my arm. Totally shocked, we held our breaths and clung to each other as if watching a natural disaster unfold before our eyes.

In the meantime, Ted, in a bright yellow suit, wrapped his arms around Mary's middle, and Dad latched onto Ted's belt. They dug in their heels as Evo dragged all three of them down the aisle. Ted grabbed one of Mary's feet and pried it loose. Mary swung her foot back and cold-cocked him right between the eyebrows with her orthopedic shoe. He stiffened like a frozen banana and Dad let him go. Ted teetered for a moment and dropped like a stone right there in the aisle beside him.

Flash. Joy got a picture of Dead Butz lying among the rose petals with a square red mark in the middle of his forehead. Someone stuck a beer in his hand and Ted looked like he'd started the party a little early. Joy snapped that one, too.

My mother looked aghast. "Joy, that's not very nice. Poor Ted is out cold!"

Joy raised a brow and gave Mom an evil grin. "One never knows when one has need of good blackmail photos, Ger."

"Oh yeah, you're right. Better take another one just in case."

Fred and I snapped out of our shock-induced paralysis and caught up with Evo. A glowering J.J. still covered up what became revealed as a sparkly thong on Mary's boney butt. Mag came up behind Fred and grabbed both of us. Classy as always, she choked, "Oh man, that is just sooo *wrong!*"

Shouts of "Oh, my God!" and "Cover that thing up," echoed through the crowd.

The three of us sprang into action. Mag and I each grabbed an arm and Fred grabbed a foot. Separating Mary from Evo was like peeling apart wet Velcro. I would never have guessed the tremendous amount of force it took to peel one seventy-eight pound geriatric off of one six-foot-three and two hundred forty-pound groom. Mary continued sniveling about beautiful weddings as we carried her into the house.

As we passed Mom and Joy, the camera flashed again. Mary flinched and her pink purse fell out of her hand. A fifth of whiskey rolled across the grass. Joy picked it up and shoved it at Mom. "Look, Ger, Mary's been tipping. No wonder she's more demented than usual. She's probably drunk off her ass!"

Mom uncapped the whiskey and took a swig. "Yep, it's whiskey all right. Here, check it out."

Mom handed the bottle back to Joy. She tipped the bottle back and slugged some down. "If that don't beat all," she huffed. "Bitch didn't even share with her friends." She took another drink, capped the bottle, stuffed it in her own purse, and grabbed Mom's arm. They stuck their respective noses in the air and stepped daintily across the lawn. I swore I heard mutterings of, "At least it won't go to waste."

34

Hours later, with the last piece of cake boxed, the party winded down. Only family and close friends remained as we sat around the fireplace in Fred's living room. The smell of the crackling fire combined with the rich aromas of coffee created a peaceful ambience, and I relaxed for the first time that day.

By general consensus, we avoided talking about the "*South American Incident*" during the wedding. Evo put his coffee on the table and leaned forward, resting his forearms on his thighs. "I've heard through Ramon Nunez that the draining of the leaching ponds at the Devil's Eye Mine has been completed. They hauled it out of the mountains tankard by tankard. Nunez paid to run a fence down the mountain to the lagoon to keep wildlife away from the toxins until they can be eradicated. They still have major cleaning up to do, but at least the threat of overflow is now gone. Chavez is pleading for his life, and his bodyguard has finally been extradited to South America. The two of them can have fun together in prison for the next ninety years or so.

Fred asked, "What about Hank? Did you hear anything about Hank?"

"Hank turned state's evidence and will probably get off pretty clean. Then they'll ship him up here."

Sam sighed. "Well, that makes me feel much better about a lot of things." She squeezed Evo's hand. "At least we can get back to normal when we get home." She leaned forward. "Now that you have your doctorate, Tony, we can expand the Tombopata operation."

Tony looked at the carpet and ran his finger around the rim of his glass. "Uh, Sam, Evo, I've decided I'm not going back for a while. Ian has offered me a job at his new facility, and I've accepted. I didn't want to tell you until after the wedding, but I'm staying here for the time being."

Fred's eyes grew huge and she spazzed next to me. Her arm hit my back and her wine went down the back of my pants. Jumping forward, I barked my shin on the ottoman and howled in pain. "Dammit, Fred! This is a new suit you just wrecked! Now I have to get home so I can get this stain out. What's wrong with you?"

Fred continued to mutter unintelligible words as she slapped at the stain, dragging me into the kitchen and trying to shove my butt under the faucet. I fought my way free of her and stood dripping on her kitchen floor.

Evo strolled in, carrying yet another one of his now famous Gander Mountain outfits. "Thought you could use these, Buzz."

I shouted my thanks, grabbed the sweats, and ran to the bathroom. I came out as Evo asked Fred if Tony's choice to stay upset her.

Fred stuttered and stammered, making no sense at all. I pulled the waistband of Evo's sweats to the vicinity of my neck, and as I hopped on one foot, I measured the situation. "Yo, Fred, is the problem that Tony will be staying here, or with Tony in general?"

She shook her head no and chewed her fingernail.

"Is it that he's going to work with Ian?"

Fred bit off her thumb nail and shook her head no. "Just leave it alone, Buzz. It's nothing, I'm a little surprised, that's all."

"But, Fred.'

"Leave it, I said!"

"Fine, be that way. I'll leave it. Matter of fact, I'll just take my wine soaked self home." I yanked my wet suit out of the sink. I stomped to the back door and called my dogs. They came bounding through house, slowing in the living room in order to check out any snacks they missed. They zipped out the front door. "Ungrateful wretches," I said.

Mom smiled. "They're just ready to go home, Buzz. It's been a long day for everyone. She patted Dad's knee. "Come on, Bill Miller, let's hit the road."

J.J. hopped up and bounded out the door. "Hey, Buzz, don't forget me. You drove, remember?"

"Oh, yeah. Sorry, I forgot. Come on, Green, the kids are already at the car, so pile in." When we were settled and pulling out of the driveway I turned to him and asked if he wanted to be dropped off first.

J.J. looked at me with an odd expression. "I'm going to your house, Buzz, it's our regular movie night. We're going to get into our jams, cuddle up in that great big leather chair of yours, spoon up some ice cream, and watch *Young Frankenstein*."

"Sounds like a great night to me, I thought you might be too tired. Let's go."

I pulled into my driveway and the dogs piled out. It was a race to the front door, and J.J. made it through first. "I'll get the movie, you get the food."

"Oh, J.J., I forgot that Wesley barks at Frau Blucher. He'll wreck the whole movie." I came through the door and saw that J.J. had made a pit stop. *Young Frankenstein* was in the VCR and I yelled through the bathroom door. "James Green, I'm warning you!"

J.J. opened the door and walked right up to my nose. He tapped the end and said, "Never fear, Buzzy dear, I shall share my ice cream with Baron von Wesley and he will never know Frau Blucher is on the television. Come on, Buzz, *Young Frankenstein*!"

"Oh, all right. I'll get the ice cream, but you get Wes."

"I'll start the movie. The dogs watched us bounce in and

out of the room, excited because they knew our movie night ritual, and they got to snuggle with us and eat cool snacks.

J.J. and I collided as we dove over opposite arms of the chair. Hill crawled up and sat in the crook of my legs. Wes hopped up behind J.J., his butt hanging over the arm. J.J. threw his arm across my shoulders and pulled me closer. "What's up with this, Green, are you making more room for the dogs, or have you just discovered how irresistible I am?"

"I couldn't reach the remote," he deadpanned as he snatched it out of my hand and started the movie.

I popped open the carton of ice cream and dunked in both spoons. J.J. dimmed the lights and snuggled in close. We each had a spoonful of butter pecan heading toward our mouths when the opening credits began to roll.

Wesley's head popped up and he let fly with a frenzy of barking. "Aw man, stop. The movie hasn't even started yet."

Woo, Woo, Woowoowoo

"Shut him up, J.J. Stuff him with ice cream or something!"

"Wes, come here, boy."

Woo, Wuh, Wuh, Woo, Woo.

"J.J., I told you he would do this."

"Wesley, enough now, here's a treat. You can stop barking now and watch the movie."

Wuh, wuff, (sneeze) Woo, Woo, Woo.

"Forget the treat Wes. Stop it now! J.J., how are we going to watch the movie over that din? Wes is going crazy!"

Woo, Woo.

I clicked off the movie and Wes shut up, proudly grinning and wagging his tail.

I pushed start and Wes took up the chorus. *Woo, Woowoowoo.*

I clicked stop and Wes stopped.

I sighed and gave J.J. the "I told you so" look. J.J. tried hard not to laugh and failed miserably. "Please don't tell me the dog knows the musical score."

"I guess he does. Want to try a different movie?"

"Either that or lock up the dog and wear headphones, I guess."

"What movie does Wes like?"

"How about *Turner and Hooch*? Wes and Hillary both love the French Mastiff that plays Hooch." I rifled through the VHS tapes and put the movie in.

We settled back and Wes draped himself across J.J.'s lap. He had ice cream on the tip of his nose. Hilary leaned over and delicately licked it off. J.J. and I shared a look over their heads like the proud parents of precocious children. The movie began and Wesley's attention diverted to the television. His tail began a rhythmic thumping as we all settled in to watch the movie.

As the final credits rolled up the screen, I yawned and stretched. J.J. yawned and stretched. Hilary woke and yawned and stretched. She delicately passed gas and gave me a dirty look. Wes took one whiff and jumped to the floor.

J.J. fanned the air with both hands. "Well, *that* was pleasant. We should take the kids to the movies more often."

"Any more often and the dogs will start repeating the dialog."

"True, true."

I got up and headed toward the kitchen. "Hey, I'm going to let these two out one last time tonight. Help yourself to whatever you want."

J.J. shot me an evil grin and waggled his eyebrows. "Okay, thanks. I'll come with you."

I unlocked the back door I stepped out with the dogs. "Oh, no need, I–"

I looked over my shoulder. J.J. stood only about two inches away. My stomach flipped and I swallowed hard. "I, uh, ah, uh, what?"

To this day I don't know whether he moved closer or it

was my imagination, but all sound ceased and the picture in front of me blurred around the edges. I felt a moment of panic, and the image of J.J. panned in until I could only see his sea green eyes. They crinkled at the corners and I was a goner. "You told me to help myself to what I want," he said softly.

I felt myself sinking fast. "Well, spit it out, Green—what *do* you want?"

"You, Miss Buzz, only you."

I stared at him like an idiot. *Oh crap, Miller. You're in trouble now.*

He smiled and drew my arms around his neck. I sighed. The light clicked out and the velvet darkness settled around us. "Miss Buzz, it doesn't get any better than this."

I settled in closer and looked at his beautiful mouth. "I think it's about to."

Pffft. The raunchy smell rose quickly and choked us.

"Hilary," we yelled and J.J. opened the door to let us all back in the house.

I flopped on the couch and crossed my arms. Wes lumbered up and laid his head in my lap and I rubbed his ears. I smiled. Wes grinned.

"Want to know what I think, Wes? I think Hill just killed the most romantic moment in the life of Buzz Miller. You don't think she does that on purpose, do you?" Wes just grinned and wagged his tail.

I sighed and headed for the kitchen. Wes saw a snacking opportunity and followed in my wake. "Just goes to show, no matter how you look at it, my love life really stinks."

Wes grinned as I dished him up some ice cream.

"Ahem, just what is your definition of *stinks*, Buzz Miller?"

I spun, ice cream carton in one hand, bowl in the other. "I uh, that is…"

J.J. smiled and his arms wrapped around me. He tilted me

off balance and his lips met mine. Emotion welled from the depths of my being and I could feel it burn its way from me to him.

It could have been seconds or minutes—I neither knew, nor cared. When we finally came up for air, J.J. stared at me and slowly straightened. Still holding me he said, "What the heck was that?"

"I don't know, but it was beautiful in a terrifying way."

J.J. blinked. "You're telling me."

He loosened his hold and ran a hand through his hair. I bent to give Wes his ice cream.

Straightening, I thought this would be where J.J. would put everything into perspective, and we would go back to being best friends. I pasted a false smile on my face and prepared for the worst.

J.J. closed the back door and flipped off the kitchen light. He took my hand and pulled me toward him. I dragged my feet. "J.J., are you sure we're moving in the right direction here?"

"Yup."

"Are you sure the whole wedding thing didn't, you know, inspire this—thing?"

"Nope." He led me toward the door.

"Well then J.J., I think this is the beginning of a beautiful friendsh—"

We stopped at the door to the living room. We heard a plop behind us, then slurping noises. J.J. went to hit the light switch and slid in the ice cream which Wes had knocked off the counter. I dove for the container and ice cream ran down my arm.

"Damn. Now I need a shower."

J.J. scraped ice cream off his pants and grinned. "A perfect place to continue this conversation."

He pushed me out the door and down the hall. Contented slurping noises resumed from the kitchen.

Gale Borger is the author of the hilarious Miller Sisters Mysteries, Totally Buzzed and Totally Fishy. Her short story, Totally Decked, delighted readers Christmas season, 2010. Gale is published by Echelon Press.

The Olive Branch Mystery series begins with Part #1, *Death of a Garden Hoe.* This is the first installment of six eBooks designed to encourage reluctant readers to "dig in" and read. Part #2, *Digging up Dirt, is followed by Kill me Over the Garden Gate, You Say Tomahto, and I Say You're Dead, Hosta la Vista, Baby.,* and *Everything's Coming up Roses.*

Gale has a Bachelor's degree in Criminal Justice Administration, and a Master's Degree in Education. She lives in Southeastern Wisconsin with her husband Bob, their sometimes-seen college student (dragging a trombone and her dirty laundry behind her), two dogs, two cats, about 1,000 tropical fish, a Pac-man frog, two turtles, and more flowers in her yard than grass.

Visit Gale at *http://galeborgerbooks.com*

CPSIA information can be obtained at www.ICGtesting.com
Printed in the USA
243021LV00001B/1/P